*Everyman, I will go with thee,
and be thy guide*

Anthony Trollope

THE WARDEN

Edited by
HUGH OSBORNE *and* DAVID SKILTON
University of Wales, Cardiff

Introduction and critical material by
BARBARA DENNIS
Saint David's University College, Lampeter

EVERYMAN
J. M. DENT · LONDON
CHARLES E. TUTTLE
VERMONT

David Skilton, University of Wales, Cardiff, is
Consultant Editor for the Everyman Trollope

Introduction, chronology and other critical apparatus
© J. M. Dent 1994

The Warden first published in Everyman by J. M. Dent in 1968

This edition first published in Everyman in 1994

J. M. Dent
Orion Publishing Group
Orion House, 5 Upper St Martin's Lane,
London WC2H 9EA
and
Charles E. Tuttle Co. Inc.
28 South Main Street
Rutland, Vermont 05701, USA

Typeset in Sabon by CentraCet Limited, Cambridge
Printed in Great Britain by
The Guernsey Press Co. Ltd, Guernsey, C.I.

British Library Cataloguing-in-Publication Data
is available upon request.

ISBN 0 460 87416 0

CONTENTS

NOTE ON THE AUTHOR AND EDITORS

ANTHONY TROLLOPE was born in London in 1817, the fourth surviving child of a failing barrister with a difficult personality and grandiose expectations. He spent a miserable childhood and youth. Because of his poverty he felt himself an outcast at Harrow and Winchester, where he was a scholastic failure. After his father went bankrupt, his mother supported the family by her writing. Through a family contact, Anthony was found a clerkship in the Post Office, and he was posted to Ireland, where he became a reliable and energetic public servant. He married Rose Heseltine in 1844. Until retiring in 1867 he combined full-time Post Office work, reorganising large parts of the postal service of Great Britain, Ireland and the West Indies, with a huge literary output, and with life in society and on the hunting field. He published his first novel in 1847, but had only just become well-known on his return to London in 1859. He was immensely popular in the 1860s, and made new efforts after 1870 to retain his market position. When he died in 1882 he had written nine volumes of stories and sketches, nine works of non-fiction and forty-seven novels, including two six-volume cycles, the *Chronicles of Barset-shire* and the Palliser novels. He journeyed extensively in Europe, North America, Australia, New Zealand and South Africa, writing fiction and factual books about his travels. His autobiography was published posthumously in 1883.

DAVID SKILTON was educated at King's College, Cambridge and the University of Copenhagen. After holding posts at the Universities of Stockholm and Glasgow and at Lampeter, he is now Professor of English at Cardiff, and Head of the School of English Studies, Communication and Philosophy there. His books include *Anthony Trollope and His Contemporaries* (1972), *Defoe to the Victorians* (1985), *The Early and Mid-Victorian Novel* (1993) and editions of numerous Victorian novels.

HUGH OSBORNE is Research Assistant at the School of English, Communications and Philosophy at the University of Wales, Cardiff.

BARBARA DENNIS is the author of *Reform and Intellectual Debate in Victorian England* (with David Skilton, 1987) and *Charlotte Yonge: Novelist of the Oxford Movement* (1992), and the editor of Charlotte Yonge, *The Daisy Chain* (1988), and Charlotte Yonge, *The Heir of Radcliffe* (forthcoming). She has lectured at Queen's University, Kingston, Ontario, and at the University of Durham, and is currently Chairman of Victorian Studies and Lecturer in English at the University of Wales, Lampeter.

CHRONOLOGY OF TROLLOPE'S LIFE

Year	Age	Life
1815		Born at Keppel St, Russell Square, London, on Monday 24 April
1823	8	Attends Harrow as a day boy until 1825
1825	10	Attends private school at Sunbury, Middlesex, until 1827
1827	12	Attends Winchester until 1830
1830	15	Returns to Harrow until 1834
1834	19	Family flees creditors to Belgium. Enters General Post Office as a clerk
1840	25	Suffers a serious illness
1841	26	Appointed surveyor's clerk in the Central District of Ireland
1843	28	Starts to write *The Macdermots of Ballycloran* (pub. 1847)
1844	29	Marries Rose Heseltine (1821–1917)

CHRONOLOGY OF HIS TIMES

Year	Literary Context	Historical Events
1815	Austen, *Emma*	Battle of Waterloo
1817	Coleridge, *Biographia Literaria*	
1818	Scott, *The Heart of Midlothian* M. Shelley, *Frankenstein*	
1819		Peterloo massacre
1820	P. Shelley, *Prometheus Unbound*	Death of George III
1821	P. Shelley, *Defence of Poetry*	
1829		Catholic Emancipation Act passed
1830	Tennyson, *Poems, Chiefly Lyrical* Cobbett, *Rural Rides*	
1832		Reform Act passed
1833		Establishment of Oxford Movement
1837	Dickens, *Pickwick Papers*	Accession to throne of Victoria
1838	Carlyle, *Sartor Resartus* Dickens, *Nicholas Nickleby*	Emergence of Chartism
1840	Dickens, *The Old Curiosity Shop*	Introduction of the Penny Post
1841		Peel becomes Prime Minister
1842	Tennyson, *Poems in Two Volumes*	Collapse of Chartist movement
1843	Dickens, *Martin Chuzzlewit*	Peel sends troops to Ireland
1844	Barrett, *Poems*	O'Connell tried for conspiracy

Year   Age   Life

Year	Literary Context	Historical Events
1846		Ireland devastated by famine Peel resigns after corn-law repeal
1847	Thackeray, *Vanity Fair*	
1848	E. Brontë, *Wuthering Heights* Macaulay, *History of England* Marx/Engels, *Communist Manifesto*	Revolution sweeps Europe
1850	Tennyson, *In Memoriam*	
1851		Opening of Great Exhibition
1852	Thackeray, *The History of Henry Esmond*	
1855	Dickens, *Little Dorrit*	Civil Service exams introduced
1857	Eliot, *Scenes of Clerical Life*	
1859	Eliot, *Adam Bede* Darwin, *The Origin of Species*	
1860	Dickens, *Great Expectations* Eliot, *The Mill on the Floss*	
1861	Eliot, *Silas Marner*	American Civil War begins
1862	Mill, *Utilitarianism*	Unification of Italy
1863	Thackeray dies	
1864	Browning, *Dramatis Personae*	
1865		American Civil War ends
1866	Swinburne, *Poems and Ballads* Eliot, *Felix Holt, The Radical*	Hyde Park riot
1867	Bagehot, *The English Constitution* Marx, *Das Kapital*	Second Reform Act passed
1868	Collins, *The Moonstone* Browning, *The Ring and the Book*	
1869	Arnold, *Culture and Anarchy* Mill, *The Subjection of Women*	
1870	Dickens dies D. G. Rossetti, *Poems*	Franco-Prussian War Start of Irish Home Rule movement. Married Women's Property Act

Year	Age	Life
1871	56	*The Eustace Diamonds* July 1871–February 1873. Travels to Australia and New Zealand, May 1871–December 1872
1872	57	*The Golden Lion of Granpere* January–August
1873	58	*Lady Anna* April 1873–April 1874. *Phineas Redux* July 1873–January 1874. *Australia and New Zealand. Harry Heathcote*
1874	59	*The Way We Live Now* February 1874–September 1875
1875	60	*The Prime Minister* November 1875–June 1876. Travels to Australia and USA, March–October. Starts *An Autobiography* (compl. 1876, pub. 1883)
1876	61	*The American Senator* May 1876–July 1877
1877	62	*Is He Popenjoy?* October 1877–July 1878. Travels to South Africa
1878	63	*John Caldigate* April 1878–June 1879. *An Eye for an Eye* August 1878–June 1879. *South Africa*
1879	64	*Cousin Henry* March–May. *The Duke's Children* October 1879–July 1880. *Thackeray*
1880	65	*Dr Wortle's School* May–December
1881	66	*Ayala's Angel. The Fixed Period* October 1881–March 1882. *Marion Fay* December 1881–June 1882
1882	67	*Kept in the Dark* May–December. *Mr Scarborough's Family* May 1882–June 1883. *The Landleaguers* November 1882–October 1883. Dies 6 December, at Welbeck Street, Cavendish Square, London
1883		*An Autobiography*
1884		*An Old Man's Love*

Year	Literary Context	Historical Events
1871	Darwin, *The Descent of Man*	
1872	Eliot, *Middlemarch*	
1874	Hardy, *Far From the Madding Crowd*	Irish Home Rule movement grows
1876	Eliot, *Daniel Deronda*	Victoria made Empress of India
1878	Swinburne, *Poems and Ballads: second series*	Congress of Berlin
1879	James, *Daisy Miller*	Irish National Land League formed
1880	Eliot dies	Charles Parnell tried for conspiracy
1881	James, *Portrait of a Lady* James, *Washington Square*	Land League outlawed
1884		Third Reform Act passed

INTRODUCTION

'A novel', writes Anthony Trollope in *An Autobiography* (1883), 'should give a picture of common life enlivened by humour and sweetened by pathos.' And while a novelist must please, or he will be nothing, yet 'he must teach whether he wish to teach or no. How shall he teach lessons of virtue and at the same time make himself a delight to his readers?'

He answered his own question so successfully in *The Warden* that (as he put it himself) the novel, the first of the Barsetshire series, has delighted readers since its first appearance in 1866 even while it 'preached [its] sermon as perhaps no clergyman can preach it'. It was not his first novel (he had written three others in the ten previous years), but the first to meet with even grudging success: '[T]he novel-reading world did not go mad about *The Warden*; but I soon felt it had not failed as the others had failed.' It marked the beginnings of his career as a popular novelist, which was confirmed by the sequel, *Barchester Towers*, in 1857. He even made money by it – £9 8s 8d in the first year. (Trollope remarked that, in terms of remuneration, 'stone-breaking would have done better'.)

It is easy to see in *The Warden* the enlivening humour and sweetening pathos in the context of familiar life that Trollope claimed were the basis of a successful novel. His own directions for a novel are amply fulfilled in the broad humour of Dr Grantly, still living in the eighteenth century, and the satirical attacks on three prominent contemporary bishops in his sons, Charles James, Henry and Samuel; and in the devotion of Eleanor to her father, or the touching regard of the old bishop for his lifetime friend, the precentor. But *The Warden* also succeeds in much more profound terms. Then, as now, readers warmed to Mr Harding, the moral centre of the novel, in his dilemma when his public position as warden of Hiram's Hospital is challenged first by society and then – more importantly – by his private conscience. The end, as he emerges with his integrity intact, no longer warden but simply the precentor and rector of 'the smallest possible parish', St Cuthbert's, is triumphant.

It was a new departure from the way the contemporary novel was developing. The conventions of the form, now by the middle of the century quite the most popular of all kinds of writing, seemed at this point to require a scenario in which the hero, initially in some way at odds with society, learns to conform and accept the mores of society, which in turn rewards him with recognition and accords him an authoritative voice. The story has concerned his education in this process of enlightenment, and his final endorsement of society's values: the individual is shown working towards the harmony of society by embracing the values of the social group. Charles Dickens exemplifies the trend with novels like *David Copperfield* (1850), and lesser novelists, often no less widely read at the time, confirm the trend. Charlotte M. Yonge's Philip Edmonton, in her phenomenally popular *Heir of Redclyffe* (1853), is a typical hero.

The Warden adopts a reverse procedure: Mr Harding moves from strength to strength in the reader's eyes as he detaches himself from society and stands triumphantly by his own personal code. It is shared by no one except Eleanor. Trollope has made it clear that rightness does not (necessarily) reside in conventional principles or institutions – that is, in 'society' as represented by Dr Grantly, Tom Towers or John Bold – but does reside in personal integrity. Mr Harding is never more authoritative than when he relinquishes his £800 a year as warden of Hiram's Hospital for the comparative poverty of St Cuthbert's parish, 'with a clear income of seventy-five pounds a year'. The approval of society is normally represented by the obvious success of financial gain, and by such standards Mr Harding's decision represents ignominy. By a paradox Trollope reverses all expectations.

In all his novels (well over forty of them) Trollope never wrote one more topical than *The Warden*, which is almost a paradigm of the politics and culture of the early 1850s. The story of how the idea for the novel came to him in the close of the cathedral at Salisbury, as he toured the southern counties inspecting the rural postal system, is well known. He had spent a significant part of his miserable schooldays at Winchester close by the cathedral there and near the ancient almshouse at St Cross, in the early 1850s the setting for a notorious financial scandal occupying the leader-writers of *The Times* (the '*Jupiter*') like Tom Towers regularly and frequently. The Master of St Cross was the Rev. Thomas North, nephew of the Prime Minister, who had succeeded to the title of Lord Guilford, and was possibly the wealthiest dignitary in the Church of England. He held, simultaneously, the wealthy parish of St Mary's, Southampton and a prebendal stall at Winchester Cathedral, as well as three smaller livings; and among his preferments the Mastership of St Cross alone was worth from £2,000 to £3,000 per annum – a part of which, anyway, he spent in regular and protracted residence abroad in France, Germany and Italy. Affairs had come to light when a disinterested searcher after truth, the Rev. Henry Holloway, inspected the accounts. Between 1849 and 1853 the scandal had been before the eyes of the public continually.

The scandal at Winchester was merely the most notorious among many. Reform was in the air. John Bold at Barchester, with his 'special mission for reforming ... all abuses; state abuses, church abuses, corporation abuses ... abuses in medical practices, and general abuses in the world at large' is Trollope's representative of many real reformers. The Rev. Henry Holloway had set the cat among the pigeons at St Cross, and the Rev. Mr Whiston was doing the same at Rochester. Trollope refers to them both, and others, repeatedly. As the Headmaster of the Cathedral Grammar School at Rochester, Mr Whiston had consulted the statutes relating to the endowments of the school to find a great deal of 'deviation from the Founder's intentions in the present Cathedral system'.[1] The endowment required that twenty boys be maintained and paid at the school, and that four students be similarly supported at the universities: but 'at present ... neither the four students, nor the twenty boys, are maintained at the costs and charges of the church, and they receive only the same numerical sums of money as in 1542, viz. £5 and £2 13s 4d respectively'[2] – the rest of the money had long been diverted into the pockets of the Dean and Chapter of the cathedral, whose stipends had, anyway, increased tenfold. In 1849 Mr Whiston, thwarted by the refusal of either Dean or Bishop to 'comply with their statutes in this important matter',[3] published his findings in a weighty pamphlet, *Cathedral Trusts and their Fulfilment* – and promply lost his job.

Rochester and Winchester were not, of course, alone in their disregard of the responsibilities, stated or implied, which accompanied their endowments. Mr Whiston had cast a level eye at other ancient cathedrals – Canterbury, Ely, Worcester, Durham – and he concluded from the abuses he found: 'Surely cathedrals were not endowed to teach morality like this, or to be pattern churches of such flagrant selfishness'.[4] A similar John Bold figure in the diocese of Hereford, for instance, one James Martin, had complained to the bishop there a little earlier of the absenteeism and gross pluralism, and by implication the abuse of cathedral endowments, which affected his own parish, where the young Elizabeth Barrett was a fellow-parishioner. A nephew of the late bishop had been presented to the parishes of Colwall and Coddington, where he lived 'in a state of beggary, drunkenness, and infamy scarcely credible by any but the two hundred parishioners intrusted to his care'.[5] When another non-resident pluralist was subsequently preferred to the parish, James Martin indignantly brought this matter, and others, to the attention of the bishop. He had scant hope of redress, however, for his lordship, although he drew his large stipend from the endowment of the cathedral, was rarely in his diocese. His own presentation to the see was largely a sinecure, for he had long been Warden of Winchester (Winchester again), where he preferred to reside, and as James Martin pointed out tartly, 'Your constant residence in a distant part of the kingdom . . . [has] probably left you less attentive to your duties here as Bishop of Hereford than you otherwise would or ought to be'![6] *The Times* had published his letter; but the energies of leader-writers were elsewhere, and more public attention was deflected. Nevertheless, reform was in the air, and eager James Martins and John Bolds all over the country multiplied to identify and initiate them.

Oxford was, it can be claimed, the *fons et origo* of it all. It had been (and still was) at the centre of reforms in the Church and in the universities. (Trollope himself reflected in *An Autobiography*, 'No doubt the increased industry of the bishops has come, as has the increased industry of public officers, from the demand of the people whom they are called to serve. But in no way and by no means has more been done to create this energy than by [the] movement at Oxford.') Throughout *The Warden* the narrator refers ironically or ruefully to the august body of convocation, the great legislative body of the university. The central event to which Trollope refers, and from which, many say, all the succeeding reforms were born, had begun in Oxford in 1833 when general reforming conscience was raised by Keble's famous Assize Sermon in St Mary's Church. It was the inauguration of the Oxford Movement, the series of strategies orchestrated by the old High Church to re-Catholicise the English Church. Trollope identified the movement as *the* reforming source in society: the Oxford leaders 'stirred up throughout the country so strong a feeling of religion [and] gave rise by their works to so much thought on a matter which had been allowed for years to go on almost without any thought . . .' (*An Autobiography*).

In the early days of the ascetic leadership of Keble, Newman and Pusey, tract after tract had poured from the pens of the clergy in Oxford, and then from pens nationwide as the reforming fervour spread. By the time of *The Warden* the movement was in its second phase. In 1855 it was ten years since Newman's conversion to the Roman Church, and the reforming movement which for him was concerned exclusively with liturgy, dogma and the ancient rubrics of the Prayer Book now concerned itself as much with the externals of worship – the ceremonies and ornaments and processions which characterised later Ritualists. After Newman's departure, and Keble's retirement from the scene, the leader of the party was seen as Edward Pusey, and its adherents were known, in a derogatory way, as 'Puseyites'. Newman's conversion in 1845 had led to renewed suspicion that the reformers at Oxford were 'Romanisers', and the hostility with which they were regarded is suggested by Trollope's satirical attack on Dickens in chapter 15 of *The Warden*: in Dickens's supposed novel, *The Almshouse*, the daughter of the demonic Master there, is, we are told, 'addicted to Puseyism and the curate'. Trollope, already about his Post Office career in Ireland at the outset of the movement, was no Tractarian sympathiser. More than forty years later, he records what he sees as the more important and long-lasting effects of the reformers:

But the wiggeries and vestments [of the Ritualists] have been simply the dross which has come from their fused gold. If you will make water really boil, some will commonly boil over. They have built new churches, and cleansed old churches, and opened closed churches. They have put on fuel and poked the fire, till heat really does issue from it. (*An Autobiography*)

The reforming influence at Oxford, noted by press and novel, was spread through society as much by this kind of written word as by other obvious channels used by the Church. In 1866, ten years after *The Warden* appeared, and as he was beginning the last in the series of Barsetshire novels, *The Last Chronicle of Barset*, Trollope started on a group of articles for the *Pall Mall Gazette* on 'Clergymen of the Church of England', in which he comments with generally sympathetic urbanity and wit on the role and nature of different officers of the Established Church. The ten 'characters' represent a range of contemporary clergymen, from 'The Modern Archbishop' and 'The Normal Dean of the Present Day' to 'The Town Incumbent' and 'The Curate in a Popular Parish'. Though no single one directly represents the warden of a charity like Hiram's Hospital, the composite features of the clergy present a version of Trollope's view of the cloth.

The Church, so much in the news in the middle decades of the century, is an institution in which Trollope can explore a favourite theme of Victorian novelists, the attempted reconciliation of society and the individual, and his own personal concern with the clash between private integrity and public morality. They are both central features of *The Warden*. Trollope's later version of the dilemmas which can face the modern clergyman, and the portrait nearest to Mr Harding is 'The Clergyman Who Subscribes for Colenso'. This man, too, must somehow bridge the gap between what is required of him by the institution he serves, and the dictates of his own conscience. The thinking clergyman, confronted with the challenge that the Church now requires him to teach doctrine 'hardly compatible with the life of an Englishman in the nineteenth century'[7] must somehow discharge his duties to his parishioners while maintaining his own intellectual integrity. If he 'subscribes for Colenso' (the heterodox Bishop of Natal who had been deprived of his see for questioning the literal truth of the Old Testament), he announces to the clerical world that he is prepared 'henceforward to be recognised as little better than an infidel – certainly as an enemy in the camp'.[8] If he declines to subscribe, under the pressure of his less liberal brethren, his conscience will taunt him to distraction. In the fictional world of Barset, but in the context of the same topicalities, the resolution of the tormented Mr Harding, faced with a similar choice, is unequivocal and unflinching.

Mr Harding's biblical certainties are, we suppose, undisturbed, but the ethics of his personal life as a clergyman are deeply troubled. He is Trollope's model for 'the free-thinking clergyman of the present time' and the 'meek, old-world clergyman [who] dares no longer teach . . . all that his father taught before him',[9] a demonstration that the values of personal integrity in a world that teaches compromise are always paramount.

Trollope was no anti-reformist, in fact, despite his profound sympathy with the Warden. There is no question but that Trollope thinks Tom Towers is right to take issue with the principle of Mr Harding's salary, or that the Rev. Henry Holloway, or the Rev. Mr Whiston are right to protest against the abuses at St Cross and Rochester. But Archdeacon Grantly is not wrong to defend the status quo with the best means at his command, here Sir Abraham Haphazard QC, 'a thorough churchman, a sound conservative'. None of them are bad men; each behaves consistently according to his principles. Trollope's sympathy in *The Warden* is for the individual who is caught in the cross-fire between the old school of thought represented by the Archdeacon and the new school of thought represented by the *Jupiter*, the individual who is suddenly called on to confront issues which affect him deeply but in apparently mutually irreconcilable ways. The simple case put in simple terms by Mr Popular Sentiment (Dickens), of a warden who is 'the demon of the book, the Mephistophiles of the drama', and Dr Pessimist Anticant (Carlyle) in his 'monthly pamphlet on the decay of the world', which in the month in question is on *Modern Charity*, only serves to demonstrate what Trollope is choosing not to do. Of course reform is necessary, and there can be no question of it. But Trollope's main aim here is to demonstrate how one man comes to terms with the clash between social morality and private integrity.

This was the real burden of Trollope's sermon – a plea for understanding among his readers for the individuals behind the issues. In terms of Mr Harding's private view of the wardenship, he has been an exemplary officer, administering the estate of John Hiram more than conscientiously, giving the twelve old bedesmen an allowance increased from his own pocket, and, more importantly, supplying them with the individual care and attention unmentioned in the Founder's will. He has accepted the salary accompanying the post without questioning John Hiram's intentions, and has never, we are told, thought to make any connection between Barchester and 'the well-known case of the Hospital at St Cross' or 'the struggles of Mr Whiston at Rochester'.

John Bold, on the other hand, is a 'new man' born in an age of reform and coming to maturity in the decade of Carlyle's most powerful influence – conditioned therefore by the sustained attacks 'condemnatory of all things in these modern times' that Carlyle had begun with *Past and Present* (1843) and that reached their virulent climax in *Latter-Day Pamphlets* (1850). It was an age when the power of journalism was increasingly forceful. *Latter-Day Pamphlets* appeared monthly, Dickens's novels were published in periodical form, and the daily press thundered like Jove at the abuses it exposed. Trollope describes in his autobiography how his sympathy grew for the unwitting objects of newspaper vehemence, particularly those in the ecclesiastical scandals which filled *The Times*: 'Though I had been much struck by the injustice . . . I had also been angered by the undeserved severity of the newspapers towards the recipients of such incomes, who could hardly be considered to be the chief sinners in the matter . . .' The implication here is that what the *Jupiter* does not do – what Mr Popular Sentiment and Dr Pessimist Anticant do not do – is consider the individuals casually destroyed by their attacks. (It is significant that Tom Towers never visits Barchester or Hiram's Hospital and never makes any attempt to verify his accusation in a meeting with Mr Harding.)

The importance of the individual, however insignificant the individual may be, is at the heart of Trollope's message. Mr Harding is barely aware of society as a ruling force, but he knows the names of the poor old men under his care and loves and cares for them as Abel Handy, Greg Moody, Matthew Spriggs, Jonathan Crumple. He himself whom, on an early reading, we may have seen as helpless, weak, even faintly ridiculous, emerges on a further reading a figure of unguessed-at dignity, courage and firmness of purpose, and never more so than when he is the discredited ex-warden.

The rhetoric of Trollope's fiction works to persuade us that the values he esteems are to be sought not primarily in the community addressed by the *Jupiter*. At the end of the novel Hiram's Hospital is not reformed – the warden's place remains unfilled, half the old bedesmen have gone lonely to their graves, and the rest are rent with dissension as they jockey for positions in a hospital now 'disordered and ugly'. The warden's garden, we are told, once 'the prettiest spot in Barsetshire', is now in symbolic ruin. It is

> a wretched wilderness, the drives and paths are covered with weeds, the flower beds are bare, and the unshorn lawn is now a mass of long grass and unwholesome moss. The beauty of the place is gone, its attractions have withered.

The two opposing voices of society, John Bold and Archdeacon Grantly, have formed an uneasy alliance, and 'do not often revert to the feud of the hospital'. Mr Harding meanwhile, now untouched and untroubled by either, and with his integrity intact, maintains a serene detachment at his lodgings over the chemist's shop, 'the one spot on earth which he calls his own'.

BARBARA DENNIS

References

1. *Cathedral Trusts and their Fulfilment*, p. iii.
2. Ibid., p. 1.
3. Ibid., Preface.
4. Ibid., p. 28.
5. *Diary By Elizabeth Barrett Browning*, p. 290.
6. Ibid., pp. 288–9.
7. 'The Clergyman who Subscribes for Colenso', p. 123.
8. Ibid., p. 130.
9. Ibid., pp. 120–1.

Bibliography

Anthony Trollope, *An Autobiography*, 1883
Anthony Trollope, *Clergymen of the Church of England*, 1866 (Leicester, Leicester University Press, 1974)

Anthony Trollope, *The Warden*, 1855

Rev. T. Whiston, *Cathedral Churches and their Fulfilment*, 1849.

P. Kelly and R. Hudson (eds), *Diary By Elizabeth Barrett Browning* (Columbus, Ohio State University Press, 1969)

NOTE ON THE TEXT

The Warden was written between 29 July 1853 and autumn 1854, but the manuscript is not known to have survived. The present text is based upon that of the first edition, published by Longman in 1855. Various small errors have been corrected, and, in line with other Everyman Paperbacks, the point has been dropped after 'Mr', 'Mrs', 'Dr', etc. Other 'Victorianisms' have been similarly emended: 'to-day' now reads 'today', for instance, and '8000*l*.' now reads '£8000'. The first edition contains some small errors concerning proper names, mistakes which could have been either Trollope's or the typesetter's ('Guildford' instead of 'Guilford', 'Horseman' instead of 'Horsman', and so on), and these too have been silently corrected.

The Warden is one of the few novels that Trollope actually returned to and revised, when it was reprinted by Chapman & Hall in 1878, in their eight-volume edition of the 'Chronicles of Barsetshire'. The changes, however, were very slight, and most of them have been incorporated into the explanatory notes.

The most important changes are the insertion of the Horace quotation on p. 133, the updating and regularising of the *Jupiter*'s circulation figures (pp. 60 and 118) and the series of footnotes commenting on Mr Harding's visit to London (pp. 138–42). The former is interesting because it demonstrates that, by 1878, Trollope was comparatively certain of the sociocultural make-up of his readership; the implicit assumption that his target readers will readily understand the quotation indicates that it is more than likely that Trollope expected them to be members of a (classically) educated middle class. Such certainty is absent from the 1855 edition, when Trollope was still largely unknown as a novelist, and necessarily ignorant of the readership to which he would eventually appeal. Similarly, the latter changes seem to indicate that Trollope was aware of the quintessential contemporaneity that gave *The Warden* its initial (moderate) success; and, again mindful of his readership, the changes ensure that the novel was now addressed to those readers of 1878, rather than to his original readers of 1855, thus framing it in some sort of historical context. [H.O.]

THE WARDEN

CHAPTER I

Hiram's Hospital

The Rev. Septimus Harding was, a few years since, a beneficed clergyman residing in the cathedral town of——; let us call it Barchester. Were we to name Wells or Salisbury,* Exeter, Hereford, or Gloucester, it might be presumed that something personal was intended; and as this tale will refer mainly to the cathedral dignitaries of the town in question, we are anxious that no personality may be suspected. Let us presume that Barchester is a quiet town in the West of England, more remarkable for the beauty of its cathedral and the antiquity of its monuments, than for any commercial prosperity; that the west end of Barchester is the cathedral close; and that the aristocracy of Barchester are the bishop, dean, and canons,* with their respective wives and daughters.

Early in life Mr Harding found himself located at Barchester. A fine voice and a taste for sacred music had decided the position in which he was to exercise his calling, and for many years he performed the easy but not highly paid duties of a minor canon. At the age of forty a small living in the close vicinity of the town increased both his work and his income, and at the age of fifty he became precentor of the cathedral.*

Mr Harding had married early in life, and was the father of two daughters. The eldest, Susan, was born soon after his marriage; the other, Eleanor, not till ten years later. At the time at which we introduce him to our readers he was living as precentor at Barchester with his youngest daughter, then twenty-four years of age; having been many years a widower, and having married his eldest daughter to a son of the bishop, a very short time before his installation to the office of precentor.

Scandal at Barchester affirmed that had it not been for the beauty of his daughter, Mr Harding would have remained a minor canon; but here probably Scandal lied, as she so often does; for even as a minor canon no one had been more popular among his reverend brethren in the close, than Mr Harding; and

Scandal, before she had reprobated Mr Harding for being made precentor by his friend the bishop, had loudly blamed the bishop for having so long omitted to do something for his friend Mr Harding. Be this as it may, Susan Harding, some twelve years since, had married the Rev. Dr Theophilus* Grantly, son of the bishop, archdeacon of Barchester,* and rector of Plumstead Episcopi, and her father became, a few months later, precentor of Barchester Cathedral, that office, being, as is not usual, in the bishop's gift.

Now there are peculiar circumstances connected with the precentorship which must be explained. In the year 1434 there died at Barchester one John Hiram, who had made money in the town as a wool-stapler,* and in his will he left the house in which he died and certain meadows and closes near the town, still called Hiram's Butts, and Hiram's Patch, for the support of twelve superannuated wool-carders,* all of whom should have been born and bred and spent their days in Barchester; he also appointed that an alms-house should be built for their abode, with a fitting residence for a warden, which warden was also to receive a certain sum annually out of the rents of the said butts and patches. He, moreover, willed, having had a soul alive to harmony, that the precentor of the cathedral should have the option of being also warden of the alms-houses, if the bishop in each case approved.

From that day to this the charity had gone on and prospered – at least, the charity had gone on, and the estates had prospered. Wool-carding in Barchester there was no longer any; so the bishop, dean, and warden, who took it in turn to put in the old men, generally appointed some hangers-on of their own; worn-out gardeners, decrepit grave-diggers, or octogenarian sextons, who thankfully received a comfortable lodging and one shilling and fourpence a day, such being the stipend to which, under the will of John Hiram, they were declared to be entitled. Formerly, indeed, – that is, till within some fifty years of the present time, – they received but sixpence a day, and their breakfast and dinner was found them at a common table by the warden, such an arrangement being in stricter conformity with the absolute wording of old Hiram's will: but this was thought to be inconvenient, and to suit the tastes of neither warden nor bedesmen,* and the daily one shilling and fourpence was substituted with the common consent of all parties, including the bishop and the corporation of Barchester.

Such was the condition of Hiram's twelve old men when Mr Harding was appointed warden; but if they may be considered as well-to-do in the world according to their condition, the happy warden was much more so. The patches and butts which, in John Hiram's time, produced hay or fed cows, were now covered with rows of houses; the value of the property had gradually increased from year to year, and century to century, and was now presumed by those who knew anything about it to bring in a very nice income; and by some who knew nothing about it, to have increased to an almost fabulous extent.

The property was farmed by a gentleman in Barchester, who also acted as the bishop's steward — a man whose father and grandfather had been stewards to the bishops of Barchester, and farmers of John Hiram's estate. The Chadwicks had earned a good name in Barchester; they had lived respected by bishops, deans, canons, and precentors; they had been buried in the precincts of the cathedral; they had never been known as griping, hard men, but had always lived comfortably, maintained a good house, and held a high position in Barchester society. The present Mr Chadwick was a worthy scion of a worthy stock, and the tenants living on the butts and patches, as well as those on the wide episcopal domains of the see, were well pleased to have to do with so worthy and liberal a steward.

For many, many years, — records hardly tell how many, probably from the time when Hiram's wishes had been first fully carried out, — the proceeds of the estate had been paid by the steward or farmer to the warden, and by him divided among the bedesmen; after which division he paid himself such sums as became his due. Times had been when the poor warden got nothing but his bare house, for the patches had been subject to floods, and the land of Barchester butts was said to be unproductive; and in these hard times, the warden was hardly able to make out the daily dole for his twelve dependants. But by degrees things mended; the patches were drained, and cottages began to rise upon the butts, and the wardens, with fairness enough, repaid themselves for the evil days gone by. In bad times the poor men had had their due, and therefore in good times they could expect no more. In this manner the income of the warden had increased; the picturesque house attached to the hospital had been enlarged and adorned, and the office had become one of the most coveted of the snug clerical sinecures attached to our church. It was now wholly in the bishop's gift, and though the dean and chapter, in former days, made a stand on the subject, they had thought it more conducive to their honour to have a rich precentor appointed by the bishop, than a poor one appointed by themselves. The stipend of the precentor of Barchester was eighty pounds a year. The income arising from the wardenship of the hospital was eight hundred, besides the value of the house.

Murmurs, very slight murmurs, had been heard in Barchester, – few indeed, and far between – that the proceeds of John Hiram's property had not been fairly divided: but they can hardly be said to have been of such a nature as to have caused uneasiness to any one: still the thing had been whispered, and Mr Harding had heard it. Such was his character in Barchester, so universal was his popularity, that the very fact of his appointment would have quieted louder whispers than those which had been heard; but Mr Harding was an open-handed, just-minded man, and feeling that there might be truth in what had been said, he had, on his instalment, declared his intention of adding twopence a day to each man's pittance, making a sum of sixty-two pounds eleven shillings and fourpence,* which he was to pay out of his own pocket. In doing so, however, he distinctly and repeatedly observed to the men, that though he promised for himself, he could not promise for his successors, and that the extra twopence could only be looked on as a gift from himself, and not from the trust. The bedesmen, however, were most of them older than Mr Harding, and were quite satisfied with the security on which their extra income was based.

This munificence on the part of Mr Harding had not been unopposed. Mr Chadwick had mildly but seriously dissuaded him from it; and his strong-minded son-in-law, the archdeacon, the man of whom alone Mr Harding stood in awe, had urgently, nay, vehemently, opposed so impolitic a concession; but the warden had made known his intention to the hospital before the archdeacon had been able to interfere, and the deed was done.

Hiram's Hospital, as the retreat is called, is a picturesque building enough, and shows the correct taste with which the ecclesiastical architects of those days were imbued. It stands on the banks of the little river, which flows nearly round the cathedral close, being on the side furthest from the town. The London road crosses the river by a pretty one-arched bridge, and, looking from this bridge, the stranger will see the windows of the old men's rooms, each pair of windows separated by a small buttress. A broad gravel walk runs between the building and the river, which is always trim and cared for; and at the end of the walk, under the parapet of the approach to the bridge, is a large and well-worn seat, on which, in mild weather, three or four of Hiram's bedesmen are sure to be seen seated. Beyond this row of buttresses, and further from the bridge, and also further from the water which here suddenly bends, are the pretty oriel windows of Mr Harding's house, and his well-mown lawn. The entrance to the hospital is from the London road, and is made through a ponderous gateway under a heavy stone arch, unnecessary, one would suppose, at any time, for the protection of twelve old men, but greatly conducive to the good appearance of Hiram's charity. On passing through this portal, never closed to any one from six a.m. till ten p.m., and never open afterwards, except on application to a huge, intricately hung, medieval bell, the handle of which no uninitiated intruder can possibly find, the six doors of the old men's abodes are seen, and beyond them is a slight iron screen, through which the more happy portion of the Barchester élite pass into the Elysium* of Mr Harding's dwelling.

Mr Harding is a small man, now verging on sixty years, but bearing few of the signs of age; his hair is rather grizzled, though not grey, his eye is very mild, but clear and bright, though the double glasses which are held swinging from his hand, unless when fixed upon his nose, show that time has told upon his sight: his hands are delicately white, and both hands and feet are small; he always wears a black frock coat, black knee-breeches, and black gaiters, and somewhat scandalises some of his more hyper-clerical brethren by a black neck-handkerchief.*

Mr Harding's warmest admirers cannot say that he was ever an industrious man; the circumstances of his life have not called on him to be so; and yet he can hardly be called an idler. Since his appointment to his precentorship, he has published, with all possible additions of vellum, typography, and gilding, a collection of our ancient church music, with some correct dissertations on Purcell, Crotch, and Nares.* He has greatly improved the choir of Barchester, which, under his dominion, now rivals that of any cathedral in England. He has taken something more than his fair share in the cathedral services, and has played the violoncello daily to such audiences as he could collect, or, *faute de mieux*,* to no audience at all.

We must mention one other peculiarity of Mr Harding. As we have before stated, he has an income of eight hundred a year, and has no family but his one daughter; and yet he is never quite at ease in money matters. The vellum and gilding of *Harding's Church Music*, cost more than any one knows, except the author, the publisher, and the Rev. Theophilus Grantly, who allows none of his father-in-law's extravagances to escape him. Then he is generous to his daughter, for whose service he keeps a small carriage and pair of ponies. He is, indeed, generous to all, but especially to the twelve old men who are in a peculiar manner under his care. No doubt with such an income Mr Harding should be above the world, as the saying is; but at any rate, he is not above Archdeacon Theophilus Grantly, for he is always more or less in debt to his son-in-law, who has, to a certain extent, assumed the arrangement of the precentor's pecuniary affairs.

The Barchester Reformer

Mr Harding has been now precentor of Barchester for ten years; and, alas, the murmurs respecting the proceeds of Hiram's estate are again becoming audible. It is not that anyone begrudges to Mr Harding the income which he enjoys, and the comfortable place which so well becomes him; but such matters have begun to be talked of in various parts of England. Eager pushing politicians have asserted in the House of Commons, with very telling indignation, that the grasping priests of the Church of England are gorged with the wealth which the charity of former times has left for the solace of the aged, or the education of the young. The well-known case of the Hospital of St Cross,* has even come before the law courts of the country, and the struggles of Mr Whiston, at Rochester,* have met with sympathy and support. Men are beginning to say that these things must be looked into.

Mr Harding, whose conscience in the matter is clear, and who has never felt that he had received a pound from Hiram's will to which he was not entitled, has naturally taken the part of the church in talking over these matters with his friend, the bishop, and his son-in-law, the archdeacon. The archdeacon, indeed, Dr Grantly, has been somewhat loud in the matter: he is a personal friend of the dignitaries of the Rochester Chapter, and has written letters in the public press on the subject of that turbulent Dr Whiston, which, his admirers think, must well nigh set the question at rest. It is also known at Oxford, that he is the author of the pamphlet signed 'Sacerdos'* on the subject of the Earl of Guildford and St Cross, in which it is so clearly argued that the manners of the present times do not admit of a literal adhesion to the very words of the founder's will, but that the interests of the church for which the founder was so deeply concerned, are best consulted in enabling its bishops to reward those shining lights, whose services have been most signally serviceable to Christianity. In answer to this, it is asserted that Henry de Blois, founder of St Cross, was not greatly interested in the welfare of the reformed church, and that the masters of St Cross, for many years past, cannot be called shining lights in the service of Christianity; it is, however, stoutly maintained, and no doubt felt, by all the archdeacon's friends, that his logic is conclusive, and has not, in fact, been answered.

With such a tower of strength to back both his arguments and his conscience, it may be imagined that Mr Harding has never felt any compunction as to receiving his quarterly sum of two hundred pounds. Indeed, the subject has never presented itself to his mind in that shape. He has talked not unfrequently, and heard very much about the wills of old founders and the incomes arising from their estates, during the last year or two; he did even, at one moment, feel a doubt (since expelled by his son-in-laws's logic) as to whether Lord Guildford was clearly entitled to receive so enormous an income as he does from the revenues of St Cross, but that he himself was overpaid with his modest eight hundred pounds; – he who, out of that, voluntarily gave up sixty-two pounds eleven shillings and fourpence a year to his twelve old nieghbours; – he who, for the money, does his precentor's work as no precentor has done it before, since Barchester Cathedral was built; – such an idea has never sullied his quiet, or disturbed his conscience.

Nevertheless, Mr Harding is becoming uneasy at the rumour which he knows to prevail in Barchester on the subject. He is aware that, at any rate, two of his old men have been heard to say, that if every one had his own, they might each have their hundred pounds a year, and live like gentlemen, instead of a beggarly one shilling and sixpence a day; and that they had slender cause to be thankful for a miserable dole of twopence, when Mr Harding and Mr Chadwick, between them, ran away with thousands of pounds which old good John Hiram never intended for the like of them. It is the ingratitude of this which stings Mr Harding. One of this discontented pair, Abel Handy, was put into the hospital by himself; he had been a stonemason in Barchester, and had broken his thigh by a fall from a scaffolding, while employed about the cathedral; and Mr Harding had given him the first vacancy in the hospital after the occurrence, although Dr Grantly had been very anxious to put into it an insufferable clerk of his at Plumstead Episcopi, who had lost all his teeth, and whom the archdeacon hardly knew how to get rid of by other means. Dr Grantly has not forgotten to remind Mr Harding how well satisfied with his one and sixpence a day old Joe Mutters would have been, and how injudicious it was on the part of Mr Harding to allow a radical from the town to get into the concern. Probably Dr Grantly forgot, at the moment, that the charity was intended for broken-down journeymen of Barchester.

There is living at Barchester, a young man, a surgeon, named John Bold, and both Mr Harding and Dr Grantly are well aware that to him is owing the pestilent rebellious feeling which has shown itself in the hospital; yes, and the renewal, too, of that disagreeable talk about Hiram's estates which is now again prevalent in Barchester. Nevertheless, Mr Harding and Mr Bold are acquainted with each other; we may say, are friends, considering the great disparity in their years. Dr Grantly, however, has a holy horror of the impious demagogue, as on one occasion he called Bold, when speaking of him to the precentor; and being a more prudent far-seeing man than Mr Harding, and possessed of a stronger head, he already perceives that this John Bold will work great trouble in Barchester. He considers that he is to be regarded as an enemy, and thinks that he should not be admitted into the camp on anything like friendly terms. As John Bold will occupy much of our attention, we must endeavour to explain who he is, and why he takes the part of John Hiram's bedesmen.

John Bold is a young surgeon, who passed many of his boyish years at Barchester. His father was a physician in the city of London, where he made a moderate fortune, which he invested in houses in that city. The Dragon of Wantly inn* and posting-house, belonged to him, also four shops in the High Street, and a moiety of the new row of genteel villas (so called in the advertisements), built outside the town just beyond Hiram's Hospital. To one of these Dr Bold retired to spend the evening of his life, and to die; and here his son John spent his holidays, and afterwards his Christmas vacation, when he went from school to study surgery in the London hospitals. Just as John Bold was entitled to write himself surgeon and apothecary,* old Dr Bold died, leaving his Barchester property to his son, and a certain sum in the three per cents to his daughter Mary, who is some four or five years older than her brother.

John Bold determined to settle himself at Barchester, and look after his own property, as well as the bones and bodies of such of his neighbours as would call upon him for assistance in their troubles. He therefore put up a large brass plate, with 'John Bold, Surgeon,' on it, to the great disgust of the nine practitioners who were already trying to get a living out of the bishop, dean and canons; and began house-keeping with the aid of his sister. At this time he was not more than twenty-four years old; and though he has now been three years in Barchester, we have not heard that he has done much harm to the nine worthy practitioners. Indeed, their dread of him died away; for in three years he had not taken three fees.

Nevertheless, John Bold is a clever man, and would, with practice, be a clever surgeon; but he has got quite into another line of life. Having enough to live on, he has not been forced to work for bread; he has declined to subject himself to what he calls the drudgery of the profession, by which, I believe, he means the general work of a practising surgeon; and has found other employment. He frequently binds up the bruises and sets the limbs of such of the poorer classes as profess his way of thinking – but this he does for love. Now I will not say that the archdeacon is strictly correct in stigmatising John Bold as a demagogue, for I hardly know how extreme must be a man's opinions befor he can be justly so called; but Bold is a strong reformer. His passion is the reform of all abuses; state abuses, church abuses, corporation abuses (he has got himself elected a town councillor of Barchester, and has so worried three consecutive mayors, that it became somewhat difficult to find a fourth), abuses in medical practice, and general abuses in the world at large. Bold is thoroughly sincere in his patriotic endeavours to mend mankind, and there is something to be admired in the energy with which he devotes himself to remedying evil and stopping injustice; but I fear that he is too much imbued with the idea that he has a special mission for reforming. It would be well if one so young had a little more diffidence himself, and more trust in the honest purposes of others – if he could be brought to believe that old customs need not necessarily be evil, and that changes may possibly be dangerous; but no, Bold has all the ardour, and all the self-assurance of a Danton,* and hurls his anathemas* against time-honoured practices with the violence of a French Jacobin.*

No wonder that Dr Grantly should regard Bold as a firebrand, falling, as he has done, almost in the centre of the quiet ancient close of Barchester Catherdral. Dr Grantly would have him avoided as the plague; but the old Doctor and Mr Harding were fast friends. Young Johnny Bold used to play as a boy on Mr Harding's lawn; he has many a time won the precentor's heart by listening with rapt attention to his sacred strains; and since those days, to tell the truth at once, he has nearly won another heart within the same walls.

Eleanor Harding has not plighted her troth to John Bold, nor has she, perhaps, owned to herself how dear to her the young reformer is; but she cannot endure that anyone should speak harshly of him. She does not dare to defend him when her brother-in-law is so loud against him; for she, like her father, is somewhat afraid of Dr Grantly; but she is beginning greatly to dislike the archdeacon. She persuades her father that it would be both unjust and injudicious to banish his young friend because of his politics; she cares little to go to houses where she will not meet him, and, in fact, she is in love.

Nor is there any good reason why Eleanor Harding should not love John Bold. He has all those qualities which are likely to touch a girl's heart. He is brave, eager, and amusing; well-made and good-looking; young and enterprising; his character is in all respects good; he has sufficient income to support a wife; he is her father's friend; and, above all, he is in love with her: then why should not Eleanor Harding be attached to John Bold?

Dr Grantly, who has as many eyes as Argus,* and has long seen how the wind blows in that direction, thinks there are various strong reasons why this should not be so. He has not thought it wise as yet to speak to his father-in-law on the subject, for he knows how foolishly indulgent is Mr Harding in everything that concerns his daughter; but he has discussed the matter with his all-trusted helpmate, within that sacred recess formed by the clerical bed-curtains at Plumstead Episcopi.

How much sweet solace, how much valued counsel has our archdeacon received within that sainted enclosure! 'Tis there alone that he unbends, and comes down from his high church pedestal to the level of a mortal man. In the world Dr Grantly never lays aside that demeanour which so well becomes him. He has all the dignity of an ancient saint with the sleekness of a modern bishop; he is always the same; he is always the archdeacon; unlike Homer, he never nods.* Even with his father-in-law, even with the bishop and dean, he maintains that sonorous tone and lofty deportment which strikes awe into the young hearts of Barchester, and absolutely cows the whole parish of Plumstead Episcopi. 'Tis only when he has exchanged that ever-new shovel hat* for a tasselled nightcap, and those shining black habiliments for his accustomed *robe de nuit*, that Dr Grantly talks, and looks, and thinks like an ordinary man.

Many of us have often thought how severe a trial of faith must this be to the wives of our great church dignitaries. To us these men are personifications of St Paul; their very gait is a speaking sermon; their clean and sombre apparel exacts from us faith and submission, and the cardinal virtues seem to hover around their sacred hats. A dean or archbishop, in the garb of his order, is sure of our reverence, and a well got-up bishop fills our very souls with awe. But how can this feeling be perpetuated in the bosoms of those who see the bishops without their aprons,* and the archdeacon even in a lower state of *dishabille*?*

Do we not all know some reverend, all but sacred, personage before whom our tongue ceases to be loud, and our step to be elastic? But were we once to see him stretch himself beneath the bed-clothes, yawn widely, and bury his face upon his pillow, we could chatter before him as glibly as before a doctor or a lawyer. From some such cause, doubtless, it arose that our archdeacon listened to the counsels of his wife, though he considered himself entitled to give counsel to every other being whom he met.

'My dear,' he said, as he adjusted the copious folds of his nightcap, 'there was that John Bold at your father's again today. I must say your father is very imprudent.'

'He is imprudent – he always was,' replied Mrs Grantly, speaking from under the comfortable bed-clothes. 'There's nothing new in that.'

'No, my dear, there's nothing new – I know that; but, at the present juncture of affairs, such imprudence is – is – I'll tell you what, my dear, if he does not take care what he's about, John Bold will be off with Eleanor.'

'I think he will, whether papa takes care or no; and why not?'

'Why not!' almost screamed the archdeacon, giving so rough a pull at his nightcap as almost to bring it over his nose; 'why not! – that pestilent, interfering upstart, John Bold – the most vulgar young person I ever met! Do you know that he is meddling with your father's affairs in a most uncalled for – most——' And being at a loss for an epithet sufficiently injurious, he finished his expressions of horror by muttering, 'Good heavens!' in a manner that had been found very efficacious in clerical meetings of the diocese. He must for the moment have forgotten where he was.

'As to his vulgarity, archdeacon' (Mrs Grantly had never assumed a more familiar term than this in addressing her husband), 'I don't agree with you. Not that I like Mr Bold – he is a great deal too conceited for me; but then Eleanor does, and it would be the best thing in the world for papa if they were to marry. Bold would never trouble himself about Hiram's Hospital if he were papa's son-in-law.' And the lady turned herself round under the bed-clothes, in a manner to which the doctor was well accustomed, and which told him, as plainly as words, that as far as she was concerned the subject was over for that night.

'Good heavens!' murmured the doctor again – he was evidently much put beside himself.

Dr Grantly is by no means a bad man; he is exactly the man which such an education as his was most likely to form; his intellect being sufficient for such a place in the world, but not sufficient to put him in advance of it. He performs with a rigid constancy such of the duties of a parish clergyman as are, to his thinking, above the sphere of his curate, but it is as an archdeacon that he shines.

We believe, as a general rule, that either a bishop or his archdeacons have sinecures: where a bishop works, archdeacons have but little to do, and *vice versa*. In the diocese of Barchester the Archdeacon of Barchester does the work. In that capacity he is diligent, authoritative, and as his friends particularly boast, judicious. His great fault is an overbearing assurance of the virtues and claims of his order, and his great foible is an equally strong confidence in the dignity of his own manner and the eloquence of his own words. He is a moral man, believing the precepts which he teaches, and believing also that he acts up to them; though we cannot say that he would give his coat to the man who took his cloak, or that he is prepared to forgive his brother even seven times.* He is severe enough in exacting his dues, considering that any laxity in this respect would endanger the security of the church; and, could he have his way, he would consign to darkness and perdition, not only every individual reformer, but every committee and every commission that would even dare to ask a question respecting the appropriation of church revenues.*

'They are church revenues: the laity admit it. Surely the church is able to administer her own revenues.' 'Twas thus he was accustomed to argue, when the sacrilegious doings of Lord John Russell* and others were discussed either at Barchester or at Oxford.*

It was no wonder that Dr Grantly did not like John Bold, and that his wife's suggestion, that he should become closely connected with such a man dismayed him. To give him his due, the archdeacon never wanted courage; he was quite willing to meet his enemy on any field, and with any weapon. He had that belief in his own arguments that he felt sure of success, could he only be sure of a fair fight on the part of his adversary. He had no idea that John Bold could really prove that the income of the hospital was malappropriated; why, then, should peace be sought for on such base terms? What! bribe an unbelieving enemy of the church with the sister-in-law of one dignitary, and the daughter of another – with a young lady whose connections with the diocese and chapter of Barchester were so close as to give her an undeniable claim to a husband endowed with some of its sacred wealth! When Dr Grantly talks of unbelieving enemies, he does not mean to imply want of belief in the doctrines of the church, but an equally dangerous scepticism as to its purity in money matters.

Mrs Grantly is not usually deaf to the claims of the high order to which she belongs. She and her husband rarely disagree as to the tone with which the church should be defended; how singular, then, that in such a case as this she should be willing to succumb! The archdeacon again murmurs 'Good heavens!' as he lays himself beside her, but he does so in a voice audible only to himself, and he repeats it till sleep relieves him from deep thought.

Mr Harding himself has seen no reason why his daughter should not love John Bold. He has not been unobservant of her feelings, and perhaps his deepest regret at the part which he fears Bold is about to take regarding the hospital, arises from a dread that he may be separated from his daughter, or that she may be separated from the man she loves. He has never spoken to Eleanor about her lover; he is the last man in the world to allude to such a subject unconsulted, even with his own daughter; and had he considered that he had ground to disapprove of Bold, he would have removed her, or forbidden him his house; but he saw no such ground. He would probably have preferred a second clerical son-in-law, for Mr Harding, also, is attached to his order; and, failing in that, he would at any rate have wished that so near a connection should have thought alike with him on church matters. He would not, however, reject the man his daughter loved because he differed on such subjects with himself.

Hitherto Bold had taken no steps in the matter in any way annoying to Mr Harding personally. Some months since, after a severe battle, which cost him not a little, he gained a victory over a certain old turnpike woman in the neighbourhood, of whose charges another old woman had complained to him. He got the act of Parliament relating to the trust, found that his *protégée* had been wrongly taxed, rode through the gate himself, paying the toll, then brought an action against the gate-keeper, and proved that all people coming up a certain by-lane, and going down a certain other by-lane, were toll free. The fame of his success spread widely abroad, and he began to be looked on as the upholder of the rights of the poor of Barchester. Not long after this success, he heard from different quarters that Hiram's bedesmen were treated as paupers, whereas the property to which they were, in effect, heirs, was very large; and he was instigated by the lawyer whom he had employed in the case of the turpike, to call upon Mr Chadwick for a statement as to the funds of the estate.

Bold had often expressed his indignation at the malappropriation of church funds in general, in the hearing of his friend the precentor; but the conversation had never referred to anything at Barchester; and when Finney, the attorney, induced him to interfere with the affairs of the hospital, it was against Mr Chadwick that his efforts were to be directed. Bold soon found that if he interfered with Mr Chadwick as steward, he must also interfere with Mr Harding as warden; and though he regretted the situation in which this would place him, he was not the man to flinch from his undertaking from personal motives.

As soon as he had determined to take the matter in hand, he set about his work with his usual energy. He got a copy of John

Hiram's will, of the wording of which he made himself perfectly master. He ascertained the extent of the property, and as nearly as he could the value of it; and made out a schedule of what he was informed was the present distribution of its income. Armed with these particulars, he called on Mr Chadwick, having given that gentleman notice of his visit; and asked him for a statement of the income and expenditure of the hospital for the last twenty-five years.

This was of course refused, Mr Chadwick alleging that he had no authority for making public the concerns of a property in managing which he was only a paid servant.

'And who is competent to give you that authority, Mr Chadwick?' asked Bold.

'Only those who employ me, Mr Bold,' said the steward.

'And who are those, Mr Chadwick?' demanded Bold.

Mr Chadwick begged to say that if these inquiries were made merely out of curiosity, he must decline answering them; if Mr Bold had any ulterior proceeding in view, perhaps it would be desirable that any necessary information should be sought for in a professional way by a professional man. Mr Chadwick's attorneys were Messrs Cox and Cummins, of Lincoln's Inn. Mr Bold took down the address of Cox and Cummins, remarked that the weather was cold for the time of the year, and wished Mr Chadwick good morning. Mr Chadwick said it was cold for June, and bowed him out.

He at once went to his lawyer, Finney. Now, Bold was not very fond of his attorney, but, as he said, he merely wanted a man who knew the forms of law, and who would do what he was told for his money. He had no idea of putting himself in the hands of a lawyer. He wanted law from a lawyer as he did a coat from a tailor, because he could not make it so well himself; and he thought Finney the fittest man in Barchester for his purpose. In one respect, at any rate, he was right: Finney was humility itself.

Finney advised an instant letter to Cox and Cummins, mindful of his six-and-eightpence.* 'Slap at them at once, Mr Bold; demand categorically and explicitly a full statement of the affairs of the hospital.'

'Suppose I were to see Mr Harding first,' suggested Bold.

'Yes, yes, by all means,' said the acquiescing Finney; 'though, perhaps, as Mr Harding is no man of business, it may lead –

lead to some little difficulties; but perhaps you're right. Mr Bold, I don't think seeing Mr Harding can do any harm.' Finney saw from the expression of his client's face that he intended to have his own way.

CHAPTER 3

The Bishop of Barchester

Bold at once repaired to the hospital. The day was now far advanced, but he knew that Mr Harding dined in the summer at four, that Eleanor was accustomed to drive in the evening, and that he might therefore probably find Mr Harding alone. It was between seven and eight when he reached the slight iron gate leading into the precentor's garden, and though, as Mr Chadwick observed, the day had been cold for June, the evening was mild, and soft, and sweet. The little gate was open. As he raised the latch he heard the notes of Mr Harding's violoncello from the far end of the garden, and, advancing before the house and across the lawn, he found him playing: and not without an audience. The musician was seated in a garden-chair just within the summer-house, so as to allow the violoncello which he held between his knees to rest upon the dry stone flooring; before him stood a rough music desk, on which was open a page of that dear sacred book, that much-laboured and much-loved volume of church music, which had cost so many guineas; and around sat, and lay, and stood, and leaned, ten of the twelve old men who dwelt with him beneath old John Hiram's roof. The two reformers were not there. I will not say that in their hearts they were conscious of any wrong done or to be done to their mild warden, but latterly they had kept aloof from him, and his music was no longer to their taste.

It was amusing to see the positions, and eager listening faces of these well-to-do old men. I will not say that they all appreciated the music which they heard, but they were intent on appearing to do so; pleased at being where they were, they were determined, as far as in them lay, to give pleasure in return; and they were not unsuccessful. It gladdened the precentor's heart to think that the old bedesmen whom he loved so well, admired the strains which were to him so full of almost ecstatic joy; and he used to boast that such was the air of the hospital, as to make it a precinct specially fit for the worship of St Cecilia.*

Immediately before him, on the extreme corner of the bench which ran round the summer-house, sat one old man, with his handkerchief smoothly lain upon his knees, who did enjoy the moment, or acted enjoyment well. He was one on whose large frame many years, for he was over eighty, had made small havoc, – he was still an upright, burly, handsome figure, with an open ponderous brow, round which clung a few, though very few, thin grey locks. The coarse black gown of the hospital, the breeches, and buckled shoes became him well; and as he sat with his hands folded on his staff, and his chin resting on his hands, he was such a listener as most musicians would be glad to welcome.

This man was certainly the pride of the hospital. It had always been the custom that one should be selected as being to some extent in authority over the others; and though Mr Bunce, for such was his name, and so he was always designated by his inferior brethren, had no greater emoluments than they, he had assumed, and well knew how to maintain, the dignity of his elevation. The precentor delighted to call him his sub-warden, and was not ashamed, occasionally, when no other guest was there, to bid him sit down by the same parlour fire, and drink the full glass of port which was placed near him. Bunce never went without the second glass, but no entreaty ever made him take a third.

'Well, well, Mr Harding; you're too good, much too good,' he'd always say, as the second glass was filled; but when that was drunk, and the half-hour over, Bunce stood erect, and with a benediction which his patron valued, retired to his own abode. He knew the world too well to risk the comfort of such halcyon moments, by prolonging them till they were disagreeable.

Mr Bunce, as it may be imagined, was most strongly opposed to innovation. Not even Dr Grantly had a more holy horror of those who would interfere in the affairs of the hospital; he was every inch a churchman, and though he was not very fond of Dr Grantly personally, that arose from there not being room in the hospital for two people so much alike as the doctor and himself, rather than from any dissimilarity in feeling. Mr Bunce was inclined to think that the warden and himself could manage the hospital without further assistance; and that, though the bishop was the constitutional visitor, and as such entitled to special reverence from all connected with John Hiram's will, John

Hiram never intended that his affairs should be interfered with by an archdeacon.*

At the present moment, however, these cares were off his mind, and he was looking at his warden, as though he thought the music heavenly, and the musician hardly less so.

As Bold walked silently over the lawn, Mr Harding did not at first perceive him, and continued to draw his bow slowly across the plaintive wires; but he soon found from his audience that some stranger was there, and looking up, began to welcome his young friend with frank hospitality.

'Pray, Mr Harding; pray don't let me disturb you,' said Bold; 'you know how fond I am of sacred music.'

'Oh! it's nothing,' said the precentor, shutting up the book, and then opening it again as he saw the delightfully imploring look of his old friend Bunce. Oh, Bunce, Bunce, Bunce, I fear that after all thou art but a flatterer. 'Well, I'll just finish it then; it's a favourite little bit of Bishop's* and then, Mr Bold, we'll have a stroll and a chat till Eleanor comes in and gives us tea.' And so Bold sat down on the soft turf to listen, or rather to think how, after such sweet harmony, he might best introduce a theme of so much discord, to disturb the peace of him who was so ready to welcome him kindly.

Bold thought that the performance was soon over, for he felt that he had a somewhat difficult task, and he almost regretted the final leave-taking of the last of the old men, slow as they were in going through their adieus.

Bold's heart was in his mouth, as the precentor made some ordinary but kind remark as to the friendliness of the visit.

'One evening call,' said he, 'is worth ten in the morning; real social talk never begins till after dinner. That's why I dine early, so as to get as much as I can of it.'

'Quite true, Mr Harding,' said the other; 'but I fear I've reversed the order of things, and I owe you much apology for troubling you on business at such an hour; but it is on business that I have called just now.'

Mr Harding looked blank and annoyed; there was something in the tone of the young man's voice, which told him that the interview was intended to be disagreeable, and he shrank back at finding his kindly greeting so repulsed.

'I wish to speak to you about the hospital,' continued Bold.

'Well, well, anything I can tell you I shall be most happy——'

'It's about the accounts.'

'Then, my dear fellow, I can tell you nothing, for I'm as ignorant as a child. All I know is, that they pay me £800 a year. Go to Chadwick, he knows all about the accounts; and now tell me, will poor Mary Jones ever get the use of her limb again?'

'Well, I think she will, if she's careful; but, Mr Harding, I hope you won't object to discuss with me what I have to say about the hospital.'

Mr Harding gave a deep, long-drawn sigh. He did object, very strongly object, to discuss any such subject with John Bold; but he had not the business tact of Mr Chadwick, and did not know how to relieve himself from the coming evil; he sighed sadly, but made no answer.

'I have the greatest regard for you, Mr Harding,' continued Bold; 'the truest respect, the most sincere——'

'Thank ye, thank ye, Mr Bold,' interjaculated the precentor somewhat impatiently; 'I'm much obliged, but never mind that; I'm as likely to be in the wrong as another man – quite as likely.'

'But, Mr Harding, I must express what I feel, lest you should think there is personal enmity in what I'm going to do.'

'Personal enmity! Going to do! Why you're not going to cut my throat, nor put me into the Ecclesiastical Court——'

Bold tried to laugh, but he couldn't. He was quite in earnest, and determined in his course, and couldn't make a joke of it. He walked on awhile in silence before he recommenced his attack, during which Mr Harding, who had still the bow in his hand, played rapidly on an imaginary violoncello. 'I fear there is reason to think that John Hiram's will is not carried out to the letter, Mr Harding,' said the young man at last; 'and I have been asked to see into it.'

'Very well, I've no objection on earth; and now we need not say another word about it.'

'Only one word more, Mr Harding. Chadwick has referred me to Cox and Cummins, and I think it my duty to apply to them for some statement about the hospital. In what I do I may appear to be interfering with you, and I hope you will forgive me for doing so.'

'Mr Bold,' said the other, stopping, and speaking with some solemnity, 'if you act justly, say nothing in this matter but the truth, and use no unfair weapons in carrying out your purposes, I shall have nothing to forgive. I presume you think I am not entitled to the income I receive from the hospital, and that others are entitled to it. Whatever some may do, I shall never attribute to you base motives because you hold an opinion opposed to my own, and adverse to my interests: pray do what you consider to be your duty; I can give you no assistance, neither will I offer you any obstacle. Let me, however, suggest to you, that you can in no wise forward your views nor I mine, by any discussion between us. Here comes Eleanor and the ponies, and we'll go in to tea.'

Bold, however, felt that he could not sit down at ease with Mr Harding and his daughter after what had passed, and therefore excused himself with much awkward apology; and merely raising his hat and bowing as he passed Eleanor and the pony chair, left her in disappointed amazement at his departure.

Mr Harding's demeanour certainly impressed Bold with a full conviction, that the warden felt that he stood on strong grounds, and almost made him think that he was about to interfere without due warrant in the private affairs of a just and honourable man; but Mr Harding himself was anything but satisfied with his own view of the case.

In the first place, he wished for Eleanor's sake to think well of Bold and to like him, and yet he could not but feel disgusted at the arrogance of his conduct. What right had he to say that John Hiram's will was not fairly carried out? But then the question would arise within his heart, Was that will fairly acted on? Did John Hiram mean that the warden of his hospital should receive considerably more out of the legacy than all the twelve old men together for whose behoof the hospital was built? Could it be possible that John Bold was right, and that the reverend warden of the hospital had been for the last ten years and more the unjust recipient of an income legally and equitably belonging to others? What if it should be proved before the light of day that he, whose life had been so happy, so quiet, so respected, had absorbed £8000, to which he had no title, and which he could never repay? I do not say that he feared that such was really the case, but the first shade of doubt now fell across his mind, and from this evening, for many a long, long day, our good, kind, loving warden was neither happy nor at ease.

Thoughts of this kind, these first moments of much misery, oppressed Mr Harding as he sat sipping his tea, absent and ill at ease. Poor Eleanor felt that all was not right, but her ideas as to the cause of the evening's discomfort did not go beyond her lover, and his sudden and uncivil departure: she thought there must have been some quarrel between Bold and her father, and she was half angry with both, though she did not attempt to explain to herself why she was so.

Mr Harding thought long and deeply over these things, both before he went to bed, and after it, as he lay awake, questioning within himself the validity of his claim to the income which he enjoyed. It seemed clear at any rate that, however unfortunate he might be at having been placed in such a position, no one could say that he ought either to have refused the appointment first, or to have rejected the income afterwards. All the world – meaning the ecclesiastical world as confined to the English church – knew that the wardenship of the Barchester Hospital was a snug sinecure, but no one had ever been blamed for accepting it. To how much blame, however, would he have been open had he rejected it! How mad would he have been thought had he declared, when the situation was vacant and offered to him, that he had scruples as to receiving £800 a year from John Hiram's property, and that he had rather some stranger should possess it! How would Dr Grantly have shaken his wise head, and have consulted with his friends in the close as to some decent retreat for the coming insanity of the poor minor canon! If he was right in accepting the place, it was clear to him also that he would be wrong in rejecting any part of the income attached to it. The patronage was a valuable appanage* of the bishopric; and surely it would not be his duty to lessen the value of that preferment which had been bestowed on himself; surely he was bound to stand by his order.

But somehow these arguments, though they seemed logical, were not satisfactory. Was John Hiram's will fairly carried out? that was the true question: and if not, was it not his especial duty to see that this was done, – his especial duty, whatever injury it might do to his order, – however ill such duty might be received by his patron and his friends? At the idea of his friends, his mind turned unhappily to his son-in-law: he knew well how strongly he would be supported by Dr Grantly, if he could bring himself to put his case into the archdeacon's hands, and to allow him to fight the battle; but he knew also that he would find no sympathy there for his doubts, no friendly feeling, no inward comfort. Dr Grantly would be ready enough to take up his

cudgel against all comers on behalf of the church militant,* but
he would do so on the distasteful ground of the church's
infallibility. Such a contest would give no comfort to Mr
Harding's doubts; he was not so anxious to prove himself right,
as to be so.

I have said before that Dr Grantly was the working man of
the diocese, and that his father the bishop was somewhat
inclined to an idle life: so it was; but the bishop, though he had
never been an active man, was one whose qualities had rendered
him dear to all who knew him. He was the very opposite to his
son; he was a bland and a kind old man, opposed by every
feeling to authoritative demonstrations and episcopal ostenta-
tion. It was perhaps well for him, in his situation, that his son
had early in life been able to do that which he could not well do
when he was younger, and which he could not have done at all
now that he was over seventy. The bishop knew how to entertain
the clergy of his diocese, to talk easy small talk with the rectors'
wives, and put curates at their ease; but it required the strong
hand of the archdeacon to deal with such as were refractory
either in their doctrines or their lives.

The bishop and Mr Harding loved each other warmly. They
had grown old together, and had together spent many, many
years in clerical pursuits and clerical conversation. When one of
them was a bishop and the other only a minor canon they were
even then much together; but since their children had married,
and Mr Harding had become warden and precentor, they were
all in all to each other. I will not say that they managed the
diocese between them, but they spent much time in discussing
the man who did, and in forming little plans to mitigate his
wrath against church delinquents, and soften his aspirations for
church dominion.

Mr Harding determined to open his mind, and confess his
doubts to his old friend; and to him he went on the morning
after John Bold's uncourteous visit.

Up to this period no rumour of these cruel proceedings against
the hospital had reached the bishop's ears. He had doubtless
heard that men existed who questioned his right to present to a
sinecure of £800 a year, as he had heard from time to time of
some special immorality or disgraceful disturbance in the usually
decent and quiet city of Barchester: but all he did, and all he
was called on to do, on such occasions, was to shake his head,

and to beg his son, the great dictator, to see that no harm happened to the church.

It was a long story that Mr Harding had to tell before he made the bishop comprehend his own view of the case; but we need not follow him through the tale. At first the bishop counselled but one step, recommended but one remedy, had but one medicine in his whole pharmacopeia strong enough to touch so grave a disorder – he prescribed the archdeacon. 'Refer him to the archdeacon,' he repeated, as Mr Harding spoke of Bold and his visit. 'The archdeacon will set you quite right about that,' he kindly said, when his friend spoke with hesitation of the justness of his cause. 'No man has got up all that so well as the archdeacon;' but the dose, though large, failed to quiet the patient; indeed it almost produced nausea.

'But, bishop,' said he, 'did you ever read John Hiram's will?'

The bishop thought probably he had, thirty-five years ago, when first instituted to his see, but could not state positively: however, he very well knew that he had the absolute right to present to the wardenship, and that the income of the warden had been regularly settled.

'But, bishop, the question is, who has the power to settle it? If, as this young man says, the will provides that the proceeds of the property are to be divided into shares, who has the power to alter these provisions?' The bishop had an indistinct idea that they altered themselves by the lapse of years; that a kind of ecclesiastical statute of limitation barred the rights of the twelve bedesmen to any increase of income arising from the increased value of property. He said something about tradition; more of the many learned men who by their practice had confirmed the present arrangement; then went at some length into the propriety of maintaining the due difference in rank and income between a beneficed clergyman, and certain poor old men who were dependent on charity; and concluded his argument by another reference to the archdeacon.

The precentor sat thoughtfully gazing at the fire, and listening to the good-natured reasoning of his friend. What the bishop said had a sort of comfort in it, but it was not a sustaining comfort. It made Mr Harding feel that many others – indeed, all others of his own order – would think him right; but it failed to prove to him that he truly was so.

'Bishop,' said he, at last, after both had sat silent for a while,

'I should deceive you and myself too, if I did not tell you that I am very unhappy about this. Suppose that I cannot bring myself to agree with Dr Grantly! – that I find, after inquiry, that the young man is right, and that I am wrong – what then?'

The two men were sitting near each other – so near, that the bishop was able to lay his hand upon the other's knee, and he did so with a gentle pressure. Mr Harding well knew what that pressure meant. The bishop had no further argument to adduce; he could not fight for the cause as his son would do; he could not prove all the precentor's doubts to be groundless; but he could sympathise with his friend, and he did so; and Mr Harding felt that he had received that for which he came. There was another period of silence, after which, the bishop asked with a degree of irritable energy, very unusual with him, whether this 'pestilent intruder'* (meaning John Bold) had any friends in Barchester.

Mr Harding had fully made up his mind to tell the bishop everything; to speak of his daughter's love, as well as his own troubles; to talk of John Bold in his double capacity of future son-in-law and present enemy; and though he felt it to be sufficiently disagreeable, now was his time to do it.

'He is very intimate at my own house, bishop.' The bishop stared; he was not so far gone in orthodoxy and church-military as his son, but still he could not bring himself to understand how so declared an enemy of the establishment could be admitted on terms of intimacy into the house, not only of so firm a pillar as Mr Harding, but one so much injured as the warden of the hospital.

'Indeed, I like Mr Bold much, personally,' continued the disinterested victim; 'and to tell you the "truth,"' – he hesitated as he brought out the dreadful tidings, – 'I have sometimes thought it not improbable that he would be my second son-in-law.' The bishop did not whistle; we believe that they lose the power of doing so on being consecrated; and that in these days one might as easily meet a corrupt judge as a whistling bishop; but he looked as though he would have done so, but for his apron.

What a brother-in-law for the archdeacon! what an alliance for Barchester close! what a connexion for even the episcopal palace! The bishop, in his simple mind, felt no doubt that John Bold, had he so much power, would shut up all cathedrals, and probably all parish churches; distribute all tithes among Methodists, Baptists, and other savage tribes; utterly annihilate the sacred bench,* and make shovel hats and lawn sleeves as illegal as cowls, sandals and sackcloth!* Here was a nice man to be initiated into the comfortable arcana* of ecclesiastical snuggeries; one who doubted the integrity of parsons, and probably disbelieved the Trinity!*

Mr Harding saw what an effect his communication had made, and almost repented the openness of his disclosure; he, however, did what he could to moderate the grief of his friend and patron. 'I did not say that there is any engagement between them. Had there been, Eleanor would have told me: I know her well enough to be assured that she would have done so; but I see that they are fond of each other; and as a man and a father, I have had no objection to urge against their intimacy.'

'But, Harding,' said the bishop, 'how are you to oppose him, if he is your son-in-law?'

'I don't mean to oppose him; it is he who opposes me: if anything is to be done in defence, I suppose Chadwick will do it. I suppose – '

'Oh, the archdeacon will see to that: were the young man twice his brother-in-law, the archdeacon will never be deterred from doing what he feels to be right.'

Mr Harding reminded the bishop that the archdeacon and the reformer were not yet brothers, and very probably never would be; exacted from him a promise that Eleanor's name should not be mentioned in any discussion between the father bishop and son archdeacon respecting the hosital; and then took his departure, leaving his poor old friend bewildered, amazed, and confounded.

CHAPTER 4

Hiram's Bedesmen

The parties most interested in the movement which is about to set Barchester by the ears, were not the foremost to discuss the merit of the question, as is often the case; but when the bishop, the archdeacon, the warden, the steward and Messrs Cox and Cummins, were all busy with the matter, each in his own way, it is not to be supposed that Hiram's bedesmen themselves were altogether passive spectators. Finney, the attorney, had been among them, asking sly questions, and raising immoderate hopes, creating a party hostile to the warden, and establishing a corps in the enemy's camp, as he figuratively calls it to himself. Poor old men; whoever may be righted or wronged by this inquiry, they at any rate will assuredly be only injured; to them it can only be an unmixed evil. How can their lot be improved? all their wants are supplied; every comfort is administered; they have warm houses, good clothes, plentiful diet, and rest after a life of labour; and above all, that treasure so inestimable in declining years, a true and kind friend to listen to their sorrows, watch over their sickness, and administer comfort as regards this world, and the world to come!

John Bold sometimes thinks of this, when he is talking loudly of the rights of the bedesmen, whom he has taken under his protection; but he quiets the suggestion within his breast with the high-sounding name of justice – 'fiat justitia ruat coelum.'* These old men should, by rights, have one hundred pounds a year instead of one shilling and sixpence a day, and the warden should have two hundred or three hundred pounds instead of eight hundred pounds. What is unjust must be wrong; what is wrong should be righted; and if he declined the task, who else would do it?

'Each one of you is clearly entitled to one hundred pounds a year by common law:' such had been the important whisper made by Finney into the ears of Abel Handy, and by him retailed to his eleven brethren.

Too much must not be expected from the flesh and blood even of John Hiram's bedesmen, and the positive promise of one hundred a year to each of the twelve old men, had its way with most of them. The great Bunce was not to be wiled away, and was upheld in his orthodoxy by two adherents. Abel Handy, who was the leader of the aspirants after wealth, had, alas, a stronger following. No less than five of the twelve soon believed that his views were just, making with their leader a moiety of the hospital. The other three, volatile unstable minds, vacillated between the two chieftains, now led away by the hope of gold, now anxious to propitiate the powers that still existed.

It had been proposed to address a petition to the bishop as visitor, praying his lordship to see justice done to the legal recipients of John Hiram's Charity, and to send copies of this petition and of the reply it would elicit, to all the leading London papers, and thereby to obtain notoriety for the subject. This it was thought would pave the way for ulterior legal proceedings. It would have been a great thing to have had the signatures and marks of all the twelve injured legatees; but this was impossible: Bunce would have cut his hand off sooner than have signed it. It was then suggested by Finney that if even eleven could be induced to sanction the document, the one obstinate recusant* might have been represented as unfit to judge on such a question, – in fact, as being *non compos mentis*,* – and the petition would have been taken as representing the feeling of the men. But this could not be done: Bunce's friends were as firm as himself, and as yet only six crosses adorned the document. It was the more provoking, as Bunce himself could write his name legibly, and one of those three doubting souls had for years boasted of like power, and possessed, indeed, a Bible, in which he was proud to show his name written by himself some thirty years ago – 'Job Skulpit;' but it was thought that Job Skulpit, having forgotten his scholarship, on that account recoiled from the petition, and that the other doubters would follow as he led them. A petition signed by half the hospital would have but a poor effect.

It was in Skulpit's room that the petition was now lying, waiting such additional signatures as Abel Handy, by his eloquence, could obtain for it. The six marks it bore were duly attested, thus: – Abel + Handy, Greg^y + Moody, Mathew + Spriggs etc., and places were duly designated in pencil for those brethren who were now expected to join: for Skulpit alone was left a spot on which his genuine signature might be written in fair clerklike style. Handy had brought in the document, and spread it out on the small deal table, and was now standing by it persuasive and eager. Moody had followed with an inkhorn, carefully left behind by Finney; and Spriggs bore aloft, as though it were a sword, a well-worn ink-black pen, which from time to time he endeavoured to thrust into Skulpit's unwilling hand.

With the learned man were his two abettors in indecision, William Gazy and Jonathan Crumple. If ever the petition were to be forwarded, now was the time, so said Mr Finney; and great was the anxiety on the part of those whose one hundred pounds a year, as they believed, mainly depended on the document in question.

'To be kept out of all that money,' as the avaricious Moody had muttered to his friend Handy, 'by an old fool saying that he can write his own name like his betters.'

'Well Job,' said Handy, trying to impart to his own sour, ill-omened visage a smile of approbation, in which he greatly failed; 'so you're ready now, Mr Finney says; here's the place, d'ye see,' – and he put his huge brown finger down on the dirty paper, – 'name or mark, it's all one. Come along, old boy; if so be we're to have the spending of this money, why the sooner the better – that's my maxim.'

'To be sure,' said Moody; 'we a'n't none of us so young: we can't stay waiting for old Catgut no longer.'

It was thus these miscreants named our excellent friend: the nickname he could easily have forgiven, but the allusion to the divine source of all his melodious joy would have irritated even him. Let us hope he never knew the insult.

'Only think, old Billy Gazy,' said Spriggs, who rejoiced in greater youth than his brethren, but having fallen into a fire when drunk, had had one eye burnt out, one cheek burnt through, and one arm nearly burnt off, and who, therefore, in regard to personal appearance, was not the most prepossessing of men; 'a hundred a year, and all to spend: only think, old Billy Gazy;' and he gave a hideous grin that showed off his misfortunes to their full extent.

Old Billy Gazy was not alive to much enthusiasm – even these golden prospects did not arouse him to do more than rub his poor old bleared eyes with the cuff of his bedesman's gown, and gently mutter; 'he didn't know, not he; he didn't know.'

'But you'd know, Jonathan,' continued Spriggs, turning to the other friend of Skulpit's, who was sitting on a stool by the table, gazing vacantly at the petition. Jonathan Crumple was a meek, mild man, who had known better days; his means had been wasted by bad children, who had made his life wretched till he had been received into the hospital, of which he had not long been a member. Since that day he had known neither sorrow nor trouble, and this attempt to fill him with new hopes was, indeed, a cruelty.

'A hundred a year's a nice thing, for sartain, neighbour Spriggs,' said he: 'I once had nigh to that myself, but it didn't do me no good.' And he gave a low sigh, as he thought of the children of his own loins who had robbed him.

'And shall have again, Joe,' said Handy; 'and will have some one to keep it right and tight for you this time.'

Crumple sighed again – he had learned the impotency of worldy wealth, and would have been satisfied, if left untempted, to have remained happy with one and sixpence a day.

'Come, Skulpit,' repeated Handy, getting impatient, 'you're not going to go along with old Bunce in helping that parson to rob us all. Take the pen, man, and right yourself. Well,' he added, seeing that Skulpit still doubted, 'to see a man as is afraid to stand by hisself, is, to my thinking, the meanest thing as is.'

'Sink them all for parsons, says I,' growled Moody; 'hungry beggars, as never thinks their bellies full till they have robbed all and every thing.'

'Who's to harm you, man?' argued Spriggs: 'let them look never so black at you, they can't get you put out when you're once in – no, not old Catgut, with Calves to help him!' I am sorry to say the archdeacon himself was designated by this scurrilous allusion to his nether person.

'A hundred a year to win, and nothing to lose,' continued Handy, 'my eyes! – Well, how a man's to doubt about sich a bit of cheese as that passes me – but some men is timorous – some men is born with no pluck in them – some men is cowed at the very first sight of a gen'leman's coat and waistcoat.'

Oh, Mr Harding, if you had but taken the archdeacon's advice in that disputed case, when Joe Mutters was this ungrateful demagogue's rival candidate!

'Afraid of a parson,' growled Moody, with a look of ineffable scorn; 'I tell ye what I'd be afraid of – I'd be afraid of not getting nothing from 'em but just what I could take by might and right – that's the most I'd be afraid on of any parson of 'em all.'

'But,' said Skulpit, apologetically, 'Mr Harding's not so bad – he did give us twopence a day, didn't he now?'

'Twopence a day!' exclaimed Spriggs with scorn, opening awfully the red cavern of his lost eye.

'Twopence a day!' muttered Moody with a curse; 'sink his twopence!'

'Twopence a day!' exclaimed Handy; 'and I'm to go, hat in hand, and thank a chap for twopence a day, when he owes me a hundred pounds a year: no, thank ye; that may do for you, but it won't for me. Come, I say Skulpit, are you a going to put your mark to this here paper, or are you not?'

Skulpit looked round in wretched indecision to his two friends. 'What d'ye think, Billy Gazy?' said he.

But Billy Gazy couldn't think: he made a noise like the bleating of an old sheep, which was intended to express the agony of his doubt, and again muttered that 'he didn't know.'

'Take hold, you old cripple,' said Handy, thrusting the pen into poor Billy's hand: 'there, so – ugh! you old fool, you've been and smeared it all – there – that'll do for you, – that's as good as the best name as ever was written:' and a big blotch of ink was presumed to represent Billy Gazy's acquiescence.

'Now Jonathan,' said Handy, turning to Crumple.

'A hundred a year's a nice thing, for sartain,' again argued Crumple. 'Well, neighbour Skulpit, how's it to be?'

'Oh, please yourself,' said Skulpit; 'please yourself, and you'll please me.'

The pen was thrust into Crumple's hand, and a faint, wandering, meaningless sign was made, betokening such sanction and authority as Jonathan Crumple was able to convey.

'Come Joe,' said Handy, softened by success, 'don't let 'em have to say that old Bunce has a man like you under his thumb – a man that always holds his head in the hospital as high as Bunce himself, though you're never axed to drink wine, and sneak, and tell lies about your betters, as he does.'

Skulpit held the pen, and made little flourishes with it in the air, but still hesitated.

'And if you'll be said by me,' continued Handy, 'you'll not

write your name to it at all, but just put your mark like the others,' – the cloud began to clear from Skulpit's brow: – 'we all know you can do it if you like, but maybe you wouldn't like to seem uppish, you know.'

'Well, the mark would be best,' said Skulpit: 'one name and the rest marks, wouldn't look well, would it?'

'The worst in the world,' said Handy; 'there – there:' and stooping over the petition, the learned clerk made a huge cross on the place left for his signature.

'That's the game,' said Handy, triumphantly pocketing the petition: 'we're all in a boat now, that is, the nine of us; and as for old Bunce, and his cronies, they may——' But as he was hobbling off to the door, with a crutch on one side and a stick on the other, he was met by Bunce himself.

'Well, Handy, and what may old Bunce do?' said the grey-haired, upright senior.

Handy muttered something, and was departing; but he was stopped in the doorway by the huge frame of the newcomer.

'You've been doing no good here, Abel Handy,' said he, ''tis plain to see that; and 'tisn't much good, I'm thinking, you ever do.'

'I mind my own business, Master Bunce,' muttered the other, 'and do you do the same. It a'n't nothing to you what I does – and your spying and poking here won't do no good nor yet no harm.'

'I suppose then, Joe,' continued Bunce, not noticing his opponent, 'if the truth must out, you've stuck your name to that petition of theirs at last.'

Skulpit looked as though he were about to sink into nothing with shame.

'What is it to you what he signs?' said Handy. 'I suppose if we all wants to ax for our own, we needn't ax leave of you first, Mr Bunce, big a man as you are: and as to your sneaking in here, into Job's room when he's busy, and where you're not wanted – '

'I've knowed Job Skulpit, man and boy, sixty years,' said Bunce, looking at the man of whom he spoke, 'and that's ever since the day he was born. I knowed the mother that bore him, when she and I were little wee things, picking daisies together in the close yonder; and I've lived under the same roof with him more nor ten years; and after that I may come into his room without axing leave, and yet no sneaking neither.'

'So you can, Mr Bunce,' said Skulpit; 'so you can, any hour, day or night.'

'And I'm free also to tell him my mind,' continued Bunce, looking at the one man and addressing the other; 'and I tell him now that he's done a foolish and a wrong thing: he's turned his back upon one who is his best friend; and is playing the game of others, who care nothing for him, whether he be poor or rich, well or ill, alive or dead. A hundred a year? Are the lot of you soft enough to think that if a hundred a year be to be given, it's the likes of you that will get it?' – and he pointed to Billy Gazy, Spriggs, and Crumple. 'Did any of us ever do anything worth half the money? Was it to make gentlemen of us we were brought in here, when all the world turned against us, and we couldn't longer earn our daily bread? A'n't you all as rich in your ways as he in his?' – and the orator pointed to the side on which the warden lived. 'A'n't you getting all you hoped for, ay, and more than you hoped for? Wouldn't each of you have given the dearest limb of his body to secure that which now makes you so unthankful?'

'We wants what John Hiram left us,' said Handy; 'we wants what's ourn by law; it don't matter what we expected; what's ourn by law should be ourn, and by goles* we'll have it.'

'Law!' said Bunce, with all the scorn he knew how to command, – 'law! Did ye ever know a poor man yet was the better for law, or for a lawyer? Will Mr Finney ever be as good to you, Job, as that man has been? Will he see to you when you're sick, and comfort you when you're wretched? Will he – '

'No, nor give you port wine, old boy, on cold winter nights! he won't do that, will he?' asked Handy: and laughing at the severity of his own wit, he and his colleagues retired, carrying with them, however, the now powerful petition.

There is no help for spilt milk; and Mr Bunce could only retire to his own room, disgusted at the frailty of human nature – Job Skulpit scratched his head – Jonathan Crumple again remarked, that, 'for sartain, sure a hundred a year was very nice' – and Billy Gazy again rubbed his eyes, and lowly muttered that 'he didn't know.'

CHAPTER 5

Dr Grantly Visits the Hospital

Though doubt and hesitation disturbed the rest of our poor warden, no such weakness perplexed the nobler breast of his son-in-law. As the indomitable cock preparing for the combat sharpens his spurs, shakes his feathers, and erects his comb, so did the archdeacon arrange his weapons for the coming war, without misgiving and without fear. That he was fully confident of the justice of his cause let no one doubt. Many a man can fight his battle with good courage, but with a doubting conscience; such was not the case with Dr Grantly. He did not believe in the Gospel with more assurance than he did in the sacred justice of all ecclesiastical revenues. When he put his shoulder to the wheel to defend the income of the present and future precentors of Barchester, he was animated by as strong a sense of a holy cause, as that which gives courage to a missionary in Africa, or enables a sister of mercy to give up the pleasures of the world for the wards of a hospital. He was about to defend the holy of holies from the touch of the profane; to guard the citadel of his church from the most rampant of its enemies; to put on his good armour in the best of fights; and secure, if possible, the comforts of his creed for coming generations of ecclesiastical dignitaries. Such a work required no ordinary vigour; and the archdeacon was, therefore, extraordinarily vigorous: it demanded a buoyant courage, and a heart happy in its toil; and the archdeacon's heart was happy, and his courage was buoyant.

He knew that he would not be able to animate his father-in-law with feelings like his own, but this did not much disturb him. He preferred to bear the brunt of the battle alone, and did not doubt that the warden would resign himself into his hands with passive submission.

'Well, Mr Chadwick,' he said, walking into the steward's office a day or two after the signing of the petition as commemorated in the last chapter; 'anything from Cox and Cummins this morning?' Mr Chadwick handed him a letter, which he read, stroking the tight-gaitered calf of his right leg as he did so. Messrs Cox and Cummins merely said that they had as yet received no notice from their adversaries; that they could recommend no preliminary steps; but that should any proceeding really be taken by the bedesmen, it would be expedient to consult that very eminent Queen's Counsel, Sir Abraham Haphazard.*

'I quite agree with them,' said Dr Grantly, refolding the letter. 'I perfectly agree with them. Haphazard is no doubt the best man; a thorough churchman, a sound conservative, and in every respect the best man we could get – he's in the house, too, which is a great thing.'

Mr Chadwick quite agreed.

'You remember how completely he put down that scoundrel Horsman* about the Bishop of Beverley's income;* how completely he set them all adrift in the earl's case.' Since the question of St Cross had been mooted by the public, one noble lord had become 'the earl,' par excellence,* in the doctor's estimation. 'How he silenced that fellow at Rochester.* Of course we must have Haphazard; and I'll tell you what, Mr Chadwick, we must take care to be in time, or the other party will forestall us.'

With all his admiration for Sir Abraham, the doctor seemed to think it not possible that that great man might be induced to lend his gigantic powers to the side of the church's enemies.

Having settled this point to his satisfaction, the doctor stepped down to the hospital, to learn how matters were going on there; and as he walked across the hallowed close, and looked up at the ravens who cawed with a peculiar reverence as he wended his way, he thought with increased acerbity of those whose impiety would venture to disturb the goodly grace of cathedral institutions.

And who has not felt the same? We believe that Mr Horsman himself would relent, and the spirit of Sir Benjamin Hall* give way, were those great reformers to allow themselves to stroll by moonlight round the towers of some of our ancient churches. Who would not feel charity for a prebendary, when walking the quiet length of that long aisle at Winchester, looking at those decent houses, that trim grassplot, and feeling, as one must, the solemn, orderly comfort of the spot! Who could be hard upon a dean while wandering round the sweet close of Hereford, and owning that in that precinct, tone and colour, design and form, solemn tower and storied window, are all in unison, and all perfect! Who could lie basking in the cloisters of Salisbury, and gaze on Jewel's library,* and that unequalled spire, without feeling that bishops should sometimes be rich.

The tone of our archdeacon's mind must not astonish us; it has been the growth of centuries of church ascendancy; and though some fungi now disfigure the tree, though there be much dead wood, for how much good fruit have not we to be thankful? Who, without remorse, can batter down the dead branches of an old oak, now useless, but ah! still so beautiful, or drag out the fragments of the ancient forest, without feeling that they sheltered the younger plants, to which they are now summoned to give way in a tone so peremptory and so harsh?

The archdeacon, with all his virtues, was not a man of delicate feeling; and after having made his morning salutations in the warden's drawing-room, he did not scruple to commence an attack on 'pestilent' John Bold in the prescence of Miss Harding, though he rightly guessed that that lady was not indifferent to the name of his enemy.

'Nelly, my dear, fetch me my spectacles from the back room,' said her father, anxious to save both her blushes and her feelings.

Eleanor brought the spectacles, while her father was trying, in ambiguous phrases, to explain to her too-practical brother-in-law that it might be as well not to say anything about Bold before her, and then retreated. Nothing had been explained to her about Bold and the hospital; but, with a woman's instinct, she knew that things were going wrong.

'We must soon be doing something,' commenced the archdeacon, wiping his brows with a large, bright-coloured handkerchief, for he had felt busy, and had walked quick, and it was a broiling summer's day. 'Of course you have heard of the petition?'

Mr Harding owned, somewhat unwillingly, that he had heard of it.

'Well,' – the archdeacon looked for some expression of opinion, but none coming, he continued, – 'We must be doing something, you know; we mustn't allow these people to cut the ground from under us while we sit looking on.' The archdeacon, who was a practical man, allowed himself the use of everyday expressive modes of speech when among his closest intimates, though no one could soar into a more intricate labyrinth of refined phraseology when the church was the subject, and his lower brethren were his auditors.

The warden still looked mutely in his face, making the slightest possible passes with an imaginary fiddle bow, and stopping, as he did so, sundry imaginary strings with the fingers of his other hand. 'Twas his constant consolation in conversational troubles. While these vexed him sorely, the passes would be short and slow, and the upper hand would not be seen to work; nay the strings on which it operated would sometimes lie concealed in the musician's pocket, and the instrument on which he played would be beneath his chair; but as his spirit warmed to the subject, – as his trusting heart, looking to the bottom of that which vexed him, would see its clear way out, – he would rise to a higher melody, sweep the unseen strings with a bolder hand, and swiftly fingering the cords from his neck, down along his waistcoat, and up again to his very ear, create an ecstatic strain of perfect music, audible to himself and to St Cecilia, and not without effect.

'I quite agree with Cox and Cummins,' continued the archdeacon: 'they say we must secure Sir Abraham Haphazard. I shall not have the slightest fear in leaving the case in Sir Abraham's hands.'

The warden played the slowest and saddest of tunes: it was but a dirge on one string.

'I think Sir Abraham will not be long in letting Master Bold know what he's about. I fancy I hear Sir Abraham cross-questioning him at the Common Pleas.'

The warden thought of his income being thus discussed, his modest life, his daily habits, and his easy work; and nothing issued from that single cord, but a low wail of sorrow. 'I suppose they've sent this petition up to my father.' The warden didn't know; he imagined they would do so this very day.

'What I can't understand is, how you let them do it, with such a command as you have in the place, or should have with such a man as Bunce; I cannot understand why you let them do it.'

'Do what?' asked the warden.

'Why, listen to this fellow Bold, and that other low pettifogger, Finney – and get up this petition too: why didn't you tell Bunce to destroy the petition?'

'That would have been hardly wise,' said the warden.

'Wise – yes, it would have been very wise if they'd done it among themselves. I must go up to the palace and answer it now, I suppose; it's a very short answer they'll get, I can tell you.'

'But why shouldn't they petition, doctor?'

'Why shouldn't they!' responded the archdeacon, in a loud brazen voice, as though all the men in the hospital were expected to hear him through the walls; 'why shouldn't they! I'll let them know why they shouldn't: by-the-by, warden, I'd like to say a few words to them all together.'

The warden's mind misgave him, and even for a moment he forgot to play. He by no means wished to delegate to his son-in-law his place and authority of warden; he had expressly determined not to interfere in any step which the men might wish to take in the matter under dispute; he was most anxious neither to accuse them nor to defend himself. All these things he was aware the archdeacon would do in his behalf, and that not in the mildest manner; and yet he knew not how to refuse the permission requested.

'I'd so much sooner remain quiet in the matter,' said he, in an apologetic voice.

'Quiet!' said the archdeacon, still speaking with his brazen trumpet; 'do you wish to be ruined in quiet?'

'Why, if I am to be ruined, certainly.'

'Nonsense, warden; I tell you something must be done – we mut act; just let me ring the bell, and send the men word that I'll speak to them in the quad.'

Mr Harding knew not how to resist, and the disagreeable order was given. The quad, as it was familiarly called, was a small quadrangle, open on one side to the river, and surrounded on the others by the high wall of Mr Harding's garden, by one gable end of Mr Harding's house, and by the end of the row of buildings which formed the residences of the bedesmen. It was flagged all round, and the centre was stoned; small stone gutters ran from the four corners of the square to a grating in the centre; and attached to the end of Mr Harding's house was a conduit with four cocks covered over from the weather, at which the old men got their water, and very generally performed their morning toilet. It was a quiet, sombre place, shaded over by the trees of the warden's garden. On the side towards the river, there stood a row of stone seats, on which the old men would sit and gaze at the little fish, as they flitted by in the running stream. On the other side of the river was a rich, green meadow, running up to and joining the deanery, and as little open to the public, as the garden of the dean itself. Nothing, therefore, could be more private than the quad of the hospital; and it was there that the archdeacon determined to convey to them his sense of their refractory proceedings.

The servant soon brought in word that the men were assembled in the quad, and the archdeacon, big with his purpose, rose to address them.

'Well, warden, of course you're coming,' said he, seeing that Mr Harding did not prepare to follow him.

'I wish you'd excuse me,' said Mr Harding.

'For heaven's sake, don't let us have division in the camp,' replied the archdeacon: 'let us have a long pull and a strong pull, but above all a pull altogether;* come, warden, come; don't be afraid of your duty.'

Mr Harding was afraid; he was afraid that he was being led to do that which was not his duty: he was not, however, strong enough to resist, so he got up and followed his son-in-law.

The old men were assembled in groups in the quadrangle – eleven of them at least, for poor old Johnny Bell was bedridden, and couldn't come; he had, however, put his mark to the petition, as one of Handy's earliest followers. 'Tis true he could not move from the bed where he lay; 'tis true he had no friend on earth, but those whom the hospital contained; and of those the warden and his daughter were the most constant and most appreciated; 'tis true that every thing was administered to him which his failing body could require, or which his faint appetite could enjoy; but still his dull eye had glistened for a moment at the idea of possessing a hundred pounds a year 'to his own cheek,'* as Abel Handy had eloquently expressed it; and poor old Johnny Bell had greedily put his mark to the petition.

When the two clergymen appeared, they all uncovered their heads. Handy was slow to do it, and hesitated; but the black coat and waistcoat, of which he had spoken so irreverently in Skulpit's room, had its effect even on him, and he too doffed his hat. Bunce, advancing before the others, bowed lowly to the archdeacon, and with affectionate reverence expressed his wish, that the warden and Miss Eleanor were quite well; 'and the doctor's lady,' he added, turning to the archdeacon, 'and the children at Plumstead, and my lord;' and having made his speech, he also retired among the others, and took his place with the rest upon the stone benches.

As the archdeacon stood up to make his speech, erect in the middle of that little square, he looked like an ecclesiastical statue placed there, as a fitting impersonation of the church militant here on earth;* his shovel hat, large, new, and well-pronounced, a churchman's hat in every inch, declared the profession as plainly as does the Quaker's broad brim; his heavy eyebrow, large open eyes, and full mouth and chin expressed the solidity of his order; the broad chest, amply covered with fine cloth, told how well to do was its estate; one hand ensonced within his pocket, evinced the practical hold which our mother church keeps on her temporal possessions; and the other, loose for action, was ready to fight if need be in her defence; and below these the decorous breeches, and neat black gaiters showing so admirably that well-turned leg, betokened the decency, the outward beauty, and grace of our church establishment.

'Now my men,' he began, when he had settled himself well in his position; 'I want to say a few words to you. Your good friend, the warden here, and myself, and my lord the bishop, on whose behalf I wish to speak to you, would all be very sorry, very sorry indeed, that you should have any just ground of complaint. Any just ground of complaint on your part would be removed at once by the warden, or by his lordship, or by me on his behalf, without the necessity of any petition on your part.' Here the orator stopped for a moment, expecting that some little murmers of applause would show that the weakest of the men were beginning to give way; but no such murmurs came. Bunce, himself, even sat with closed lips, mute and unsatisfactory. 'Without the necessity of any petition at all,' he repeated. 'I'm told you have addressed a petition to my lord.' He paused for a reply from the men, and after a while, Handy plucked up courage, and said, 'Yes, we has.'

'You have addressed a petition to my lord, in which, as I am informed, you express an opinion that you do not receive from Hiram's estate all that is your due.' Here most of the men expressed their assent. 'Now what is it you ask for? what is it you want that you hav'n't got here? what is it – '

'A hundred a year,' muttered old Moody, with a voice as if it came out of the ground.

'A hundred a year!' ejaculated the archdeacon militant, defying the impudence of these claimants with one hand stretched out and closed, while with the other he tightly grasped, and secured within his breeches pocket, that symbol of the church's wealth which his own loose half-crowns not unaptly represented. 'A hundred a year! Why, my men, you must be mad; and you talk about John Hiram's will! When John Hiram built a hospital for worn-out old men, worn-out old labouring men, infirm old men past their work, cripples, blind, bed-ridden, and such like, do you think he meant to make gentlemen of them? Do you think John Hiram intended to give a hundred a year to old single men, who earned perhaps two shillings or half-a-crown a day for themselves and families in the best of their time? No, my men, I'll tell you what John Hiram meant; he meant that twelve poor old worn-out labourers, men who could no longer support themselves, who had no friends to support them, who must starve and perish miserably if not protected by the hand of charity; he meant that twelve such men as these should come in here in their poverty and wretchedness, and find within these walls shelter and food before their death, and a little leisure to make their peace with God. That was what John Hiram meant: you have not read John Hiram's will, and I doubt whether those wicked men who are advising you have done so. I have; I know what his will was; and I tell you that that was his will, and that that was his intention.'

Not a sound came from the eleven bedesmen, as they sat listening to what, according to the archdeacon, was their intended estate. They grimly stared upon his burly figure, but did not then express, by word or sign, the anger and disgust to which such language was sure to give rise.

'Now let me ask you,' he continued, 'do you think you are worse off than John Hiram intended to make you? Have you not shelter, and food, and leisure? Have you not much more? Have you not every indulgence which you are capable of enjoying? Have you not twice better food, twice a better bed, ten times more money in your pocket than you were ever able to earn for yourselves before you were lucky enough to get into this place? And now you send a petition to the bishop, asking for a hundred pounds a year! I tell you what, my friends; you are deluded, and made fools of by wicked men who are acting for their own ends. You will never get a hundred pence a year more than what you have now: it is very possible that you may get less; it is very possible that my lord the bishop, and your warden may make changes – '

'No, no, no,' interrupted Mr Harding, who had been listening with indescribable misery to the tirade of his son-in-law; 'no, my friends. I want no changes, – at least no changes that shall make you worse off than you now are, as long as you and I live together.'

'God bless you, Mr Harding,' said Bunce; and 'God bless you, Mr Harding, God bless you sir, we know you was always our friend,' was exclaimed by enough of the men to make it appear that the sentiment was general.

The archdeacon had been interrupted in his speech before he had quite finished it; but he felt that he could not recommence with dignity after this little ebullition, and he led the way back into the garden, followed by his father-in-law.

'Well,' said he, as soon as he found himself within the cool retreat of the warden's garden; 'I think I spoke to them plainly.' And he wiped the perspiration from his brow; for making a speech under a broiling mid-day sun in summer, in a full suit of thick black cloth, is warm work.

'Yes, you were plain enough,' replied the warden, in a tone which did not express approbation.

'And that's everything,' said the other, who was clearly well satisfied with himself; 'that's everything: with those sort of people one must be plain, or one will not be understood. Now, I think they did understand me – I think they knew what I meant.'

The warden agreed. He certainly thought they had understood to the full what had been said to them.

'They know pretty well what they have to expect from us; they know how we shall meet any refractory spirit on their part; they know that we are not afraid of them. And now I'll just step into Chadwick's, and tell him what I've done; and then I'll go up to the palace, and answer this petition of theirs.'

The warden's mind was very full – full nearly to overcharging itself; and had it done so – had he allowed himself to speak the thoughts which were working within him, he would indeed have astonished the archdeacon by the reprobation he would have expressed as to the proceeding of which he had been so unwilling a witness. But different feelings kept him silent; he was as yet

afraid of differing from his son-in-law – he was anxious beyond
measure to avoid even a semblance of rupture with any of his
order, and was painfully fearful of having to come to an open
quarrel with any person on any subject. His life had hitherto
been so quiet, so free from strife; his little early troubles had
required nothing but passive fortitude; his subsequent prosperity
had never forced upon him any active cares – had never brought
him into disagreeable contact with any one. He felt that he
would give almost anything – much more than he knew he
ought to do – to relieve himself from the storm which he feared
was coming. It was so hard that the pleasant waters of his little
stream should be disturbed and muddied by rough hands; that
his quiet paths should be made a battlefield; that the unobtrusive
corner of the world which had been allotted to him, as though
by Providence, should be invaded and desecrated, and all within
it made miserable and unsound.

Money he had none to give; the knack of putting guineas
together had never belonged to him; but how willingly, with
what a foolish easiness, with what happy alacrity, would he
have abandoned the half of his income for all time to come,
could he by so doing have quietly dispelled the clouds that were
gathering over him – could he have thus compromised the
matter between the reformer and the conservative, between his
possible son-in-law, Bold, and his positive son-in-law, the
archdeacon.

And this compromise would not have been made from any
prudential motive of saving what would yet remain, for Mr
Harding still felt little doubt but he should be left for life in
quiet possession of the good things he had, if he chose to retain
them. No; he would have done so from the sheer love of quiet,
and from a horror of being made the subject of public talk. He
had very often been moved to pity – to that inward weeping of
the heart for others' woes; but none had he ever pitied more
than that old lord, whose almost fabulous wealth, drawn from
his church preferments, had become the subject of so much
opprobrium, of such public scorn; that wretched clerical octogenarian Croesus,* whom men would not allow to die in peace
– whom all the world united to decry and to abhor.

Was he to suffer such a fate? Was his humble name to be
bandied in men's mouths, as the gormandiser of the resources
of the poor, as of one who had filched from the charity of other

ages wealth which had been intended to relieve the old and the infirm? Was he to be gibbeted in the press, to become a by-word for oppression, to be named as an example of the greed of the English church? Should it ever be said that he had robbed those old men, whom he so truly and so tenderly loved in his heart of hearts? As he slowly paced, hour after hour, under those noble lime trees, turning these sad thoughts within him, he became all but fixed in his resolve that some great step must be taken to relieve him from the risk of so terrible a fate.

In the meanwhile, the archdeacon, with contented mind and unruffled spirit, went about his business. He said a word or two to Mr Chadwick, and then finding, as he expected, the petition lying in his father's library, he wrote a short answer to the men, in which he told them that they had no evils to redress, but rather great mercies for which to be thankful; and having seen the bishop sign it, he got into his broughham* and returned home to Mrs Grantly, and Plumstead Episcopi.

CHAPTER 6

The Warden's Tea Party

After much painful doubting, on one thing only could Mr Harding resolve. He determined that at any rate he would take no offence, and that he would make this question no cause of quarrel either with Bold or with the bedesmen. In furtherance of this resolution, he himself wrote a note to Mr Bold, the same afternoon, inviting him to meet a few friends and hear some music on an evening named in the next week. Had not this little party been promised to Eleanor, in his present state of mind he would probably have avoided such gaiety; but the promise had been given, the invitations were to be written, and when Eleanor consulted her father on the subject, she was not ill pleased to hear him say, 'Oh, I was thinking of Bold, so I took it into my head to write to him myself, but you must write to his sister.'

Mary Bold was older than her brother, and, at the time of our story, was just over thirty. She was not an unattractive young woman, though by no means beautiful. Her great merit was the kindliness of her disposition. She was not very clever, nor very animated, nor had she apparently the energy of her brother; but she was guided by a high principle of right and wrong; her temper was sweet, and her faults were fewer in number than her virtues. Those who casually met Mary Bold thought little of her; but those who knew her well loved her well, and the longer they knew her the more they loved her. Among those who were fondest of her was Eleanor Harding, and though Eleanor had never openly talked of her brother, each understood the other's feelings about him. The brother and sister were sitting together when the two notes were brought in.

'How odd,' said Mary, 'that they should send two notes. Well, if Mr Harding becomes fashionable, the world is going to change.'

Her brother understood immediately the nature and intention of the peace offering; but it was not so easy for him to behave well in the matter, as it was for Mr Harding. It is much less difficult for the sufferer to be generous than for the oppressor. John Bold felt that he could not go to the warden's party: he never loved Eleanor better than he did now; he had never so strongly felt how anxious he was to make her his wife as now, when so many obstacles to his doing so appeared in view. Yet here was her father himself, as it were clearing away those very obstacles, and still he felt that he could not go to the house any more as an open friend.

As he sat thinking of these things with the note in his hand, his sister was waiting for his decision.

'Well,' said she, 'I suppose we must write separate answers, and both say we shall be very happy.'

'You'll go, of course, Mary,' said he; to which she readily assented. 'I cannot,' he continued, looking serious and gloomy; 'I wish I could, with all my heart.'

'And why not, John?' said she. She had as yet heard nothing of the new-found abuse which her brother was about to reform; at least, nothing which connected it with her brother's name.

He sat thinking for awhile till he determined that it would be best to tell her at once what it was that he was about: it must be done sooner or later.

'I fear I cannot go to Mr Harding's house any more as a friend, just at present.'

'Oh, John! Why not? Ah, you've quarrelled with Eleanor!'

'No, indeed,' said he; 'I've no quarrel with her as yet.'

'What is it, John?' said she, looking at him with an anxious, loving face, for she knew well how much of his heart was there in that house which he said he could no longer enter.

'Why,' said he at last, 'I've taken up the case of these twelve old men of Hiram's Hospital, and of course that brings me into contact with Mr Harding. I may have to oppose him, interfere with him, perhaps injure him.'

Mary looked at him steadily for some time before she committed herself to reply, and then merely asked him what he meant to do for the old men.

'Why, it's a long story, and I don't know that I can make you understand it. John Hiram made a will, and left his property in charity for certain poor old men, and the proceeds, instead of going to the benefit of these men, goes chiefly into the pocket of the warden, and the bishop's steward.'

'And you mean to take away from Mr Harding his share of it?'

'I don't know what I mean yet. I mean to inquire about it. I mean to see who is entitled to this property. I mean to see, if I can, that justice be done to the poor of the city of Barchester generally, who are, in fact, the legatees under the will. I mean, in short, to put the matter right, if I can.'

'And why are you to do this, John?'

'You might ask the same question of anybody else,' said he; 'and according to that, the duty of righting these poor men would belong to nobody. If we are to act on that principle, the weak are never to be protected, injustice is never to be opposed, and no one is to struggle for the poor!' And Bold began to comfort himself in the warmth of his own virtue.

'But is there no one to do this but you, who have known Mr Harding so long? Surely, John, as a friend, as a young friend, so much younger than Mr Harding – '

'That's woman's logic, all over, Mary. What has age to do with it? Another man might plead that he was too old; and as to his friendship, if the thing itself be right, private motives should never be allowed to interfere. Because I esteem Mr Harding, is that a reason that I should neglect a duty which I owe to these old men? or should I give up a work which my conscience tells me is a good one, because I regret the loss of his society?'

'And Eleanor, John?' said the sister, looking timidly into her brother's face.

'Eleanor, that is, Miss Harding, if she thinks fit – that is, if her father – or rather, if she – or, indeed, he, – if they find it necessary – but there is no necessity now to talk about Eleanor Harding; but this I will say, that if she has the kind of spirit for which I give her credit, she will not condemn me for doing what I think to be a duty.' And Bold consoled himself with the consolation of a Roman.*

Mary sat silent for awhile, till at last her brother reminded her that the notes must be answered, and she got up, and placed her desk before her, took out her pen and her paper, wrote on it slowly, –

Pakenham Villas, Tuesday morning.

My dear Eleanor,
  I –

and then stopped, and looked at her brother.

'Well, Mary, why don't you write it?'

'Oh, John,' said she, 'dear John, pray think better of this.'

'Think better of what?' said he.

'Of this, about the hospital, – of all this about Mr Harding, – of what you say about those old men. Nothing can call upon you, – no duty can require you to set yourself against your oldest, your best friend. Oh, John, think of Eleanor; you'll break her heart and your own.'

'Nonsense, Mary; Miss Harding's heart is as safe as yours.'

'Pray, pray, for my sake, John, give it up. You know how dearly you love her.' And she came and knelt before him on the rug. 'Pray give it up. You are going to make yourself, and her, and her father miserable: you are going to make us all miserable. And for what? For a dream of justice. You will never make those twelve men happier than they now are.'

'You don't understand it, my dear girl,' said he, smoothing her hair with his hand.

'I do understand it, John. I understand that this is a chimera – a dream that you have got. I know well that no duty can require you to do this mad – this suicidal thing. I know you love Eleanor Harding with all your heart, and I tell you now that she loves you as well. If there was a plain, a positive duty before you, I would be the last to bid you neglect it for any woman's love; but this – oh, think again, before you do anything to make it necessary that you and Mr Harding should be at variance.' He did not answer, as she knelt there, leaning on his knees, but by his face she thought that he was inclined to yield. 'At any rate let me say that you will go to this party. At any rate do not break with them while your mind is in doubt.' And she got up, hoping to conclude her note in the way she desired.

'My mind is not in doubt,' at last he said, rising; 'I could never respect myself again, were I to give way now, because Eleanor Harding is beautiful. I do love her: I would give a hand to hear her tell me what you have said, speaking on her behalf; but I cannot for her sake go back from the task which I have commenced. I hope she may hereafter acknowledge and respect my motives, but I cannot now go as a guest to her father's house.' And the Barchester Brutus* went out to fortify his own resolution by meditations on his own virtue.

Poor Mary Bold sat down, and sadly finished her note, saying that she would herself attend the party, but that her brother was unavoidably prevented from doing so. I fear that she did not admire as she should have done the self-devotion of his singular virtue.

The party went off as such parties do: there were fat old ladies, in fine silk dresses, and slim young ladies, in gauzy muslin frocks; old gentlemen stood up with their backs to the empty fireplace, looking by no means so comfortable as they would have done in their own armchairs at home; and young gentlemen, rather stiff about the neck, clustered near the door, not as yet sufficiently in courage to attack the muslin frocks, who awaited the battle, drawn up in a semicircular array. The warden endeavoured to induce a charge, but failed signally, not having the tact of a general: his daughter did what she could to comfort the forces under her command, who took in refreshing rations of cake and tea, and patiently looked for the coming engagement: but she herself, Eleanor, had no spirit for the work; the only enemy whose lance she cared to encounter was not there, and she and others were somewhat dull.

Loud above all voices was heard the clear sonorous tones of the archdeacon as he dilated to brother parsons of the danger of the church, of the fearful rumours of mad reforms even at Oxford,* and of the damnable heresies of Dr Whiston.*

Soon, however, sweeter sounds began timidly to make themselves audible. Little movements were made in a quarter, notable for round stools and music stands. Wax candles were arranged in sconces,* big books were brought from hidden recesses, and the work of the evening commenced.

How often were those pegs twisted and retwisted before our friend found that he had twisted them enough; how many discordant scrapes gave promise of the coming harmony! How much the muslin fluttered and crumpled before Eleanor and another nymph were duly seated at the piano; how closely did that tall Apollo* pack himself against the wall, with his flute, long as himself, extending high over the heads of his pretty neighbours; into how small a corner crept that round and florid little minor canon, and there with skill amazing found room to tune his accustomed fiddle!

And now the crash begins:* away they go in full flow of harmony together – up hill and down dale – now louder and louder, then lower and lower: now loud, as though stirring the battle; then low, as though mourning the slain. In all, through all, and above all, is heard the violoncello. Ah, not for nothing were those pegs twisted and retwisted – listen, listen! Now alone that saddest of instruments tells its touching tale. Silent, and in awe, stand fiddle, flute, and piano, to hear the sorrows of their wailing brother. 'Tis but for a moment: before the melancholy of those low notes has been fully realised, again comes the full force of all the band – down go the pedals, away rush twenty fingers scouring over the bass notes with all the impetus of passion. Apollo blows till his stiff neckcloth is no better than a rope, and the minor canon works both arms till he falls in a syncope* of exhaustion against the wall.

How comes it that now, when all should be silent, when courtesy, if not taste, should make men listen – how is it at this moment the black-coated corps leave their retreat and begin skirmishing? One by one they creep forth, and fire off little guns timidly, and without precision. Ah, my men, efforts such as these will take no cities, even though the enemy should be never so open to assault. At length a more deadly artillery is brought to bear; slowly, but with effect, the advance is made; the muslin ranks are broken, and fall into confusion; the formidable array of chairs gives way; the battle is no longer between opposing regiments, but hand to hand, and foot to foot with single combatants, as in the glorious days of old, when fighting was really noble. In corners, and under the shadow of curtains, behind sofas and half hidden by doors, in retiring windows, and sheltered by hanging tapestry, are blows given and returned, fatal, incurable, dealing death.

Apart from this another combat arises, more sober and more serious. The archdeacon is engaged against two prebendaries,* a pursy full-blown rector assisting him, in all the perils and all the enjoyments of short whist.* With solemn energy do they watch the shuffled pack, and, all-expectant, eye the coming trump. With what anxious nicety do they arrange their cards, jealous of each other's eyes! Why is that lean doctor so slow – cadaverous man with hollow jaw and sunken eye, ill beseeming the richness of his mother church! Ah, why so slow, thou meagre doctor? See how the archdeacon, speechless in his agony, deposits on the board his cards, and looks to heaven or to the ceiling for support. Hark, how he sighs, as with thumbs in his waistcoat pocket he seems to signify that the end of such torment is not yet even nigh at hand! Vain is the hope if hope there be, to disturb that meagre doctor. With care precise he places every card, weighs well the value of each mighty ace, each guarded king, and comfort-giving queen; speculates on knave and ten, counts all his suits, and sets his price upon the whole. At length a card is led, and quick three others fall upon the board. The little doctor leads again, while with lustrous eye his partner absorbs the trick. Now thrice has this been done – thrice has constant fortune favoured the brace of prebendaries, ere the archdeacon rouses himself to the battle: but at the fourth assault he pins to the earth a prostrate king, laying low his crown and sceptre, bushy beard, and lowering brow, with a poor deuce.

'As David did Goliath,' says the archdeacon, pushing over the four cards to his partner. And then a trump is led, then another trump; then a king – and then an ace – and then a long ten, which brings down from the meagre doctor his only remaining tower of strength – his cherished queen of trumps.

'What, no second club?' says the archdeacon to his partner.

'Only one club,' mutters from his inmost stomach the pursy rector, who sits there red-faced, silent, impervious, careful, a safe but not a brilliant ally.

But the archdeacon cares not for many clubs, or for none. He dashes out his remaining cards with a speed most annoying to his antagonists, pushes over to them some four cards as their allotted portion, shoves the remainder across the table to the red-faced rector: calls out 'two by cards and two by honours, and the odd trick last time,' marks a treble under the candlestick, and has dealt round the second pack before the meagre doctor has calculated his losses.

And so went off the warden's party, and men and women arranging shawls and shoes declared how pleasant it had been; and Mrs Goodenough, the red-faced rector's wife, pressing the warden's hand, declared she had never enjoyed herself better; which showed how little pleasure she allowed herself in this world, as she had sat the whole evening through in the same chair without occupation, not speaking, and unspoken to. And Matilda Johnson, when she allowed young Dickson of the bank to fasten her cloak round her neck, thought that two hundred pounds a year and a little cottage would really do for happiness; besides he was sure to be manager some day. And Apollo folding his flute into his pocket, felt that he had acquitted himself with honour; and the archdeacon pleasantly jingled his gains; but the meagre doctor went off without much audible speech, muttering ever and anon as he went 'three and thirty points,' 'three and thirty points!'

And so they all were gone, and Mr Harding was left alone with his daughter.

What had passed between Eleanor Harding and Mary Bold need not be told. It is indeed a matter of thankfulness that neither the historian nor the novelist hears all that is said by their heroes or heroines, – or how would three volumes or twenty suffice! In the present case so little of this sort have I overheard, that I live in hopes of finishing my work within 300 pages, and of completing that pleasant task – a novel in one volume; but something had passed between them, and as the warden blew out the wax candles, and put his instrument into its case, his daughter stood sad and thoughtful by the empty fireplace, determined to speak to her father, but irresolute as to what she would say.

'Well, Eleanor,' said he, 'are you for bed?'

'Yes,' said she, moving, 'I suppose so; but, papa – Mr Bold was not here tonight: do you know why not?'

'He was asked; I wrote to him myself,' said the warden.

'But do you know why he did not come, papa?'

'Well, Eleanor, I could guess; but it's no use guessing at such things, my dear. What makes you look so earnest about it?'

'Oh papa, do tell me,' she exclaimed, throwing her arms round him, and looking into his face; 'what is it he is going to do? What is it all about? Is there any – any – any – ' she didn't well know what word to use – 'any danger?'

'Danger, my dear, what sort of danger?'

'Danger to you, danger of trouble, and of loss, and of – Oh papa, why hav'n't you told me of all this before?'

Mr Harding was not the man to judge harshly of any one, much less of the daughter whom he now loved better than any living creature; but still he did judge her wrongly at this moment. He knew that she loved John Bold; he fully sympathised in her affection; day after day he thought more of the matter, and, with the tender care of a loving father, tried to arrange in his own mind how matters might be so managed that his daughter's heart should not be made the sacrifice to the dispute which was likely to exist between him and Bold. Now, when she spoke to him for the first time on the subject, it was natural that he should think more of her than of himself, and that he should imagine that her own cares, and not his, were troubling her.

He stood silent before her awhile, as she gazed up into his face, and then kissing her forehead he placed her on the sofa.

'Tell me, Nelly, he said (he only called her Nelly in his kindest, softest, sweetest moods, and yet all his moods were kind and sweet), 'tell me, Nelly, do you like Mr Bold – much?'

She was quite taken aback by the question. I will not say that she had forgotten herself, and her own love in thinking about John Bold, and while conversing with Mary: she certainly had not done so. She had been sick at heart to think, that a man of whom she could not but own to herself that she loved him, of whose regard she had been so proud, that such a man should turn against her father to ruin him. She had felt her vanity hurt, that his affection for her had not kept him from such a course; had he really cared for her, he would not have risked her love by such an outrage; but her main fear had been for her father, and when she spoke of danger, it was of danger to him and not to herself.

She was taken aback by the question altogether: 'Do I like him, papa?'

'Yes, Nelly, do you like him? Why shouldn't you like him; but that's a poor word – do you love him?' She sat still in his arms without answering him. She certainly had not prepared herself for an avowal of affection, intending, as she had done, to abuse John Bold herself, and to hear her father do so also. 'Come, my love,' said he, 'let us make a clean breast of it: do you tell me what concerns yourself, and I will tell you what concerns me and the hospital.'

And then, without waiting for an answer, he described to her, as he best could, the accusation that was made about Hiram's will; the claims which the old men put forward; what he considered the strength and what the weakness of his own position; the course which Bold had taken, and that which he presumed he was about to take; and then by degrees, without further question, he presumed on the fact of Eleanor's love, and spoke of that love as a feeling which he could in no way disapprove: he apologised for Bold, excused what he was doing; nay praised him for his energy and intentions: made much of his good qualities, and harped on none of his foibles; then, reminding his daughter how late it was, and comforting her with much assurance which he hardly felt himself, he sent her to her room, with flowing eyes and a full heart.

When Mr Harding met his daughter at breakfast the next morning, there was no further discussion on the matter, nor was the subject mentioned between them for some days. Soon after the party Mary Bold called at the hospital, but there were various persons in the drawing-room at the time, and she therefore said nothing about her brother. On the day following, John Bold met Miss Harding in one of the quiet sombre shaded walks of the close: he was most anxious to see her, but unwilling to call at the warden's house, and had in truth waylaid her in her private haunts.

'My sister tells me,' said he, abruptly hurrying on with his premeditated speech, 'my sister tells me that you had a delightful party the other evening. I was so sorry I could not be there.'

'We were all sorry,' said Eleanor, with dignified composure.

'I believe, Miss Harding, you understood why, at this moment — 'And Bold hesitated, muttered, stopped, commenced his explanation again, and again broke down.

Eleanor would not help him in the least.

'I think my sister explained to you, Miss Harding?'

'Pray don't apologise, Mr Bold; my father will, I am sure, always be glad to see you, if you like to come to the house now as formerly; nothing has occurred to alter his feelings; of your own views you are, of course, the best judge.'

'Your father is all that is kind and generous; he always was so, but you, Miss Harding, yourself — I hope you will not judge me harshly, because — '

'Mr Bold,' said she, 'you may be sure of one thing; I shall always judge my father to be right, and those who oppose him I shall judge to be wrong. If those who do not know him oppose him, I shall have charity enough to believe that they are wrong, through error of judgment; but should I see him attacked by those who ought to know him, and to love him, and revere him, of such I shall be constrained to form a different opinion.' And then curtseying low she sailed on, leaving her lover in anything but a happy state of mind.

CHAPTER 7

The *Jupiter*

Though Eleanor Harding rode off from John Bold on a high horse, it must not be supposed that her heart was so elate as her demeanour. In the first place, she had a natural repugnance to losing her lover; and in the next, she was not quite so sure that she was in the right as she pretended to be. Her father had told her, and that now repeatedly, that Bold was doing nothing unjust or ungenerous, and why then should she rebuke him, and throw him off, when she felt herself so ill able to bear his loss? – but such is human nature, and young-lady-nature especially. As she walked off from him beneath the shady elms of the close, her look, her tone, every motion and gesture of her body, belied her heart; she would have given the world to have taken him by the hand, to have reasoned with him, persuaded him, cajoled him, coaxed him out of his project; to have overcome him with all her female artillery, and to have redeemed her father at the cost of herself; but pride would not let her do this, and she left him without a look of love or a word of kindness.

Had Bold been judging of another lover and of another lady he might have understood all this as well as we do; but in matters of love men do not see clearly in their own affairs. They say that faint heart never won fair lady; and it is amazing to me how fair ladies are won, so faint are often men's hearts! Were it not for the kindness of their nature, that seeing the weakness of our courage they will occasionally descend from their impregnable fortresses, and themselves aid us in effecting their own defeat, too often would they escape unconquered if not unscathed, and free of body if not of heart.

Poor Bold crept off quite crestfallen; he felt that as regarded Eleanor Harding his fate was sealed, unless he could consent to give up a task to which he had pledged himself, and which indeed it would not be easy for him to give up. Lawyers were engaged, and the question had to a certain extent been taken up by the public; besides, how could a high-spirited girl like Eleanor

Harding really learn to love a man for neglecting a duty which he assumed! Could she allow her affection to be purchased at the cost of his own self-respect?

As regarded the issue of his attempt at reformation in the hospital, Bold had no reason hitherto to be discontented with his success. All Barchester was by the ears about it. The bishop, the archdeacon, the warden, the steward, and several other clerical allies, had daily meetings, discussing their tactics, and preparing for the great attack. Sir Abraham Haphazard had been consulted, but his opinion was not yet received: copies of Hiram's will, copies of wardens' journels, copies of leases, copies of accounts, copies of everything that could be copied, and of some that could not, had been sent to him; and the case was assuming most creditable dimensions. But above all, it had been mentioned in the daily *Jupiter*.* That all powerful organ of the press in one of its leading thunderbolts launched at St Cross, had thus remarked: Another case, of smaller dimensions indeed, but of similar import, is now likely to come under public notice. We are informed that the warden or master of an old almshouse attached to Barchester Cathedral is in receipt of twenty-five times the annual income appointed for him by the will of the founder, while the sum yearly expended on the absolute purposes of the charity has always remained fixed. In other words, the legatees under the founder's will have received no advantage from the increase in the value of the property during the last four centuries, such increase having been absorbed by the so-called warden. It is impossible to conceive a case of greater injustice. It is no answer to say that some six or nine or twelve old men receive as much of the goods of this world as such old men require. On what foundation, moral or divine, traditional or legal, is grounded the warden's claim to the large income he receives for doing nothing? The contentment of these almsmen, if content they be, can give him no title to this wealth! Does he ever ask himself, when he stretches wide his clerical palm to receive the pay of some dozen of the working clergy, for what service he is so remunerated? Does his conscience ever entertain the question of his right to such subsidies? Or is it possible that the subject never so presents itself to his mind; that he has received for many years, and intends, should God spare him, to receive for years to come, these fruits of the industrious piety of past ages, indifferent as to any right on his own part, or of any injustice to others! We must express an opinion that nowhere but in the Church of England, and only there among its priests, could such a state of moral indifference be found.'

I must for the present leave my readers to imagine the state of Mr Harding's mind after reading the above article. They say that forty thousand copies of the *Jupiter* are daily sold, and that each copy is read by five persons at the least. Two hundred thousand readers then would hear this accusation against him;* two hundred thousand hearts would swell with indignation at the griping injustice, the bare-faced robbery of the warden of Barchester Hospital! And how was he to answer this? How was he to open his inmost heart to this multitude, to these thousands, the educated, the polished, the picked men of his own country; how show them that he was no robber, no avaricious lazy priest scrambling for gold, but a retiring humble-spirited man who had innocently taken what had innocently been offered to him?

'Write to the *Jupiter*,' suggested the bishop.

'Yes,' said the archdeacon, more worldly wise than his father, 'yes, and be smothered with ridicule; tossed over and over again with scorn; shaken this way and that, as a rat in the mouth of a practised terrier. You will leave out some word or letter in your answer, and the ignorance of the cathedral clergy will be harped upon; you will make some small mistake, which will be a falsehood, or some admission, which will be self-condemnation; you will find yourself to have been vulgar, ill-tempered, irreverent, and illiterate, and the chances are ten to one, but that being a clergyman you will have been guilty of blasphemy! A man may have the best of causes, the best of talents, and the best of tempers; he may write as well as Addison,* or as strongly as Junius;* but even with all this he cannot successfully answer, when attacked by the *Jupiter*. In such matters it is omnipotent. What the Czar is in Russia, or the mob in America, that the *Jupiter* is in England. Answer such an article! No, warden; whatever you do, don't do that. We were to look for this sort of thing you know; but we need not draw down on our heads more of it than is necessary.'

The article in the *Jupiter*, while it so greatly harassed our poor warden, was in immense triumph to some of the opposite party. Sorry as Bold was to see Mr Harding attacked so personally, it still gave him a feeling of elation to find his cause taken up by so powerful an advocate: and as to Finney, the attorney, he was beside himself. What! to be engaged in the same cause and on the same side with the *Jupiter*; to have the views he had recommended seconded, and furthered, and battled for by the *Jupiter*! Perhaps to have his own name mentioned as that of the learned gentlemen whose efforts had been so successful on behalf of the poor of Barchester! He might be examined before committees of the House of Commons, with heaven knows how much a day for his personal expenses – he might be engaged for years on such a suit! There was no end to the glorious golden dreams which this leader in the *Jupiter* produced in the soaring mind of Finney.

And the old bedesmen, they also heard of this article, and had a glimmering, indistinct idea of the marvellous advocate which had now taken up their cause. Abel Handy limped hither and thither through the rooms, repeating all that he understood to have been printed, with some additions of his own which he thought should have been added. He told them how the *Jupiter* had declared that their warden was no better than a robber, and that what the *Jupiter* said was acknowledged by the world to be true. How the *Jupiter* had affirmed that each one of them – 'each one of us, Jonathan Crumple, think of that,' – had a clear right to a hundred a year; and that if the *Jupiter* had said so, it was better than a decision of the Lord Chancellor;* and then he carried about the paper, supplied by Mr Finney, which, though none of them could read it, still afforded in its very touch and aspect positive corroboration of what was told them, and Jonathan Crumple pondered deeply over his returning wealth; and Job Skulpit saw how right he had been in signing the petition, and said so many scores of times; and Spriggs leered fearfully with his one eye; and Moody, as he more nearly approached the coming golden age, hated more deeply than ever those who still kept possession of what he so coveted. Even Billy Gazy and poor bedridden Bell became active and uneasy, and the great Bunce stood apart with lowering brow, with deep grief seated in his heart, for he perceived that evil days were coming.

It had been decided, the archdeacon advising, that no remonstrance, explanation, or defence should be addressed from the Barchester conclave to the Editor of the *Jupiter*, but hitherto that was the only decision to which they had come.

Sir Abraham Haphazard was deeply engaged in preparing a bill for the mortification of papists, to be called the 'Convent

Custody Bill,' the purport of which was to enable any protestant clergyman over fifty years of age to search any nun whom he suspected of being in possession of treasonable papers, or jesuitical symbols:* and as there were to be a hundred and thirty-seven clauses in the bill, each clause containing a separate thorn for the side of the papist, and as it was known the bill would be fought inch by inch, by fifty maddened Irishmen, the due construction and adequate dovetailing of it did consume much of Sir Abraham's time. The bill had all its desired effect. Of course it never passed into law; but it so completely divided the ranks of the Irish members, who had bound themselves together to force on the ministry a bill for compelling all men to drink Irish whisky, and all woman to wear Irish poplins, that for the remainder of the session the Great Poplin and Whisky League was utterly harmless.*

   Thus it happened that Sir Abraham's opinion was not at once forthcoming, and the uncertainty, the expectation, and suffering of the folk of Barchester was maintained at a high pitch.

Chapter 8

Plumstead Episcopi

The reader must now be requested to visit the rectory of Plumstead Episcopi; and as it is as yet still early morning, to ascend again with us into the bedroom of the archdeacon. The mistress of the mansion was at her toilet; on which we will not dwell with profane eyes, but proceed into a small inner room, where the doctor dressed and kept his boots and sermons; and here we will take our stand premising that the door of the room was so open as to admit of a conversation between our reverend Adam and his valued Eve.

'It's all your own fault, archdeacon,' said the latter; 'I told you from the beginning how it would end, and papa has no one to thank but you.'

'Good gracious, my dear,' said the doctor, appearing at the door of his dressing-room, with his face and head enveloped in the rough towel which he was violently using; 'how can you say so? I am doing my very best.'

'I wish you had never done so much,' said the lady, interrupting him; 'if you'd just have let John Bold come and go there, as he and papa liked, he and Eleanor would have been married by this time, and we should not have heard one word about all this affair.'

'But, my dear – '

'Oh, it's all very well, archdeacon, and of course you're right; I don't for a moment think you'll ever admit that you could be wrong; but the fact is, you've brought this young man down upon papa by huffing him as you have done.'

'But, my love – '

'And all because you didn't like John Bold for a brother-in-law. How is she ever to do better? papa hasn't got a shilling; and though Eleanor is well enough, she has not at all a taking style of beauty. I'm sure I don't know how she's to do better than marry John Bold, or as well indeed,' added the anxious sister, giving the last twist to her last shoestring.

Dr Grantly felt keenly the injustice of this attack; but what could he say? He certainly had huffed John Bold; he certainly had objected to him as a brother-in-law, and a very few months ago the very idea had excited his wrath: but now matters were changed; John Bold had shown his power, and, though he was as odious as ever to the archdeacon, power is always respected, and the reverend dignitary began to think that such an alliance might not have been imprudent. Nevertheless, his motto was still 'no surrender;' he would still fight it out; he still believed confidently in Oxford, in the bench of bishops, in Sir Abraham Haphazard, and in himself; and it was only when alone with his wife that doubts of defeat ever beset him. He once more tried to communicate this confidence to Mrs Grantly, and for the twentieth time began to tell her of Sir Abraham.

'Oh, Sir Abraham!' said she, collecting all her house keys into her basket before she descended; 'Sir Abraham won't get Eleanor a husband; Sir Abraham won't get papa another income when he has been worreted* out of the hospital. Mark what I tell you, archdeacon: while you and Sir Abraham are fighting, papa will lose his preferment; and what will you do then with him and Eleanor on your hands? besides, who's to pay Sir Abraham? I suppose he won't take the case up for nothing?' And so the lady descended to family worship among her children and servants, the pattern of a good and prudent wife.

Dr Grantly was blessed with a happy, thriving family. There were, first, three boys, now at home from school for the holidays. They were called, respectively, Charles James, Henry, and Samuel.* The two younger (there were five in all) were girls; the elder, Florinda, bore the name of the Archbishop of York's wife, whose godchild she was; and the younger had been christened Grizzel, after a sister of the Archbishop of Canterbury. The boys were all clever, and gave good promise of being well able to meet the cares and trials of the world; and yet they were not alike in their dispositions, and each had his individual character, and each his separate admirers among the doctor's friends.

Charles James was an exact and careful boy; he never committed himself;* he well knew how much was expected from the eldest son of the Archdeacon of Barchester, and was therefore mindful not to mix too freely with other boys. He had not the great talents of his younger brothers, but he exceeded them in judgment and propriety of demeanour; his fault, if he had one, was an over-attention to words instead of things; there was a thought too much *finesse* about him, and, as even his father sometimes told him, he was too fond of a compromise.*

The second was the archdeacon's favourite son, and Henry was indeed a brilliant boy.* The versatility of his genius was surprising, and the visitors at Plumstead Episcopi were often amazed at the marvellous manner in which he would, when called on, adapt his capacity to apparently most uncongenial pursuits. He appeared once before a large circle as Luther the reformer, and delighted them with the perfect manner in which he assumed the character; and within three days he again astonished them by acting the part of a Capuchin friar to the very life. For this last exploit his father gave him a golden guinea, and his brothers said the reward had been promised beforehand in the event of the performance being successful.* He was also sent on a tour into Devonshire; a treat which the lad was most anxious of enjoying. His father's friends there, however, did not appreciate his talents, and sad accounts were sent home of the perversity of his nature.* He was a most courageous lad, game to the backbone. It was soon known, both at home, where he lived, and within some miles of Barchester Cathedral, and also at Westminster, where he was at school, that young Henry could box well and would never own himself beat; other boys would fight while they had a leg to stand on, but he would fight with no leg at all. Those backing him would sometimes think him crushed by the weight of blows and faint with loss of blood, and his friends would endeavour to withdraw him from the contest; but no, Henry never gave in, was never weary of the battle. The ring was the only element in which he seemed to enjoy himself; and while other boys were happy in the number of their friends, he rejoiced most in the multitude of his foes.

His relations could not but admire his pluck, but they sometimes were forced to regret that he was inclined to be a bully; and those not so partial to him as his father was, observed with pain that, though he could fawn to the masters and the archdeacon's friends, he was imperious and masterful to the servants and the poor.

But perhaps Samuel was the general favourite; and dear little Soapy, as he was familiarly called, was as engaging a child as ever fond mother petted. He was soft and gentle in his manners, and attractive in his speech; the tone of his voice was melody, and every action was a grace; unlike his brothers, he was courteous to all, he was affable to the lowly, and meek even to the very scullery maid. He was a boy of great promise, minding his books and delighting the hearts of his masters. His brothers, however, were not particularly fond of him; they would complain to their mother that Soapy's civility all meant something; they thought that his voice was too often listened to at Plumstead Episcopi, and evidently feared that, as he grew up, he would have more weight in the house than either of them; there was, therefore, a sort of agreement among them to put young Soapy down. This, however, was not so easy to be done; Samuel, though young, was sharp; he could not assume the stiff decorum of Charles James, nor could he fight like Henry; but he was a perfect master of his own weapons, and contrived, in the teeth of both of them, to hold the place which he had assumed. Henry declared that he was a false, cunning creature; and Charles James, though he always spoke of him as his dear brother Samuel, was not slow to say a word against him when opportunity offered. To speak the truth, Samuel was a cunning boy, and those even who loved him best could not but own that for one so young, he was too adroit in choosing his words, and too skilled in modulating his voice.*

The two little girls Florinda and Grizzel were nice little girls enough, but they did not possess the strong sterling qualities of their brothers; their voices were not often heard at Plumstead Episcopi; they were bashful and timid by nature, slow to speak before company even when asked to do so; and though they looked very nice in their clean white muslin frocks and pink sashes, they were but little noticed by the archdeacon's visitors.

Whatever of submissive humility may have appeared in the gait and visage of the archdeacon during his colloquy with his wife in the sanctum of their dressing-rooms, was dispelled as he entered his breakfast-parlour with erect head and powerful step. In the presence of a third person he assumed the lord and master; and that wise and talented lady too well knew the man to whom her lot for life was bound, to stretch her authority beyond the point at which it would be borne. Strangers at Plumstead Episcopi, when they saw the imperious brow with which he commanded silence from the large circle of visitors, children, and servants who came together in the morning to hear him read the word of God, and watched how meekly that wife seated herself behind her basket of keys with a little girl on each side, as she caught that commanding glance; strangers, I say, seeing this, could little guess that some fifteen minutes since she had stoutly held her ground against him, hardly allowing him to open his mouth in his own defence. But such is the tact and talent of women!

And now let us observe the well-furnished breakfast-parlour at Plumstead Episcopi, and the comfortable air of all the belongings of the rectory. Comfortable they certainly were, but neither gorgeous nor even grand; indeed, considering the money that had been spent there, the eye and taste might have been better served; there was an air of heaviness about the rooms which might have been avoided without any sacrifice of propriety; colours might have been better chosen and lights more perfectly diffused: but perhaps in doing so the thorough clerical aspect of the whole might have been somewhat marred; at any rate, it was not without ample consideration that those thick, dark, costly carpets were put down; those embossed, but sombre papers hung up; those heavy curtains draped so as to half-exclude the light of the sun: nor were these old-fashioned chairs, bought at a price far exceeding that now given for more modern goods, without a purpose. The breakfast-service on the table was equally costly and equally plain; the apparent object had been to spend money without obtaining brilliancy or splendour. The urn was of thick and solid silver, as were also the tea-pot, coffee-pot, cream-ewer, and sugar-bowl; the cups were old, dim dragon china, worth about a pound a piece, but very despicable in the eyes of the uninitiated. The silver forks were so heavy as to be disagreeable to the hand, and the bread-basket was of a weight really formidable to any but robust persons. The tea consumed was the very best, the coffee the very blackest, the cream the very thickest; there was dry toast and buttered toast, muffins and crumpets; hot bread and cold bread, white bread and brown bread, home-made bread and bakers' bread, wheaten bread and oaten bread, and if there be other breads than these, they were there; there were eggs in napkins, and crispy bits of bacon under silver covers; and there were little fishes in a little box, and devilled kidneys frizzling on a hot-water dish; which, by the bye, were placed closely contiguous to the plate of the worthy archdeacon himself. Over and above this, on a snow-white napkin, spread upon the sideboard, was a huge ham and a huge sirloin; the latter having laden the dinner table on the previous evening. Such was the ordinary fare at Plumstead Episcopi.

And yet I have never found the rectory a pleasant house. The fact that man shall not live by bread alone* seemed to be somewhat forgotten: and noble as was the appearance of the host, and sweet and good-natured as was the face of the hostess, talented as were the children, and excellent as were the viands and the wines, in spite of these attractions, I generally found the rectory somewhat dull. After breakfast the archdeacon would retire, of course to his clerical pursuits. Mrs Grantly, I presume, inspected her kitchen, though she had a first-rate housekeeper, with sixty pounds a year; and attended to the lessons of Florinda and Grizzel, though she had an excellent governess with thirty pounds a year: but at any rate she disappeared: and I never could make companions of the boys. Charles James, though he always looked as though there was something in him, never seemed to have much to say; and what he did say he would always unsay the next minute. He told me once, that he considered cricket, on the whole, to be a gentleman-like game for boys, provided they would play without running about; and that fives, also, was a seemly game, so that those who played it never heated themselves. Henry once quarrelled with me for taking his sister Grizzel's part, in a contest between them as to the best mode of using a watering-pot for the garden flowers; and from that day to this he has not spoken to me, though he speaks at me often enough. For half an hour or so I certainly did like Sammy's gentle speeches; but one gets tired of honey, and I found that he preferred the more admiring listeners whom he met in the kitchen-garden and back precincts of the establishment; besides, I think I once caught Sammy fibbing.

On the whole, therefore, I found the rectory a dull house, though it must be admitted that everything there was of the very best.

After breakfast, on the morning of which we are writing, the archdeacon, as usual, retired to his study, intimating that he was going to be very busy, but that he would see Mr Chadwick if he called. On entering this sacred room he carefully opened the paper case on which he was wont to compose his favourite sermons, and spread on it a fair sheet of paper, and one partly written on; he then placed his inkstand, looked at his pen, and folded his blotting-paper; having done so, he got up again from his seat, stood with his back to the fireplace, and yawned comfortably, stretching out vastly his huge arms, and opening his burly chest. He then walked across the room and locked the door; and having so prepared himself, he threw himself into his easy chair, took from a secret drawer beneath his table a volume of Rabelais,* and began to amuse himself with the witty mischief of Panurge;* and so passed the archdeacon's morning on that day.

He was left undisturbed at his studies for an hour or two, when a knock came to the door, and Mr Chadwick was announced. Rabelais retired into the secret drawer, the easy chair seemed knowingly to betake itself off, and when the archdeacon quickly undid his bolt, he was discovered by the steward working, as usual, for that church of which he was so useful a pillar. Mr Chadwick had just come from London, and was, therefore, known to be the bearer of important news.

'We've got Sir Abraham's opinion at last,' said Mr Chadwick, as he seated himself.

'Well, well, well!' exclaimed the archdeacon impatiently.

'Oh, it's as long as my arm,' said the other; 'it can't be told in a word, but you can read it;' and he handed him a copy, in heaven knows how many spun-out folios, of the opinion which the attorney-general had managed to cram on the back and sides of the case as originally submitted to him.

'The upshot is,' said Chadwick, 'that there's a screw loose in their case, and we had better do nothing. They are proceeding against Mr Harding and myself, and Sir Abraham holds that, under the wording of the will, and subsequent arrangements legally sanctioned, Mr Harding and I are only paid servants. The defendants should have been either the Corporation of Barchester, or possibly the chapter or your father.'

'W – hoo,' said the archdeacon; 'so Master Bold is on a wrong scent, is he?'

'That's Sir Abraham's opinion; but any scent almost would be a wrong scent. Sir Abraham thinks that if they'd taken the corporation, or the chapter, we could have baffled them. The bishop, he thinks, would be the surest shot; but even there we could plead that the bishop is only visitor, and that he has never made himself a consenting party to the performance of other duties.'

'That's quite clear,' said the archdeacon.

'Not quite so clear,' said the other. 'You see the will says, "My lord, the bishop, being graciously pleased to see that due justice be done." Now, it may be a question whether, in accepting and administering the patronage, your father has not accepted also the other duties assigned. It is doubtful, however; but even if they hit that nail – and they are far off from that yet, – the point is so nice, as Sir Abraham says, that you would force them into fifteen thousand pounds' cost before they could bring it to an issue! and where's that sum of money to come from?'

The archdeacon rubbed his hands with delight; he had never doubted the justice of his case, but he had begun to have some dread of unjust success on the part of his enemies. It was delightful to him thus to hear that their cause was surrounded with such rocks and shoals; such causes of shipwreck unseen by the landsman's eye, but visible enough to the keen eyes of practical law mariners. How wrong his wife was to wish that Bold should marry Eleanor! Bold! why, if he should be ass enough to persevere, he would be a beggar before he knew whom he was at law with!

'That's excellent, Chadwick – that's excellent! I told you Sir Abraham was the man for us;' and he put down on the table the copy of the opinion, and patted it fondly.

'Don't you let that be seen, though, archdeacon.'

'Who? – I! – not for worlds,' said the doctor.

'People will talk, you know, archdeacon.'

'Of course, of course,' said the doctor.

'Because, if that gets abroad, it would teach them how to fight their own battle.'

'Quite true,' said the doctor.

'No one here in Barchester ought to see that but you and I, archdeacon.'

'No, no, certainly no one else,' said the archdeacon, pleased with the closeness of the confidence; 'no one else shall.'

'Mrs Grantly is very interested in the matter, I know,' said Mr Chadwick.

Did the archdeacon wink, or did he not? I am inclined to think he did not quite wink; but that without such, perhaps, unseemly gesture he communicated to Mr Chadwick, with the corner of his eye, intimation that, deep as was Mrs Grantly's interest in the matter, it should not procure for her a perusal of that document; and at the same time he partly opened the small drawer, above spoken of, deposited the paper on the volume of Rabelais, and showed to Mr Chadwick the nature of the key which guarded these hidden treasures. The careful steward then expressed himself contented. Ah! vain man! he could fasten up his Rabelais, and other things secret, with all the skill of Bramah or of Chubb;* but where could he fasten up the key which solved these mechanical mysteries? It is probable to us that the contents of no drawer in that house were unknown to its mistress, and we think, moreover, that she was entitled to all such knowledge.

'But,' said Mr Chadwick, 'we must, of course, tell your father and Mr Harding so much of Sir Abraham's opinion as will satisfy them that the matter is doing well.'

'Oh, certainly, – yes, of course,' said the doctor.

'You had better let them know that Sir Abraham is of opinion that there is no case at any rate against Mr Harding; and that as the action is worded at present, it must fall to the ground; they must be nonsuited* if they carry it on; you had better tell Mr Harding, that Sir Abraham is clearly of opinion that he is only a servant, and as such, not liable – or if you like it, I'll see Mr Harding myself.'

'Oh, I must see him tomorrow, and my father too, and I'll explain to them exactly so much, – you won't go before lunch, Mr Chadwick: well, if you will, you must, for I know your time is precious;' and he shook hands with the diocesan steward, and bowed him out.

And the archdeacon had again recourse to his drawer, and twice read through the essence of Sir Abraham Haphazard's law-enlightened and law-bewildered brains. It was very clear that to Sir Abraham, the justice of the old men's claim or the justice of Mr Harding's defence were ideas that had never presented themselves. A legal victory over an opposing party was the service for which Sir Abraham was, as he imagined, to be paid: and that he, according to his lights, had diligently laboured to achieve, and with probable hope of success. Of the intense desire which Mr Harding felt to be assured on fit authority, that he was wronging no man, that he was entitled in true equity to his income, that he might sleep at night without pangs of conscience, that he was no robber, no spoiler of the poor; that he and all the world might be openly convinced that he was not the man which the *Jupiter* had described him to be; of such longings on the part of Mr Harding, Sir Abraham was entirely ignorant; nor, indeed, could it be looked on as part of his business to gratify such desires. Such was not the system on which his battles were fought, and victories gained. Success was his object, and he was generally successful. He conquered his enemies by their weakness rather than by his own strength, and it had been found almost impossible to make up a case, in which Sir Abraham, as an antagonist, would not find a flaw.

The archdeacon was delighted with the closeness of the reasoning. To do him justice, it was not a selfish triumph that he desired; he would personally lose nothing by defeat, or at least what he might lose did not actuate him; but neither was it love of justice which made him so anxious, nor even mainly solicitude for his father-in-law. He was fighting a part of a never-ending battle against a never-conquered foe – that of the church against its enemies.

He knew Mr Harding could not pay all the expense of these doings; for these long opinions of Sir Abraham's, these causes to be pleaded, these speeches to be made, these various courts through which the case was, he presumed, to be dragged. He knew that he and his father must at least bear the heavier portion of this tremendous cost; but to do the archdeacon justice, he did not recoil from this. He was a man fond of obtaining money, greedy of a large income, but open-handed enough in expending it, and it was a triumph to him to foresee the success of this measure, although he might be called on to pay so dearly for it himself.

CHAPTER 9

The Conference

On the following morning the archdeacon was with his father betimes, and a note was sent down to the warden begging his attendance at the palace. Dr Grantly, as he cogitated on the matter, leaning back in his brougham as he journeyed into Barchester, felt that it would be difficult to communicate his own satisfaction either to his father or his father-in-law. He wanted success on his own side and discomfiture on that of his enemies. The bishop wanted peace on the subject; a settled peace if possible, but peace at any rate till the short remainder of his own days had spun itself out; but Mr Harding required, not only success and peace, but he also demanded that he might stand justified before the world.

The bishop, however, was comparatively easy to deal with; and before the arrival of the other, the dutiful son had persuaded his father that all was going on well, and then the warden arrived.

It was Mr Harding's wont, whenever he spent a morning at the palace, to seat himself immediately at the bishop's elbow, the bishop occupying a huge armchair fitted up with candlesticks, a reading table, a drawer, and other paraphernalia, the position of which chair was never moved, summer or winter; and when, as was very usual, the archdeacon was there also, he confronted the two elders, who thus were enabled to fight the battle against him together; and together submit to defeat, for such was their constant fate.

Our warden now took his accustomed place, having greeted his son-in-law as he entered, and then affectionately inquired after his friend's health. There was a gentleness about the bishop to which the soft womanly affection of Mr Harding particularly endeared itself, and it was quaint to see how the two mild old priests pressed each other's hands, and smiled and made little signs of love.

'Sir Abraham's opinion has come at last,' began the archdeacon. Mr Harding had heard so much, and was most anxious to know the result.

'It is quite favourable,' said the bishop, pressing his friend's arm. 'I am so glad.'

Mr Harding looked at the mighty bearer of the important news for confirmation of these glad tidings.

'Yes,' said the archdeacon, 'Sir Abraham has given most minute attention to the case; indeed, I knew he would; – most minute attention, and his opinion is – and as to his opinion on such a subject being correct, no one who knows Sir Abraham's character, can doubt – his opinion is, that they hav'n't got a leg to stand on.'

'But as how, archdeacon?'

'Why, in the first place: – but you're no lawyer, warden, and I doubt you won't understand it; the gist of the matter is this: – Under Hiram's will two paid guardians have been selected for the hospital; the law will say two paid servants, and you and I won't quarrel with the name.'

'At any rate I will not if I am one of the servants,' said Mr Harding. 'A rose you know – .'*

'Yes, yes,' said the archdeacon, impatient of poetry at such a time. 'Well, two paid servants, we'll say; one to look after the men, and the other to look after the money. You and Chadwick are these two servants, and whether either of you be paid too much, or too little, more or less in fact than the founder willed, it's as clear as daylight that no one can fall foul of either of you for receiving an allotted stipend.'

'That does seem clear,' said the bishop, who had winced visibly under the words servants and stipend, which, however, appeared to have caused no uneasiness to the archdeacon.

'Quite clear,' said he, 'and very satisfactory. In point of fact, it being necessary to select such servants for the use of the hospital, the pay to be given to them must depend on the rate of pay for such services, according to their market value at the period in question; and those who manage the hospital must be the only judges of this.'

'And who does manage the hospital?' asked the warden.

'Oh, let them find that out; that's another question; the action is brought against you and Chadwick, and that's your defence, and a perfect and full defence it is. Now that I think very satisfactory.'

'Well,' said the bishop, looking inquiringly up into his friend's face, who sat silent awhile, and apparently not so well satisfied.

'And conclusive,' continued the archdeacon; 'if they press it to a jury, which they won't do, no twelve men in England will take five minutes to decide against them.'

'But according to that,' said Mr Harding, 'I might as well have sixteen hundred a year as eight, if the managers choose to allot it to me; and as I am one of the managers, if not the chief manager, myself, that can hardly be a just arrangement.'

'Oh, well, all that's nothing to the question; the question is, whether this intruding fellow, and a lot of cheating attorneys and pestilent dissenters, are to interfere with an arrangement which every one knows is essentially just and serviceable to the church. Pray don't let us be splitting hairs, and that amongst ourselves, or there'll never be an end of the cause or the cost.'

Mr Harding again sat silent for awhile, during which the bishop once and again pressed his arm, and looked in his face to see if he could catch a gleam of a contented and eased mind; but there was no such gleam, and the poor warden continued playing sad dirges on invisible stringed instruments in all manner of positions: he was ruminating in his mind on this opinion of Sir Abraham, looking to it wearily and earnestly for satisfaction, but finding none. At last he said, 'Did you see the opinion, archdeacon?'

The archdeacon said he had not – that was to say, he had – that was, he had not seen the opinion itself; he had seen what had been called a copy, but he could not say whether of a whole or part; nor could he say that what he had seen were the *ipsissima verba** of the great man himself; but what he had seen contained exactly the decision which he had announced, and which he again declared to be to his mind extremely satisfactory.

'I should like to see the opinion,' said the warden; 'that is, a copy of it.'

'Well, I suppose you can if you make a point of it; but I don't see the use myself; of course it is essential that the purport of it should not be known, and it is therefore unadvisable to multiply copies.'

'Why should it not be known?' asked the warden.

'What a question for a man to ask!' said the archdeacon, throwing up his hands in token of his surprise; 'but it is like you – a child is not more innocent than you are in matters of business. Can't you see that if we tell them that no action will lie against you, but that one may possibly lie against some other person or persons, that we shall be putting weapons into their hands, and be teaching them how to cut our own throats?'

The warden again sat silent, and the bishop again looked at him wistfully: 'The only thing we have now to do,' continued the archdeacon, 'is to remain quiet, hold our peace, and let them play their own game as they please.'

'We are not to make known then,' said the warden, 'that we have consulted the attorney-general, and that we are advised by him that the founder's will is fully and fairly carried out.'

'God bless my soul!' said the archdeacon, 'how odd it is that you will not see that all we are to do is to do nothing: why should we say anything about the founder's will? We are in possession; and we know that they are not in a position to put us out: surely that is enough for the present.'

Mr Harding rose from his seat and paced thoughtfully up and down the library, the bishop the while watching him painfully at every turn, and the archdeacon continuing to pour forth his convictions that the affair was in a state to satisfy any prudent mind.

'And the *Jupiter*?' said the warden, stopping suddenly.

'Oh! the *Jupiter*,' answered the other. 'The *Jupiter* can break no bones. You must bear with that; there is much of course which it is our bounden duty to bear; it cannot be all roses for us here,' and the archdeacon looked exceedingly moral; 'besides the matter is too trivial, of too little general interest to be mentioned again in the *Jupiter*, unless we stir up the subject:' and the archdeacon again looked exceedingly knowing and worldly wise.

The warden continued his walk; the hard and stinging words of that newspaper article, each one of which had thrust a thorn as it were into his inmost soul, were fresh in his memory: he had read it more than once, word by word, and what was worse, he fancied it was as well known to every one as to himself. Was he to be looked on as the unjust griping priest he had been there described? Was he to be pointed at as the consumer of the bread of the poor, and to be allowed no means of refuting such charges, of clearing his begrimed name, of standing innocent in the world, as hitherto he had stood? Was he to bear all this, to receive as usual his now hated income, and be known as one of those greedy priests who by their rapacity have brought disgrace on their church? and why? Why should he bear all this? why should he die, for he felt that he could not live, under such a weight of obloquy? As he paced up and down the room he resolved in his misery and enthusiasm that he could with pleasure, if he were allowed, give up his place, abandon his pleasant home, leave the hospital, and live poorly, happily, and with an unsullied name, on the small remainder of his means.

He was a man somewhat shy of speaking of himself, even before those who knew him best, and whom he loved the most; but at last it burst forth from him, and with a somewhat jerking eloquence he declared that he could not, would not, bear this misery any longer.

'If it can be proved,' said he at last, 'that I have a just and honest right to this, as God well knows I always deemed I had; if this salary or stipend be really my due, I am not less anxious than another to retain it. I have the well-being of my child to look to. I am too old to miss without some pain the comforts to which I have been used; and I am, as others are, anxious to prove to the world that I have been right, and to uphold the place I have held; but I cannot do it at such a cost as this. I cannot bear this. Could you tell me to do so?' and he appealed, almost in tears, to the bishop, who had left his chair, and was now leaning on the warden's arm as he stood on the further side of the table facing the archdeacon. 'Could you tell me to sit there at ease, indifferent, and satisfied, while such things as these are said loudly of me in the world?'

The bishop could feel for him and sympathise with him, but he could not advise him, he could only say, 'No, no, you shall be asked to do nothing that is painful; you shall do just what your heart tells you to be right; you shall do whatever you think best yourself. Theophilus, don't advise him, pray don't advise the warden to do anything which is painful.'

But the archdeacon, though he could not sympathise, could advise; and he saw that the time had come when it behoved him to do so in a somewhat peremptory manner.

'Why, my lord,' he said speaking to his father: and when he called his father 'my lord,' the good old bishop shook in his shoes, for he knew that an evil time was coming. 'Why, my lord, there are two ways of giving advice; there is advice that may be good for the present day; and there is advice that may be good for days to come: now I cannot bring myself to give the former, if it be incompatible with the other.'

'No, no, no, I suppose not,' said the bishop, reseating himself, and shading his face with his hands. Mr Harding sat down with his back to the further wall, playing to himself some air fitted for so calamitous an occasion, and the archdeacon said out his say standing, with his back to the empty fireplace.

'It is not to be supposed, but that much pain will spring out of this unnecessarily raised question. We must all have foreseen that, and the matter has in no wise gone on worse than we expected; but it will be weak, yes, and wicked also, to abandon the cause and own ourselves wrong, because the inquiry is painful. It is not only ourselves we have to look to: to a certain extent the interest of the church is in our keeping. Should it be found that one after another of those who hold preferment abandoned it whenever it might be attacked, is it not plain that such attacks would be renewed till nothing was left us? and, that if so deserted, the Church of England must fall to the ground altogether? If this be true of many, it is true of one. Were you, accused as you now are, to throw up the wardenship, and to relinquish the preferment which is your property, with the vain object of proving yourself disinterested, you would fail in that object, you would inflict a desperate blow on your brother clergymen, you would encourage every cantankerous dissenter in England to make a similar charge against some source of clerical revenue, and you would do your best to dishearten those who are most anxious to defend you and uphold your position. I can fancy nothing more weak, or more wrong. It is not that you think that there is any justice in these charges, or that you doubt your own right to the wardenship: you are convinced of your own honesty, and yet would yield to them through cowardice.'

'Cowardice!' said the bishop, expostulating. Mr Harding sat unmoved, gazing on his son-in-law.

'Well, would it not be cowardice? would he not do so because he is afraid to endure the evil things which will be falsely spoken of him? Would that not be cowardice? And now let us see the extent of the evil which you dread. The *Jupiter* publishes an article which a great many, no doubt, will read; but of those who understand the subject how many will believe the *Jupiter*? Every one knows what its object is; it has taken up the case against Lord Guildford and against the Dean of Rochester,* and that against half a dozen bishops; and does not every one know that it would take up any case of the kind, right or wrong, false or true, with known justice or known injustice, if by doing so it could further its own views? Does not all the world know this of the *Jupiter*? Who that really knows you will think the worse of you for what the *Jupiter* says? And why care for those who do not know you? I will say nothing of your own comfort, but I do say that you could not be justified in throwing up, in a fit of passion, for such it would be, the only maintenance that Eleanor has; and if you did so, if you really did vacate the wardenship, and submit to ruin, what would that profit you? If you have no future right to the income, you have had no past right to it; and the very fact of your abandoning your position, would create a demand for repayment of that which you have already received and spent.'

The poor warden groaned as he sat perfectly still, looking up at the hard-hearted orator who thus tormented him, and the bishop echoed the sound faintly from behind his hands; but the archdeacon cared little for such signs of weakness, and completed his exhortation.

'But let us suppose the office to be left vacant, and that your own troubles concerning it were over; would that satisfy you? Are your only aspirations in the matter confined to yourself and family? I know they are not. I know you are as anxious as any of us for the church to which we belong; and what a grievous blow would such an act of apostasy give her! You owe it to the church of which you are a member and a minister, to bear with this affliction, however severe it may be: you owe it to my father, who instituted you, to support his rights: you owe it to those who preceded you to assert the legality of their position: you owe it to those who are to come after you, to maintain uninjured for them that which you received uninjured from others; and you owe to us all the unflinching assistance of perfect brotherhood in this matter, so that upholding one another we may support our great cause without blushing and without disgrace.'

And so the archdeacon ceased, and stood self-satisfied, watching the effect of his spoken wisdom.

The warden felt himself, to a certain extent, stifled; he would have given the world to get himself out into the open air without speaking to, or noticing those who were in the room with him; but this was impossible. He could not leave without saying something, and he felt himself confounded by the archdeacon's eloquence. There was a heavy, unfeeling, unanswerable truth in what he had said; there was so much practical, but odious common sense in it, that he neither knew how to assent or to differ. If it were necessary for him to suffer, he felt that he could endure without complaint and without cowardice, providing that he was self-satisfied of the justice of his own cause. What he could not endure was, that he should be accused by others, and not acquitted by himself. Doubting, as he had begun to doubt, the justice of his own position in the hospital, he knew that his own self-confidence would not be restored because Mr Bold had been in error as to some legal form; nor could he be satisfied to escape, because, through some legal fiction, he who received the greatest benefit from the hospital might be considered only as one of its servants.

The archdeacon's speech had silenced him – stupefied him – annihilated him; anything but satisfied him. With the bishop it fared not much better. He did not discern clearly how things were, but he saw enough to know that a battle was to be prepared for; a battle that would destroy his few remaining comforts, and bring him with sorrow to the grave.

The warden still sat, and still looked at the archdeacon, till his thoughts fixed themselves wholly on the means of escape from his present position, and he felt like a bird fascinated by gazing on a snake.

'I hope you agree with me,' said the archdeacon at last, breaking the dread silence; 'my lord, I hope *you* agree with me.'

Oh what a sigh the bishop gave! 'My lord, I hope you agree with me,' again repeated the merciless tyrant.

'Yes, I suppose so,' groaned the poor old man, slowly.

'And you, warden?'

Mr Harding was now stirred to action – he must speak and move, so he got up and took one turn before he answered.

'Do not press me for an answer just at present; I will do nothing lightly in the matter, and of whatever I do I will give you and the bishop notice.' And so without another word he took his leave, escaping quickly through the palace hall, and down the lofty steps, nor did he breathe freely till he found himself alone under the huge elms of the silent close. Here he walked long and slowly, thinking on his case with a troubled air, and trying in vain to confute the archdeacon's argument. He then went home, resolved to bear it all — ignominy, suspense, disgrace, self doubt, and heart-burning — and to do as those would have him, who he still believed were most fit and most able to counsel him aright.

CHAPTER 10

Tribulation

Mr Harding was a sadder man than he had ever yet been when he returned to his own house. He had been wretched enough on that well remembered morning when he was forced to expose before his son-in-law the publisher's account for ushering into the world his dear book of sacred music; when after making such payments as he could do unassisted, he found that he was a debtor of more than three hundred pounds: but his sufferings then were as nothing to his present misery; – then he had done wrong, and he knew it, and was able to resolve that he would not sin in like manner again; but now he could make no resolution, and comfort himself by no promises of firmness. He had been forced to think that his lot had placed him in a false position, and he was about to maintain that position against the opinion of the world and against his own convictions.

He had read with pity, amounting almost to horror, the strictures which had appeared from time to time against the Earl of Guildford as master of St Cross, and the invectives that had been heaped on rich diocesan dignitaries and overgrown sine-cure pluralists. In judging of them, he judged leniently; the whole bias of his profession had taught him to think that they were more sinned against than sinning,* and that the animosity with which they had been pursued was venomous and unjust; but he had not the less regarded their plight as most miserable. His hair had stood on end and his flesh had crept as he read the things which had been written; he had wondered how men could live under such a load of disgrace; how they could face their fellow creatures while their names were bandied about so injuriously and so publicly – and now this lot was to be his – he, that shy retiring man, who had so comforted himself in the hidden obscurity of his lot, who had so enjoyed the unassuming warmth of his own little corner, he was now to be dragged forth into the glaring day, and gibbeted before ferocious multitudes.

He entered his own house a crestfallen, humiliated man, without a hope of overcoming the wretchedness which affected him.

He wandered into the drawing-room where was his daughter; but he could not speak to her now, so he left it, and went into the book room. He was not quick enough to escape Eleanor's glance, or to prevent her from seeing that he was disturbed; and in a little while she followed him. She found him seated in his accustomed chair, with no book open before him, no pen ready in his hand, no ill-shapen notes of blotted music lying before him as was usual, none of those hospital accounts with which he was so precise and yet so unmethodical: he was doing nothing, thinking of nothing, looking at nothing; he was merely suffering.

'Leave me Eleanor, my dear,' he said, 'leave me my darling for a few minutes, for I am busy.'

Eleanor saw well how it was, but she did leave him, and glided silently back to her drawing-room. When he had sat awhile, thus alone and unoccupied, he got up to walk again – he could make more of his thoughts walking than sitting, and was creeping out into his garden, when he met Bunce on the threshold.

'Well, Bunce,' said he, in a tone that for him was sharp, 'what is it? do you want me?'

'I was only coming to ask after your reverence,' said the old bedesman, touching his hat; 'and to inquire about the news from London,' he added after a pause.

The warden winced, and put his hand to his forehead and felt bewildered.

'Attorney Finney has been there this morning,' continued Bunce, 'and by his looks I guess he is not so well pleased as he once was, and it has got abroad somehow that the archdeacon has had down great news from London, and Handy and Moody are both as black as devils; and I hope,' said the man, trying to assume a cheery tone, 'that things are looking up, and that there'll be an end soon to all this stuff which bothers your reverence so sorely.'

'Well, I wish there may be, Bunce.'

'But about the news, your reverence?' said the old man, almost whispering.

Mr Harding walked on, and shook his head impatiently. Poor Bunce little knew how he was tormenting his patron.

'If there was anything to cheer you, I should be so glad to know it,' said he, with a tone of affection which the warden in all his misery could not resist.

He stopped, and took both the old man's hands in his. 'My friend,' said he, 'my dear old friend, there is nothing: there is no news to cheer me – God's will be done:' and two small hot tears broke away from his eyes and stole down his furrowed cheeks.

'Then God's will be done,' said the other solemnly, 'but they told me that there was good news from London, and I came to wish your reverence joy; but God's will be done;' and so the warden again walked on, and the bedesman looking wistfully after him, and receiving no encouragement to follow, returned sadly to his own abode.

For a couple of hours the warden remained thus in the garden, now walking, now standing motionless on the turf, and then, as his legs got weary, sitting unconsciously on the garden seats, and then walking again. And Eleanor, hidden behind the muslin curtains of the window, watched him through the trees as he now came in sight, and then again was concealed by the turnings of the walk; and thus the time passed away till five, when the warden crept back to the house and prepared for dinner.

It was but a sorry meal. The demure parlour-maid as she handed the dishes and changed the plates, saw that all was not right, and was more demure than ever: neither father nor daughter could eat, and the hateful food was soon cleared away, and the bottle of port placed upon the table.

'Would you like Bunce to come in, papa?' said Eleanor, thinking that the company of the old man might lighten his sorrow.

'No my dear, thank you, not today; but are not you going out, Eleanor, this lovely afternoon? don't stay in for me, my dear.'

'I thought you seemed so sad, papa.'

'Sad,' said he irritated; 'well, people must all have their share of sadness here; I am not more exempt than another: but kiss me, dearest, and go now; I will, if possible, be more sociable when you return.'

And Eleanor was again banished from her father's sorrow. Ah! her desire now was not to find him happy, but to be allowed to share his sorrows; not to force him to be sociable, but to persuade him to be trustful.

She put on her bonnet as desired, and went up to Mary Bold; this was now her daily haunt, for John Bold was up in London among lawyers and church reformers, diving deep into other questions than that of the wardenship of Barchester; supplying information to one member of parliament, and dining with another; subscribing to funds for the abolition of clerical incomes, and seconding at that great national meeting at the Crown and Anchor a resolution to the effect, that no clergyman of the Church of England, be he who he might, should have more than a thousand a year, and none less than two hundred and fifty. His speech on this occasion was short, for fifteen had to speak, and the room was hired for two hours only, at the expiration of which the Quakers and Mr Cobden were to make use of it for an appeal to the public in aid of the Emperor of Russia;* but it was sharp and effective: at least he was told so by a companion with whom he now lived much, and on whom he greatly depended – one Tom Towers,* a very leading genius, and supposed to have high employment on the staff of the *Jupiter*.

So Eleanor, as was now her wont, went up to Mary Bold, and Mary listened kindly, while the daughter spoke much of her father, and, perhaps kinder still, found a listener in Eleanor, while she spoke about her brother. In the meantime the warden sat alone, leaning on the arm of his chair; he had poured out a glass of wine, but had done so merely from habit, for he left it untouched: there he sat gazing at the open window, and thinking, if he can be said to have thought, of the happiness of his past life. All manner of past delights came before his mind, which at the time he had enjoyed without considering them; his easy days, his absence of all kind of hard work, his pleasant shady home, those twelve old neighbours whose welfare till now had been the source of so much pleasant care, the excellence of his children, the friendship of the dear old bishop, the solemn grandeur of those vaulted aisles, through which he loved to hear his own voice pealing; and then that friend of friends, that choice ally that had never deserted him, that eloquent companion that would always, when asked, discourse such pleasant music, that violoncello of his – ah, how happy he had been! but it was over now; his easy days and absence of work had been the crime which brought on him his tribulation; his shady home was pleasant no longer; maybe it was no longer his; the old neighbours, whose welfare had been so desired by him, were his enemies; his daughter was as wretched as himself, and even the bishop was made miserable by his position. He could never again lift up his voice boldly as he had hitherto done among his brethren, for he felt that he was disgraced; and he feared even to touch his bow, for he knew how grievous a sound of wailing, how piteous a lamentation, it would produce.

He was still sitting in the same chair and the same posture, having hardly moved a limb for two hours, when Eleanor came back to tea, and succeeded in bringing him with her into the drawing-room.

The tea seemed as comfortless as the dinner, though the warden, who had hitherto eaten nothing all day, devoured the plateful of bread and butter, unconscious of what he was doing.

Eleanor had made up her mind to force him to talk to her, but she hardly knew how to commence: she must wait till the urn was gone, till the servant would no longer be coming in and out.

At last everything was gone, and the drawing-room door was permanently closed; then Eleanor, getting up and going round to her father, put her arm round his neck, and said, 'Papa, won't you tell me what it is?'

'What what is, my dear?'

'This new sorrow that torments you; I know you are unhappy, papa.'

'New sorrow! It's no new sorrow, my dear, we have all our cares sometimes,' and he tried to smile, but it was a ghastly failure; 'but I shouldn't be so dull a companion; come, we'll have some music.'

'No papa, not tonight – it would only trouble you tonight:' and she sat upon his knee, as she sometimes would in their gayest moods, and with her arm round his neck, she said, 'Papa, I will not leave you till you talk to me; oh, if you only knew how much good it would do to you, to tell me of it all.'

The father kissed his daughter, and pressed her to his heart; but still he said nothing: it was so hard to him to speak of his own sorrows; he was so shy a man even with his own child.

'Oh, papa, do tell me what it is; I know it is about the hospital, and what they are doing up in London, and what that cruel newspaper has said; but if there be such cause for sorrow, let us be sorrowful together; we are all in all to each other now: dear, dear papa, do speak to me.'

Mr Harding could not well speak now, for the warm tears were running down his cheeks like rain in May, but he held his child close to his heart, and squeezed her hand as a lover might, and she kissed his forehead and his wet cheeks, and lay upon his bosom, and comforted him as a woman only can do.

'My own child,' he said, as soon as his tears would let him speak; 'my own, own child, why should you too be unhappy before it is necessary: it may come to that, that we must leave this place, but till that time comes, why should your young days be clouded?'

'And is that all, papa? If that be all, let us leave it, and have light hearts elsewhere: if that be all, let us go. Oh, papa, you and I could be happy if we had only bread to eat, so long as our hearts were light.'

And Eleanor's face was lighted up with enthusiasm as she told her father how he might banish all his care; and a gleam of joy shot across his brow as this idea of escape again presented itself, and he again fancied for a moment that he could spurn away from him the income which the world envied him; that he could give the lie to that wielder of the tomahawk who had dared to write such things of him in the *Jupiter*. That he could leave Sir Abraham, and the archdeacon, and Bold, and the rest of them with their lawsuit among them, and wipe his hands altogether of so sorrow-stirring a concern. Ah, what happiness might there be in the distance, with Eleanor and him in some small cottage, and nothing left of their former grandeur but their music! Yes, they would walk forth with their music books, and their instruments, and shaking the dust from off their feet as they went, leave the ungrateful place.* Never did a poor clergyman sigh for a warm benefice more anxiously than our warden did now to be rid of his.

'Give it up, papa,' she said again, jumping from his knees and standing on her feet before him, looking boldly into his face; 'give it up, papa.'

Oh, it was sad to see how that momentary gleam of joy passed away; how the look of hope was dispersed from that sorrowful face, as the remembrance of the archdeacon came back upon our poor warden, and he reflected that he could not stir from his now hated post. He was as a man bound with iron, fettered with adamant: he was in no respect a free agent; he had no choice. 'Give it up!' Oh if he only could: what an easy way that were out of all his troubles!

'Papa don't doubt about it,' she continued, thinking that his hesitation arose from his unwillingness to abandon so comfortable a home; 'is it on my account that you would stay here? Do you think that I cannot be happy without a pony-carriage and a fine drawing-room? Papa, I never can be happy here, as long as there is a question as to your honour in staying here; but I could be gay as the day is long in the smallest tiny little cottage, if I could see you come in and go out with a light heart. Oh! papa, your face tells so much; though you won't speak to me with your voice, I know how it is with you every time I look at you.'

How he pressed her to his heart again with almost a spasmodic pressure! how he kissed her as the tears fell like rain from his old eyes! how he blessed her, and called her by a hundred soft sweet names which now came new to his lips! how he chid himself for ever having been unhappy with such a treasure in his house, such a jewel on his bosom, with so sweet a flower in the choice garden of his heart! and then the floodgates of his tongue were loosed, and, at length, with unsparing detail of circumstances, he told her all that he wished, and all that he could not do. He repeated those arguments of the archdeacon, not agreeing in their truth, but explaining his inability to escape from them; how it had been declared to him that he was bound to remain where he was by the interests of his order, by gratitude to the bishop, by the wishes of his friends, by a sense of duty, which, though he could not understand it, he was fain to acknowledge. He told her how he had been accused of cowardice, and though he was not a man to make much of such a charge before the world, now in the full candour of his heart, he explained to her that such an accusation was grievous to him; that he did think it would be unmanly to desert his post, merely to escape his present sufferings, and that, therefore, he must bear as best he might the misery which was prepared for him.

And did she find these details tedious? Oh, no – she encouraged him to dilate on every feeling he expressed, till he laid bare the inmost corners of his heart to her. They spoke together of the archdeacon, as two children might of a stern, unpopular, but still respected schoolmaster, and of the bishop as a parent kind as kind could be, but powerless against an omnipotent pedagogue.

And then, when they had discussed all this, when the father had told all to the child, she could not be less confiding than he had been; and as John Bold's name was mentioned between them, she owned how well she had learned to love him, – 'had loved him once,' she said, 'but she would not, could not do so now – no, even had her troth been plighted to him, she would have taken it back again – had she sworn to love him as his wife, she would have discarded him and not felt herself forsworn, when he proved himself the enemy of her father.'

But the warden declared that Bold was no enemy of his, and encouraged her love; and gently rebuked, as he kissed her, the stern resolve she had made to cast him off; and then he spoke to her of happier days when their trials would all be over; and declared that her young heart should not be torn asunder to please either priest or prelate, dean or archdeacon. No, not if all Oxford were to convocate together,* and agree as to the necessity of the sacrifice.

And so they greatly comforted each other – and in what sorrow will not such mutual confidence give consolation! – and with a last expression of tender love they parted, and went comparatively happy to their rooms.

Iphigenia

When Eleanor laid her head on her pillow that night, her mind was anxiously intent on some plan by which she might extricate her father from his misery; and, in her warm-hearted enthusiasm, self-sacrifice was decided on as the means to be adopted. Was not so good an Agamemnon worthy of an Iphigenia?* She would herself personally implore John Bold to desist from his undertaking; she would explain to him her father's sorrows, the cruel misery of his position; she would tell him how her father would die if he were thus dragged before the public and exposed to such unmerited ignominy; she would appeal to his old friendship, to his generosity, to his manliness, to his mercy; if need were she would kneel to him for the favour she would ask; but before she did this, the idea of love must be banished. There must be no bargain in the matter. To his mercy, to his generosity, she could appeal; but as a pure maiden, hitherto even unsolicited, she could not appeal to his love, nor under such circumstances could she allow him to do so. Of course when so provoked, he would declare his passion; that was to be expected; there had been enough between them to make such a fact sure; but it was equally certain that he must be rejected. She could not be understood as saying, Make my father free and I am the reward. There would be no sacrifice in that − not so had Jephthah's daughter* saved her father − not so could she show to that kindest, dearest of parents how much she was able to bear for his good. No; to one resolve must her whole soul be bound; and so resolving, she felt that she could make her great request to Bold with as much self-assured confidence as she could have done to his grandfather.

And now I own I have fears for my heroine: not as to the upshot of her mission − not in the least as to that; as to the full success of her generous scheme, and the ultimate result of such a project, no one conversant with human nature and novels can have a doubt; but as to the amount of sympathy she may receive from those of her own sex. Girls below twenty and old ladies above sixty will do her justice; for in the female heart the soft springs of sweet romance reopen after many years, and again gush out with waters pure as in earlier days, and greatly refresh the path that leads downwards to the grave. But I fear that the majority of those between these two eras will not approve of Eleanor's plan. I fear that unmarried ladies of thirty-five will declare that there can be no probability of so absurd a project being carried through; that young women on their knees before their lovers are sure to get kissed, and that they would not put themselves in such a position did they not expect it; that Eleanor is going to Bold, only because circumstances prevent Bold from coming to her; that she is certainly a little fool, or a little schemer, but that in all probability she is thinking a good deal more about herself than her father.

Dear ladies, you are right as to your appreciation of the circumstances, but very wrong as to Miss Harding's character. Miss Harding was much younger than you are, and could not, therefore, know, as you may do, to what dangers such an encounter might expose her. She may get kissed. I think it very probable that she will; but I give my solemn word and positive assurance, that the remotest idea of such a catastrophe never occurred to her, as she made the great resolve now alluded to.

And then she slept; and then she rose refreshed, and met her father with her kindest embrace and most loving smiles; and on the whole their breakfast was by no means so triste* as had been their dinner the day before; and then, making some excuse to her father for so soon leaving him, she started on the commencement of her operations.

She knew that John Bold was in London, and that, therefore, the scene itself could not be enacted today; but she also knew that he was soon to be home, probably on the next day, and it was necessary that some little plan for meeting him should be concerted with his sister Mary. When she got up to the house, she went as usual into the morning sitting-room, and was startled by perceiving, by a stick, a great coat, and sundry parcels which were lying about, that Bold must already have returned.

'John has come back so suddenly,' said Mary, coming into the room; 'he has been travelling all night.'

'Then I'll come up again some other time,' said Eleanor, about to beat a retreat in her sudden dismay.

'He's out now, and will be for the next two hours,' said the other; 'he's with that horrid Finney; he only came to see him, and he returns by the mail train tonight.'

Returns by the mail train tonight, thought Eleanor to herself, as she strove to screw up her courage* – away again tonight – then it must be now or never; and she again sat down, having risen to go.

She wished the ordeal could have been postponed: she had fully made up her mind to do the deed, but she had not made up her mind to do it this very day; and now she felt ill at ease, astray, and in difficulty.

'Mary,' she began, 'I must see your brother before he goes back.'

'Oh yes, of course,' said the other; 'I know he'll be delighted to see you; and she tried to treat it as a matter of course, but she was not the less surprised; for Mary and Eleanor had daily talked over John Bold and his conduct, and his love, and Mary would insist on calling Eleanor her sister, and would scold her for not calling Bold by his christian name; and Eleanor would half confess her love, but like a modest maiden would protest against such familiarities even with the name of her lover: and so they talked hour after hour, and Mary Bold, who was much the elder, looked forward with happy confidence to the day when Eleanor would not be ashamed to call her, her sister. She was, however, fully sure that just at present Eleanor would be much more likely to avoid her brother than to seek him.

'Mary, I must see your brother, now, today, and beg from him a great favour,' and she spoke with a solemn air, not at all usual to her; and then she went on, and opened to her friend all her plan, her well-weighed scheme for saving her father from a sorrow which would, she said, if it lasted, bring him to his grave. 'But Mary,' she continued, 'you must now, you know, cease any joking about me and Mr Bold; you must now say no more about that; I am not ashamed to beg this favour from your brother, but when I have done so, there can never be anything further between us;' and this she said with a staid and solemn air, quite worthy of Jephthah's daughter or of Iphigenia either.

It was quite clear that Mary Bold did not follow the argument: that Eleanor Harding would appeal, on behalf of her father, to

Bold's better feelings, seemed to Mary quite natural; it seemed quite natural that he should relent, overcome by such filial tears, and by so much beauty; but, to her thinking, it was at any rate equally natural, that having relented, John should put his arm round his mistress's waist, and say, 'Now having settled that, let us be man and wife, and all will end happily!' Why his good nature should not be rewarded, when such rewards would operate to the disadvantage of none, Mary, who had more sense than romance, could not understand; and she said as much.

Eleanor, however, was firm, and made quite an eloquent speech to support her own view of the question: she could not condescend, she said, to ask such a favour on any other terms than those proposed. Mary might, perhaps, think her high-flown, but she had her own ideas, and she could not submit to sacrifice her self-respect.

'But I am sure you love him, – don't you?' pleaded Mary; 'and I am sure he loves you better than anything in the world.'

Eleanor was going to make another speech, but a tear came to each eye, and she could not; so she pretended to blow her nose, and walked to the window, and made a little inward call on her own courage, and finding herself somewhat sustained, said sententiously, – 'Mary, this is nonsense.'

'But you do love him,' said Mary, who had followed her friend to the window, and now spoke with her arms close wound round the other's waist. 'You do love him with all your heart, – you know you do; I defy you to deny it.'

'I – ' commenced Eleanor, turning sharply round to refute the charge; but the intended falsehood stuck in her throat,* and never came to utterance. She could not deny her love, so she took plentifully to tears, and leant upon her friend's bosom and sobbed there, and protested that, love or no love, it would make no difference in her resolve, and called Mary, a thousand times, the most cruel of girls, and swore her to secrecy by a hundred oaths, and ended by declaring that the girl who could betray her friend's love, even to a brother, would be as black a traitor as a soldier in a garrison who should open the city gates to the enemy. While they were yet discussing the matter, Bold returned, and Eleanor was forced into sudden action: she had either to accomplish or abandon her plan; and having slipped into her friend's bedroom, as the gentleman closed the hall door, she washed the marks of tears from her eyes, and resolved within herself to go through with it. 'Tell him I am here,' said she, 'and coming in; and mind, whatever you do, don't leave us.' So Mary informed her brother, with a somewhat sombre air, that Miss Harding was in the next room, and was coming to speak to him.

Eleanor was certainly thinking more of her father than herself, as she arranged her hair before the glass, and removed the traces of sorrow from her face, and yet I should be untrue if I said that she was not anxious to appear well before her lover: why else was she so sedulous with that stubborn curl that would rebel against her hand, and smooth so eagerly her ruffled ribands? why else did she damp her eyes to dispel the redness, and bite her pretty lips to bring back the colour? Of course she was anxious to look her best, for she was but a mortal angel after all. But had she been immortal, had she flitted back to the sitting room on a cherub's wings, she could not have had a more faithful heart, or a truer wish to save her father at any cost to herself.

John Bold had not met her since the day when she left him in dudgeon in the cathedral close. Since that his whole time had been occupied in promoting the cause against her father, and not unsuccessfully. He had often thought of her, and turned over in his mind a hundred schemes for showing her how disinterested was his love. He would write to her and beseech her not to allow the performance of a public duty to injure him in her estimation; he would write to Mr Harding, explain all his views, and boldly claim the warden's daughter, urging that the untoward circumstances between them need be no bar to their ancient friendship, or to a closer tie; he would throw himself on his knees before his mistress; he would wait and marry the daughter when the father had lost his home and his income; he would give up the lawsuit and go to Australia, with her of course, leaving the *Jupiter* and Mr Finney to complete the case between them. Sometimes as he woke in the morning fevered and impatient, he would blow out his brains and have done with all his cares – but this idea was generally consequent on an imprudent supper enjoyed in company with Tom Towers.

How beautiful Eleanor appeared to him as she slowly walked into the room! Not for nothing had all those little cares been taken. Though her sister, the archdeacon's wife, had spoken slightingly of her charms, Eleanor was very beautiful when seen aright. Hers was not of those impassive faces, which have the beauty of a marble bust; finely chiselled features, perfect in every line, true to the rules of symmetry, as lovely to a stranger as to a friend, unvarying unless in sickness, or as age affects them. She had no startling brilliancy of beauty, no pearly whiteness, no radiant carnation: she had not the majestic contour that rivets attention, demands instant wonder, and then disappoints by the coldness of its charms. You might pass Eleanor Harding in the street without notice, but you could hardly pass an evening with her and not lose your heart.

She had never appeared more lovely to her lover than she now did. Her face was animated though it was serious, and her full dark lustrous eyes shone with anxious energy; her hand trembled as she took his, and she could hardly pronounce his name, when she addressed him. Bold wished with all his heart that the Australian scheme was in the act of realisation, and that he and Eleanor were away together, never to hear further of the lawsuit.

He began to talk, asked after her health – said something about London being very stupid, and more about Barchester being very pleasant: declared the weather to be very hot, and then inquired after Mr Harding.

'My father is not very well,' said Eleanor.

John Bold was very sorry, so sorry: he hoped it was nothing serious, and put on the unmeaningly solemn face, which people usually use on such occasions.

'I especially want to speak to you about my father, Mr Bold; indeed, I am now here on purpose to do so. Papa is very unhappy, very unhappy indeed, about this affair of the hospital: you would pity him, Mr Bold, if you could see how wretched it has made him.'

'Oh Miss Harding!'

'Indeed you would, – any one would pity him: but a friend, an old friend as you are – indeed you would. He is an altered man; his cheerfulness has all gone, and his sweet temper, and his kind happy tone of voice; you would hardly know him if you saw him, Mr Bold, he is so much altered; and – and – if this goes on, he will die.' Here Eleanor had recourse to her handkerchief, and so also had her auditors; but she plucked up her courage and went on with her tale. 'He will break his heart, and die. I am sure, Mr Bold, it was not you who wrote those cruel things in the newspaper – '

John Bold eagerly protested that it was not, but his heart smote him as to his intimate alliance with Tom Towers.

'No, I am sure it was not; and papa has not for a moment thought so; you would not be so cruel – but it has nearly killed him. Papa cannot bear to think that people should so speak of him, and that everybody should hear him so spoken of: – they have called him avaricious, and dishonest, and they say he is robbing the old men, and taking the money of the hospital for nothing.'

'I have never said so, Miss Harding. I – '

'No,' continued Eleanor, interrupting him, for she was now in the full floodtide of her eloquence; 'no, I am sure you have not, but others have said so; and if this goes on, if such things are written again, it will kill papa. Oh! Mr Bold, if you only knew the state he is in! Now papa does not care much about money.'

Both her auditors, brother and sister, assented to this, and declared on their own knowledge that no man lived less addicted to filthy lucre* than the warden.

'Oh! it's so kind of you to say so, Mary, and of you too, Mr Bold. I couldn't bear that people should think unjustly of papa. Do you know he would give up the hospital altogether, only he cannot. The archdeacon says it would be cowardly, and that he would be deserting his order, and injuring the church. Whatever may happen, papa will not do that: he would leave the place tomorrow willingly, and give up his house, and the income and all, if the archdeacon – ' Eleanor was going to say 'would let him,' but she stopped herself before she had compromised her father's dignity; and giving a long sigh, she added – 'Oh, I do so wish he would.'

'No one who knows Mr Harding personally, accuses him for a moment,' said Bold.

'It is he that has to bear the punishment; it is he that suffers,' said Eleanor; 'and what for? what has he done wrong? how has he deserved this persecution? he that never had an unkind thought in his life, he that never said an unkind word!' and here she broke down, and the violence of her sobs stopped her utterance.

Bold, for the fifth or sixth time, declared that neither he nor any of his friends imputed any blame personally to Mr Harding.

'Then why should he be persecuted?' ejaculated Eleanor

through her tears, forgetting in her eagerness that her intention had been to humble herself as a suppliant before John Bold – 'why should he be singled out for scorn and disgace? why should he be made so wretched? Oh! Mr Bold,' – and she turned towards him as though the kneeling scene were about to be commenced – 'oh! Mr Bold, why did you begin all this? you whom we all so – so – valued!'

To speak the truth, the reformer's punishment was certainly come upon him, for his present plight was not enviable; he had nothing for it but to excuse himself by platitudes about public duty, which it is by no means worthwhile to repeat, and to reiterate his eulogy on Mr Harding's character. His position was certainly a cruel one: had any gentlemen called upon him on behalf of Mr Harding he could of course have declined to enter upon the subject; but how could he do so with a beautiful girl, with the daughter of the man whom he had injured, with his own love?

In the meantime Eleanor recollected herself, and again summoned up her energies.

'Mr Bold,' said she, 'I have come here to implore you to abandon this proceeding.'

He stood up from his seat, and looked beyond measure distressed.

'To implore you to abandon it, to implore you to spare my father, to spare either his life or his reason, for one or the other will pay the forfeit if this goes on. I know how much I am asking, and how little right I have to ask anything; but I think you will listen to me as it is for my father. Oh, Mr Bold, pray, pray do this for us – pray do not drive to distraction a man who has loved you so well.'

She did not absolutely kneel to him, but she followed him as he moved from his chair, and laid her soft hands imploringly upon his arm. Ah! at any other time how exquisitely valuable would have been that touch! but now he was distraught, dumb-founded, and unmanned. What could he say to that sweet suppliant; how explain to her that the matter now was probably beyond his control; how tell her that he could not quell the storm which he had raised?

'Surely, surely, John, you cannot refuse her,' said his sister.

'I would give her my soul,' said he, 'if it would serve her.'

'Oh, Mr Bold,' said Eleanor, 'do not speak so; I ask nothing for myself; and what I ask for my father, it cannot harm you to grant.'

'I would give her my soul, if it would serve her,' said Bold, still addressing his sister; 'everything I have is hers, if she will accept it; my house, my heart, my all; every hope of my breast is centred in her: her smiles are sweeter to me than the sun, and when I see her in sorrow as she now is, every nerve in my body suffers. No man can love better than I love her.'

'No, no, no,' ejaculated Eleanor, 'there can be no talk of love between us; will you protect my father from the evil you have brought upon him?'

'Oh, Eleanor, I will do anything; let me tell you how I love you!'

'No, no, no,' she almost screamed; 'this is unmanly of you, Mr Bold. Will you, will you, will you leave my father to die in peace in his quiet home?' and seizing him by his arm and hand, she followed him across the room towards the door. 'I will not leave you till you promise me; I'll cling to you in the street; I'll kneel to you before all the people. You shall promise me this, you shall promise me this, you shall – ' And she clung to him with fixed tenacity, and reiterated her resolve with hysterical passion.

'Speak to her, John; answer her,' said Mary, bewildered by the unexpected vehemence of Eleanor's manner; 'you cannot have the cruelty to refuse her.'

'Promise me, promise me,' said Eleanor; 'say that my father is safe – one word will do. I know how true you are; say one word, and I will let you go.'

She still held him, and looked eagerly into his face, with her hair dishevelled, and her eyes all blood-shot. She had no thought now of herself, no care now for her appearance, and yet he thought he had never seen her half so lovely; he was amazed at the intensity of her beauty, and could hardly believe that it was she whom he had dared to love. 'Promise me,' said she; 'I will not leave you till you have promised me.'

'I will,' said he at length, 'I do – all I can do, I will do.'

'Then may God Almighty bless you for ever and ever!' said Eleanor; and falling on her knees with her face on Mary's lap, she wept and sobbed like a child: her strength had carried her through her allotted task, but now it was well nigh exhausted.

In a while she was partly recovered, and got up to go, and

would have gone, had not Bold made her understand that it was necessary for him to explain to her how far it was in his power to put an end to the proceedings which had been taken against Mr Harding. Had he spoken on any other subject, she would have vanished, but on that she was bound to hear him; and now the danger of her position commenced. While she had an active part to play, while she clung to him as a suppliant, it was easy enough for her to reject his proffered love, and cast from her his caressing words; but now – now that he had yielded, and was talking to her calmly and kindly as to her father's welfare, it was hard enough for her to do so. Then Mary Bold assisted her, but now she was quite on her brother's side. Mary said but little, but every word she did say gave some direct and deadly blow. The first thing she did was to make room for her brother between herself and Eleanor on the sofa: as the sofa was full large for three, Eleanor could not resent this, nor could she show suspicion by taking another seat; but she felt it to be a most unkind proceeding. And then Mary would talk as though they three were joined in some close peculiar bond together; as though they were in future always to wish together, contrive together, and act together; and Eleanor could not gainsay this; she could not make another speech, and say, 'Mr Bold and I are mere strangers, Mary, and are always to remain so!'

He explained to her that, though undoubtedly the proceeding against the hospital had commenced solely with himself, many others were now interested in the matter, some of whom were much more influential than himself: that it was to him alone, however, that the lawyers looked for instruction as to their doings, and, more important still, for the payment of their bills; and he promised that he would at once give them notice that it was his intention to abandon the cause. He thought, he said, that it was not probable that any active steps would be taken after he had seceded from the matter, though it was possible that some passing allusion might still be made to the hospital in the daily *Jupiter*. He promised, however, that he would use his best influence to prevent any further personal allusion being made to Mr Harding. He then suggested that he would on that afternoon ride over himself to Dr Grantly, and inform him of his altered intentions on the subject, and with this view, he postponed his immediate return to London.

This was all very pleasant, and Eleanor did enjoy a sort of

triumph in the feeling that she had attained the object for which she had sought this interview; but still the part of Iphigenia was to be played out. The gods had heard her prayer, granted her request, and were they not to have their promised sacrifice? Eleanor was not a girl to defraud them wilfully; so, as soon as she decently could, she got up for her bonnet.

'Are you going so soon?' said Bold, who half-an-hour since would have given a hundred pounds that he was in London, and she still at Barchester.

'Oh yes!' said she. 'I am so much obliged to you; papa will feel this to be so kind' (she did not quite appreciate all her father's feelings); 'of course I must tell him, and I will say that you will see the archdeacon.'

'But may I not say one word for myself?' said Bold.

'I'll fetch you your bonnet, Eleanor,' said Mary, in the act of leaving the room.

'Mary, Mary,' said she, getting up and catching her by her dress, 'don't go, I'll get my bonnet myself;' but Mary, the traitress, stood fast by the door, and permitted no such retreat. Poor Iphigenia!

And with a volley of impassioned love, John Bold poured forth the feelings of his heart, swearing, as men do, some truths and many falsehoods; and Eleanor repeated with every shade of vehemence the 'No, no, no,' which had had a short time since so much effect; but now, alas! its strength was gone. Let her be never so vehement, her vehemence was not respected; all her 'No, no, no's' were met with counter asseverations, and at last were overpowered. The ground was cut from under her on every side: she was pressed to say whether her father would object; whether she herself had any aversion (aversion! God help her, poor girl! the word nearly made her jump into his arms); any other preference (this she loudly disclaimed); whether it was impossible that she should love him (Eleanor could not say that it was impossible): and so at last, all her defences demolished, all her maiden barriers swept way, she capitulated, or rather marched out with the honours of war, vanquished evidently, palpably vanquished, but still not reduced to the necessity of confessing it.

And so the altar on the shore of the modern Aulis* reeked with no sacrifice.

CHAPTER 12

Mr Bold's Visit to Plumstead

Whether or no the ill-natured prediction made by certain ladies in the beginning of the last chapter, was or was not carried out to the letter, I am not in a position to state; Eleanor, however, certainly did feel herself to have been baffled, as she returned home with all her news to her father. Certainly she had been victorious, certainly she had achieved her object, certainly she was not unhappy, and yet she did not feel herself triumphant. Everything would run smooth now. Eleanor was not at all addicted to the Lydian school of romance; she by no means objected to her lover because he came in at the door under the name of Absolute, instead of pulling her out of a window under the name of Beverley;* and yet she felt that she had been imposed upon, and could hardly think of Mary Bold with sisterly charity. 'I did think I could have trusted Mary,' she said to herself over and over again. 'Oh that she should have dared to keep me in the room when I tried to get out!' Eleanor, however, felt that the game was up, and that she had now nothing further to do, but to add to the budget of news which was prepared for her father, that John Bold was her accepted lover.

We will, however, now leave her on her way, and go with John Bold to Plumstead Episcopi, merely premising that Eleanor on reaching home will not find things so smooth as she fondly expected; two messengers had come, one to her father, and the other to the archdeacon, and each of them much opposed to her quiet mode of solving all their difficulties; the one in the shape of a number of the *Jupiter*, and the other in that of a further opinion from Sir Abraham Haphazard.

John Bold got on his horse and rode off to Plumstead Episcopi; not briskly and with eager spur, as men do ride when self-satisfied with their own intentions, but slowly, modestly, thoughtfully, and somewhat in dread of the coming interview. Now and again he would recur to the scene which was just over, support himself by the remembrance of the silence that gives consent, and exult as a happy lover; but even this feeling was not without a shade of remorse. Had he not shown himself childishly weak thus to yield up the resolve of many hours of thought to the tears of a pretty girl? How was he to meet his lawyer? How was he to back out of a matter in which his name was already so publicly concerned? What, oh what! was he to say to Tom Towers? While meditating these painful things he reached the lodge leading up to the archdeacon's glebe,* and for the first time in his life found himself within the sacred precincts.

All the doctor's children were together on the slope of the lawn close to the road, as Bold rode up to the hall door. They were there holding high debate on matters evidently of deep interest at Plumstead Episcopi, and the voices of the boys had been heard before the lodge gate was closed.

Florinda and Grizzel, frightened at the sight of so well-known an enemy to the family, fled on the first appearance of the horseman, and ran in terror to their mother's arms; not for them was it, tender branches, to resent injuries, or as members of a church militant to put on armour against its enemies: but the boys stood their ground like heroes, and boldly demanded the business of the intruder.

'Do you want to see anybody here, sir?' said Henry, with a defiant eye and a hostile tone, which plainly said that at any rate no one there wanted to see the person so addressed; and as he spoke he brandished aloft his garden water-pot, holding it by the spout, ready for the braining of any one.

'Henry,' said Charles James slowly, and with a certain dignity of diction, 'Mr Bold of course would not have come without wanting to see some one; if Mr Bold has a proper ground for wanting to see some person here, of course he has a right to come.'

But Samuel stepped lightly up to the horse's head, and offered his services. 'Oh, Mr Bold,' said he, 'papa, I'm sure, will be glad to see you; I suppose you want to see papa. Shall I hold your horse for you? Oh, what a very pretty horse!' and he turned his head and winked funnily at his brothers; 'papa has heard such good news about the old hospital today. We know you'll be glad to hear it, because you're such a friend of grandpapa Harding, and so much in love with aunt Nelly!'

'How d'ye do, lads?' said Bold, dismounting; 'I want to see your father if he's at home.'

'Lads!' said Henry, turning on his heel and addressing himself to his brother, but loud enough to be heard by Bold; 'lads, indeed! if we're lads, what does he call himself?'

Charles James condescended to say nothing further, but cocked his hat with much precision, and left the visitor to the care of his youngest brother.

Samuel stayed till the servant came, chatting and patting the horse; but as soon as Bold had disappeared through the front door, he stuck a switch under the animal's tail to make him kick, if possible.

The church reformer soon found himself *tête à tête* with the archdeacon in that same room, in that sanctum sanctorum* of the rectory, to which we have already been introduced. As he entered he heard the click of a certain patent lock, but it struck him with no surprise: the worthy clergyman was no doubt hiding from eyes profane his last much-studied sermon, for the archdeacon, though he preached but seldom, was famous for his sermons. No room, Bold thought, could have been more becoming for a dignitary of the church; each wall was loaded with theology; over each separate bookcase was printed in small gold letters the names of those great divines whose works were ranged beneath: beginning from the early fathers in due chronological order, there were to be found the precious labours of the chosen servants of the church down to the last pamphlet written in opposition to the consecration of Dr Hampden;* and raised above this were to be seen the busts of the greatest among the great: Chrysostom, St Augustine, Thomas à Becket, Cardinal Wolsey, Archbishop Laud, and Dr Phillpotts.*

Every appliance that could make study pleasant and give ease to the over-toiled brain was there: chairs made to relieve each limb and muscle; reading-desks and writing-desks to suit every attitude; lamps and candles mechanically contrived to throw their light on any favoured spot, as the student might desire; a shoal of newspapers to amuse the few leisure moments which might be stolen from the labours of the day; and then from the window a view right through a bosky vista along which ran a broad green path from the rectory to the church, at the end of which the tawny-tinted fine old tower was seen with all its variegated pinnacles and parapets. Few parish churches in

England are in better repair, or better worth keeping so, than that at Plumstead Episcopi; and yet it is built in a faulty style: the body of the church is low – so low, that the nearly flat leaden roof would be visible from the churchyard, were it not for the carved parapet with which it is surrounded. It is cruciform, though the transepts are irregular, one being larger than the other; and the tower is much too high in proportion to the church: but the colour of the building is perfect; it is that rich yellow grey which one finds nowhere but in the south and west of England, and which is so strong a characteristic of most of our old houses of Tudor architecture. The stone work also is beautiful; the mullions of the windows and the thick tracery of the Gothic workmanship is as rich as fancy can desire; and though in gazing on such a structure, one knows by rule that the old priests who built it, built it wrong, one cannot bring oneself to wish that they should have made it other than it is.

When Bold was ushered into the book-room, he found its owner standing with his back to the empty fireplace ready to receive him, and he could not but perceive that that expansive brow was elated with triumph, and that those full heavy lips bore more prominently than usual an appearance of arrogant success.

'Well, Mr Bold,' said he, – 'well, what can I do for you? Very happy, I can assure you, to do anything for such a friend of my father-in-law.'

'I hope you'll excuse my calling, Dr Grantly.'

'Certainly, certainly,' said the archdeacon; 'I can assure you, no apology is necessary from Mr Bold; only let me know what I can do for him.'

Dr Grantly was standing himself, and he did not ask Bold to sit, and therefore he had to tell his tale standing, leaning on the table, with his hat in his hand. He did, however, manage to tell it; and as the archdeacon never once interrupted him, or even encouraged him by a single word, he was not long in coming to the end of it.

'And so, Mr Bold, I'm to understand, I believe, that you are desirous of abandoning this attack upon Mr Harding.'

'Oh, Dr Grantly, there has been no attack, I can assure you – '

'Well, well, we won't quarrel about words; I should call it an attack – most men would so call an endeavour to take away from a man every shilling of income that he has to live upon; but it shan't be an attack, if you don't like it; you wish to abandon this – this little game of backgammon you've begun to play.'

'I intend to put an end to the legal proceedings which I have commenced.'

'I understand,' said the archdeacon. 'You've already had enough of it; well, I can't say that I am surprised; carrying on a losing lawsuit where one had nothing to gain, but everything to pay, is not pleasant.'

Bold turned very red in the face. 'You misinterpret my motives,' said he; 'but, however, that is of little consequence. I did not come to trouble you with my motives, but to tell you a matter of fact. Good morning, Dr Grantly.'

'One moment – one moment,' said the other. 'I don't exactly appreciate the taste which induced you to make any personal communication to me on the subject; but I dare say I'm wrong, I dare say your judgment is the better of the two; but as you have done me the honour – as you have, as it were, forced me into a certain amount of conversation on a subject which had better, perhaps, have been left to our lawyers, you will excuse me if I ask you to hear my reply to your communication.'

'I am in no hurry, Dr Grantly.'

'Well, I am, Mr Bold; my time is not exactly leisure time, and, therfore, if you please, we'll go to the point at once – you're going to abandon this lawsuit?' – and he paused for a reply.

'Yes, Dr Grantly, I am.'

'Having exposed a gentleman who was one of your father's warmest friends, to all the ignomiy and insolence which the press could heap upon his name; having somewhat ostentatiously declared that it was your duty as a man of high public virtue to protect those poor old fools whom you have humbugged there at the hospital, you now find that the game costs more than it's worth, and so you make up your mind to have done with it. A prudent resolution, Mr Bold; but it is a pity you should have been so long coming to it. Has it struck you that we may not now choose to give over? that we may find it necessary to punish the injury you have done to us? Are you aware, sir, that we have gone to enormous expense to resist this iniquitous attempt of yours?'

Bold's face was now furiously red, and he nearly crushed his hat between his hands; but he said nothing.

'We have found it necessary to employ the best advice that money could procure. Are you aware, sir, what may be the probable cost of securing the services of the attorney-general?'

'Not in the least, Dr Grantly.'

'I dare say not, sir. When you recklessly put this affair into the hands of your friend Mr Finney, whose six and eightpences and thirteen and fourpences may, probably, not amount to a large sum, you were indifferent as to the cost and suffering which such a proceeding might entail on others; but are you aware, sir, that these crushing costs must now come out of your own pocket?'

'Any demand of such a nature which Mr Harding's lawyer may have to make, will doubtless be made to my lawyer.'

'Mr Harding's lawyer and my lawyer! Did you come here merely to refer me to the lawyers? Upon my word I think the honour of your visit might have been spared! And now, sir, I'll tell you what my opinion is – my opinion is, that we shall not allow you to withdraw this matter from the courts.'

'You can do as you please, Dr Grantly; good morning.'

'Hear me out, sir,' said the archdeacon; 'I have here in my hands the last opinion given in this matter by Sir Abraham Haphazard. I dare say you have already heard of this – I dare say it has had something to do with your visit here today.'

'I know nothing whatever of Sir Abraham Haphazard or his opinion.'

'Be that as it may, here it is; he declares most explicitly that under no phasis* of the affair whatever have you a leg to stand upon; that Mr Harding is as safe in his hospital as I am here in my rectory; that a more futile attempt to destroy a man was never made, than this which you have made to ruin Mr Harding. Here,' and he slapped the paper on the table, 'I have this opinion from the very first lawyer in the land; and under these circumstances you expect me to make you a low bow for your kind offer to release Mr Harding from the toils of your net! Sir, your net is not strong enough to hold him; sir, your net has fallen to pieces, and you knew that well enough before I told you – and now, sir, I'll wish you good morning, for I'm busy.'

Bold was now choking with passion; he had let the archdeacon run on, because he knew not with what words to interrupt him; but now that he had been so defied and insulted, he could not leave the room without some reply.

'Dr Grantly,' he commenced.

'I have nothing further to say or to hear,' said the archdeacon; 'I'll do myself the honour to order your horse:' and he rang the bell.

'I came here, Dr Grantly, with the warmest, kindest feelings – '

'Oh, of course you did; nobody doubts it.'

'With the kindest feelings – and they have been most grossly outraged by your treatment.'

'Of course they have – I have not chosen to see my father-in-law ruined; what an outrage that has been to your feelings!'

'The time will come, Dr Grantly, when you will understand why I called upon you today.'

'No doubt, no doubt. Is Mr Bold's horse there? That's right, open the front door – good morning, Mr Bold;' and the doctor stalked into his own drawing-room, closing the door behind him, and making it quite impossible that John Bold should speak another word.

As he got on his horse, which he was fain to do feeling like a dog turned out of a kitchen, he was again greeted by little Sammy.

'Goodbye, Mr Bold; I hope we may have the pleasure of seeing you again before long; I am sure papa will always be glad to see you.'

That was certainly the bitterest moment in John Bold's life; not even the remembrance of his successful love could comfort him; nay, when he thought of Eleanor, he felt that it was that very love which had brought him to such a pass. That he should have been so insulted, and be unable to reply! That he should have given up so much to the request of a girl, and then have had his motives so misunderstood! That he should have made so gross a mistake at this visit of his to the archdeacon's! He bit the top of his whip, till he penetrated the horn of which it was made: he struck the poor animal in his anger, and then was doubly angry with himself at his futile passion. He had been so completely checkmated, so palpably overcome! and what was he to do? He could not continue his action after pledging himself to abandon it; nor was there any revenge in that – it was the very step to which his enemy had endeavoured to goad him!

He threw the reins to the servant who came to take his horse, and rushed upstairs into his drawing-room, where his sister Mary was sitting.

'If there be a devil,' said he, 'a real devil here on earth, it is Dr Grantly.' He vouchsafed her no further intelligence, but again seizing his hat, he rushed out, and took his departure for London without another word to any one.

CHAPTER 13

The Warden's Decision

The meeting between Eleanor and her father was not so stormy as that described in the last chapter, but it was hardly more successful. On her return from Bold's house, she found her father in a strange state. He was not sorrowful and silent as he had been on that memorable day when his son-in-law lectured him as to all that he owed to his order; nor was he in his usual quiet mood. When Eleanor reached the hospital, he was walking quickly to and fro upon the lawn, and she soon saw that he was much excited.

'I am going to London, my dear,' he said as soon as he saw her.

'London, papa!'

'Yes my dear, to London; I will have this matter settled some way: there are some things, Eleanor, which I cannot bear.'

'Oh, papa, what is it?' said she, leading him by the arm into the house – 'I had such good news for you, and now you make me fear I am too late;' and then, before he could let her know what had caused this sudden resolve, or could point to the fatal paper which lay on the table, she told him that the lawsuit was over, that Bold had commissioned her to assure her father in his name that it would be abandoned, that there was no further cause for misery, that the whole matter might be looked on as though it had never been discussed. She did not tell him with what determined vehemence she had obtained this concession in his favour, nor did she mention the price she was to pay for it.

The warden did not express himself peculiarly gratified at this intelligence, and Eleanor, though she had not worked for thanks, and was by no means disposed to magnify her own good offices,* felt hurt at the manner in which her news was received.

'Mr Bold can act as he thinks proper, my love,' said he; 'if Mr Bold thinks that he has been wrong, of course he will discontinue what he is doing; but that cannot change my purpose.'

'Oh, papa!' she exclaimed, all but crying with vexation – 'I thought you would have been so happy – I thought all would have been right now.'

'Mr Bold,' continued he, 'has set great people to work; so great that I doubt they are now beyond his control. Read that, my dear:' and the warden, doubling up a number of the *Jupiter*, pointed to the peculiar article which she was to read. It was to the last of the three leaders, which are generally furnished daily for the support of the nation, that Mr Harding directed her attention. It dealt some heavy blows on various clerical delinquents; on families who had received their tens of thousands yearly for doing nothing; on men who, as the article stated, rolled in wealth which they had neither earned nor inherited, and which was in fact stolen from the poorer clergy. It named some sons of bishops, and grandsons of archbishops; men great in their way, who had redeemed their disgrace in the eyes of many by the enormity of their plunder; and then having disposed of these leviathans, it descended to Mr Harding.

'We alluded some few weeks since to an instance of similar injustice, though in a more humble scale, in which the warden of an almshouse at Barchester has become possessed of the income of the greater part of the whole institution. Why an almshouse should have a warden we cannot pretend to explain, nor can we say what special need twelve old men can have for the services of a separate clergyman, seeing that they have twelve reserved seats for themselves in Barchester Cathedral. But be this as it may, let the gentleman call himself warden or precentor, or what he will, let him be never so scrupulous in exacting religious duties from his twelve dependants, or never so negligent as regards the services of the cathedral, it appears palpably clear that he can be entitled to no portion of the revenue of the hospital, excepting that which the founder set apart for him; and it is equally clear that the founder did not intend that three fifths of his charity should be so consumed.

'The case is certainly a paltry one after the tens of thousands with which we have been dealing, for the warden's income is after all but a poor eight hundred a year: eight hundred a year is not magnificent preferment of itself, and the warden may, for anything we know, be worth much more to the church; but if so, let the church pay him out of funds justly at its own disposal.

'We allude to the question of the Barchester almshouse at the present moment, because we understand that a plea has been set up which will be peculiarly revolting to the minds of English churchmen. An action has been taken against Mr Warden Harding, on behalf of the almsmen, by a gentleman acting solely on public grounds, and it is to be argued that Mr Harding takes nothing but what he receives as a servant of the hospital, and that he is not himself responsible for the amount of stipend given to him for his work. Such a plea would doubtless be fair, if any one questioned the daily wages of a bricklayer employed on the building, or the fee of the charwoman who cleans it; but we cannot envy the feeling of a clergyman of the Church of England who could allow such an argument to be put into his mouth.

'If this plea be put forward, we trust Mr Harding will be forced as a witness to state the nature of his employment; the amount of work that he does; the income which he receives, and the source from whence he obtained his appointment. We do not think he will receive much public sympathy to atone for the annoyance of such an examination.'

As Eleanor read the article her face flushed with indignation, and when she had finished it, she almost feared to look up at her father.

'Well, my dear,' said he, 'what do you think of that – is it worthwhile to be a warden at that price?'

'Oh, papa – dear papa.'

'Mr Bold can't unwrite that my dear – Mr Bold can't say that that shan't be read by every clergyman at Oxford; nay, by every gentleman in the land:' and then he walked up and down the room, while Eleanor in mute despair followed him with her eyes – 'and I'll tell you what, my dear,' he continued, speaking now very calmly, and in a forced manner very unlike himself. 'Mr Bold can't dispute the truth of every word in that article you have just read – nor can I.' Eleanor stared at him, as though she scarcely understood the words he was speaking. 'Nor can I, Eleanor: that's the worst of all, or would be so if there were no remedy; I have thought much of all this since we were together last night;' and he came and sat beside her, and put his arm round her waist as he had done then. 'I have thought much of what the archdeacon has said, and of what this paper says; and I do believe I have no right to be here.'

'No right to be warden of the hospital, papa?'

'No right to be warden with eight hundred a year; no right to

be warden with such a house as this; no right to spend in luxury
money that was intended for charity. Mr Bold may do as he
pleases about his suit, but I hope he will not abandon it for my
sake.'

Poor Eleanor! this was hard upon her. Was it for this she had
made her great resolve! For this that she had laid aside her quiet
demeanour, and taken upon her the rants of a tragedy heroine!
One may work and not for thanks, but yet feel hurt at not
receiving them; and so it was with Eleanor: one may be
disinterested in one's good actions, and yet feel discontented
that they are not recognised. Charity may be given with the left
hand so privily that the right hand does not know it, and yet the
left hand may regret to feel that it has no immediate reward.*
Eleanor had had no wish to burden her father with a weight of
obligation, and yet she had looked forward to much delight
from the knowledge that she had freed him from his sorrows:
now such hopes were entirely over; all that she had done was of
no avail; she had humbled herself to Bold in vain; the evil was
utterly beyond her power to cure!

She had thought also how gently she would whisper to her
father all that her lover had said to her about herself, and how
impossible she had found it to reject him: and then she had
anticipated her father's kindly kiss and close embrace as he gave
his sanction to her love. Alas, she could say nothing of this now.
In speaking of Mr Bold, her father put him aside as one whose
thoughts and sayings and acts could be of no moment. Gentle
reader, did you ever feel yourself snubbed? Did you ever, when
thinking much of your own importance, find yourself suddenly
reduced to a nonentity? Such was Eleanor's feeling now.

'They shall not put forward this plea on my behalf,' continued
the warden. 'Whatever may be the truth of the matter, that at
any rate is not true; and the man who wrote that article is right
in saying that such a plea is revolting to an honest mind. I will
go up to London, my dear, and see these lawyers myself, and if
no better excuse can be made for me than that, I and the hospital
will part.'

'But the archdeacon, papa?'

'I can't help it, my dear; there are some things which a man
cannot bear, – I cannot bear that' – and he put his hand upon
the newspaper.

'But will the archdeacon go with you?'

To tell the truth Mr Harding had made up his mind to steal a march upon the archdeacon. He was aware that he could take no steps without informing his dread son-in-law, but he had resolved that he would send out a note to Plumstead Episcopi detailing his plans, but that the messenger should not leave Barchester till he himself had started for London; so that he might be a day before the doctor, who, he had no doubt, would follow him. In that day, if he had luck, he might arrange it all; he might explain to Sir Abraham that he, as warden, would have nothing further to do with the defence about to be set up; he might send in his official resignation to his friend the bishop, and so make public the whole transaction, that even the doctor would not be able to undo what he had done. He knew too well the doctor's strength and his own weakness to suppose he could do this, if they both reached London together; indeed, he would never be able to get to London, if the doctor knew of his intended journey in time to prevent it.

'No, I think not,' said he; 'I think I shall start before the archdeacon could be ready – I shall go early tomorrow morning.'

'That will be best, papa,' said Eleanor, showing that her father's ruse was appreciated.

'Why, yes, my love: the fact is, I wish to do all this before the archdeacon can – can interfere. There is a great deal of truth in all he says – he argues very well, and I can't always answer him; but there is an old saying, Nelly, "every one knows where his own shoe pinches!"* He'll say that I want moral courage, and strength of character, and power of endurance, and it's all true; but I'm sure I ought not to remain here, if I have nothing better to put forward than a quibble: so, Nelly, we shall have to leave this pretty place.'

Eleanor's face brightened up, as she assured her father how cordially she agreed with him.

'True, my love,' said he, now again quite happy and at ease in his manner. 'What good to us is this place or all the money, if we are to be ill-spoken of?'

'Oh, papa, I am so glad.'

'My darling child. It did cost me a pang at first, Nelly, to think that you should lose your pretty drawing-room, and your ponies, and your garden: the garden will be the worst of all – but there is a garden at Crabtree, a very pretty garden.'

Crabtree Parva was the name of the small living which Mr Harding had held as a minor canon, and which still belonged to him. It was only worth some eighty pounds a year, and a small house and glebe, all of which were now handed over to Mr Harding's curate; but it was to Crabtree glebe that Mr Harding thought of retiring. This parish must not be mistaken for that other living, Crabtree Canonicorum as it is called. Crabtree Canonicorum is a very nice thing; there are only two hundred parishioners; there are four hundred acres of glebe; and the great and small tithes, which both go to the rector, are worth four hundred pounds a year more. Crabtree Canonicorum is in the gift of the dean and chapter, and is at this time possessed by the Honourable and Rev. Dr Vesey Stanhope, who also fills the prebendal stall of Goosegorge in Barchester Chapter, and holds the united rectory of Eiderdown and Stogpingum, or Stoke Pinquium as it should be written. This is the same Dr Vesey Standhope, whose hospitable villa on the Lake of Como is so well known to the élite of English travellers, and whose collection of Lombard butterflies is supposed to be unique.*

'Yes,' said the warden musing, 'there is a very pretty garden at Crabtree, but I shall be sorry to disturb poor Smith.' Smith was the curate of Crabtree, a gentleman who was maintaining a wife and half a dozen children on the income arising from his profession.

Eleanor assured her father that as far as she was concerned, she could leave her house and her ponies without a single regret: she was only so happy that he was going, – going where he would escape all this dreadful turmoil.

'But we will take the music, my dear.'

And so they went on planning their future happiness, and plotting how they would arrange it all without the interposition of the archdeacon, and at last they again became confidential, and then the warden did thank her for what she had done, and Eleanor, lying on her father's shoulder, did find an opportunity to tell her secret: and the father gave his blessing to his child, and said that the man whom she loved was honest, good, and kind-hearted, and right-thinking in the main – one who wanted only a good wife to put him quite upright; – 'a man, my love,' he ended by saying, 'to whom I firmly believe that I can trust my treasure with safety.'

'But what will Dr Grantly say?'

'Well, my dear, it can't be helped – we shall be out at Crabtree then.'

And Eleanor ran upstairs to prepare her father's clothes for his journey; and the warden returned to his garden to make his last adieus to every tree, and shrub, and shady nook that he knew so well.

CHAPTER 14

Mount Olympus

Wretched in spirit, groaning under the feeling of insult, self-condemning, and ill-satisfied in every way, Bold returned to his London lodgings. Ill as he had fared in his interview with the archdeacon, he was not less under the necessity of carrying out his pledge to Eleanor; and he went about his ungracious task with a heavy heart.

The attorneys whom he had employed in London received his instructions with surprise and evident misgiving: however, they could only obey, and mutter something of their sorrow that such heavy costs should only fall upon their own employer, – especially as nothing was wanting but perseverance to throw them on the opposite party. Bold left the office which he had latterly so much frequented, shaking the dust from off his feet; and before he was down the stairs, an edict had already gone forth for the preparation of the bill.

He next thought of the newspapers. The case had been taken up by more than one; and he was well aware that the key note had been sounded by the *Jupiter*. He had been very intimate with Tom Towers, and had often discussed with him the affairs of the hospital. Bold could not say that the articles in the paper had been written at his own instigation; he did not even know as a fact that they had been written by his friend. Tom Towers had never said that such a view of the case, or such a side in the dispute, would be taken by the paper with which he was connected. Very discreet in such matters was Tom Towers, and altogether indisposed to talk loosely of the concerns of that mighty engine of which it was his high privilege to move in secret some portion. Nevertheless, Bold believed that to him were owing those dreadful words which had caused such panic at Barchester, – and he conceived himself bound to prevent their repetition. With this view he betook himself from the attorneys' to that laboratory where, with amazing chemistry, Tom Towers compounded thunderbolts for the destruction of all that is evil, and for the furtherance of all that is good, in this and other hemispheres.

Who has not heard of Mount Olympus* – that high abode of all the powers of type, that favoured seat of the great goddess Pica,* that wondrous habitation of gods and devils,* from whence, with ceaseless hum of steam and never-ending flow of Castalian ink,* issue forth fifty thousand nightly edicts for the governance of a subject nation?

Velvet and gilding do not make a throne, nor gold and jewels a sceptre. It is a throne because the most exalted one sits there – and a sceptre because the most mighty one wields it. So it is with Mount Olympus. Should a stranger make his way thither at dull noonday, or during the sleepy hours of the silent afternoon, he would find no acknowledged temple of power and beauty, no fitting fane* for the great Thunderer, no proud façades and pillared roofs to support the dignity of this greatest of earthly potentates. To the outward and uninitiated eye, Mount Olympus is a somewhat humble spot – undistinguished, unadorned, – nay, almost mean. It stands alone, as it were, in a mighty city, close to the densest throng of men, but partaking neither of the noise nor the crowd; a small secluded, dreary spot, tenanted, one would say, by quite unambitious people at the easiest rents. 'Is this Mount Olympus?' asks the unbelieving stranger. 'Is it from these small, dark, dingy buildings that those infallible laws proceed which cabinets are called upon to obey; by which bishops are to be guided, lords and commons controlled, – judges instructed in law, generals in strategy, admirals in naval tactics, and orange-women in the management of their barrows?' 'Yes, my friend – from these walls. From here issue the only known infallible bulls* for the guidance of British souls and bodies. This little court is the Vatican of England. Here reigns a pope, self-nominated, self-consecrated – ay, and much stranger too, – self-believing! – a pope whom, if you cannot obey him, I would advise you to disobey as silently as possible; a pope hitherto afraid of no Luther; a pope who manages his own inquisition, who punishes unbelievers as no most skilful inquisitor of Spain ever dreamt of doing – one who can excommunicate thoroughly, fearfully, radically; put you beyond the pale of men's charity; make you odious to your dearest friends, and turn you into a monster to be pointed at by the finger!'

Oh heavens! and this is Mount Olympus!

It is a fact amazing to ordinary mortals that the *Jupiter* is never wrong. With what endless care, with what unsparing labour, do we not strive to get together for our great national council the men most fitting to compose it. And how we fail! Parliament is always wrong: look at the *Jupiter*, and see how futile are their meetings, how vain their council, how needless all their trouble! With what pride do we regard our chief ministers, the great servants of state, the oligarchs of the nation on whose wisdom we lean, to whom we look for guidance in our difficulties! But what are they to the writers of the *Jupiter*? They hold council together and with anxious thought painfully elaborate their country's good; but when all is done, the *Jupiter* declares that all is nought. Why should we look to Lord John Russell* – why should we regard Palmerston and Gladstone,* when Tom Towers without a struggle can put us right? Look at our generals, what faults they make; at our admirals, how inactive they are. What money, honesty, and science can do, is done; and yet how badly are our troops brought together, fed, conveyed, clothed, armed, and managed. The most excellent of our good men do their best to man our ships, with the assistance of all possible external appliances, but in vain. All, all is wrong – alas! alas! Tom Towers, and he alone, knows all about it. Why, oh why, ye earthly ministers, why have ye not followed more closely this heaven-sent messenger that is among us?

Were it not well for us in our ignorance that we confided all things to the *Jupiter*? Would it not be wise in us to abandon useless talking, idle thinking, and profitless labour? Away with majorities in the House of Commons, with verdicts from judicial bench given after much delay, with doubtful laws, and the fallible attempts of humanity! Does not the *Jupiter*, coming forth daily with fifty thousand impressions* full of unerring decision on every mortal subject, set all matters sufficiently at rest? Is not Tom Towers here, able to guide us and willing?

Yes indeed, – able and willing to guide all men in all things, so long as he is obeyed as autocrat should be obeyed – with undoubting submission: only let not ungrateful ministers seek other colleagues than those whom Tom Towers may approve; let church and state, law and physic, commerce and agriculture – the arts of war, and the arts of peace, all listen and obey, and all will be made perfect. Has not Tom Towers an all-seeing eye?

From the diggings of Australia to those of California, right round the habitable globe, does he not know, watch, and chronicle the doings of every one? From a bishopric in New Zealand to an unfortunate director of a North-West passage, is he not the only fit judge of capability? From the sewers of London to the Central Railway of India, – from the palaces of St Petersburg to the cabins of Connaught, nothing can escape him. Britons have but to read, to obey, and be blessed. None but the fools doubt the wisdom of the *Jupiter*; none but the mad dispute its facts.

No established religion has ever been without its unbelievers, even in the country where it is the most firmly fixed; no creed has been without scoffers; no church has so prospered as to free itself entirely from dissent. There are those who doubt the *Jupiter*! They live and breathe the upper air, walking here unscathed, though scorned – men, born of British mothers and nursed on English milk, who scruple not to say that Mount Olympus has its price, that Tom Towers can be bought for gold!

Such is Mount Olympus, the mouthpiece of all the wisdom of this great country. It may probably be said that no place in this nineteenth century is more worthy of notice. No treasury mandate armed with the signatures of all the government has half the power of one of those broadsheets, which fly forth from hence so abundantly, armed with no signature at all.

Some great man, some mighty peer – we'll say a noble duke – retires to rest feared and honoured by all his countrymen – fearless himself, if not a good man, at any rate a mighty man – too mighty to care much what men may say about his want of virtue. He rises in the morning degraded, mean, and miserable; an object of men's scorn, anxious only to retire as quickly as may be to some German obscurity, some unseen Italian privacy, or, indeed, anywhere out of sight. What has made this awful change? what has so afflicted him? An article has appeared in the *Jupiter*; some fifty lines of a narrow column has destroyed all his grace's equanimity, and banished him for ever from the world. No man knows who wrote the bitter words, the clubs talk confusedly of the matter, whispering to each other this and that name; while Tom Towers walks quietly along Pall Mall, with his coat buttoned close against the east wind, as though he were a mortal man, and not a god dispensing thunderbolts from Mount Olympus.

It was not to Mount Olympus that our friend Bold betook himself. He had before now wandered round that lonely spot, thinking how grand a thing it was to write articles for the *Jupiter*; considering within himself whether by any stretch of the powers within him he could ever come to such distinction; wondering how Tom Towers would take any little humble offering of his talents; calculating that Tom Towers himself must have once had a beginning, have once doubted as to his own success. Towers could not have been born a writer in the *Jupiter*. With such ideas, half ambitious and half awestruck, had Bold regarded the silent-looking workshop of the gods; but he had never yet by word or sign attempted to influence the slightest word of his unerring friend. On such a course was he now intent; and not without much inward palpitation did he betake himself to the quiet abode of wisdom, where Tom Towers was to be found o' mornings inhaling ambrosia and sipping nectar* in the shape of toast and tea.

Not far removed from Mount Olympus, but somewhat nearer to the blessed regions of the West, is the most favoured abode of Themis.* Washed by the rich tide which now passes from the towers of Caesar to Barry's halls of eloquence; and again back, with new offerings of a city's tribute,* from the palaces of peers to the mart of merchants, stand those quiet walls which Law has delighted to honour by its presence. What a world within a world is the Temple! how quiet are its 'entangled walks,' as some one lately has called them, and yet how close to the densest concourse of humanity! how gravely respectable its sober alleys, though removed but by a single step from the profanity of the Strand and the low iniquity of Fleet Street! Old St Dunstan,* with its bell-smiting bludgeoners, has been removed; the ancient shops with their faces full of pleasant history are passing away one by one; the bar itself is to go* — its doom has been pronounced by the *Jupiter*; rumour tells us of some huge building that is to appear in these latitudes dedicated to law, subversive of the courts of Westminster, and antagonistic to the Rolls and Lincoln's Inn; but nothing yet threatens the silent beauty of the Temple: it is the medieval court of the metropolis.

Here, on the choicest spot of this choice ground, stands a lofty row of chambers, looking obliquely upon the sullied Thames; before the windows, the lawn of the Temple Gardens stretches with that dim yet delicious verdure so refreshing to the eyes of Londoners. If doomed to live within the thickest of London smoke, you would surely say that that would be your chosen spot. Yes, you, you whom I now address, my dear, middle-aged bachelor friend, can nowhere be so well domiciled as here. No one here will ask whether you are out or at home; alone or with friends: here no Sabbatarian will investigate your Sundays, no censorious landlady will scrutinise your empty bottle, no valetudinarian* neighbour will complain of late hours. If you love books, to what place are books so suitable? The whole spot is redolent of typography. Would you worship the Paphian goddess,* the groves of Cyprus are not more taciturn than those of the Temple. Wit and wine are always here, and always together; the revels of the Temple are as those of polished Greece, where the wildest worshipper of Bacchus never forgot the dignity of the god whom he adored.* Where can retirement be so complete as here? where can you be so sure of all the pleasures of society?

It was here that Tom Towers lived, and cultivated with eminent success the tenth Muse who now governs the periodical press.* But let it not be supposed that his chambers were such, or so comfortless, as are frequently the gaunt abodes of legal aspirants. Four chairs, a half-filled deal bookcase with hangings of dingy green baize, an old office table covered with dusty papers, which are not moved once in six months, and an older Pembroke* brother with rickety legs, for all daily uses – a despatcher for the preparation of lobsters and coffee, and an apparatus for the cooking of toast and mutton chops; such utensils and luxuries as these did not suffice for the well being of Tom Towers. He indulged in four rooms on the first floor, each of which was furnished, if not with the splendour, with probably more than the comfort of Stafford House.* Every addition that science and art have lately made to the luxuries of modern life was to be found there. The room in which he usually sat was surrounded by bookshelves carefully filled; nor was there a volume there which was not entitled to its place in such a collection, both by its intrinsic worth and exterior splendour: a pretty portable set of steps in one corner of the room showed that those even on the higher shelves were intended for use. The chamber contained but two works of art – the one, an admirable bust of Sir Robert Peel, by Power,* declared the individual politics of our friend; and the other, a singularly long figure of a female devotee, by Millais,* told equally plainly the school of art to which he was addicted. This picture was not hung, as pictures usually are, against the wall; there was no inch of wall vacant for such a purpose: it had a stand or desk erected for its own accommodation; and there on her pedestal, framed and glazed, stood the devotional lady looking intently at a lily as no lady ever looked before.*

Our modern artists, whom we style Pre-Raphaelites, have delighted to go back, not only to the finish and peculiar manner, but also to the subjects of the early painters. It is impossible to give them too much praise for the elaborate perseverance with which they have equalled the minute perfections of the masters from whom they take their inspiration: nothing probably can exceed the painting of some of these latter-day pictures. It is, however, singular into what faults they fall as regards their subjects: they are not quite content to take the old stock groups — a Sebastian with his arrows, a Lucia with her eyes in a dish, a Lorenzo with a gridiron, or the virgin with two children.* But they are anything but happy in their change. As a rule, no figure should be drawn in a position which it is impossible to suppose any figure should maintain. The patient endurance of St Sebastian, the wild ecstasy of St John in the Wilderness, the maternal love of the virgin, are feelings naturally portrayed by a fixed posture; but the lady with the stiff back and bent neck, who looks at her flower, and is still looking from hour to hour, gives us an idea of pain without grace, and abstraction without a cause.

It was easy, from his rooms, to see that Tom Towers was a Sybarite,* though by no means an idle one. He was lingering over his last cup of tea, surrounded by an ocean of newspapers, through which he had been swimming, when John Bold's card was brought in by his tiger.* This tiger never knew that his master was at home, though he often knew that he was not, and thus Tom Towers was never invaded but by his own consent. On this occasion, after twisting the card twice in his fingers, he signified to his attendant imp that he was visible; and the inner door was unbolted, and our friend announced.

I have before said that he of the *Jupiter* and John Bold were intimate. There was no very great difference in their ages, for Towers was still considerably under forty; and when Bold had been attending the London hospitals, Towers, who was not then the great man that he had since become, had been much with

him. Then they had often discussed together the objects of their
ambition and future prospects; then Tom Towers was struggling
hard to maintain himself, as a briefless barrister, by short-hand
reporting for any of the papers that would engage him; then he
had not dared to dream of writing leaders for the *Jupiter*, or
canvassing the conduct of Cabinet ministers. Things had altered
since that time: the briefless barrister was still briefless, but he
now despised briefs: could he have been sure of a judge's seat,
he would hardly have left his present career. It is true he wore
no ermine, bore no outward marks of a world's respect; but
with what a load of inward importance was he charged! It is
true his name appeared in no large capitals; on no wall was
chalked up 'Tom Towers for ever' – 'Freedom of the Press and
Tom Towers:' but what member of Parliament had half his
power? It is true that in far-off provinces men did not talk daily
of Tom Towers, but they read the *Jupiter*, and acknowledged
that without the *Jupiter* life was not worth having. This kind of
hidden but still conscious glory suited the nature of the man. He
loved to sit silent in a corner of his club and listen to the loud
chattering of politicians, and to think how they all were in his
power – how he could smite the loudest of them, were it worth
his while to raise his pen for such a purpose. He loved to watch
the great men of whom he daily wrote, and flatter himself that
he was greater than any of them. Each of them was responsible
to his country, each of them must answer if inquired into, each
of them must endure abuse with good humour, and insolence
without anger. But to whom was he, Tom Towers, responsible?
No one could insult him; no one could inquire into him. He
could speak out withering words, and no one could answer him:
ministers courted him, though perhaps they knew not his name;
bishops feared him; judges doubted their own verdicts unless he
confirmed them; and generals, in their councils of war, did not
consider more deeply what the enemy would do, than what the
Jupiter would say. Tom Towers never boasted of the *Jupiter*; he
scarcely ever named the paper even to the most intimate of his
friends; he did not even wish to be spoken of as connected with
it; but he did not the less value his privileges, or think the less of
his own importance. It is probable that Tom Towers considered
himself the most powerful man in Europe; and so he walked on
from day to day, studiously striving to look a man, but knowing
within his breast that he was a god.

CHAPTER 15

Tom Towers, Dr Anticant, and Mr Sentiment

'Ah, Bold! how are you? You haven't breakfasted?'

'Oh yes, hours ago. And how are you?'

When one Eskimo meets another, do the two, as an invariable rule, ask after each other's health? is it inherent in all human nature to make this obliging inquiry? Did any reader of this tale ever meet any friend or acquaintance without asking some such question, and did any one ever listen to the reply? Sometimes a studiously courteous questioner will show so much thought in the matter as to answer it himself, by declaring that had he looked at you he needn't have asked; meaning thereby to signify that you are an absolute personification of health: but such persons are only those who premeditate small effects.

'I suppose you're busy?' inquired Bold.

'Why, yes, rather; or I should say rather not: I have a leisure hour in the day, this is it.'

'I want to ask you if you can oblige me in a certain matter.'

Towers understood in a moment, from the tone of his friend's voice, that the certain matter referred to the newspaper. He smiled, and nodded his head, but made no promise.

'You know this lawsuit that I've been engaged in?' said Bold.

Tom Towers intimated that he was aware of the action which was pending about the hospital.

'Well, I've abandoned it.'

Tom Towers merely raised his eyebrows, thrust his hands into his trousers' pockets, and waited for his friend to proceed.

'Yes, I've given it up. I needn't trouble you with all the history; but the fact is that the conduct of Mr Harding – Mr Harding is the – '

'Oh yes, the master of the place; the man who takes all the money and does nothing,' said Tom Towers, interrupting him.

'Well, I don't know about that; but his conduct in the matter has been so excellent, so little selfish, so open, that I cannot proceed in the matter to his detriment.' Bold's heart misgave him as to Eleanor as he said this; and yet he felt that what he said was not untrue. 'I think nothing should now be done till the wardenship be vacant.'

'And be again filled,' said Towers, 'as it certainly would, before any one heard of the vacancy; and the same objection would again exist. It's an old story that of the vested rights of the incumbent; but suppose the incumbent has only a vested wrong, and that the poor of the town have a vested right, if they only knew how to get at it: is not that something the case here?'

Bold couldn't deny it, but thought it was one of those cases which required a good deal of management before any real good could be done. It was a pity that he had not considered this before he crept into the lion's mouth, in the shape of an attorney's office.

'It will cost you a good deal, I fear,' said Towers.

'A few hundreds,' said Bold – 'perhaps three hundred; I can't help that, and am prepared for it.'

'That's philosophical; it's quite refreshing to hear a man talking of his hundreds in so purely indifferent a manner. But I'm sorry you are giving the matter up; it injures a man to commence a thing of this kind, and not carry it through. Have you seen that?' and he threw a small pamphlet across the table, which was all but damp from the press.

Bold had not seen it nor heard of it; but he was well acquainted with the author of it – a gentleman whose pamphlets, condemnatory of all things in these modern days, had been a good deal talked about of late.

Dr Pessimist Anticant* was a Scotchman, who had passed a great portion of his early days in Germany; he had studied there with much effect, and had learnt to look with German subtlety into the root of things, and to examine for himself their intrinsic worth and worthlessness.* No man ever resolved more bravely than he to accept as good nothing that was evil; to banish from him as evil nothing that was good. 'Tis a pity that he should not have recognised the fact, that in this world no good is unalloyed, and that there is but little evil that has not in it some seed of what is goodly.

Returning from Germany, he had astonished the reading public by the vigour of his thoughts, put forth in the quaintest language. He cannot write English, said the critics. No matter, said the public; we can read what he does write, and that without yawning. And so Dr Pessimist Anticant became popular. Popularity spoilt him for all further real use, as it has done many another. While, with some diffidence, he confined his objurgations to the occasional follies or shortcomings of mankind; while he ridiculed the energy of the squire devoted to the slaughter of partridges, or the mistake of some noble patron who turned a poet into a gauger of beer barrels,* it was all well; we were glad to be told our faults and to look forward to the coming millennium, when all men, having sufficiently studied the works of Dr Anticant, would become truthful and energetic. But the doctor mistook the signs of the times* and the minds of men, instituted himself censor of things in general, and began the great task of reprobating everything and everybody, without further promise of any millennium at all. This was not so well; and, to tell the truth, our author did not succeed in his undertaking. His theories were all beautiful, and the code of morals that he taught us certainly an improvement on the practices of the age. We all of us could, and many of us did, learn much from the doctor while he chose to remain vague, mysterious, and cloudy; but when he became practical, the charm was gone.

His allusion to the poet and the partridges was received very well. 'Oh, my poor brother,' said he, 'slaughtered partridges a score of brace to each gun, and poets gauging ale barrels, with sixty pounds a-year, at Dumfries, are not the signs of a great era! perhaps of the smallest possible era yet written of. Whatever economies we pursue, political or other, let us see at once that this is the maddest of the uneconomic: partridges killed by our land magnates at, shall we say, a guinea a-head, to be retailed in Leadenhall at one shilling and ninepence, with one poacher in limbo for every fifty birds! our poet, maker, creator, gauging ale, and that badly, with no leisure for making or creating, only a little leisure for drinking, and such like beer-barrel avocations! Truly, a cutting of blocks with fine razors while we scrape our chins so uncomfortably with rusty knives! Oh, my political economist, master of supply and demand, division of labour and high pressure – oh, my loud-speaking friend, tell me, if so much be in you, what is the demand for poets in these kingdoms of Queen Victoria, and what the vouchsafed supply?'

This was all very well; this gave us some hope. We might do better with our next poet, when we got one; and though the partridges might not be abandoned, something could perhaps be done as to the poachers. We were unwilling, however, to take lessons in politics from so misty a professor; and when he came to tell us that the heroes of Westminster were naught, we began to think that he had written enough.* His attack upon despatch boxes was not thought to have much in it; but as it is short, the doctor shall again be allowed to speak his sentiments: –

'Could utmost ingenuity in the management of red tape avail anything to men lying gasping – we may say, all but dead; could despatch boxes with never-so-much velvet lining and Chubb's patent,* be of comfort to a people *in extremis*, I also, with so many others, would, with parched tongue, call on the name of Lord John Russell; or, my brother, at your advice, on Lord Aberdeen; or, my cousin, on Lord Derby, at yours; being, with my parched tongue, indifferent in such matters. 'Tis all one. Oh, Derby! Oh, Gladstone! Oh, Palmerston! Oh, Lord John! Each comes running with serene face and despatch box. Vain physicians! though there were hosts of such, no despatch box will cure this disorder! What! are these other doctors' new names, disciples who have not burdened their souls with tape? Well, let us call again. Oh, Disraeli, great oppositionist, man of the bitter brow! or, Oh, Molesworth,* great reformer, thou who promisest Utopia. They come; each with the serene face, and each – alas, me! alas, my country! – each with a despatch box!

'Oh, the serenity of Downing Street!

'My brothers, when hope was over on the battle field, when no dimmest chance of victory remained, the ancient Roman could hide his face within his toga, and die gracefully. Can you and I do so now? If so, 'twere best for us; if not, oh my brothers, we must die disgracefully, for hope of life and victory I see none left to us in this world below. I for one cannot trust much of serene face and despatch box!'

There might be truth in this, there might be depth of reasoning; but Englishmen did not see enough in the argument to induce them to withdraw their confidence from the present arrangements of the government, and Dr Anticant's monthly pamphlet on the decay of the world* did not receive so much attention as his earlier works. He did not confine himself to politics in these publications, but roamed at large over all matters of public interest, and found everything bad. According to him nobody was true, and not only nobody, but nothing; a man could not take off his hat to a lady without telling a lie — the lady would lie again in smiling. The ruffles of the gentleman's shirt would be fraught with deceit, and the lady's flounces full of falsehood. Was ever anything more severe than that attack of his on chip bonnets, or the anathemas with which he endeavoured to dust the powder out of the bishops' wigs?

The pamphlet which Tom Towers now pushed across the table was entitled 'Modern Charity,' and was written with the view of proving how much in the way of charity was done by our predecessors — how little by the present age; and it ended by a comparison between ancient and modern times, very little to the credit of the latter.*

'Look at this,' said Towers, getting up and turning over the pages of the pamphlet, and pointing to a passage near the end; 'your friend the warden, who is so little selfish, won't like that, I fear.' Bold read as follows: —

'Heavens, what a sight! Let us with eyes wide open see the godly man of four centuries since, the man of the dark ages: let us see how he does his godlike work, and, again, how the godly man of these latter days does his.

'Shall we say that the former is one walking painfully through the world, regarding, as a prudent man, his worldly work, prospering in it as a diligent man will prosper, but always with an eye to that better treasure to which thieves do not creep in?* Is there not much nobility in that old man, as, leaning on his oaken staff, he walks down the high street of his native town, and receives from all courteous salutation and acknowledgment of his worth? A noble old man, my august inhabitants of Belgrave Square* and such like vicinity — a very noble old man, though employed no better than in the wholesale carding of wool.

'This carding of wool, however, did in those days bring with it much profit, so that our ancient friend, when dying, was declared, in whatever slang then prevailed, to cut up exceeding well. For sons and daughters there was ample sustenance, with assistance of due industry; for friends and relatives some relief for grief at this great loss; for aged dependants comfort in declining years. This was much for one old man to get done in that dark fifteenth century. But this was not all: coming generations of poor woolcarders should bless the name of this rich one; and a hospital should be founded and endowed with his wealth for the feeding of such of the trade as could not, by diligent carding, any longer duly feed themselves.

'Twas thus that an old man in the fifteenth century did his godlike work to the best of his power, and not ignobly, as appears to me.

'We will not take our godly man of latter days. He shall no longer be a woolcarder, for such are not now men of mark. We will suppose him to be one of the best of the good – one who has lacked no opportunities. Our old friend was, after all, but illiterate; our modern friend shall be a man educated in all seemly knowledge; he shall, in short, be that blessed being – a clergyman of the Church of England!

'And now, in what perfectest manner does he in this lower world get his godlike work done and put out of hand? Heavens! in the strangest of manners. Oh, my brother! in a manner not at all to be believed but by the most minute testimony of eyesight. He does it by the magnitude of his appetite – by the power of his gorge; his only occupation is to swallow the bread prepared with so much anxious care for these impoverished carders of wool – that, and to sing indifferently through his nose once in the week some psalm more or less long – the shorter the better, we should be inclined to say.

'Oh, my civilised friends! – great Britons that never will be slaves,* men advanced to infinite state of freedom and knowledge of good and evil – tell me, will you, what becoming monument you will erect to an highly educated clergyman of the Church of England?'

Bold certainly thought that his friend would not like that: he could not conceive anything that he would like less than this. To what a world of toil and trouble had he, Bold, given rise by his indiscreet attack upon the hospital!

'You see,' said Towers, 'that this affair has been much talked of, and the public are with you. I am sorry you should give the matter up. Have you seen the first number of the "Almshouse"?'

No; Bold had not seen the 'Almshouse.' He had seen advertisements of Mr Popular Sentiment's new novel* of that name, but had in no way connected it with Barchester Hospital, and had never thought a moment on the subject.

'It's a direct attack on the whole system,' said Towers. 'It'll go a long way to put down Rochester, and Barchester, and Dulwich, and St Cross,* and all such hotbeds of peculation.*

It's very clear that Sentiment has been down to Barchester, and got up the whole story there; indeed, I thought he must have had it all from you. It's very well done, as you'll see: his first numbers always are.'

Bold declared that Mr Sentiment had got nothing from him, and that he was deeply grieved to find that the case had become so notorious.

'The fire has gone too far to be quenched,' said Towers; 'the building must go now; and as the timbers are all rotten, why, I should be inclined to say, the sooner the better. I expected to see you get some *éclat* in the matter.'

This was all wormwood to Bold. He had done enough to make his friend the warden miserable for life, and had then backed out just when the success of his project was sufficient to make the question one of real interest. How weakly he had managed his business! He had already done the harm, and then stayed his hand when the good which he had in view was to be commenced. How delightful would it have been to have employed all his energy in such a cause – to have been backed by the *Jupiter*, and written up to by two of the most popular authors of the day! The idea opened a view into the very world in which he wished to live. To what might it not have given rise? what delightful intimacies – what public praise – to what Athenian banquets and rich flavour of Attic salt?*

This, however, was now past hope. He had pledged himself to abandon the cause; and could he have forgotten the pledge, he had gone too far to retreat. He was now, this moment, sitting in Tom Towers' room with the object of deprecating any further articles in the *Jupiter*, and, greatly as he disliked the job, his petition to that effect must be made.

'I couldn't continue it,' said he, 'because I found I was in the wrong.'

Tom Towers shrugged his shoulders. How could a successful man be in the wrong! 'In that case,' said he, 'of course you must abandon it.'

'And I called this morning to ask you also to abandon it,' said Bold.

'To ask me,' said Tom Towers with the most placid of smiles, and a consummate look of gentle surprise, as though Tom Towers was well aware that he of all men was the last to meddle in such matters.

'Yes,' said Bold, almost trembling with hesitation. 'The *Jupiter*, you know, has taken the matter up very strongly. Mr Harding has felt what it has said deeply; and I thought that if I could explain to you that he personally has not been to blame, these articles might be discontinued.'

How calmly impassive was Tom Towers' face, as this innocent little proposition was made! Had Bold addressed himself to the doorposts in Mount Olympus, they would have shown as much outward sign of assent or dissent. His quiescence was quite admirable; his discretion certainly more than human.

'My dear fellow,' said he, when Bold had quite done speaking, 'I really cannot answer for the *Jupiter*.'

'But if you saw that these articles were unjust, I think you would endeavour to put a stop to them: of course nobody doubts that you could, if you chose.'

'Nobody and everybody are always very kind, but unfortunately are generally very wrong.'

'Come, come, Towers,' said Bold, plucking up his courage, and remembering that for Eleanor's sake he was bound to make his best exertion; 'I have no doubt in my own mind but that you wrote the articles yourself; and very well written they were: it will be a great favour if you will in future abstain from any personal allusion to poor Harding.'

'My dear Bold,' said Tom Towers, 'I have a sincere regard for you. I have known you for many years, and value your friendship; I hope you will let me explain to you, without offence, that none who are connected with the public press can with propriety listen to interference.'

'Interference!' said Bold, 'I don't want to interfere.'

'Ah, but my dear fellow, you do; what else is it? You think that I am able to keep certain remarks out of a newspaper. Your information is probably incorrect, as most public gossip on such subjects is; but, at any rate, you think I have such power, and you ask me to use it: now that is interference.'

'Well, if you choose to call it so.'

'And now suppose for a moment that I had this power, and used it as you wish: isn't it clear that it would be a great abuse? Certain men are employed in writing for the public press; and if they are induced either to write or to abstain from writing by private motives, surely the public press would soon be of little value. Look at the recognised worth of different newspapers, and see if it does not mainly depend on the assurance which the public feel that such a paper is, or is not, independent. You alluded to the *Jupiter*: surely you cannot but see that the weight of the *Jupiter* is too great to be moved by any private request, even though it should be made to a much more influential person than myself: you've only to think of this, and you'll see that I am right.'

The discretion of Tom Towers was boundless: there was no contradicting what he said, no arguing against such propositions. He took such high ground that there was no getting on it. 'The public is defrauded,' said he, 'whenever private considerations are allowed to have weight.' Quite true, thou greatest oracle of the middle of the nineteenth century, thou sententious proclaimer of the purity of the press – the public is defrauded when it is purposely misled. Poor public! how often is it misled! against what a world of fraud has it to contend!

Bold took his leave and got out of the room as quickly as he could, inwardly denouncing his friend Tom Towers as a prig and a humbug. 'I know he wrote those articles,' said Bold to himself; 'I know he got his information from me. He was ready enough to take my word for gospel when it suited his own views, and to see Mr Harding up before the public as an impostor on no other testimony than my chance conversation; but when I offer him real evidence opposed to his own views, he tells me that private motives are detrimental to public justice! Confound his arrogance! What is any public question but a conglomeration of private interests? What is any newspaper article but an expression of the views taken by one side? Truth! it takes an age to ascertain the truth of any question! The idea of Tom Towers talking of public motives and purity of purpose! Why, it wouldn't give him a moment's uneasiness to change his politics tomorrow, if the paper required it.'

Such were John Bold's inward exclamations as he made his way out of the quiet labyrinth of the Temple; and yet there was no position of worldly power so coveted in Bold's ambition as that held by the man of whom he was thinking. It was the impregnability of the place which made Bold so angry with the possessor of it, and it was the same quality which made it appear so desirable.

Passing into the Strand, he saw in a bookseller's window an announcement of the first number of the 'Almshouse;' so he purchased a copy, and hurrying back to his lodgings, proceeded to ascertain what Mr Popular Sentiment had to say to the public on the subject which had lately occupied so much of his own attention.

In former times great objects were attained by great work. When evils were to be reformed, reformers set about their heavy task with grave decorum and laborious argument. An age was occupied in proving a grievance, and philosophical researches were printed in folio pages, which it took a life to write, and an eternity to read. We get on now with a lighter step, and quicker:* ridicule is found to be more convincing than argument, imaginary agonies touch more than true sorrows, and monthly novels convince, when learned quartos fail to do so. If the world is to be set right, the work will be done by shilling numbers.*

Of all such reformers Mr Sentiment is the most powerful. It is incredible the number of evil practices he has put down: it is to be feared he will soon lack subjects, and that when he has made the working classes comfortable, and got bitter beer put into proper-sized pint bottles, there will be nothing further for him left to do. Mr Sentiment is certainly a very powerful man, and perhaps not the less so that his good poor people are so very good; his hard rich people so very hard; and the genuinely honest so very honest. Namby-pamby* in these days is not thrown away if it be introduced in the proper quarters. Divine peeresses are not longer interesting, though possessed of every virtue; but a pattern peasant or an immaculate manufacturing hero may talk as much twaddle as one of Mrs Radcliffe's heroines, and still be listened to.* Perhaps, however, Mr Sentiment's great attraction is in his second-rate characters. If his heroes and heroines walk upon stilts, as heroes and heroines, I fear, ever must, their attendant satellites are as natural as though one met them in the street: they walk and talk like men and women, and live among our friends a rattling, lively life; yes, live, and will live till the names of their callings shall be forgotten in their own, and Bucket and Mrs Gamp will be the only words left to us to signify a detective police officer or a monthly nurse.*

'The Almshouse' opened with a scene in a clergyman's house. Every luxury to be purchased by wealth was described as being there: all the appearances of household indulgence generally found among the most self-indulgent of the rich were crowded

into this abode. Here the reader was introduced to the demon
of the book, the Mephistopheles* of the drama. What story was
ever written without a demon? what novel, what history, what
work of any sort, what world, would be perfect without existing
principles both of good and evil? The demon of the 'Almshouse'
was the clerical owner of this comfortable abode. He was a man
well stricken in years, but still strong to do evil: he was one who
looked cruelly out of a hot, passionate, bloodshot eye; who had
a huge red nose with a carbuncle, thick lips, and a great double,
flabby chin, which swelled out into solid substance, like a turkey
cock's comb, when sudden anger inspired him: he had a hot,
furrowed, low brow, from which a few grizzled hairs were not
yet rubbed off by the friction of his handkerchief: he wore a
loose unstarched white handkerchief, black loose ill-made
clothes, and huge loose shoes, adapted to many corns and
various bunions: his husky voice told tales of much daily port
wine, and his language was not so decorous as became a
clergyman. Such was the master of Mr Sentiment's 'Almshouse.'
He was a widower, but at present accompanied by two daughters, and a thin and somewhat insipid curate. One of the young
ladies was devoted to her father and the fashionable world, and
she of course was the favourite; the other was equally addicted
to Puseyism* and the curate.

The second chapter of course introduced the reader to the
more especial inmates of the hospital. Here were discovered
eight old men; and it was given to be understood that four
vacancies remained unfilled, through the perverse ill-nature of
the clerical gentleman with the double chin. The state of these
eight paupers was touchingly dreadful: sixpence-farthing a-day
had been sufficient for their diet when the almshouse was
founded; and on sixpence-farthing a-day were they still doomed
to starve, though food was four times as dear, and money four
times as plentiful. It was shocking to find how the conversation
of these eight starved old men in their dormitory shamed that of
the clergyman's family in his rich drawing-room. The absolute
words they uttered were not perhaps spoken in the purest
English, and it might be difficult to distinguish from their dialect
to what part of the country they belonged; the beauty of the
sentiment, however, amply atoned for the imperfection of the
language; and it was really a pity that these eight old men could

not be sent through the country as moral missionaries, instead of being immured and starved in that wretched almshouse.

Bold finished the number; and as he threw it aside, he thought that that at least had no direct appliance to Mr Harding, and that the absurdly strong colouring of the picture would disenable the work from doing either good or harm. He was wrong. The artist who paints for the million must use glaring colours, as no one knew better than Mr Sentiment when he described the inhabitants of his almshouse; and the radical reform which has now swept over such establishments has owed more to the twenty numbers of Mr Sentiment's novel, than to all the true complaints which have escaped from the public for the last half century.

A Long Day in London

The warden had to make use of all his very moderate powers of intrigue to give his son-in-law the slip, and get out of Barchester without being stopped on his road. No schoolboy ever ran away from school with more precaution and more dread of detection; no convict, slipping down from a prison wall, ever feared to see the gaoler more entirely than Mr Harding did to see his son-in-law, as he drove up in the pony carriage to the railway station, on the morning of his escape to London.*

The evening before he went, he wrote a note to the archdeacon, explaining that he should start on the morrow on his journey; that it was his intention to see the attorney-general if possible, and to decide on his future plans in accordance with what he heard from that gentleman; he excused himself for giving Dr Grantly no earlier notice, by stating that his resolve was very sudden; and having entrusted this note to Eleanor, with the perfect, though not expressed, understanding that it was to be sent over to Plumstead Episcopi without haste, he took his departure.

He also prepared and carried with him a note for Sir Abraham Haphazard, in which he stated his name, explaining that he was the defendant in the case of 'The Queen on behalf of the Woolcarders of Barchester *v*. Trustees under the will of the late John Hiram,' for so was the suit denominated, and begged the illustrious and learned gentleman to vouchsafe to him ten minutes' audience at any hour on the next day. Mr Harding calculated that for that one day he was safe; his son-in-law, he had no doubt, would arrive in town by an early train, but not early enough to reach the truant till he should have escaped from his hotel after breakfast; and could he thus manage to see the lawyer on that very day, the deed might be done before the archdeacon could interfere.

On his arrival in town the warden drove, as was his wont, to the Chapter Hotel and Coffee House, near St Paul's. His visits to London of late had not been frequent; but in those happy days when Harding's church music was going through the press, he had been often there; and as the publisher's house was in Paternoster Row, and the printer's press in Fleet Street, the Chapter Hotel and Coffee House had been convenient. It was a quiet, sombre, clerical house, beseeming such a man as the warden, and thus he afterwards frequented it. Had he dared, he would on this occasion have gone elsewhere to throw the archdeacon further off the scent; but he did not know what violent steps his son-in-law might take for his recovery if he were not found at his usual haunt, and he deemed it not prudent to make himself the object of a hunt through London.

Arrived at his inn, he ordered dinner, and went forth to the attorney-general's chambers. There he learnt that Sir Abraham was in Court, and would not probably return that day. He would go direct from Court to the House; all appointments were, as a rule, made at the chambers; the clerk could by no means promise an interview for the next day; was able, on the other hand, to say that such interview was, he thought, impossible; but that Sir Abraham would certainly be at the House in the course of the night, when an answer from himself might possibly be elicited.

To the House Mr Harding went, and left his note, not finding Sir Abraham there. He added a most piteous entreaty that he might be favoured with an answer that evening, for which he would return. He then journeyed back sadly to the Chapter Coffee House, digesting his great thoughts, as best he might, in a clattering omnibus, wedged in between a wet old lady and a journeyman glazier, returning from his work with his tools in his lap. In melancholy solitude he discussed his mutton chop and pint of port. What is there in this world more melancholy than such a dinner? A dinner, though alone, in a country hotel may be worthy of some energy; the waiter, if you are known, will make much of you; the landlord will make you a bow, and perhaps put the fish on the table; if you ring you are attended to, and there is some life about it. A dinner at a London eatinghouse is also lively enough, if it have no other attraction. There is plenty of noise and stir about it, and the rapid whirl of voices and rattle of dishes disperses sadness. But a solitary dinner in an old, respectable, sombre, solid London inn, where nothing makes any noise but the old waiter's creaking shoes;

where one plate slowly goes and another slowly comes without a sound; where the two or three guests would as soon think of knocking each other down as of speaking; where the servants whisper, and the whole household is disturbed if an order be given above the voice – what can be more melancholy than a mutton chop and a pint of port in such a place?

Having gone through this, Mr Harding got into another omnibus, and again returned to the House. Yes, Sir Abraham was there, and was that moment on his legs, fighting eagerly for the hundred and seventh clause of the Convent Custody Bill. Mr Harding's note had been delivered to him; and if Mr Harding would wait some two or three hours, Sir Abraham could be asked whether there was any answer. The House was not full, and perhaps Mr Harding might get admittance into the Strangers' Gallery, which admission, with the help of five shillings, Mr Harding was able to effect.*

This bill of Sir Abraham's had been read a second time and passed into committee. A hundred and six clauses had already been discussed, and had occupied only four mornings and five evening sittings: nine of the hundred and six clauses were passed, fifty-five were withdrawn by consent, fourteen had been altered so as to mean the reverse of the original proposition, eleven had been postponed for further consideration, and seventeen had been directly negatived. The hundred and seventh ordered the bodily searching of nuns for Jesuitical symbols by aged clergymen, and was considered to be the real mainstay of the whole bill. No intention had ever existed to pass such a law as that proposed, but the government did not intend to abandon it till their object was fully attained by the discussion of this clause. It was known that it would be insisted on with terrible vehemence by Protestant Irish members, and as vehemently denounced by the Roman Catholic; and it was justly considered that no further union between the parties would be possible after such a battle. The innocent Irish fell into the trap as they always do, and whisky and poplins became a drug in the market.*

A florid-faced gentleman with a nice head of hair, from the south of Ireland, had succeeded in catching the speaker's eye by the time that Mr Harding had got into the gallery, and was denouncing the proposed sacrilege, his whole face glowing with a fine theatrical frenzy.

'And is this a Christian country?' said he. (Loud cheers;

counter cheers from the ministerial benches. 'Some doubt as to that,' from a voice below the gangway.) 'No, it can be no Christian country, in which the head of the bar, the lagal adviser (loud laughter and cheers) – yes, I say the lagal adviser of the crown (great cheers and laughter), – can stand up in his seat in this house (prolonged cheers and laughter), and attempt to lagalise indacent assaults on the bodies of religious ladies.' (Deafening cheers and laughter, which were prolonged till the honourable member resumed his seat.)*

When Mr Harding had listened to this and much more of the same kind for about three hours, he returned to the door of the house, and received back from the messenger his own note, with the following words scrawled in pencil on the back of it: – 'Tomorrow, 10 p.m. – my chambers. A. H.'

He was so far successful, – but 10 p.m.: what an hour Sir Abraham had named for a legal interview! Mr Harding felt perfectly sure that long before that Dr Grantly would be in London. Dr Grantly could not, however, know that this interview had been arranged, nor could he learn it unless he managed to get hold of Sir Abraham before that hour; and as this was very improbable, Mr Harding determined to start from his hotel early, merely leaving word that he should dine out, and unless luck were much against him, he might still escape the archdeacon till his return from the attorney-general's chambers.

He was at breakfast at nine, and for the twentieth time consulted his 'Bradshaw,'* to see at what earliest hour Dr Grantly could arrive from Barchester. As he examined the columns, he was nearly petrified by the reflection that perhaps the archdeacon might come up by the night mail-train! His heart sank within him at the horrid idea, and for a moment he felt himself dragged back to Barchester without accomplishing any portion of his object. Then he remembered that had Dr Grantly done so, he would have been in the hotel, looking for him long since.

'Waiter,' said he, timidly.

The waiter approached, creaking in his shoes, but voiceless.

'Did any gentleman – a clergyman, arrive here by the night mail-train?'

'No, sir, not one,' whispered the waiter, putting his mouth nearly close to the warden's ear.

Mr Harding was reassured.

'Waiter,' said he again, and the waiter again creaked up; 'If any one calls for me, I am going to dine out, and shall return about eleven o'clock.'

The waiter nodded, but did not this time vouchsafe any reply; and Mr Harding, taking up his hat, proceeded out to pass a long day in the best way he could, somewhere out of sight of the archdeacon.

'Bradshaw' had told him twenty times that Dr Grantly could not be at Paddington station till 2 p.m., and our poor friend might therefore have trusted to the shelter of the hotel for some hours longer with perfect safety; but he was nervous. There was no knowing what steps the archdeacon might take for his apprehension: a message by electric telegraph might desire the landlord of the hotel to set a watch upon him; some letter might come which he might find himself unable to disobey; at any rate, he could not feel himself secure in any place at which the archdeacon could expect to find him; and at 10 a.m. he started forth to spend twelve hours in London.

Mr Harding had friends in town, had he chosen to seek them; but he felt that he was in no humour for ordinary calls, and he did not now wish to consult with any one as to the great step which he had determined to take. As he had said to his daughter, no one knows where the shoe pinches but the wearer. There are some points on which no man can be contented to follow the advice of another – some subjects on which a man can consult his own conscience only. Our warden had made up his mind that it was good for him at any cost to get rid of this grievance; his daughter was the only person whose concurrence appeared necessary to him, and she did concur with him most heartily. Under such circumstances he would not, if he could help it, consult any one further, till advice would be useless. Should the archdeacon catch him, indeed, there would be much advice, and much consultation of a kind not to be avoided; but he hoped better things; and as he felt that he could not now converse on indifferent subjects, he resolved to see no one till after his interview with the attorney-general.

He determined to take sanctuary in Westminster Abbey, so he again went thither in an omnibus, and finding that the doors were not open for morning service, he paid his twopence, and went in as a sight-seer.* It occurred to him that he had no definite place of rest for the day, and that he should be absolutely worn out before his interview if he attempted to walk about from 10 a.m. to 10 p.m., so he sat himself down on a stone step, and gazed up at the figure of William Pitt,* who looks as though he had just entered the church for the first time in his life, and was anything but pleased at finding himself there.

He had been sitting unmolested about twenty minutes, when the verger asked him whether he wouldn't like to walk round. Mr Harding didn't want to walk anywhere, and declined, merely observing that he was waiting for the morning service. The verger seeing that he was a clergyman, told him that the doors of the choir were now open, and showed him into a seat. This was a great point gained; the archdeacon would certainly not come to morning service at Westminster Abbey, even though he were in London; and here the warden could rest quietly, and, when the time came, duly say his prayers.

He longed to get up from his seat, and examine the music-books of the choristers, and the copy of the litany from which the service was chanted, to see how far the little details at Westminster corresponded with those at Barchester, and whether he thought his own voice would fill the church well from the Westminster precentor's seat. There would, however, be impropriety in such meddling, and he sat perfectly still, looking up at the noble roof, and guarding against the coming fatigues of the day.

By degrees two or three people entered: the very same damp old woman who had nearly obliterated him in the omnibus, or some other just like her; a couple of young ladies, with their veils down, and gilt crosses conspicuous on their prayer-books; an old man on crutches; a party who were seeing the abbey, and thought they might as well hear the service for their twopence, as opportunity served; and a young woman with her prayer-book done up in her handkerchief, who rushed in late, and, in her hurried entry, tumbled over one of the forms, and made such a noise that every one, even the officiating minor canon, was startled, and she herself was so frightened by the echo of her own catastrophe, that she was nearly thrown into fits by the panic.

Mr Harding was not much edified by the manner of the service. The minor canon in question hurried in, somewhat late, in a surplice not in the neatest order, and was followed by a dozen choristers, who were also not as trim as they might have been: they all jostled into their places with a quick hurried step, and the service was soon commenced. Soon commenced, and soon over, for there was no music, and time was not unnecessarily lost in the chanting.* On the whole, Mr Harding was of opinion that things were managed better at Barchester, though even there he knew that there was room for improvement.

It appears to us a question whether any clergyman can go through our church service with decorum, morning after morning, in an immense building, surrounded by not more than a dozen listeners. The best actors cannot act well before empty benches, and though there is, of course, a higher motive in one case than the other, still even the best of clergymen cannot but be influenced by their audience; and to expect that a duty should be well done under such circumstances, would be to require from human nature more than human power.

When the two ladies with the gilt crosses, the old man with his crutch, and the still palpitating housemaid were going, Mr Harding found himself obliged to go too. The verger stood in his way, and looked at him and looked at the door, and so he went. But he returned again in a few minutes, and re-entered with another twopence. There was no other sanctuary so good for him.

As he walked slowly down the nave, and then up one aisle, and then again down the nave and up the other aisle, he tried to think gravely of the step he was about to take. He was going to give up eight hundred a year voluntarily; and doom himself to live for the rest of his life on about a hundred and fifty. He knew that he had hitherto failed to realise this fact as he ought to do. Could he maintain his own independence and support his daughter on a hundred and fifty pounds a year without being a burden on any one? His son-in-law was rich, but nothing could induce him to lean on his son-in-law after acting, as he intended to do, in most direct opposition to his counsel. The bishop was rich, but he was about to throw away the bishop's best gift, and that in a manner to injure materially the patronage of the giver: he could neither expect nor accept anything further from the bishop. There would be not only no merit, but positive disgrace, in giving up his wardenship, if he were not prepared to meet the world without it. Yes, he must from this time forward bound all his human wishes for himself and his daughter to the poor extent of so limited an income. He knew he had not thought sufficiently of this, that he had been carried away by enthusiasm, and had hitherto not brought home to himself the full reality of his position.

He thought most about his daughter, naturally. It was true that she was engaged, and he knew enough of his proposed son-in-law to be sure that his own altered circumstances would make no obstacle to such a marriage; nay, he was sure that the very fact of his poverty would induce Bold more anxiously to press the matter; but he disliked counting on Bold in this emergency, brought on, as it had been, by his doing. He did not like saying to himself, Bold has turned me out of my house and income, and, therefore, he must relieve me of my daughter; he preferred reckoning on Eleanor as the companion of his poverty and exile, – as the sharer of his small income.

Some modest provision for his daughter had been long since made. His life was insured for three thousand pounds, and this sum was to go to Eleanor. The archdeacon, for some years past, had paid the premium, and had secured himself by the immediate possession of a small property which was to have gone to Mrs Grantly after her father's death. This matter, therefore, had been out of the warden's hands long since, as, indeed, had all the business transactions of his family, and his anxiety was, therefore, confined to his own life income.

Yes. A hundred and fifty per annum was very small, but still it might suffice; but how was he to chant the litany at the cathedral on Sunday mornings, and get the service done at Crabtree Parva? True, Crabtree Church was not quite a mile and a half from the cathedral; but he could not be in two places at once! Crabtree was a small village, and afternoon service might suffice, but still this went against his conscience; it was not right that his parishioners should be robbed of any of their privileges on account of his poverty. He might, to be sure, make some arrangement for doing weekday service at the cathedral, but he had chanted the litany at Barchester so long, and had a conscious feeling that he did it so well, that he was unwilling to give up the duty.

Thinking of such things, turning over in his own mind together small desires and grave duties, but never hesitating for a moment as to the necessity of leaving the hospital, Mr Harding walked up and down the abbey, or sat still meditating on the same stone step, hour after hour. One verger went and another

came, but they did not disturb him; every now and then they
crept up and looked at him, but they did so with a reverential
stare, and, on the whole, Mr Harding found his retreat well
chosen. About four o'clock his comfort was disturbed by an
enemy in the shape of hunger; it was necessary that he should
dine, and it was clear that he could not dine in the abbey; so he
left his sanctuary not willingly, and betook himself to the
neighbourhood of the Strand to look for food.

His eyes had become so accustomed to the gloom of the
church, that they were dazed when he got out into the full light
of day, and he felt confused and ashamed of himself, as though
people were staring at him. He hurried along, still in dread of
the archdeacon, till he came to Charing Cross, and then remembered that in one of his passages through the Strand he had seen
the words 'Chops and Steaks' on a placard in a shop window.
He remembered the shop distinctly; it was next door to a trunk-
seller's, and there was a cigar shop on the other side. He couldn't
go to his hotel for dinner, which to him hitherto was the only
known mode of dining in London at his own expense; and,
therefore, he would get a steak at the shop in the Strand.
Archdeacon Grantly would certainly not come to such a place
for his dinner.

He found the house easily — just as he had observed it,
between the trunks and the cigars. He was rather daunted by
the huge quantity of fish which he saw in the window. There
were barrels of oysters, hecatombs of lobsters, a few tremen-
dous-looking crabs, and a tub full of pickled salmon; not,
however, being aware of any connexion between shell-fish and
iniquity, he entered, and modestly asked a slatternly woman,
who was picking oysters out of a great watery reservoir, whether
he could have a mutton chop and a potato.

The woman looked somewhat surprised, but answered in the
affirmative, and a slipshod girl ushered him into a long back
room, filled with boxes for the accommodation of parties, in
one of which he took his seat. In a more miserable forlorn place
he could not have found himself: the room smelt of fish, and
sawdust, and stale tobacco smoke, with a slight taint of escaped
gas; everything was rough, and dirty, and disreputable; the cloth
which they put before him was abominable; the knives and
forks were bruised, and hacked, and filthy; and everything was
impregnated with fish. He had one comfort, however: he was

quite alone; there was no one there to look on his dismay; nor was it probable that any one would come to do so. It was a London supper-house. About one o'clock at night the place would be lively enough, but at the present time his seclusion was as deep as it had been in the abbey.

In about half an hour the untidy girl, not yet dressed for her evening labours, brought him his chop and potatoes, and Mr Harding begged for a pint of sherry. He was impressed with an idea which was generally prevalent a few years since, and is not yet wholly removed from the minds of men, that to order a dinner at any kind of inn, without ordering a pint of wine for the benefit of the landlord, was a kind of fraud; not punishable, indeed, by law, but not the less abominable on that account. Mr Harding remembered his coming poverty, and would willingly have saved his half-crown, but he thought he had no alternative; and he was soon put in possession of some horrid mixture procured from the neighbouring public-house.

His chop and potatoes, however, were eatable, and having got over as best he might the disgust created by the knives and forks, he contrived to swallow his dinner. He was not much disturbed: one young man, with pale face and watery fish-like eyes, wearing his hat ominously on one side, did come in and stare at him, and ask the girl, audibly enough, 'Who that old cock was;' but the annoyance went no further, and the warden was left seated on his wooden bench in peace, endeavouring to distinguish the different scents arising from lobsters, oysters, and salmon.

Unknowing as Mr Harding was in the ways of London, he felt he had somehow selected an ineligible dining-house, and that he had better leave it. It was hardly five o'clock – how was he to pass the time till ten? Five miserable hours! He was already tired, and it was impossible that he should continue walking so long. He thought of getting into an omnibus and going out to Fulham for the sake of coming back in another: this, however, would be weary work, and as he paid his bill to the woman in the shop, he asked her if there were any place near where he could get a cup of coffee. Though she did keep a shell-fish supper-house, she was very civil, and directed him to the cigar divan*on the other side of the street.

Mr Harding had not a much correcter notion of a cigar divan than he had of a London dinner-house, but he was desperately in want of rest, and went as he was directed. He thought he must have made some mistake when he found himself in a cigar shop, but the man behind the counter saw immediately that he was a stranger, and understood what he wanted. 'One shilling, sir – thank ye, sir – cigar, sir? – ticket for coffee, sir – you'll only have to call the waiter. Up those stairs, if you please, sir. Better take the cigar, sir – you can always give it to a friend you know. Well, sir, thank ye, sir – as you are so good, I'll smoke it myself.' And so Mr Harding ascended to the divan, with his ticket for coffee, but minus the cigar.

The place seemed much more suitable to his requirements than the room in which he had dined: there was, to be sure, a strong smell of tobacco, to which he was not accustomed; but after the shellfish, the tobacco did not seem disagreeable. There were quantities of books, and long rows of sofas. What on earth could be more luxurious than a sofa, a book and a cup of coffee? An old waiter came up to him, with a couple of magazines and an evening paper. Was ever anything so civil? Would he have a cup of coffee, or would he prefer a sherbet?* Sherbet! Was he absolutely in an Eastern divan, with the slight addition of all the London perodicals? He had, however, an idea that sherbet should be drunk sitting cross-legged, and as he was not quite up to this, he ordered the coffee.

The coffee came, and was unexceptionable. Why, this divan was paradise! The civil old waiter suggested to him a game of chess: though a chess player he was not equal to this, so he declined, and putting up his weary legs on the sofa, leisurely sipped his coffee, and turned over the pages of his Blackwood.* He might have been so engaged for about an hour, for the old waiter enticed him to a second cup of coffee, when a musical clock began to play. Mr Harding then closed his magazine, keeping his place with his finger, and lay, listening with closed eyes to the clock. Soon the clock seemed to turn into a violoncello, with piano accompaniments, and Mr Harding began to fancy the old waiter was the Bishop of Barchester; he was inexpressibly shocked that the bishop should have brought him his coffee, with his own hands; then Dr Grantly came in, with a basket full of lobsters, which he would not be induced to leave downstairs in the kitchen; and then the warden couldn't quite understand why so many people would smoke in the bishop's drawing-room; and so he fell fast asleep, and his dreams wandered away to his accustomed stall in Barchester Cathedral, and the twelve old men he was so soon about to leave for ever.

He was fatigued, and slept soundly for some time. Some sudden stop in the musical clock woke him at length, and he jumped up with a start, surprised to find the room quite full; it had been nearly empty when his nap began. With nervous anxiety he pulled out his watch, and found that it was half-past nine. He seized his hat, and, hurrying down stairs, started at a rapid pace for Lincoln's Inn.

It still wanted twenty minutes to ten when the warden found himself at the bottom of Sir Abraham's stairs, so he walked leisurely up and down the quiet inn to cool himself. It was a beautiful evening at the end of August. He had recovered from his fatigue; his sleep and the coffee had refreshed him, and he was surprised to find he was absolutely enjoying himself, when the inn clock struck ten. The sound was hardly over before he knocked at Sir Abraham's door, and was informed by the clerk who received him that the great man would be with him immediately.

CHAPTER 17

Sir Abraham Hapazard

Mr Harding was shown into a comfortable inner sitting-room, looking more like a gentleman's book-room than a lawyer's chambers, and there waited for Sir Abraham. Nor was he kept waiting long: in ten or fifteen minutes he heard a clatter of voices speaking quickly in the passage, and then the attorney-general entered.

'Very sorry to keep you waiting, Mr Warden,' said Sir Abraham, shaking hands with him; 'and sorry, too, to name so disagreeable an hour; but your notice was short, and as you said today, I named the very earliest hour that was not disposed of.'

Mr. Harding assured him that he was aware that it was he that should apologise.

Sir Abraham was a tall thin man, with hair prematurely grey, but bearing no other sign of age; he had a slight stoop, in his neck rather than his back, acquired by his constant habit of leaning forward as he addressed his various audiences. He might be fifty years old, and would have looked young for his age, had not constant work hardened his features, and given him the appearance of a machine with a mind. His face was full of intellect, but devoid of natural expression. You would say he was a man to use, and then have done with; a man to be sought for on great emergencies, but ill adapted for ordinary services; a man whom you would ask to defend your property, but to whom you would be sorry to confide your love. He was bright as a diamond, and as cutting, and also as unimpressionable. He knew everyone whom to know was an honour, but he was without a friend; he wanted none, however, and knew not the meaning of the word in other than its parliamentary sense.* A friend! Had he not always been sufficient to himself, and now, at fifty, was it likely that he should trust another? He was married, indeed, and had children, but what time had he for the soft idleness of conjugal felicity? His working days or term times were occupied from his time of rising to the late hour at which he went to rest, and even his vacations were more full of labour than the busiest days of other men. He never quarrelled with his wife, but he never talked to her, — he never had time to talk, he was so taken up with speaking. She, poor lady, was not unhappy; she had all that money could give her, she would probably live to be a peeress, and she really thought Sir Abraham the best of husbands.

Sir Abraham was a man of wit, and sparkled among the brightest at the dinner-tables of political grandees; indeed, he always sparkled; whether in society, in the House of Commons, or the courts of law, coruscations flew from him; glittering sparkles, as from hot steel, but no heat; no cold heart was ever cheered by warmth from him, no unhappy soul ever dropped a portion of its burden at his door.

With him success alone was praiseworthy, and he knew none so successful as himself. No one had thrust him forward; no powerful friends had pushed him along on his road to power. No, he was attorney-general, and would, in all human probability, be Lord Chancellor by sheer dint of his own industry and his own talent. Who else in all the world rose so high with so little help? A premier, indeed! Who had ever been premier without mighty friends? An archbishop! Yes, the son or grand-son of a great noble, or else, probably, his tutor. But he, Sir Abraham, had had no mighty lord at his back; his father had been a county apothecary, his mother a farmer's daughter. Why should he respect any but himself? And so he glitters along through the world, the brightest among the bright; and when his glitter is gone, and he is gathered to his fathers, no eye will be dim with a tear, no heart will mourn for its lost friend.*

'And so, Mr Warden,' said Sir Abraham, 'all our trouble about this law-suit is at an end.'

Mr Harding said he hoped so, but he didn't at all understand what Sir Abraham meant. Sir Abraham, with all his sharpness, could not have looked into his heart and read his intentions.

'All over. You need trouble yourself no further about it; of course they must pay the costs, and the absolute expense to you and Dr Grantly will be trifling – that is, compared with what it might have been if it had been continued.'

'I fear I don't quite understand you, Sir Abraham.'

'Don't you know that their attorneys have noticed us that they have withdrawn the suit?'

Mr Harding explained to the lawyer that he knew nothing of this, although he had heard in a round-about way that such an intention had been talked of; and he also at length succeeded in making Sir Abraham understand that even this did not satisfy him. The attorney-general stood up, put his hands into his breeches pockets, and raised his eyebrows, as Mr Harding proceeded to detail the grievance from which he now wished to rid himself.

'I know I have no right to trouble you personally with this matter, but as it is of most vital importance to me, as all my happiness is concerned in it, I thought I might venture to seek your own advice.'

Sir Abraham bowed, and declared his clients were entitled to the best advice he could give them; particularly a client so respectable in every way as the Warden of Barchester Hospital.

'A spoken word, Sir Abraham, is often of more value than volumes of written advice. The truth is, I am ill satisfied with this matter as it stands at present. I do see – I cannot help seeing, that the affairs of the hospital are not arranged according to the will of the founder.'

'None of such institutions are, Mr Harding, nor can they be; the altered circumstances in which we live do not admit of it.'

'Quite true – that is quite true; but I can't see that those altered circumstances give me a right to eight hundred a year. I don't know whether I ever read John Hiram's will, but were I to read it now I could not understand it. What I want you, Sir Abraham, to tell me, is this – am I, as warden, legally and distinctly entitled to the proceeds of the property, after the due maintenance of the twelve bedesmen?'

Sir Abraham declared that he couldn't exactly say in so many words that Mr Harding was legally entitled to, etc., etc., etc., and ended in expressing a strong opinion that it would be madness to raise any further question on the matter, as the suit was to be, – nay, was, abandoned.

Mr Harding, seated in his chair, began to play a slow tune on an imaginary violoncello.

'Nay, my dear sir,' continued the attorney-general; 'there is no further ground for any question; I don't see that you have the power of raising it.'

'I can resign,' said Mr Harding, slowly playing away with his right hand, as though the bow were beneath the chair in which he was sitting.

'What! throw it up altogether?' said the attorney-general, gazing with utter astonishment at his client.

'Did you see those articles in the *Jupiter*?' said Mr Harding, piteously, appealing to the sympathy of the lawyer.

Sir Abraham said he had seen them. This poor little clergyman, cowed into such an act of extreme weakness by a newspaper article, was to Sir Abraham so contemptible an object, that he hardly knew how to talk to him as to a rational being.

'Hadn't you better wait,' said he, 'till Dr Grantly is in town with you? Wouldn't it be better to postpone any serious step till you can consult with him?'

Mr Harding declared vehemently that he could not wait, and Sir Abraham began seriously to doubt his sanity.

'Of course,' said the latter, 'if you have private means sufficient for your wants, and if this – '

'I haven't a sixpence, Sir Abraham,' said the warden.

'God bless me! Why, Mr Harding, how do you mean to live?'

Mr Harding proceeded to explain to the man of law that he meant to keep his precentorship, – that was eighty pounds a year; and, also, that he meant to fall back upon his own little living of Crabtree, which was another eighty pounds. That, to be sure, the duties of the two were hardly compatible; but perhaps he might effect an exchange. And then, recollecting that the attorney-general would hardly care to hear how the service of a cathedral church is divided among the minor canons, stopped short in his explanations.

Sir Abraham listened in pitying wonder. 'I really think, Mr Harding, you had better wait for the archdeacon. This is a most serious step; one for which, in my opinion, there is not the slightest necessity; and, as you have done me the honour of asking my advice, I must implore you to do nothing without the approval of your friends. A man is never the best judge of his own position.'

'A man is the best judge of what he feels himself. I'd sooner beg my bread till my death, than read such another article as those two that have appeared, and feel, as I do, that the writer has truth on his side.'

'Have you not a daughter, Mr Harding, – an unmarried daughter?'

'I have,' said he, now standing also, but still playing away on his fiddle with his hand behind his back. 'I have, Sir Abraham; and she and I are completely agreed on this subject.'

'Pray excuse me, Mr Harding, if what I say seems impertinent: but surely it is you that should be prudent on her behalf. She is young, and does not know the meaning of living on an income of a hundred and fifty pounds a year. On her account give up this idea. Believe me, it is sheer Quixotism.'*

The warden walked away to the window, and then back to his chair; and then, irresolute what to say, took another turn at the window. The attorney-general was really extremely patient, but he was beginning to think that the interview had been long enough.

'But if this income be not justly mine, what if she and I have both to beg?' said the warden at last, sharply, and in a voice so different from that he had hitherto used, that Sir Abraham was startled. 'If so, it would be better to beg.'

'My dear sir, nobody now questions its justness.'

'Yes, Sir Abraham, one does question it, – the most important of all witnesses against me, – I question it myself. My God knows whether or no I love my daughter; but I would sooner that she and I should both beg, than that she should live in comfort on money which is truly the property of the poor. It may seem strange to you, Sir Abraham, it is strange to myself, that I should have been ten years in that happy home, and not have thought of these things, till they were so roughly dinned into my ears. I cannot boast of my conscience, when it required the violence of a public newspaper to awaken it; but, now that it is awake, I must obey it. When I came here I did not know that the suit was withdrawn by Mr Bold, and my object was to beg you to abandon my defence. As there is no action, there can be no defence; but it is, at any rate, as well that you should know that, from tomorrow, I shall cease to be the warden of the hospital. My friends and I differ on this subject, Sir Abraham, and that adds much to my sorrow: but it cannot be helped.' And, as he finished what he had to say, he played up such a tune as never before had graced the chambers of any attorney-general. He was standing up, gallantly fronting Sir Abraham, and his right arm passed with bold and rapid sweeps before him, as though he were embracing some huge instrument, which allowed him to stand thus erect; and with the fingers of his left hand he stopped, with preternatural velocity, a multitude of strings, which ranged from the top of his collar to the bottom of the lappet* of his coat. Sir Abraham listened and looked in wonder. As he had never before seen Mr Harding, the meaning of these wild gesticulations was lost upon him; but he perceived that the gentleman who had a few minutes since been so subdued as to be unable to speak without hesitation, was now impassioned – nay, almost violent.

'You'll sleep on this, Mr Harding, and tomorrow –

'I have done more than sleep upon it,' said the warden; 'I have laid awake upon it, and that night after night. I found I could not sleep upon it; now I hope to do so.'

The attorney-general had no answer to make to this; so he expressed a quiet hope that whatever settlement was finally made would be satisfactory; and Mr Harding withdrew, thanking the great man for his kind attention.

Mr Harding was sufficiently satisfied with the interview to feel a glow of comfort as he descended into the small old square of Lincoln's Inn. It was a calm, bright, beautiful night, and by the light of the moon, even the chapel of Lincoln's Inn, and the sombre row of chambers, which surround the quadrangle, looked well. He stood still a moment to collect his thoughts, and reflect on what he had done, and was about to do. He knew that the attorney-general regarded him as little better than a fool, but that he did not mind; he and the attorney-general had not much in common between them; he knew also that others, whom he did care about, would think so too; but Eleanor, he was sure, would exult in what he had done, and the bishop, he trusted, would sympathise with him.

In the meantime he had to meet the archdeacon, and so he walked slowly down Chancery Lane and along Fleet Street, feeling sure that his work for the night was not yet over. When he reached the hotel he rang the bell quietly, and with a palpitating heart; he almost longed to escape round the corner, and delay the coming storm by a further walk round St Paul's Churchyard, but he heard the slow creaking shoes of the old waiter approaching, and he stood his ground manfully.

CHAPTER 18

The Warden Is Very Obstinate

'Dr Grantly is here, sir,' greeted his ears before the door was well open, 'and Mrs Grantly; they have a sitting-room above, and are waiting up for you.'

There was something in the tone of the man's voice which seemed to indicate that even he looked upon the warden as a runaway schoolboy, just recaptured by his guardian, and that he pitied the culprit, though he could not but be horrified at the crime.

The warden endeavoured to appear unconcerned, as he said, 'Oh, indeed! I'll go upstairs at once;' but he failed signally: there was, perhaps, a ray of comfort in the presence of his married daughter; that is to say, of comparative comfort, seeing that his son-in-law was there: but how much would he have preferred that they should both have been safe at Plumstead Episcopi! However, upstairs he went, the waiter slowly preceding him; and on the door being opened the archdeacon was discovered standing in the middle of the room, erect, indeed, as usual, but oh! how sorrowful! and on a dingy sofa behind him reclined his patient wife.

'Papa, I thought you were never coming back,' said the lady; 'it's twelve o'clock.'

'Yes, my dear,' said the warden. 'The attorney-general named ten for my meeting; to be sure ten is late, but what could I do, you know? Great men will have their own way.'

And he gave his daughter a kiss, and shook hands with the doctor, and again tried to look unconcerned.

'And you have absolutely been with the attorney-general?' asked the archdeacon.

Mr Harding signified that he had.

'Good heavens, how unfortunate!' And the archdeacon raised his huge hands in the manner in which his friends are so accustomed to see him express disapprobation and astonishment. 'What will Sir Abraham think of it? Did you know that it is not customary for clients to go direct to their counsel?'

'Isn't it?' asked the warden, innocently. 'Well, at any rate, I've done it now. Sir Abraham didn't seem to think it so very strange.'

The archdeacon gave a sigh that would have moved a man-of-war.

'But, papa, what did you say to Sir Abraham?' asked the lady.

'I asked him, my dear, to explain John Hiram's will to me. He couldn't explain it in the only way which would have satisfied me, and so I resigned the wardenship.'

'Resigned it!' said the archdeacon, in a solemn voice, sad and low, but yet sufficiently audible; a sort of whisper that Macready* would have envied, and the galleries have applauded with a couple of rounds. 'Resigned it! Good heavens!' and the dignitary of the church sank back horrified into a horsehair armchair.

'At least I told Sir Abraham that I would resign; and of course I must now do so.'

'Not at all,' said the archdeacon, catching a ray of hope. 'Nothing that you say in such a way to your own counsel can be in any way binding on you; of course you were there to ask his advice. I'm sure, Sir Abraham did not advise any such step.'

Mr Harding could not say that he had.

'I am sure he disadvised you from it,' continued the reverend cross-examiner.

Mr Harding could not deny this.

'I'm sure Sir Abraham must have advised you to consult your friends.'

To this proposition also Mr Harding was obliged to assent.

'Then your threat of resignation amounts to nothing, and we are just where we were before.'

Mr Harding was now standing on the rug, moving uneasily from one foot to the other. He made no distinct answer to the archdeacon's last proposition, for his mind was chiefly engaged on thinking how he could escape to bed. That his resignation was a thing finally fixed on, a fact all but completed, was not in his mind a matter of any doubt; he knew his own weakness; he knew how prone he was to be led; but he was not weak enough to give way now, to go back from the position to which his conscience had driven him, after having purposely come to

London to declare his determination: he did not in the least doubt his resolution, but he greatly doubted his power of defending it against his son-in-law.

'You must be very tired, Susan,' said he: 'wouldn't you like to go to bed?'

But Susan didn't want to go till her husband went – she had an idea that her papa might be bullied if she were away: she wasn't tired at all, or at least she said so.

The archdeacon was pacing the room, expressing, by certain noddles* of his head, his opinion of the utter fatuity of his father-in-law.

'Why,' at last he said – and angels might have blushed at the rebuke expressed in his tone and emphasis – 'Why did you go off from Barchester so suddenly? Why did you take such a step without giving us notice, after what had passed at the palace?'

The warden hung his head, and made no reply: he could not condescend to say that he had not intended to give his son-in-law the slip; and as he had not the courage to avow it, he said nothing.

'Papa has been too much for you,' said the lady.

The archdeacon took another turn, and again ejaculated, 'Good heavens!' this time in a very low whisper, but still audible.

'I think I'll go to bed,' said the warden, taking up a side candle.

'At any rate you'll promise me to take no further step without consultation,' said the archdeacon. Mr Harding made no answer, but slowly proceeded to light his candle. 'Of course,' continued the other, 'such a declaration as that you made to Sir Abraham means nothing. Come, warden, promise me this. The whole affair, you see, is already settled, and that with very little trouble or expense. Bold has been compelled to abandon his action, and all you have to do is to remain quiet at the hospital.' Mr Harding still made no reply, but looked meekly into his son-in-law's face. The archdeacon thought he knew his father-in-law, but he was mistaken; he thought that he had already talked over a vacillating man to resign his promise. 'Come,' said he, 'promise Susan to give up this idea of resigning the wardenship.'

The warden looked at his daughter, thinking probably at the moment that if Eleanor were contented with him, he need not so much regard his other child, and said, 'I am sure Susan will not ask me to break my word, or to do what I know to be wrong.'

'Papa,' she said, 'it would be madness in you to throw up your preferment. What are you to live on?'

'God, that feeds the young ravens, will take care of me also,'* said Mr Harding, with a smile, as though afraid of giving offence by making his reference to scripture too solemn.

'Pish!' said the archdeacon, turning away rapidly; 'if the ravens persisted in refusing the food prepared for them, they wouldn't be fed.' A clergyman generally dislikes to be met in argument by any scriptural quotation; he feels as affronted as a doctor does, when recommended by an old woman to take some favourite dose, or as a lawyer when an unprofessional man attempts to put him down by a quibble.

'I shall have the living of Crabtree,' modestly suggested the warden.

'Eighty pounds a year!' sneered the archdeacon.

'And the precentorship,' said the father-in-law.

'It goes with the wardenship,' said the son-in-law. Mr Harding was prepared to argue this point, and began to do so, but Dr Grantly stopped him. 'My dear warden,' said he, 'this is all nonsense. Eighty pounds or a hundred and sixty makes very little difference. You can't live on it – you can't ruin Eleanor's prospects for ever. In point of fact, you can't resign; the bishop wouldn't accept it; the whole thing is settled. What I now want to do is to prevent any inconvenient tittle tattle, – any more newspaper articles.'

'That's what I want, too,' said the warden.

'And to prevent that,' continued the other, 'we mustn't let any talk of resignation get abroad.'

'But I shall resign,' said the warden, very, very meekly.

'Good heavens! Susan, my dear, what can I say to him?'

'But, papa,' said Mrs Grantly, getting up, and putting her arm through that of her father, 'what is Eleanor to do if you throw away your income?'

A hot tear stood in each of the warden's eyes as he looked round upon his married daughter. Why should one sister who was so rich predict poverty for another? some such idea as this was on his mind, but he gave no utterance to it. Then he thought of the pelican feeding its young with blood from its own breast, but he gave no utterance of that either; and then of Eleanor waiting for him at home, waiting to congratulate him on the end of all his trouble.

'Think of Eleanor, papa,' said Mrs Grantly.

'I do think of her,' said her father.

'And you will not do this rash thing?' The lady was really moved beyond her usual calm composure.

'It can never be rash to do right,' said he. 'I shall certainly resign this wardenship.'

'Then, Mr Harding, there is nothing before you but ruin,' said the archdeacon, now moved beyond all endurance. 'Ruin both for you and Eleanor. How do you mean to pay the monstrous expenses of this action?'

Mrs Grantly suggested that, as the action was abandoned, the costs would not be heavy.

'Indeed they will, my dear,' continued he. 'One cannot have the attorney-general up at twelve o'clock at night for nothing; – but of course your father has not thought of this.'

'I will sell my furniture,' said the warden.

'Furniture!' ejaculated the other, with a most powerful sneer.

'Come, archdeacon,' said the lady, 'we needn't mind that at present. You know you never expected papa to pay the costs.'

'Such absurdity is enough to provoke Job,'* said the archdeacon, marching quicky up and down the room. 'Your father is like a child. Eight hundred pounds a-year! – eight hundred and eighty with the house – with nothing to do. The very place for him. And to throw that up because some scoundrel writes an article in a newspaper! Well – I have done my duty. If he chooses to ruin his child I cannot help it;' and he stood still at the fireplace, and looked at himself in a dingy mirror which stood on the chimneypiece.

There was a pause for about a minute, and then the warden, finding that nothing else was coming, lighted his candle, and quietly said, 'Good night.'

'Good night, papa,' said the lady.

And so the warden retired; but, as he closed the door behind him, he heard the well-known ejaculation – slower, lower, more solemn, more ponderous than ever – 'Good heavens!'

CHAPTER 19

The Warden Resigns

The party met the next morning at breakfast; and a very sombre affair it was – very unlike the breakfasts at Plumstead Episcopi.

There were three thin, small, dry bits of bacon, each an inch long, served up under a huge old plated cover; there were four three-cornered bits of dry toast, and four square bits of buttered toast; there was a loaf of bread, and some oily-looking butter; and on the sideboard there were the remains of a cold shoulder of mutton. The archdeacon, however, had not come up from his rectory to St Paul's Churchyard to enjoy himself, and therefore nothing was said of the scanty fare.

The guests were as sorry as the viands – hardly anything was said over the breakfast table. The archdeacon munched his toast in ominous silence, turning over bitter thoughts in his deep mind. The warden tried to talk to his daughter, and she tried to answer him; but they both failed. There were no feelings at present in common between them. The warden was thinking only of getting back to Barchester, and calculating whether the archdeacon would expect him to wait for him; and Mrs Grantly was preparing herself for a grand attack which she was to make on her father, as agreed upon between herself and her husband during their curtain confabulation of that morning.

When the waiter had creaked out of the room with the last of the teacups, the archdeacon got up and went to the window, as though to admire the view. The room looked out on a narrow passage which runs from St Paul's Churchyard to Paternoster Row; and Dr Grantly patiently perused the names of the three shopkeepers whose doors were in view. The warden still kept his seat at the table, and examined the pattern of the tablecloth; and Mrs Grantly, seating herself on the sofa, began to knit.

After awhile the warden pulled his 'Bradshaw' out of his pocket, and began laboriously to consult it. There was a train for Barchester at 10 a.m. That was out of the question, for it was nearly ten already. Another at 3 p.m; another, the night-mail train, at 9 p.m. The three o'clock train would take him home to tea, and would suit very well.

'My dear,' said he, 'I think I shall go back home at three o'clock to-day. I shall get home at half-past eight. I don't think there's anything to keep me in London.'

'The archdeacon and I return by the early train tomorrow, papa; won't you wait and go back with us?'

'Why, Eleanor will expect me tonight; and I've so much to do; and – '

'Much to do!' said the archdeacon *sotto voce*;* but the warden heard him.

'You'd better wait for us, papa.'

'Thank ye, my dear! I think I'll go this afternoon.' The tamest animal will turn when driven too hard, and even Mr Harding was beginning to fight for his own way.

'I suppose you won't be back before three?' said the lady, addressing her husband.

'I must leave this at two,' said the warden.

'Quite out of the question,' said the archdeacon, answering his wife, and still reading the shopkeepers' names; 'I don't suppose I shall be back till five.'

There was another long pause, during which Mr Harding continued to study his 'Bradshaw.'

'I must go to Cox and Cummins,' said the archdeacon at last.

'Oh, to Cox and Cummins,' said the warden. It was quite a matter of indifference to him where his son-in-law went. The names of Cox and Cummins had now no interest in his ears. What had he to do with Cox and Cummins further, having already had his suit finally adjudicated upon in a court of conscience, a judgment without power of appeal fully registered, and the matter settled so that all the lawyers in London could not disturb it. The archdeacon could go to Cox and Cummins, could remain there all day in anxious discussion; but what might be said there was no longer matter of interest to him, who was so soon to lay aside the name of warden of Barchester Hospital.

The archdeacon took up his shining new clerical hat, and put on his black new clerical gloves, and looked heavy, respectable, decorous, and opulent, a decided clergyman of the Church of England, every inch of him. 'I suppose I shall see you at Barchester the day after tomorrow,' said he.

The warden supposed he would.

'I must once more beseech you to take no further steps till you see my father; if you owe me nothing,' and the archdeacon looked as though he thought a great deal were due to him, 'at least you owe so much to my father;' and, without waiting for a reply, Dr Grantly wended his way to Cox and Cummins.

Mrs Grantley waited till the last fall of her husband's foot was heard, as he turned out of the court into St Paul's Churchyard, and then commenced her task of talking her father over.

'Papa,' she began, 'this is a most serious business.'

'Indeed it is,' said the warden, ringing the bell.

'I greatly feel the distress of mind you must have endured.'

'I am sure you do, my dear;' and he ordered the waiter to bring him pen, ink, and paper.

'Are you going to write, papa?'

'Yes, my dear – I am going to write my resignation to the bishop.'

'Pray, pray, papa, put it off till our return, – pray put it off till you have seen the bishop, – dear papa! for my sake, for Eleanor's!——'

'It is for your sake and Eleanor's that I do this. I hope, at least, that my children may never have to be ashamed of their father.'

'How can you talk about shame, papa?' and she stopped while the waiter creaked in with the paper, and then slowly creaked out again; 'how can you talk about shame? you know what all your friends think about this question.'

The warden spread his paper on the table, placing it on the meagre blotting-book, which the hotel afforded, and sat himself down to write.

'You won't refuse me one request, papa?' continued his daughter; 'you won't refuse to delay your letter for two short days? – two days can make no possible difference.'

'My dear,' said he naïvely, 'if I waited till I got to Barchester, I might, perhaps, be prevented.'

'But surely you would not wish to offend the bishop?' said she.

'God forbid! The bishop is not apt to take offence, and knows me too well to take in bad part anything that I may be called on to do.'

'But, papa——'

'Susan,' he said, 'my mind on this subject is made up; it is not without much repugnance that I act in opposition to the advice of such men as Sir Abraham Haphazard and the archdeacon; but in this matter I can take no advice, I cannot alter the resolution to which I have come.'

'But two days, papa——'

'No, – nor can I delay it. You may add to my present unhappiness by pressing me, but you cannot change my purpose; it will be a comfort to me if you will let the matter rest:' and, dipping his pen into the inkstand, he fixed his eyes intently on the paper.

There was something in his manner which taught his daughter to perceive that he was in earnest; she had at one time ruled supreme in her father's house, but she knew that there were moments when, mild and meek as he was, he would have his way, and the present was an occasion of the sort. She returned, therefore, to her knitting, and very shortly after left the room.

The warden was now at liberty to compose his letter, and, as it was characteristic of the man, it shall be given at full length. The official letter, which, when written, seemed to him to be too formally cold to be sent alone to so dear a friend, was accompanied by a private note: and both are here inserted.

The letter of resignation ran as follows: –

> Chapter Hotel, St Paul's,
> London, – August, 18 – .

My Lord Bishop,

It is with the greatest pain that I feel myself constrained to resign into your Lordship's hands the wardenship of the hospital at Barchester which you so kindly conferred upon me, now nearly twelve years since.

I need not explain the circumstances which have made this step appear necessary to me. You are aware that a question has arisen as to the right of the warden to the income which has been allotted to the wardenship; it has seemed to me that this right is not well made out, and I hesitate to incur the risk of taking an income to which my legal claim appears doubtful.

The office of precentor of the cathedral is, as your Lordship is aware, joined to that of the warden; that is to say, the precentor has for many years been the warden of the hospital; there is, however, nothing to make the junction of the two offices necessary, and, unless you or the dean and chapter object to such an arrangement, I would wish to keep the precentorship. The income of this office will now be necessary to me; indeed, I do not know why I should be ashamed to say that I should have difficulty in supporting myself without it.

Your Lordship, and such others as you may please to consult on the matter, will at once see that my resignation of the wardenship need offer not the slightest bar to its occupation by another person. I am thought in the wrong by all those whom I have consulted in the matter; I have very little but an inward and an unguided conviction of my own to bring me to this step, and I shall, indeed, be hurt to find that any slur is thrown on the preferment which your kindness bestowed on me, by my resignation of it. I, at any rate for one, shall look on any successor whom you may appoint as enjoying a clerical situation of the highest respectability, and one to which your Lordship's nomination gives an indefeasible right.

I cannot finish this official letter without again thanking your Lordship for all your great kindness, and I beg to subscribe myself

Your Lordship's most obedient servant,
SEPTIMUS HARDING,

Warden of Barchester Hospital,
and Precentor of the cathedral.

He then wrote the following private note: —

My dear Bishop,

I cannot send you the accompanying official letter without a warmer expression of thanks for all your kindness than would befit a document which may to a certain degree be made public. You, I know, will understand the feeling, and, perhaps, pity the weakness which makes me resign the hospital. I am not made of calibre strong enough to withstand public attack. Were I convinced that I stood on ground perfectly firm, that I was certainly justified in taking eight hundred a year under Hiram's will, I should feel bound by duty to retain the position, however unendurable might be the nature of the assault; but, as I do not feel this conviction, I cannot believe that you will think me wrong in what I am doing.

I had at one time an idea of keeping only some moderate portion of the income; perhaps three hundred a year, and of remitting the remainder to the trustees; but it occurred to me, and I think with reason, that by so doing I should place my successors in an invidious position, and greatly damage your patronage.

My dear friend, let me have a line from you to say that you do not blame me for what I am doing, and that the officiating vicar of Crabtree Parva will be the same to you as the warden of the hospital.

I am very anxious about the precentorship; the archdeacon thinks it must go with the wardenship; I think not, and that, having it, I cannot be ousted. I will, however, be guided by you and the dean. No other duty will suit me so well, or come so much within my power of adequate performance.

'I thank you from my heart for the preferment which I am now giving up, and for all your kindness, and am, dear bishop, now as always,

Yours most sincerely,*
SEPTIMUS HARDING

London, – August, 18 – .

Having written these letters and made a copy of the former one for the benefit of the archdeacon, Mr Harding, whom we must now cease to call the warden, he having designated himself so for the last time, found that it was nearly two o'clock, and that he must prepare for his journey. Yes, from this time he never again admitted the name by which he had been so familiarly known, and in which, to tell the truth, he had rejoiced. The love of titles is common to all men, and a vicar or fellow is as pleased at becoming Mr Archdeacon or Mr Provost,* as a lieutenant at getting his captaincy, or a city tallow-chandler in becoming Sir John on the occasion of a Queen's visit to a new bridge. But warden he was no longer, and the name of precentor, though the office was to him so dear, confers in itself no sufficient distinction; our friend, therefore, again became Mr Harding.

Mrs Grantly had gone out; he had, therefore, no one to delay him by further entreaties to postpone his journey; he had soon arranged his bag, and paid his bill, and leaving a note for his daughter, in which he put the copy of his official letter, he got into a cab and drove away to the station with something of triumph in his heart.

Had he not cause for triumph? Had he not been supremely successful? Had he not for the first time in his life held his own purpose against that of his son-in-law, and manfully combated against great odds, – against the archdeacon's wife as well as the archdeacon? Had he not gained a great victory, and was it not fit that he should step into his cab with triumph?

He had not told Eleanor when he would return, but she was

on the look-out for him by every train by which he could arrive, and the pony carriage was at Barchester station when the train drew up at the platform.

'My dear,' said he, sitting beside her, as she steered her little vessel to one side of the road to make room for the clattering omnibus as they passed from the station into town; 'I hope you'll be able to feel a proper degree of respect for the vicar of Crabtree.'

'Dear papa,' said she, 'I am so glad.'

There was great comfort in returning home to that pleasant house, though he was to leave it so soon, and in discussing with his daughter all that he had done, and all that he had to do. It must take some time to get out of one house into another; the curate at Crabtree could not be abolished under six months, that is, unless other provision could be made for him; and then the furniture – the most of that must be sold to pay Sir Abraham Haphazard for sitting up till twelve at night. Mr Harding was strangely ignorant as to lawyers' bills; he had no idea, from twenty pounds to two thousand, as to the sum in which he was indebted for legal assistance. True, he had called in no lawyer himself; true, he had been no consenting party to the employment of either Cox and Cummins, or Sir Abraham; he had never been consulted on such matters; – the archdeacon had managed all this himself, never for a moment suspecting that Mr Harding would take upon him to end the matter in a way of his own. Had the lawyers' bills been ten thousand pounds, Mr Harding could not have helped it; but he was not on that account disposed to dispute his own liability. The question never occurred to him; but it did occur to him that he had very little money at his banker's, that he could receive nothing further from the hospital, and that the sale of the furniture was his only resource.

'Not all, papa,' said Eleanor, pleadingly.

'Not quite all, my dear,' said he; 'that is, if we can help it. We must have a little at Crabtree – but it can only be a little; we must put a bold front on it, Nelly; it isn't easy to come down from affluence to poverty.'

And so they planned their future mode of life; the father taking comfort from the reflection that his daughter would soon be freed from it, and she resolving that her father would soon have in her own house a ready means of escape from the solitude of the Crabtree vicarage.

When the archdeacon left his wife and father-in-law at the Chapter Coffee House to go to Messrs Cox and Cummins, he had no very defined idea of what he had to do when he got there. Gentlemen when at law, or in any way engaged in matters requiring legal assistance, are very apt to go to their lawyers without much absolute necessity; – gentlemen when doing so, are apt to describe such attendance as quite compulsory, and very disagreeable. The lawyers, on the other hand, do not at all see the necessity, though they quite agree as to the disagreeable nature of the visit; – gentlemen when so engaged are usually somewhat gravelled* at finding nothing to say to their learned friends; they generally talk a little politics, a little weather, ask some few foolish questions about their suit, and then withdraw, having passed half an hour in a small, dingy waiting-room, in company with some junior assistant-clerk, and ten minutes with the members of the firm; the business is then over for which the gentleman has come up to London, probably a distance of a hundred and fifty miles. To be sure he goes to the play, and dines at his friend's club, and has a bachelor's liberty and bachelor's recreation for three or four days; and he could not probably plead the desire of such gratifications as a reason to his wife for a trip to London.

Married ladies, when your husbands find they are positively obliged to attend their legal advisers, the nature of the duty to be performed is generally of this description.

The archdeacon would not have dreamt of leaving London without going to Cox and Cummins; and yet he had nothing to say to them. The game was up; he plainly saw that Mr Harding in this matter was not to be moved; his only remaining business on this head was to pay the bill and have done with it: and I think it may be taken for granted, that whatever the cause may be that takes a gentleman to a lawyer's chambers, he never goes there to pay his bill.

Dr Grantly, however, in the eyes of Messrs Cox and Cummins represented the spiritualities of the diocese of Barchester, as Mr Chadwick did the temporalities, and was, therefore, too great a man to undergo the half-hour in the clerks' room. It will not be necessary that we should listen to the notes of sorrow in which the archdeacon bewailed to Mr Cox the weakness of his father-in-law, and the end of all their hopes of triumph; nor need we repeat the various exclamations of surprise with which the mournful intelligence was received. No tragedy occurred, though Mr Cox, a short and somewhat bull-necked man, was very near a fit of apoplexy when he first attempted to ejaculate that fatal word – resign!

Over and over again did Mr Cox attempt to enforce on the archdeacon the propriety of urging on Mr Warden the madness of the deed he was about to do.

'Eight hundred a-year!' said Mr Cox.

'And nothing whatever to do!' said Mr Cummins, who had joined the conference.

'No private fortune, I believe,' said Mr Cox.

'Not a shilling,' said Mr Cummins, in a very low voice, shaking his head.

'I never heard such a case in all my experience,' said Mr Cox.

'Eight hundred a-year, and as nice a house as any gentleman could wish to hang up his hat in,' said Mr Cummins.

'And an unmarried daughter, I believe,' said Mr Cox, with much moral seriousness in his tone. The archdeacon only sighed as each separate wail was uttered, and shook his head, signifying that the fatuity of some people was past belief.

'I'll tell you what he might do,' said Mr Cummins, brightening up. 'I'll tell you how you might save it – let him exchange.'

'Exchange where?' said the archdeacon.

'Exchange for a living. There's Quiverful,* of Puddingdale; he has twelve children, and would be delighted to get the hospital. To be sure Puddingdale is only four hundred, but that would be saving something out of the fire: Mr Harding would have a curate, and still keep three hundred or three hundred and fifty.'

The archdeacon opened his ears and listened; he really thought the scheme might do.

'The newspapers,' continued Mr Cummins, 'might hammer away at Quiverful every day for the next six months without his minding them.'

The archdeacon took up his hat, and returned to his hotel, thinking the matter over deeply: at any rate he would sound Quiverful; a man with twelve children would do much to double his income.

Chapter 20

Farewell

On the morning after Mr Harding's return home, he received a note from the bishop full of affection, condolence, and praise. 'Pray come to me at once,' wrote the bishop, 'that we may see what had better be done; as to the hospital, I will not say a word to dissuade you; but I don't like your going to Crabtree: at any rate, come to me at once.'

Mr Harding did go to him at once; and long and confidential was the consultation between the two old friends. There they sat together the whole long day plotting to get the better of the archdeacon, and to carry out little schemes of their own, which they knew would be opposed by the whole weight of his authority.

The bishop's first idea was, that Mr Harding, if left to himself, would certainly starve – not in the figurative sense in which so many of our ladies and gentlemen do starve on incomes from one to five hundred a year; not that he would be starved as regarded dress coats, port wine, and pocket-money; but that he would positively perish of inanition* for want of bread.

'How is a man to live, when he gives up all his income?' said the bishop to himself. And then the good-natured little man began to consider how his friend might be rescued from a death so horrid and painful.

His first proposition to Mr Harding was, that they should live together at the palace. He, the bishop, positively assured Mr Harding that he wanted another resident chaplain: not a young, working chaplain, but a steady, middle-aged chaplain; one who would dine and drink a glass of wine with him, talk about the archdeacon, and poke the fire. The bishop did not positively name all these duties, but he gave Mr Harding to understand that such would be the nature of the service required.

It was not without much difficulty that Mr Harding made his friend see that this would not suit him; that he could not throw up the bishop's preferment, and then come and hang on at the bishop's table; that he could not allow people to say of him that it was an easy matter to abandon his own income, as he was able to sponge on that of another person. He succeeded, however, in explaining that the plan would not do, and then the bishop brought forward another which he had in his sleeve. He, the bishop, had in his will left certain moneys to Mr Harding's two daughters, imagining that Mr Harding would himself want no such assistance during his own lifetime. This legacy amounted to three thousand pounds each, duty free; and he now pressed it as a gift on his friend.

'The girls, you know,' said he, 'will have it just the same when you're gone – and they won't want it sooner – and as for the interest during my lifetime, it isn't worth talking about. I have more than enough.'

With much difficulty and heartfelt sorrow, Mr Harding refused also this offer. No; his wish was to support himself, however poorly, – not to be supported on the charity of any one. It was hard to make the bishop understand this; it was hard to make him comprehend that the only real favour he could confer was the continuation of his independent friendship; but at last even this was done. At any rate, thought the bishop, he will come and dine with me from time to time, and if he be absolutely starving I shall see it.

Touching the precentorship, the bishop was clearly of the opinion that it could be held without the other situation – an opinion from which no one differed; and it was therefore soon settled among all the parties concerned, that Mr Harding should still be the precentor of the cathedral.

On the day following Mr Harding's return, the archdeacon reached Plumstead full of Mr Cummins's scheme regarding Puddingdale and Mr Quiverful. On the very next morning he drove over to Puddingdale, and obtained the full consent of the wretched clerical Priam who was endeavouring to feed his poor Hecuba and a dozen of Hectors* on the small proceeds of his ecclesiastical kingdom. Mr Quiverful had no doubts as to the legal rights of the warden; his conscience would be quite clear as to accepting the income; and as to the *Jupiter*, he begged to assure the archdeacon that he was quite indifferent to any emanations from the profane portion of the periodical press.

Having so far succeeded, he next sounded the bishop; but here he was astonished by most unexpected resistance. The

bishop did not think it would do. 'Not do, why not?' and seeing
that his father was not shaken, he repeated the question in a
severer form: 'Why not do, my lord?'

His lordship looked very unhappy, and shuffled about in his
chair, but still didn't give way; he thought Puddingdale wouldn't
do for Mr Harding; it was too far from Barchester.

'Oh! of course he'll have a curate.'

The bishop also thought that Mr Quiverful wouldn't do for
the hospital; such an exchange wouldn't look well at such a
time; and, when pressed harder, he declared he didn't think Mr
Harding would accept of Puddingdale under any circumstances.

'How is he to live?' demanded the archdeacon.

The bishop, with tears in his eyes, declared that he had not
the slightest conception how life was to be sustained within him
at all.

The archdeacon then left his father, and went down to the
hospital; but Mr Harding wouldn't listen at all to the Puddingdale scheme. To his eyes it had no attraction; it savoured of
simony,* and was likely to bring down upon him harder and
more deserved strictures than any he had yet received: he
positively declined to become vicar of Puddingdale under any
circumstances.

The archdeacon waxed wroth, talked big, and looked bigger;
he said something about dependence and beggary, spoke of the
duty every man was under to earn his bread, made passing
allusions to the follies of youth and waywardness of age, as
though Mr Harding were afflicted by both, and ended by
declaring that he had done. He felt that he had left no stone
unturned to arrange matters on the best and easiest footing; that
he had, in fact, so arranged them, that he had so managed that
there was no further need of any anxiety in the matter. And how
had he been paid? His advice had been systematically rejected;
he had been not only slighted, but distrusted and avoided; he
and his measures had been utterly thrown over, as had been Sir
Abraham, who, he had reason to know, was much pained at
what had occurred. He now found it was useless to interfere any
further, and he should retire. If any further assistance were
required from him, he would probably be called on, and should
be again happy to come forward. And so he left the hospital,
and has not since entered it from that day to this.

And here we must take leave of Archdeacon Grantly. We fear

that he is represented in these pages as being worse than he is; but we have had to do with his foibles, and not with his virtues. We have seen only the weak side of the man, and have lacked the opportunity of bringing him forward on his strong ground. That he is a man somewhat too fond of his own way, and not sufficiently scrupulous in his manner of achieving it, his best friends cannot deny. That he is bigoted in favour, not so much of his doctrines as of his cloth, is also true: and it is true that the possession of a large income is a desire that sits near his heart. Nevertheless, the archdeacon is a gentleman and a man of conscience; he spends his money liberally, and does the work he has to do with the best of his ability; he improves the tone of society of those among whom he lives. His aspirations are of a healthy, if not of the highest, kind. Though never an austere man, he upholds propriety of conduct both by example and precept. He is generous to the poor, and hospitable to the rich; in matters of religion he is sincere, and yet no Pharisee;* he is in earnest, and yet no fanatic. On the whole, the Archdeacon of Barchester is a man doing more good than harm, – a man to be furthered and supported, though perhaps also to be controlled; and it is a matter of regret to us that the course of our narrative has required that we should see more of his weakness than his strength.

Mr Harding allowed himself no rest till everything was prepared for his departure from the hospital. It may be as well to mention that he was not driven to the stern necessity of selling all his furniture: he had been quite in earnest in his intention to do so, but it was soon made known to him that the claims of Messrs Cox and Cummins made no such step obligatory. The archdeacon had thought it wise to make use of the threat of the lawyer's bill, to frighten his father-in-law into compliance; but he had no intention to saddle Mr Harding with costs, which had been incurred by no means exclusively for his benefit. The amount of the bill was added to the diocesan account, and was, in fact, paid out of the bishop's pocket, without any consciousness on the part of his lordship. A great part of his furniture he did resolve to sell, having no other means to dispose of it; and the ponies and carriage were transferred, by private contract, to the use of an old maiden lady in the city.

For his present use Mr Harding took a lodging in Barchester, and thither were conveyed such articles as he wanted for daily

use – his music, books, and instruments, his own armchair, and
Eleanor's pet sofa; her teapoy* and his cellaret,* and also the
slender but still sufficient contents of his wine-cellar. Mrs
Grantly had much wished that her sister would reside at
Plumstead, till her father's house at Crabtree should be ready
for her; but Eleanor herself strongly resisted this proposal. It
was in vain urged upon her, that a lady in lodgings cost more
than a gentleman; and that, under her father's present circumstances, such an expense should be avoided. Eleanor had not
pressed her father to give up the hospital, in order that she
might live at Plumstead Rectory, and he alone in his Barchester
lodgings; nor did Eleanor think that she would be treating a
certain gentleman very fairly, if she betook herself to the house
which he would be the least desirous of entering of any in the
county. So she got a little bedroom for herself behind the sitting-
room, and just over the little back parlour of the chemist, with
whom they were to lodge. There was somewhat of a savour of
senna* softened by peppermint about the place; but, on the
whole, the lodgings were clean and comfortable.

The day had been fixed for the migration of the ex-warden,
and all Barchester were in a state of excitement on the subject.
Opinion was much divided as to the propriety of Mr Harding's
conduct. The mercantile part of the community, the mayor and
corporation, and council, also most of the ladies, were loud in
his praise. Nothing could be more noble, nothing more generous, nothing more upright. But the gentry were of a different
way of thinking, – especially the lawyers and the clergymen.
They said such conduct was very weak and undignified; that Mr
Harding evinced a lamentable want of *esprit de corps*,* as well
as courage; and that such an abdication must do much harm,
and could do but little good.

On the evening before he left, he summoned all the bedesmen
into his parlour to wish them goodbye. With Bunce he had been
in frequent communication since his return from London, and
had been at much pains to explain to the old man the cause of
his resignation, without in any way prejudicing the position of
his successor. The others, also, he had seen more or less
frequently; and had heard from most of them separately some
expression of regret at his departure; but he had postponed his
farewell till the last evening.

He now bade the maid put wine and glasses on the table; and

had the chairs arranged around the room; and sent Bunce to each of the men to request they would come and say farewell to their late warden. Soon the noise of aged scuffling feet was heard upon the gravel and in the little hall, and the eleven men who were enabled to leave their rooms were assembled.

'Come in, my friends, come in,' said the warden – he was still warden then. 'Come in, and sit down;' and he took the hand of Abel Handy, who was the nearest to him, and led the limping grumbler to a chair. The others followed slowly and bashfully: the infirm, the lame, and the blind; poor wretches! who had been so happy, had they but known it! Now their aged faces were covered with shame, and every kind word from their master was a coal of fire burning on their heads.*

When first the news had reached them that Mr Harding was going to leave the hospital, it had been received with a kind of triumph; – his departure was, as it were, a prelude to success. He had admitted his want of right to the money about which they were disputing; and as it did not belong to him, of course it did to them. The one hundred a-year to each of them was actually becoming a reality; and Abel Handy was a hero, and Bunce a faint-hearted sycophant, worthy neither honour nor fellowship. But other tidings soon made their way into the old men's rooms. It was first notified to them that the income abandoned by Mr Harding would not come to them; and these accounts were confirmed by attorney Finney. They were then informed that Mr Harding's place would be at once filled by another. That the new warden could not be a kinder man they all knew; that he would be a less friendly one most suspected; and then came the bitter information that, from the moment of Mr Harding's departure, the twopence a-day, his own peculiar gift, must of necessity be withdrawn.

And this was to be the end of all their mighty struggle – of their fight for their rights – of their petition, and their debates and their hopes! They were to change the best of masters for a possible bad one, and to lose twopence a day each man! No; unfortunate as this was, it was not the worst, or nearly the worst, as will just now be seen.

'Sit down, sit down, my friends,' said the warden. 'I want to say a word to you, and to drink your healths, before I leave you. Come up here, Moody, here is a chair for you; come, Jonathan Crumple – ' and by degrees he got the men to be seated. It was not surprising that they should hang back with faint hearts, having returned so much kindness with such deep ingratitude. Last of all of them came Bunce, and with sorrowful mien and slow step got into his accustomed seat near the fireplace.

When they were all in their places, Mr Harding rose to address them; and then finding himself not quite at home on his legs, he sat down again. 'My dear old friends,' said he, 'you all know that I am going to leave you.'

There was a sort of murmur ran round the room, intended, perhaps, to express regret at his departure; but it was but a murmur, and might have meant that or anything else.

'There has been lately some misunderstanding between us. You have thought, I believe, that you did not get all that you were entitled to, and that the funds of the hospital have not been properly disposed of. As for me, I cannot say what should be the disposition of these moneys, or how they should be managed, and I have therefore thought it best to go.'

'We never wanted to drive your reverence out of it,' said Handy.

'No, indeed, your reverence,' said Skulpit. 'We never thought it would come to this. When I signed the petition – that is, I didn't sign it, because——'

'Let his reverence speak, can't you?' said Moody.

'No,' continued Mr Harding; 'I am sure you did not wish to turn me out; but I thought it best to leave you. I am not a very good hand at a lawsuit, as you may all guess; and when it seemed necessary that our ordinary quiet mode of living should be disturbed, I thought it better to go. I am neither angry nor offended with any man in the hospital.'

Here Bunce uttered a kind of groan, very clearly expressive of disagreement.

'I am neither angry nor displeased with any man in the hospital,' repeated Mr Harding, emphatically. 'If any man has been wrong – and I don't say any man has – he has erred through wrong advice. In this country all are entitled to look for their own rights, and you have done no more. As long as your interests and my interests were at variance, I could give you no counsel on this subject; but the connexion between us has ceased; my income can no longer depend on your doings, and therefore, as I leave you, I venture to offer to you my advice.'

The men all declared that they would from henceforth be entirely guided by Mr Harding's opinion in their affairs.

'Some gentleman will probably take my place here very soon, and I strongly advise you to be prepared to receive him in a kindly spirit, and to raise no further question among yourselves as to the amount of his income. Were you to succeed in lessening what he has to receive, you would not increase your own allowance. The surplus would not go to you; your wants are adequately provided for, and your position could hardly be improved.'

'God bless your reverence, we knows it,' said Spriggs.

'It's all true, your reverence,' said Skulpit; 'we sees it all now.'

'Yes, Mr Harding,' said Bunce, opening his mouth for the first time; 'I believe they do understand it now, now that they've driven from under the same roof with them such a master as not one of them will ever know again – now that they're like to be in sore want of a friend.'

'Come, come, Bunce,' said Mr Harding, blowing his nose, and manoeuvring to wipe his eyes at the same time.

'Oh, as to that,' said Handy, 'we none of us never wanted to do Mr Harding no harm; if he's going now, it's not along of us; and I don't see for what Mr Bunce speaks up agen us that way.'

'You've ruined yourselves, and you've ruined me too, and that's why,' said Bunce.

'Nonsense, Bunce,' said Mr Harding; 'there's nobody ruined at all. I hope you'll let me leave you all friends, I hope you'll all drink a glass of wine in friendly feeling with me and with one another. You'll have a good friend, I don't doubt, in your new warden; and if ever you want any other, why after all I'm not going so far off but that I shall sometimes see you;' and then, having finished his speech, Mr Harding filled all the glasses, and himself handed each a glass to the men round him, and raising his own, said, –

'God bless you all! you have my heartfelt wishes for your welfare. I hope you may live contented, and die trusting in the Lord Jesus Christ, and thankful to Almighty God for the good things he has given you. God bless you, my friends!' and Mr Harding drank his wine.

Another murmur, somewhat more articulate than the first, passed round the circle, and this time it was intended to imply a blessing on Mr Harding. It had, however, but little cordiality in it. Poor old men! how could they be cordial with their sore consciences and shamed faces? how could they bid God bless him with hearty voices and a true benison, knowing, as they did, that their vile cabal had driven him from his happy home, and sent him in old age to seek shelter under a strange roof-tree?* They did their best, however; they drank their wine, and withdrew.

As they left the hall-door, Mr Harding shook hands with each of the men, and spoke a kind word to them about their individual cases and ailments; and so they departed, answering his questions in the fewest words, and retreated to their dens, a sorrowful repentant crew.

All but Bunce, who still remained to make his own farewell. 'There's poor old Bell,' said Mr Harding, 'I mustn't go without saying a word to him; come through with me, Bunce, and bring the wine with you;' and so they went through to the men's cottages, and found the old man propped up as usual in his bed.

'I've come to say good-bye to you, Bell,' said Mr Harding, speaking loud, for the old man was deaf.

'And are you going away, then, really?' asked Bell.

'Indeed I am, and I've brought you a glass of wine; so that we may part friends, as we lived, you know.'

The old man took the proffered glass in his shaking hands, and drank it eagerly. 'God bless you, Bell!' said Mr Harding; 'good-bye, my old friend.'

'And so you're really going?' the man again asked.

'Indeed I am, Bell.'

The poor old bedridden creature still kept Mr Harding's hand in his own, and the warden thought that he had met with something like warmth of feeling in the one of all his subjects from whom it was the least likely to be expected, for poor old Bell had nearly outlived all human feelings. 'And your reverence,' said he, and then he paused, while his old palsied head shook horribly, and his shrivelled cheeks sank lower within his jaws, and his glazy eye gleamed with a momentary light; 'and, your reverence, shall we get the hundred a-year then?'

How gently did Mr Harding try to extinguish the false hope of money which had been so wretchedly raised to disturb the quiet of the dying man! One other week and his mortal coil would be shuffled off;* in one short week would God resume his soul, and set it apart for its irrevocable doom; seven more tedious days and nights of senseless inactivity, and all would be over for poor Bell in this world; and yet, with his last audible words, he was demanding his moneyed rights, and asserting himself to be the proper heir of John Hiram's bounty! Not on him, poor sinner as he was, be the load of such sin!

Mr Harding returned to his parlour, meditating with a sick heart on what he had seen, and Bunce with him. We will not describe the parting of these two good men, for good men they were. It was in vain that the late warden endeavoured to comfort the heart of the old bedesman; poor old Bunce felt that his days of comfort were gone. The hospital had to him been a happy home, but it could be so no longer. He had had honour there, and friendship; he had recognised his master, and been recognised; all his wants, both of soul and body, had been supplied, and he had been a happy man. He wept grievously as he parted from his friend, and the tears of an old man are bitter. 'It is all over for me in this world,' said he, as he gave the last squeeze to Mr Harding's hand; 'I have now to forgive those who have injured me – and to die.'

And so the old man went out, and then Mr Harding gave way to his grief, and he too wept aloud.

CHAPTER 21

Conclusion

Our tale is now done, and it only remains to us to collect the scattered threads of our little story, and to tie them into a seemly knot. This will not be a work of labour, either to the author or to his readers; we have not to deal with many personages, or with stirring events, and were it not for the custom of the thing, we might leave it to the imagination to conceive how affairs at Barchester arranged themselves.

On the morning after the day last alluded to, Mr Harding, at an early hour, walked out of the hospital, with his daughter under his arm, and sat down quietly to breakfast at his lodgings over the chemist's shop. There was no parade about his departure; no one, not even Bunce, was there to witness it: had he walked to the apothecary's thus early to get a piece of court plaster, or a box of lozenges, he could not have done it with less appearance of an important movement. There was a tear in Eleanor's eye as she passed through the big gateway and over the bridge; but Mr Harding walked with an elastic step, and entered his new abode with a pleasant face.

'Now, my dear,' said he, 'you have everything ready, and you can make tea here just as nicely as in the parlour at the hospital.' So Eleanor took off her bonnet and made the tea. After this manner did the late Warden of Barchester Hospital accomplish his flitting, and change his residence.

It was not long before the archdeacon brought his father to discuss the subject of a new warden. Of course he looked upon the nomination as his own, and he had in his eye three or four fitting candidates, seeing that Mr Cummins's plan as to the living of Puddingdale could not be brought to bear. How can I describe the astonishment which confounded him, when his father declared that he would appoint no successor to Mr Harding? 'If we can get the matter set to rights, Mr Harding will return,' said the bishop; 'and if we cannot, it will be wrong to put any other gentleman into so cruel a position.'

It was in vain that the archdeacon argued and lectured, and even threatened; in vain he my-lorded his poor father in his sternest manner; in vain his 'good heavens!' were ejaculated in a tone that might have moved a whole synod, let alone one weak and aged bishop. Nothing would induce his father to fill up the vacancy caused by Mr Harding's retirement.

Even John Bold would have pitied the feelings with which the archdeacon returned to Plumstead: the church was falling, nay, already in ruins; its dignitaries were yielding without a struggle before the blows of its antagonists; and one of its most respected bishops, his own father — the man considered by all the world as being in such matters under his, Dr Grantly's control — had positively resolved to capitulate, and own himself vanquished!

And how fared the hospital under this resolve of its visitor? Badly indeed. It is now some years since Mr Harding left it, and the warden's house is still tenantless. Old Bell has died, and Billy Gazy; the one-eyed Spriggs has drunk himself to death, and three others of the twelve have been gathered into the church-yard mould. Six have gone, and the six vacancies remain unfilled! Yes, six have died, with no kind friend to solace their last moments, with no wealthy neighbour to administer comforts and ease the stings of death.* Mr Harding, indeed, did not desert them; from him they had such consolation as a dying man may receive from his Christian pastor; but it was the occasional kindness of a stranger which ministered to them, and not the constant presence of a master, a neighbour, and a friend.

Nor were those who remained better off than those who died. Dissensions rose among them, and contests for pre-eminence; and then they began to understand that soon one among them would be the last, — some one wretched being would be alone there in that now comfortless hospital, — the miserable relic of what had once been so good and comfortable.

The building of the hospital itself has not been allowed to go to ruins. Mr Chadwick, who still holds his stewardship, and pays the accruing rents into an account opened at a bank for the purpose, sees to that; but the whole place has become disordered and ugly. The warden's garden is a wretched wilderness, the drive and paths are covered with weeds, the flower-beds are bare, and the unshorn lawn is now a mass of long damp grass and unwholesome moss. The beauty of the place is gone; its attractions have withered. Alas! a very few years since it was the prettiest spot in Barchester, and now it is a disgrace to the city.

Mr Harding did not go out to Crabtree Parva. An arrangement was made which respected the homestead of Mr Smith and his happy family, and put Mr Harding into possession of a small living within the walls of the city. It is the smallest possible parish, containing a part of the Cathedral Close and a few old houses adjoining. The church is a singular little Gothic building, perched over a gateway, through which the Close is entered, and is approached by a flight of stone steps which leads down under the archway of the gate. It is no bigger than an ordinary room, – perhaps twenty-seven feet long by eighteen wide, – but still it is a perfect church. It contains an old carved pulpit and reading-desk, a tiny altar under a window filled with dark old-coloured glass, a font, some half-dozen pews, and perhaps a dozen seats for the poor, and also a vestry. The roof is high-pitched, and of black old oak, and the three large beams which support it run down to the side walls, and terminate in gro-tesquely carved faces – two devils and an angel on one side, two angels and a devil on the other. Such is the church of St Cuthbert at Barchester, of which Mr Harding became rector, with a clear income of seventy-five pounds a-year.

Here he performs afternoon service every Sunday, and administers the Sacrament once in every three months. His audience is not large; and, had they been so, he could not have accommodated them: but enough come to fill his six pews, and, on the front seat of those devoted to the poor is always to be seen our old friend Mr Bunce, decently arrayed in his bedesman's gown.

Mr Harding is still precentor of Barchester; and it is very rarely the case that those who attend the Sunday morning service miss the gratification of hearing him chant the Litany, as no other man in England can do it. He is neither a discontented nor an unhappy man; he still inhabits the lodgings to which he went on leaving the hospital, but he now has them to himself. Three months after that time Eleanor became Mrs Bold, and of course removed to her husband's house.

There were some difficulties to be got over on the occasion of the marriage. The archdeacon, who could not so soon overcome his grief, would not be persuaded to grace the ceremony with his presence, but he allowed his wife and children to be there. The marriage took place at the palace, and the bishop himself officiated. It was the last occasion on which he ever did so; and, though he still lives, it is not probable that he will ever do so again.

Not long after the marriage, perhaps six months, when Eleanor's bridal-honours were fading, and persons were beginning to call her Mrs Bold without twittering, the archdeacon consented to meet John Bold at a dinner-party, and since that time they have become almost friends. The archdeacon firmly believes that his brother-in-law was, as a bachelor, an infidel, an unbeliever in the great truths of our religion; but that matrimony has opened his eyes, as it has those of others. And Bold is equally inclined to think that time has softened the asperities of the archdeacon's character. Friends though they are, they do not often revert to the feud of the hospital.

Mr Harding, we say, is not an unhappy man; he keeps his lodgings, but they are of little use to him, except as being the one spot on earth which he calls his own. His time is spent chiefly at his daughter's or at the palace; he is never left alone, even should he wish to be so; and within a twelvemonth of Eleanor's marriage his determination to live at his own lodging had been so far broken through and abandoned, that he consented to have his violoncello permanently removed to his daughter's house.

Every other day a message is brought to him from the bishop. 'The bishop's compliments, and his lordship is not very well to-day, and he hopes Mr Harding will dine with him.' This bulletin as to the old man's health is a myth; for though he is over eighty he is never ill, and will probably die some day, as a spark goes out, gradually and without a struggle. Mr Harding does dine with him very often, which means going to the palace at three and remaining till ten; and whenever he does not the bishop whines, and says that the port wine is corked, and complains that nobody attends to him, and frets himself off to bed an hour before his time.

It was long before the people of Barchester forgot to call Mr Harding by his long well-known name of Warden. It had become so customary to say Mr Warden, that it was not easily dropped. 'No, no,' he always says when so addressed, 'not warden now, only precentor.'

THE END

NOTES

In preparing these notes, we have been grateful for the help provided by both the Penguin edition (ed. Robin Gilmour) and the World's Classics edition (ed. David Skilton) of the novel. We are also indebted to the copy-editor for this edition, Jenny Fellows, and to George Walter of Saint David's University College, Lampeter, for providing the information for some of the more arcane references. [H.O.]

Chapter 1

All biblical references are to the Authorised Version (1611). The abbreviation *OED* stands for *The Oxford English Dictionary*.

p. 3 **Salisbury**: in *An Autobiography* (1883), ch. 5, Trollope records that, in the course of his work for the Post Office 'I visited Salisbury, and whilst wandering there on a midsummer evening round the purlieus of the cathedral I conceived the story of The Warden, – from whence came that series of novels of which Barchester, with its bishops, deans, and archdeacon, was the central site.'

p. 3 **the bishop, dean, and canons**: see Appendix I.

p. 3 **precentor of the cathedral**: see Appendix I.

p. 4 **Theophilus**: given his fanaticism for defending the *status quo* of the Church of England, the archdeacon may be named ironically after St Theophilus of Alexandria, the hot-tempered fifth-century theologian; fiercely opposed to all non-Christian religions, Theophilus conducted virulent campaigns against the non-Christian shrines of North Africa and, with the permission of the emperor Theodosius 1, razed a great many pagan temples, subsequently using the stones of the ruins to construct Christian churches.

p. 4 **archdeacon of Barchester**: see Appendices I and II.

p. 4 **wool-stapler**: 'a merchant who buys wool from the producer, grades it, and sells it to the manufacturer' (*OED*).

p. 4 **wool-carders**: workers who use a 'card' (similar to a comb) to separate the fibres of wool, preparatory to spinning.

p. 4 **bedesmen**: a bedesman/beadsman, is one bound or endowed to pray for the souls of others, deriving from *bead*, an old and obscure word for 'prayer'.

p. 6 **a sum of sixty-two pounds eleven shillings and fourpence**: Gilmour points out that Trollope's arithmetic here is at fault; the total should be £36.10s.

p. 7 **Elysium**: in Greek mythology, the region of the blessed dead. The early Greek authors tell us that entrance to Elysium was restricted to those favoured by the gods, who conferred immortality upon those admitted. Later, however, Elysium began to be perceived in terms similar to Christian notions of Heaven, with entrance gained by the leading of a righteous life.

p. 7 **somewhat scandalises . . . black neck-handkerchief**: Mr Harding's preferred mode of dress proclaims him to be unaffected by the ostentatious clericalism favoured by High Churchmen.

p. 7 **Purcell, Crotch, and Nares**: Henry Purcell (1658?–95), William Crotch (1775–1847), and James Nares (1715–83) were all noted organists and composers of sacred music.

p. 8 *faute de mieux*: for want of better (Fr.).

Chapter 2

p. 9 **the Hospital of St Cross**: see Introduction, p. xvii.

p. 9 **Mr Whiston, at Rochester**: see Introduction, p. xvii.

p. 9 **'Sacerdos'**: priest (Lat.).

p. 11 **The Dragon of Wantly inn**: The name of the inn is appropriate to the novel's examination of Church abuse. 'The Dragon of Wantley' is a comic ballad that features in Thomas Percy's *Reliques of Ancient English Poetry* (1765) and its tale of the slaying of the dragon by 'More of More-Hall' is, as Percy points out in his introduction, a satirical allegory on a specific instance of church abuse: 'Warncliffe Lodge, and Warncliffe Wood (vulgarly pronounced Wantley), are in the parish of Penniston, in Yorkshire. The rectory of Penniston was part of the dissolved monastery of St Stephen's, Westminster; and was granted to the Duke of Norfolk's family: who therewith endowed an hospital, which he built at Sheffield, for women. The trustees let the impropriation of the great Tythes of Penniston to the Wortley family, who got a great deal by it, and wanted to get still more: for Mr Nicholas Wortley attempted to take the tythes in kind, but Mr Francis Bosville opposed him, and there was a decree in favour of the Modus in 37th Eliz . . . [T]he ballad apparently relates to the law-suit carried on concerning this claim of tythes made by the Wortley family . . .' (See *Reliques*, Vol. III, Book the Third, No. 13.)

p. 11 **entitled ... apothecary**: in other words, Bold is entitled to practise medicine and to dispense drugs.

p. 12 **Danton**: George Jacques Danton (1759–94) was one of the principal leaders of the French Revolution, and renowned as a brilliant orator. He was indicted before the Revolutionary Tribunal for financial mismanagement, and guillotined in 1794.

p. 12 **anathemas**: ecclesiastical curses; denunciations of a doctrine or practice as damnable.

p. 12 **a French Jacobin**: the Jacobins were a society of French revolutionaries, of whom Danton was one of the political leaders. They took their name from the disused convent of Saint-Jacques, which served as the headquarters for the society.

p. 13 **as many eyes as Argus**: in Greek mythology, Argus Panoptes had a hundred eyes. After he was murdered by the god Hermes, the goddess Hera placed his eyes in the tail of a peacock, to remind the world of his brutal death.

p. 13 **unlike Homer, he never nods**: cf. Horace, *Ars poetica*, 359: 'Indignor quandoque bonus dormitat Homerus' ('I'm aggrieved when sometimes even excellent Homer nods'). Horace is saying, figuratively, that Homer is occasionally careless in the composition of his poetry (using 'nods' in the sense of 'dozes off'). Hence Trollope means that the archdeacon never ceases to be vigilant in his struggles on behalf of the Church.

p. 14 **shovel-hat**: a hat with a broad brim, turned up at the sides, and projecting in front, worn by clergy of the Church of England.

p. 14 **aprons**: part of the official dress of a bishop.

p. 14 *dishabille*: undress (Fr.).

p. 15 **we cannot say ... even seven times**: an allusion to two seminal examples of Christ's teaching: Matthew 5:40 (from the Sermon on the Mount), 'And if any man will sue thee at the law, and take away thy coat, let him have thy cloke also'; and Matthew 18:21–2, 'Then came Peter to him, and said, Lord, how oft shall my brother sin against me, and I forgive him? till seven times? Jesus saith unto him, I say not unto thee, Until seven times: but, Until seventy times seven.'

pp. 15–16 **every committee ... church revenues**: instigated by Sir Robert Peel in 1835, the Ecclesiastical Duties and Revenues Commission superintended a number of reforms of the Church of England, and was distrusted by High Churchmen.

p. 16 **the sacrilegious doings of Lord John Russell**: the name of Lord John Russell (1792–1878), Whig Prime Minister from 1846 to 1852, had become anathema to the conservative High Church; driven by a deep-seated suspicion and distrust of the perceived leanings towards Catholicism displayed by the High Church, Russell began his premiership determined to appoint liberal theologians to as many positions of authority as possible. Matters came to a crisis when in 1847 Russell nominated the broadly liberal Regius Professor of Divinity at Oxford, Dr R. D. Hampden, for the bishopric of Hereford. Hampden had long been deemed heretical in his theology by the High Churchmen of Oxford, following their wilfully one-sided interpretation of his Bampton Lectures, *The Scholastic Philosophy considered in its relation to Christian Theology* (1832), and his 1834 pamphlet *Observations on Religious Dissent*. Russell's move to appoint Hampden to the see of Hereford thus prompted no fewer than fourteen bishops to oppose the government vociferously. Hampden was eventually consecrated, but not before the case of Queen Victoria versus the Archbishop of Canterbury had gone to court, to test, in Owen Chadwick's words, 'what safeguards the established church possessed if the royal supremacy were abused'. In the event, the government stretched the royal prerogative to its limit, and the High Church rebels were forced to back down. (See Owen Chadwick, *The Victorian Church, Part One: 1829–1859*, London, SCM Press, 1987, pp. 232–50.)

p. 16 **Oxford**: Oxford University, where the High Church party had its base, and from which the Oxford Movement took its name.

p. 18 **six-and-eightpence**: one-third of a pound in imperial currency; the standard minimum fee for a legal transaction.

Chapter 3

p. 20 **St Cecilia**: the patron saint of music.

pp. 21–2 **though the bishop was the constitutional visitor ... an archdeacon**: in other words, as the bishop has been the one appointed under the terms of Hiram's will to oversee the running of the hospital, he and he alone has the right to act in its affairs.

p. 22 **a favourite little bit of Bishop's**: Mr Harding is probably referring to John Bishop (1665–1737), organist at Winchester Cathedral and composer of sacred music, including numerous psalm tunes and anthems, a setting of the Morning and Evening Service and a collection of Latin compositions for use by Winchester College.

p. 25 **appanage**: endowment, perquisite, in the gift of the Bishop of Barchester.

p. 26 **the church militant**: the Church on earth considered as warring against the powers of evil (see note to p. 43 below).

p. 28 **this 'pestilent intruder'**: perhaps a glance at Acts 24:5: 'For we have found this man a pestilent fellow, and a mover of sedition among all the Jews throughout the world.' If Trollope *is* alluding to scripture here, then the satire against the Church is considerably sharpened, as the 'pestilent fellow' referred to in Acts, is, of course, St Paul, the last person one would expect the clerical hierarchy to compare with Bold, the vehement critic of the Established Church's authority.

p. 29 **the sacred bench**: the bench of bishops in the House of Lords.

p. 29 **cowls, sandals, and sackcloth**: the dress of monastic orders; the associations with Catholicism had led to them being outlawed.

p. 29 **arcana**: secrets, mysteries.

p. 29 **the Trinity**: in Christian doctrine, the perceived unity of Father, Son and Holy Spirit as three persons in one Godhead.

Chapter 4

p. 30 **'fiat justitia ruat coelum'**: let justice be done, though the heavens fall' (Lat.). The maxim was common at least as far back as 1600, but gained its widest celebrity in 1768, when quoted by Lord Mansfield as he overturned the sentence of outlawry passed on John Wilkes for publication of the *North Briton*: 'The constitution does not allow reasons of state to influence our judgement. God forbid it should! We must not regard political consequences, however formidable they might be; if rebellion was the certain consequence we are bound to say "Justitia fiat, ruat coelum."'

p. 31 **recusant**: historically, one who refused to attend Church of England services; hence, one who refuses submission to authority, or compliance with regulation.

p. 31 ***non compos mentis***: not in his right mind (Lat.).

p. 36 **by goles**: by golly.

Chapter 5

p. 38 **Sir Abraham Haphazard**: Trollope's attorney-general is named ironically; the weight of legal authority connoted by 'Abraham' (the law-giving patriarch of the Old Testament) is undermined by the less-than-confidence-inspiring 'Haphazard'.

p. 38 **that scoundrel Horsman**: Edward Horsman (1807–76), politician notoriously critical of the Church, accusing even Lord John Russell's views and policies on the relationship between Church and State as being too favourable to the bishops.

p. 38 **the Bishop of Beverley's income**: there was no Anglican Bishop of Beverley. Gilmour points out that Beverley was in fact an old Anglo-Saxon see; David Skilton suggests that Trollope could be thinking of R. M. Beverley, the dissenting pamphleteer who was a fierce critic of Church abuses. However, when Pope Pius IX finally approved, in 1850, of the instituting of thirteen Catholic bishoprics in England, Beverley and Hexham, because of their ancient origins, were deemed suitable choices for two of the sees. Nevertheless, it seems hardly likely that the archdeacon would look favourably upon any lawyer who staunchly defended the rights of a Catholic bishop.

p. 38 *par excellence*: literally, 'by excellence' (Fr.): superior to all others of the same sort.

p. 38 **that fellow at Rochester**: Robert Whiston. (See Introduction, p. xvii.)

p. 38 **Sir Benjamin Hall**: Hall (1807–76) was another politician, and an active critic of the Established Church.

p. 39 **Jewel's library**: John Jewel (1522–71), a prominent Elizabethan advocate of the authority of the Established Church, became Bishop of Salisbury in 1560, and authorised the building of the cathedral library.

p. 42 **a long pull . . . a pull altogether**: a rallying-cry apparently given by the playwright Richard Brinsley Sheridan as the conclusion to an election address at the Westminster hustings: 'From speaking of a proper member for Parliament, Mr Sh*r*d*n, somehow or other, contrived to shift the subject to himself, of whom he gave a very pleasing account indeed. He told us, in general terms, that he had done surprising things for the country; but was tender of descending to particulars; probably because the law does not oblige a criminal to convict himself . . . He concluded his harangue with this elegant exhortation. *Now my friends, let us have a long pull, a strong pull, and a pull altogether!*' (From *All the Talents; A Satirical Poem, in Three Dialogues, by Polypus* [1807; 'Polypus' = Eaton Stannard Barrett, 1786–1820].)

p. 42 **'to his own cheek'**: to/for his own satisfaction.

p. 43 **church militant here on earth**: Trollope paraphrases the *Book of Common Prayer*: 'Let us pray for the whole state of Christ's Church militant here in earth' (Holy Communion, Prayer after offertory).

p. 46 **that wretched clerical octogenarian Croesus**: referring to the Earl of Guilford (see Introduction, p. xvii); Croesus, king of Lydia 560–546 BC, amassed a huge fortune through trade, his name becoming proverbial for immense wealth.

p. 47 **brougham**: a one-horse closed carriage, named after Lord Brougham (1778–1868).

Chapter 6

p. 50 **the consolation of a Roman**: from putting the pursuit of abstract justice before personal considerations. See below.

p. 51 **the Barchester Brutus**: referring to Lucius Junius Brutus, whose name became proverbial for remorseless justice. Brutus is held to have founded the Roman Republic in 509 BC, and then to have condemned his own sons to death when they conspired to restore to the throne of Rome the deposed House of Tarquin.

p. 52 **mad reforms even at Oxford**: in 1850, Lord John Russell, suspicious of the Tractarians, and aware that Oxford University (owing to the many publicity-generating theological quarrels there) was losing its esteem with the public, appointed a Royal Commission to examine the various theological structures and strictures that governed the university. The Commission reported in 1852, and the eventual outcome was that Dissenters (Nonconformists) were finally given the right to be educated at Oxford and Cambridge.

p. 52 **the damnable heresies of Dr Whiston**: see Introduction, p. xvii.

p. 52 **sconces**: candlesticks, either bracketed or with handles.

p. 52 **Apollo**: the Greek god of light, divine retribution and music. The reference here is to the god's legendary beauty, as well as to his musical ability.

pp. 52–4 **And now the crash begins ... a poor deuce**: the passages here are an elaborate pastiche of the mock-heroic discourse of Pope's *Rape of the Lock* (1712).

p. 53 **syncope**: a fainting fit.

p. 53 **prebendaries**: see Appendix I.

p. 53 **short whist**: immediate forerunner to bridge, inasmuch as scoring only begins after the sixth trick has been taken. Honours are scored separately at the end of each game.

Chapter 7

p. 59 **the daily Jupiter**: Trollope is alluding to *The Times* newspaper. 'The Thunderer' was a common nickname for *The Times*; Jupiter, of course, was the king of the gods in Roman mythology, with a propensity for hurling thunderbolts. (See also Appendix III.)

p. 60 **They say ... against him**: for the 1878 Chapman & Hall edition of the 'Chronicles of Barsetshire', and presumably mindful of the contemporary specificity that gave *The Warden* much of its original impetus, Trollope made a number of small amendments. Here, the 1878 edition updates the circulation figures of the *Jupiter*: 'They say that eighty thousand copies of the *Jupiter* are daily sold, and that each copy is read by five persons at the least. Four hundred thousand readers etc.'

p. 60 **Addison**: Joseph Addison (1672–1719), English essayist and politician, who in 1711 co-founded the *Spectator*.

p. 60 **Junius**: the pseudonymous author of a series of virulent attacks in the form of letter-articles, appearing between 1769 and 1772, attacking George III and his ministers.

p. 61 **Lord Chancellor**: head of the judiciary in England and Wales, and Speaker of the House of Lords.

pp. 61–2 **Sir Abraham . . . jesuitical symbols**: a parody of the Recovery of Personal Liberty in Certain Cases Bill, introduced in the House in 1853, which sought to appoint commissioners to effect the liberation of any woman detained in a Roman Catholic convent 'against her Will'.

p. 62 **a bill for compelling . . . utterly harmless**: Skilton points out that the second reading of the Recovery of Personal Liberty Bill 'fell on the same day as the resumption of the debate on the Excise Duties on Spirits Bill with a controversy about allowances on Irish and Scotch spirits'. As the Scots and Irish lobbies wanted preferential allowances to stimulate artificially respective home markets, Trollope satirically compounds and ridicules this by linking the whisky debate to his imaginary proposed enforcement of the wearing of poplin by Irishwomen; poplin was a type of fabric largely manufactured in Ireland.

Chapter 8

p. 64 **worreted**: worried.

p. 64 **Charles James, Henry, and Samuel**: what follow are satirical portraits of three bishops of the contemporary Church: Charles James Blomfield (1787–1857), Bishop of London 1828–56; Henry Phillpotts (1778–1860), Bishop of Exeter 1830–69; and Samuel Wilberforce (1805–73), Bishop of Oxford 1845–69.

p. 64 **he never committed himself**: Blomfield had developed a reputation for cowardly indecision after he abstained from the vote in the Lords that defeated the first Reform Bill, in 1831. His excuse, that he was in mourning for his father, was somewhat undermined by his giving a public address at the opening of King's College, London, the very next morning after the vote. Blomfield thus found himself vilified by both the Whig and the Tory press, the former complaining that an abstention was, in the circumstances, tantamount to a vote against the bill, the latter accusing the bishop of weak-minded shilly-shallying. (See Chadwick, pp. 24–47.)

p. 65 **his fault ... compromise:** Blomfield's reputation suffered a further blow when, in 1842, he unwittingly precipitated one of the many controversies that dogged the Church throughout the latter half of the nineteenth century, over the place of ritual in the Anglican church service. Low Church in his sympathies, so naturally suspicious of the taint of popery that coloured too-strict observances of ritual, yet mindful not to appear too evangelical, he decreed that every clergyman in his diocese should obey as literally as possible the rubric of the Prayer Book (which, ambiguous in its tenets, was susceptible to being interpreted and appropriated by clergymen to jusify either High or Low Church theologies). The vastness of his diocese meant that he presided over clergymen and congregations of every caste, some of whom flagrantly disobeyed him, some of whom accepted his ruling with enthusiasm, and some of whom obeyed reluctantly, only to find themselves accused of popery by their congregations, naturally suspicious of the consequent changes (which were perceived as popish innovations). Blomfield 'began by rebuking congregations with the brusqueness which flowed from his pen. Soon he was privately advising his clergy not to obey the rubric after all. But if one of his clergy insisted on the rubric, Blomfield could hardly avoid backing him against the people. He found himself in the unusual predicament of writing private letters to some clergymen urging them to yield and public letters to other clergymen pronouncing them right in not yielding' (Chadwick, p. 216).

p. 65 **The second ... brilliant boy:** that Henry should be the archdeacon's favourite is no surprise, as Bishop Phillpotts was a Tory of the extreme right, and one of the most belligerent clergymen of the nineteenth century, shocking his fellow-bishops in the Lords with the violence of his speeches and, in Chadwick's words, 'teaching the establishment that aggression is the best defence'.

p. 65 **He appeared once ... being successful:** in other words, Phillpotts could appear at will either as a champion of Protestantism or as an apologist for Catholicism. This charge of Trollope's is slightly puzzling, as the last thing Phillpotts was was equivocal over the status and authority of the Church of England. Even so, Trollope may be referring to the troubled relationship between Britain and the Papal States that loomed large during the early 1850s. Prior to 1848, the British government was prevented by law from recognising the existence of the pope. In an effort to ease the perennially troubled Irish situation, and to facilitate support of the Italians against Austrian oppression, Russell appointed an ambassador to Rome in 1847, and in 1848 hurried a bill through parliament designed to legalise such diplomatic representation. Phillpotts was one of the few prominent Tories to oppose it. However, when the pope decided in 1850 to authorise the establishment of Catholic bishoprics in England, popular anti-Catholic prejudice reached such heights that High Churchmen like Phillpotts were deemed guilty of popery by association, and on Guy Fawkes Night of that year, the crowd at Exeter, the Gorham controversy fresh in their mind (see below), needed to be restrained from burning an effigy of Phillpotts alongside effigies of the pope and Cardinal Wiseman. (See Chadwick, pp. 284–308.)

p. 65 **He was also sent . . . perversity of his nature**: Phillpotts's natural belligerence and inflexibility initiated a number of controversies within his own diocese, most significantly the surplice riots of 1844 and – especially – the Gorham controversy, which ran from 1846 to 1850, and which created havoc within the Church of England. The former were a development of the ritual controversy started by Blomfield. To avoid creating the same sort of difficulties that the Bishop of London had made for himself, Phillpotts gave precise instructions to each of his clergy, ordering them to wear the surplice while preaching and to institute weekly collections. The parishioners within the diocese, who perceived the wearing of the surplice as reeking of popery, and who no doubt were not best pleased to be confronted suddenly with compulsory offertories, objected in the strongest possible terms; the palace at Exeter was besieged by poison-pen letters, the dean and chapter disagreed publicly with the bishop, and Phillpotts was regularly vilified in the national press until, eventually, he was forced to retract. The Gorham controversy was more protracted, and much more serious. In 1846, George Cornelius Gorham was installed in the parish of St Just with Penwith, in Cornwall. Phillpotts was soon aghast to discover that Gorham was fanatically evangelical, especially over the issue of baptism, and almost as combative as the bishop himself. In 1847 Gorham requested a move to the parish of Brampford Speke, just outside Exeter. Phillpotts refused to install him. Gorham pressed on, and asked the Court of Arches to force Phillpotts to institute him. Phillpotts, meanwhile, was declaring that Gorham's views on baptism were those of a heretic. Such talk precipitated a crisis over doctrinal definition, and Phillpotts found himself opposed not only by evangelicals, but by all those suspicious of Tractarianism in general, and all those supicious of Phillpotts in particular. The case continued, gathering momentum and attracting much adverse publicity for the Church of England, for the next three years, until eventually, in 1850, the judicial committee of the Privy Council found in favour of Gorham. (See Chadwick, pp. 250–71.)

pp. 65–6 **But perhaps Samuel . . . modulating his voice**: the reputation of Wilberforce, whose unctuous manner seemed to give the lie to his characteristic outpourings of sincerity, was another casualty of the Hampden affair (see note to p. 16 above). The majority of English clergy wanted Dr Hampden's orthodoxy firmly established before his being consecrated, and as his Oxford professorship had attached to it the living of Ewelme in the diocese of Oxford, it was permissible that Hampden might be cross-questioned under the Church Discipline Act of 1840. Wilberforce, as Bishop of Oxford, was in charge of the preliminary investigations. Wilberforce pored over Hampden's Bampton Lectures, and eventually wrote to the professor, stating that the withdrawal of the lectures and the pamphlet *Observations on Religious Dissent* would ensure the dropping of any suit against him. Hampden refused, so Wilberforce declared that the suit must go forward. However, as the Archbishop of Canterbury let it be known that he was not in favour of the suit, and as Wilberforce received word from Edward Hawkins, Provost of Oriel and supporter of Hampden, that not only was the objectionable *Observations* being sold without Hampden's consent, but that the professor was prepared to amend the more dubious passages of the Bampton Lectures, Wilberforce was relieved to be able to declare that a renewed inspection of Hampden's declarations found the professor suitably orthodox in his beliefs. The suddenness and completeness of this volte-face ensured Wilberforce's reputation for trimming, and the currency of the nickname 'Slippery Sam' (later giving way to 'Soapy Sam') increased greatly. (See Chadwick, pp. 243–5)

p. 68 **man shall not live by bread alone**: cf. Deuteronomy 8:3, and Matthew 4:4.

p. 69 **a volume of Rabelais**: François Rabelais (*c.* 1494–*c.* 1553), French monk and satirist most famous for his *Pantagruel* (1532) and *Gargantua* (1534), twin satires which mock (among other things) the church hierarchy for its unshakeable belief in its own authority. Its numerous scatological references made it highly improper reading for the Victorians. That a high-ranking clergyman of the Church of England should indulge in reading Rabelais would thus, in terms of Victorian propriety, be unthinkable.

p. 69 **Panurge**: a character in Rabelais's *Pantagruel*.

p. 71 **all the skill of Bramah or of Chubb**: Joseph Bramah (1748–1814) and Jeremiah Chubb (dates unknown), both inventors of locks so secure that professional thieves were invited to try and pick them. Bramah was so confident that his combination lock (1784) was burglar-proof, that he offered a 200-guinea prize to anybody who could pick it successfully.

p. 71 **nonsuited**: in English law, a nonsuit is the stopping of a suit, either by the voluntary withdrawal of the plaintiff, or by the judge when the plaintiff fails to make out cause of action or to bring sufficient evidence.

Chapter 9

p. 74 'A rose, you know – ': Mr Harding is about to quote from Shakespeare's *Romeo and Juliet*, II, ii, 43–4:

> What's in a name? that which we call a rose
> By any other name would smell as sweet.

p. 75 the *ipsissima verba*: the very words (Lat.).

p. 79 the case against . . . Rochester: see Introduction, p. xvii.

Chapter 10

p. 82 more sinned against than sinning: cf. *King Lear*, III, ii, 59–60.

p. 85 the Quakers . . . Emperor of Russia: the Crimean War against Russia (1854–6) was vigorously opposed by Richard Cobden (1804–65), statesman and champion of Corn Law repeal, and by his close political associate the Quaker John Bright (1811–89).

p. 85 one Tom Towers: see Appendix III.

p. 87 Yes, they would . . . the ungrateful place: see Christ's injunction to his disciples, Luke 9:5: 'And whosoever will not receive you, when ye go out of that city, shake off the very dust from your feet for a testimony against them.'

p. 89 not if all Oxford were to convocate together: the Oxford Convocation, the legislative body of the University, would often make pronouncements upon ecclesiastical matters.

Chapter 11

p. 90 Agamemnon . . . Iphigenia: the 100-strong fleet commanded by Agamemnon at the outset of the Trojan wars was prevented from leaving the port of Aulis by strong winds sent by the goddess Artemis, whom Agamemnon had offended. To appease the goddess, the Greek commander was forced to sacrifice his daughter Iphigenia.

p. 90 Jephthah's daughter: the Israelite commander Jephthah made a vow to God that if He granted the Israelites victory over the Ammonites, then 'whatsoever cometh forth of the doors of my house to meet me . . . shall surely be the Lord's, and I will offer it up for a burnt offering'. Unfortunately, he was greeted by his daughter upon his return, and after two months 'bewail[ing] her virginity upon the mountains', she was duly sacrificed. (See Judges 11:30–40.)

p. 91 triste: sad (Fr.).

p. 92 to screw up her courage: cf. *Macbeth*. I, vii, 62–3:

> But screw your courage to the sticking-place;
> And we'll not fail.

p. 93 **the intended falsehood stuck in her throat**: cf. *Macbeth*, II, ii, 32–3:

> Wherefore could not I pronounce 'Amen'?
> I had most need of blessing, and 'Amen'
> Stuck in my throat.

p. 97 **filthy lucre**: proverbial for money as a corrupting influence. The context in which it is employed here makes the clerical associations of its scriptural origins (I Timothy 3:1–3) especially pertinent: 'If a man desire the office of a bishop, he desireth a good work. A bishop then must be blameless, the husband of one wife, vigilant, sober, of good behaviour, given to hospitality, apt to teach; Not given to wine, no striker, not greedy of filthy lucre; but patient, not a brawler, not covetous.'

p. 100 **the altar on the shore of the modern Aulis**: see first note to p. 90 above.

Chapter 12

p. 101 **the Lydian school ... Beverley**: in Sheridan's comedy *The Rivals* (1775), Lydia Languish spurns the attentions of Captain Absolute, the wealthy suitor chosen for her by her aunt. Absolute assumes the identity of the penniless Ensign Beverley, and woos her successfully.

p. 102 **glebe**: the land attached to a parish church.

p. 103 **sanctum sanctorum**: literally, 'the holy of holies' (Lat.); a sanctuary, a place of privacy.

p. 103 **the last pamphlet ... Dr Hampden**: see last note to p. 16 above.

p. 103 **Chrysostom ... Dr Phillpotts**: prominent divines who championed the cause of Church authority against State interference: St John Chrysostom (*c.* 347–407) was Archbishop of Constantinople (398–404), whose preaching against the abuse of wealth led to a conspiracy against him by the empress Eudoxia and Theophilus of Alexandria (see first note to p. 4 above); St Augustine (d. 604) was the first Archbishop of Canterbury (601–4), who converted King Ethelbert to Christianity; Thomas à Becket (1118?–70), Archbishop of Canterbury (1162–70), was murdered on the orders of Henry II for defending the Church's prerogative against secular interference; Cardinal Wolsey (1474?–1530) was Henry VIII's Lord Chancellor (1515–30) and Archbishop of York (1514–30), eventually charged with high treason when he failed to get sanction from the pope for Henry's divorce from

Catherine of Aragon; William Laud (1573–1645) was the fanatical Archbishop of Canterbury (from 1633) whose vigorous persecution of Puritans led to his eventual impeachment and execution. For Phillpotts, see notes to p. 65 above.

p. 106 **phasis**: aspect; stage of advancement.

Chapter 13

p. 108 **to magnify her own good offices**: cf. Romans 11:13: 'inasmuch as I am the apostle of the Gentiles, I magnify mine office.'

p. 112 **Charity may be given ... immediate reward**: an ironically worldly adaptation of Matthew 6:3–4: 'But when thou doest alms, let not thy left hand know what thy right hand doeth: That thine alms may be in secret: and thy Father which seeth in secret himself shall reward thee openly.'

p. 113 **'every one knows where his own shoe pinches!'**: this saying dates back at least as far as Chaucer: cf. *The Merchant's Tale*, 1.1553: 'But I woot best where wryngeth me my sho.'

p. 114 **Crabtree Canonicorum is in the gift ... to be unique**: although the recommendations of the Ecclesiastical Commission became law by three acts of parliament (the Established Church Act of 1836, the Pluralities Act of 1838 and the Dean and Chapter Act of 1840), rendering the existence of such Church abuses listed here technically illegal, nevertheless the reforms tended only to be implemented after each affected living fell vacant; hence absenteeism of the sort described here, and the holding of two or more livings, were both still relatively common. (In *Barchester Towers* [1857] the evangelical Bishop Proudie insists on Dr Stanhope's return to the diocese.)

Chapter 14

p. 117 **Mount Olympus**: Trollope, merging Greek and Roman mythologies, extends his 'Jupiter' analogy, by referring to the offices of the newspaper as 'Mount Olympus', the home of the gods.

p. 117 **Pica**: a size of printer's type.

p. 117 **that wondrous habitation of gods and devils**: Trollope indulges in a bit of word-play here; a 'printer's devil' was the term for an errand-boy in a printing-office.

p. 117 **Castalian ink**: in Greek mythology the spring of Castalia, on Mount Parnassus, was said to have powers of poetic inspiration.

p. 117 **fane**: temple.

p. 117 **infallible bulls**: papal edicts.

p. 118 **Lord John Russell**: see first note to p. 16 above.

p. 118 **Palmerston and Gladstone**: Lord Palmerston (1784–1865), Home Secretary from 1852–1855, succeeded Lord Aberdeen as Prime Minister in 1855. William Gladstone (1809–98) was Chancellor of the Exchequer from 1852 to 1855.

p. 118 **fifty thousand impressions**: the 1878 edition alters this figure to eighty thousand.

p. 120 **ambrosia . . . nectar**: the food and drink of the gods.

p. 120 **Themis**: the Greek goddess of law and justice; her 'abode' is the Temple, between Fleet Street and the Thames, which housed lawyers and students attached to two of the four Inns of Court.

p. 120 **the rich tide . . . city's tribute**: Trollope's ironic description of the untreated sewage that poured into the Thames. The Tower of London was popularly supposed to have been built under the auspices of Julius Caesar; Sir Charles Barry (1795–1860) was the designer of the new Houses of Parliament, built between 1840 and 1867, after the original buildings were destroyed by fire in 1834.

p. 120 **Old St Dunstan**: the church of St Dunstan in the West, in Fleet Street, was rebuilt in 1829–33. The 'bell-smiting bludgeoners' were (and are) the figures on the church's clock, armed with clubs, which struck the hours and quarters.

p. 120 **the bar itself is to go**: Temple Bar, the archway between the Strand and Fleet Street which marked the outer limit of the City of London, was finally removed in 1878.

p. 121 **valetudinarian**: tending 'to be in weak health or to be much concerned about one's own health' (*OED*).

p. 121 **the Paphian goddess**: there was a shrine to Aphrodite, the Greek goddess of love and beauty, at Paphos in Cyprus.

p. 121 **the wildest worshipper . . . adored**: the cult of the Greek god Dionysus (Bacchus in Roman mythology) was notorious for the religious frenzy it provoked in its subscribers, as well as for the licentiousness of its orgiastic festivals, the Dionysia (Bacchanalia).

p. 121 **the tenth Muse who now governs the periodical press**: the Muses of classical mythology were nine sisters, each one representing a different branch of the arts.

p. 121 **Pembroke**: a small table with hinged flaps, supported by four legs joined to the central piece.

p. 121 **Stafford House**: the notoriously opulent town house of the Duke of Sutherland (now Lancaster House).

p. 121 **Sir Robert Peel, by Power**: Sir Robert Peel (1788–1850), Tory Prime Minister in 1834 and 1841–6. In 1846 he split his party by repealing the Corn Laws, which had served the agricultural interest by maintaining home-grown corn at artificially high prices. Trollope thought him an unprincipled opportunist, and launches a vicious attack on him in his civil service novel *The Three Clerks* (1858). Hiram Powers (1805–73) was a noted American sculptor.

p. 122 **a singularly long figure ... by Millais**: John Everett Millais (1829–96), one of the founders of the Pre-Raphaelite brotherhood, a group of artists and poets who sought to restore to British art some of the vitality of the period prior to the High Renaissance (Raphael lived from 1483 to 1520). The paintings of the Pre-Raphaelites are characterised by obsessive attention to detail, ponderous moral significance and a gaudy use of bold colours. The figures in their paintings, as Trollope here intimates, were often unnaturally willowy and stiff-looking.

p. 122 **devotional lady ... ever looked before**: Gilmour identifies this painting as being *Convent Thoughts*, which was not by Millais at all but by the artist Charles Allston Collins.

p. 122 **the old stock groups ... two children**: favourite subjects for painting by the artists of the Renaissance. St Sebastian (d. *c.* 288), according to legend, was a captain in the Roman guard under the emperor Diocletian. When it was discovered he was a Christian, he was ordered to be killed by his own archers. His martyrdom was depicted by, among others, Botticelli, Perugino, El Greco, Mantegna and Bernini. St Lucia (d. 304), another early Christian martyr, came to be thought of as the patron saint of sight (because of her name's connotations of light), and was often depicted by medieval artists carrying a dish that contained her eyes. St Lorenzo (d. 258) was one of the seven deacons of the Roman Church executed by the emperor Valerian. Legend has it that he was roasted to death on a gridiron. The Virgin is the Virgin Mary, the children are Christ and John the Baptist.

p. 122 **a Sybarite**: Sybaris was a Greek city in ancient Italy whose inhabitants were noted for luxurious living.

p. 122 **tiger**: a boy in livery, so called after the striped black-and-yellow uniform.

Chapter 15

p. 125 **Dr Pessimist Anticant**: a satirical portrait of Thomas Carlyle (1795–1881), the massively influential nineteenth-century cultural critic.

p. 125 **he had studied ... worthlessness**: after reading Madame de

Staël's *De l'Allemagne*, Carlyle became fascinated with German art and literature. His first piece of criticism on German letters was an essay, published in the *Edinburgh Review*, on Goethe's *Faust* (1822). This was followed by an ambitious translation of Goethe's *Wilhelm Meister* (1824), the widely praised *Life of Schiller* (1825), and the four-volume *German Romance: Specimens of its Chief Authors with Biographical and Critical Notices* (1827). Carlyle's collected *Critical and Miscellaneous Essays* (1838) also contained a large number of articles on German literature.

p. 126 **he ridiculed ... a gauger of beer-barrels**: Robert Burns (1759–96) settled in Dumfriesshire in 1788, and the following year secured a post as an excise officer, this enabling him to move to Dumfries in 1791. Carlyle, who was from Ecclefechan in Dumfriesshire, held Burns in extremely high regard: 'You would think it strange if I called Burns the most gifted British soul we had in all that century of his: and yet I believe the day is coming when there will be little danger in saying so.' (Lecture V, 'The Hero as Man of Letters', in *On Heroes, Hero-Worship and the Heroic in History*, 1840. In Carlyle's *Latter-Day Pamphlets* (1850), where the messianic tone that Trollope parodies here is much in evidence, Carlyle writes of Burns in terms very similar to those of the parodist: 'From the lowest and broadest stratum of Society, where the births are by the million, there was born, almost in our own memory, a Robert Burns; son of one who "had not capital for his poor moor-farm of Twenty Pounds a-year." Robert Burns never had the smallest chance to get into Parliament, much as Robert Burns deserved, for all our sakes, to have been found there. For the man, – it was not known to men purblind, sunk in their poor dim vulgar element, but might have been known to men of insight who had any loyalty or royalty of their own, – was a born king of men: full of valour, of intelligence and heroic nobleness; fit for far other work than to break his heart among poor mean mortals, gauging beer! Him no Tenpound Constituency chose, nor did any reforming Premier: in the deep-sunk British nation, overwhelmed in foggy stupor, with the loadstars all gone out for it, there was no whisper of a notion that it could be desirable to choose him, – except to come and dine with you, and in the interim to gauge. And yet heaven-born Mr Pitt, at that period, was by no means without need of Heroic intellect, for other purposes than gauging! But sorrowful strangulation by redtape, much tighter then than it now is when so many revolutionary earthquakes have tussled it, quite tied up the meagre Pitt; and he said, on hearing of this Burns and his sad hampered case, "Literature will take care of itself." – "Yes, and of you too, if you don't mind it!" answers one' (Number III, 'Downing Street').

p. 126 **the signs of the times**: Carlyle's own 'The Signs of the Times', an attack on Utilitarianism, appeared in *The Edinburgh Review* in 1829. The phrase is biblical in its origin; cf. Matthew 16:3: 'ye can discern the face of the sky; but can ye not discern the signs of the times?'

p. 127 **We were unwilling ... written enough**: referring to the anti-Parliamentary sections of *Latter-Day Pamphlets*.

p. 127 **Chubb's patent**: Jeremiah Chubb patented his 'detector' lock in 1818. This was gradually improved by his brother Charles (d. 1845), and further patents were taken out in 1824, 1828 and 1833. (See first note to p. 71 above.)

p. 127 **Lord John Russell ... Molesworth**: prominent contemporary politicians. For Russell, see first note to p. 16 above; Lord Aberdeen (1784–1860) was Prime Minister from 1852 to 1855, during the composition of *The Warden;* Lord Derby (1799–1869) was Prime Minister in 1852 and led the protectionist Tories in opposition to Peel; for Palmerston and Gladstone, see second note to p. 214 above; Benjamin Disraeli (1804–81) was Chancellor of the Exchequer in 1852, and a champion of the protectionists; Sir William Molesworth (1810–55) was a Radical politician under Aberdeen.

p. 127 **Dr Anticant's monthly pamphlet on the decay of the world**: Carlyle's *Latter-Day Pamphlets* were issued monthly.

p. 128 **a comparison ... the latter**: as Gilmour points out, Trollope here alludes to the rhetorical structure of Carlyle's *Past and Present* (1843), in which, for example, the modern St Ives workhouse is contrasted unfavourably with the medieval monastery of St Edmundsbury.

p. 128 **that better treasure to which thieves do not creep in**: cf. Matthew 6:19–21: 'Lay not up for yourselves treasure upon earth, where moth and dust doth corrupt, and where thieves break through and steal: But lay up for yourselves treasures in heaven, where neither moth nor dust corrupt, and where thieves do not break through nor steal: For where your treasure is, there will your heart be also.'

p. 128 **Belgrave Square**: fashionable district of London.

p. 129 **great Britons that never will be slaves**: a paraphrase of the verse, famously set to music by Thomas Arne (1710–78), from Act II of *Alfred: A Masque* (1740), by James Thomson (1700–48):

> Rule, Britannia, rule the waves;
> Britons never will be slaves.

p. 129 **Mr Popular Sentiment's new novel**: Mr Sentiment is Trollope's satirical portrait of Charles Dickens (1812–70). Trollope was not an especial admirer of Dickens's work, thinking that the tendency to exaggeration, and Dickens's idiosyncratic use of language, both got in the way of the realistic enterprise that Trollope saw as the principal criterion of good novelistic practice. *The Warden* is Trollope's response to the sort of fictional representation he deplored so much in Dickens's writing, just as the later *The Three Clerks* is intended as a response and a corrective to Dickens's unfair portrayal of the civil service in *Little Dorrit* (1855–7), Trollope's Weights and Measures Department being a criticism, through fiction, of Dickens's own Circumlocution Office. In *An Autobiography* (ch. 13), Trollope writes: 'I do acknowledge that Mrs Gamp, Micawber, Pecksniff, and others have become household words in every house, as though they were human beings; but to my judgement they are not human beings, nor are any of the characters human which Dickens has portrayed. It has been the peculiarity and the marvel of this man's power, that he has invested his puppets with a charm that has enabled him to dispense with human nature ... Of Dickens's style it is impossible to speak in praise. It is jerky, ungrammatical, and created by himself in defiance of rules – almost as completely as that created by Carlyle. To readers who have taught themselves to regard language, it must therefore be unpleasant.'

p. 129 **to put down Rochester ... St Cross**: see Introduction, p. xvii.

p. 129 **peculation**: embezzlement; misappropriation of funds.

p. 130 **Attic salt**: the sophisticated conversational wit that supposedly characterised the banquets in ancient Athens. The phrase originated with Pliny (*Historia naturalis*, II, xxxi, 87).

p. 133 **a lighter step, and quicker**: the 1878 edition here inserts the following quotation from Horace's *Satires*, I, x, 14: Ridiculum acri Fortius et melius magnas plerumque secat res' ('Humour very often cuts the knot of serious questions more trenchantly and successfully than severity').

p. 133 **shilling numbers**: Dickens's novels would appear in nineteen instalments (the last being a double issue), costing a shilling each.

p. 133 **Namby-pamby**: sentimental childishness.

p. 133 **Divine peeresses ... listened to**: Trollope here refers to the trite characterisation of the gothic novel that had been so popular at the start of the nineteenth century. Mrs Ann Radcliffe (1764–1823) was author of the famous gothic novel *The Mysteries of Udolpho* (1794).

p. 133 **Perhaps, however ... monthly nurse**: Bucket appears in *Bleak House* (1852–3); Mrs Gamp in *Martin Chuzzlewit* (1843).

p. 134 **Mephistopheles**: the devil who, in the Faust legend, makes the pact with Faust.

p. 134 **Puseyism**: see Introduction, p. xix, and Appendix I.

Chapter 16

p. 136 **escape to London**: the 1878 edition adds the following two lines: 'It was mean all this, and he knew that it was mean; but, for the life of him, he could not help it. Had he met the archdeacon he certainly would have lacked the courage to explain the purpose which was carrying him up to London – to explain it in full.'

p. 138 **able to effect**: the 1878 edition here inserts the following footnote: 'How these pleasant things have been altered since this was written a quarter of a century ago!'

p. 138 **drug in the market**: another footnote of 1878: 'Again what a change!'

p. 139 **'And is this . . .' . . . resumed his seat**: Trollope here parodies *Hansard*, the official record of the proceedings of the Houses of Parliament.

p. 139 **'Bradshaw'**: *Bradshaw's Railway Guides* were first issued in 1839 by George Bradshaw (1801–53), a Salford printer and mapmaker, and quickly became the standard railway timetables of the Victorian period.

p. 140 **as a sight-seer**: another footnote of 1878: 'Again what a change!'

p. 141 **William Pitt**: Pitt the younger (1759–1806) was Tory Prime Minister 1783–1801 and 1804–6. There is a monument to him over the west door of Westminster Abbey.

pp. 141–2 **Mr Harding . . . lost in the chanting**: the final footnote of 1878 occurs here: 'Again the changes which years have made should be noted.'

p. 145 **cigar divan**: cigar shop with an attached smoking room. Deriving from the Persian word *divan*, originally meaning 'inner council', later coming to signify the chamber where such councils assembled.

p. 146 **sherbet**: a chilled Eastern drink of sweetened fruit-juice and snow; imitated in the West by mixing water with effervescent fruit-flavoured powder.

p. 146 **Blackwood**: *Blackwood's Edinburgh Magazine* (or *Maga*, as it was familiarly known) was founded in 1817 by William Blackwood (1776–1834), intended as a Tory rival to the Whiggish *Edinburgh Review*. Trollope himself later contributed a number of novels to the magazine, including *Nina Balatka* (July 1866–January 1867), *Linda Tressel* (October 1867–May 1869), *John Caldigate* (April 1878–June 1879), *Dr Wortle's School* (May–December 1880) and *The Fixed Period* (October 1881–March 1881).

Chapter 17

p. 148 **knew not the meaning ... parliamentary sense**: Trollope is alluding to the Parliamentary convention whereby members in the chamber refer to one another as 'my honourable friend'.

p. 149 **and when his glitter is gone ... its lost friend**: cf. Judges 2:10: 'And also that generation were gathered unto their fathers: and there arose another generation after them, which knew not the Lord, nor yet the works which He had done for Israel.'

p. 152 **Quixotism**: absurd generosity, selflessness, or devotion to lofty ideals, from the eponymous hero of *Don Quixote de la Mancha* (1605), by Miguel de Cervantes (1547–1616).

p. 153 **lappet**: 'a loose or overlapping part of a garment, forming a flap or fold' (*OED*).

Chapter 18

p. 155 **Macready**: William Charles Macready (1793–1873) was one of the most celebrated actor-managers of his day, especially noted for his performances in Shakespearean tragedy.

p. 156 **noddles**: nodding movement of the head.

p. 157 **'God, that feeds the young ravens ...'**: cf. Psalms 147:9: 'He giveth to the beast his food, and to the young ravens which cry.'

p. 158 **enough to provoke Job**: the legend of Job's patience in the face of unmerited and unrelenting suffering is relayed in the biblical Book of Job. Despite his many afflictions, Job's piety and righteousness prevent him from cursing God.

Chapter 19

p. 160 *sotto voce*: literally, 'below the voice' (Ital.); in an undertone.

p. 164 **Yours most sincerely**: the 1878 edition emends this to 'Yours most affectionately'.

p. 164 **Mr Provost**: the dignitary set over a cathedral or collegiate church.

p. 166 **gravelled**: puzzled, irritated.

p. 167 **Quiverful**: cf. Psalms 127:3–5: 'Lo, children are an heritage of the Lord: and the fruit of the womb is his reward. As arrows are in the hand of a mighty man; so are children of the youth. Happy is the man that hath his quiver full of them.' Mr Quiverful features more prominently in *Barchester Towers* (1857).

Chapter 20

p. 168 **inanition**: 'the exhausted condition resulting from want or insufficiency of nourishment' (*OED*).

p. 169 **the wretched clerical Priam . . . Hectors**: Priam was the legendary king of Troy, Hecuba his queen, and Hector one of his fifty sons.

p. 170 **simony**: the illegal practice of buying or selling ecclesiastical preferments.

p. 171 **Pharisee**: one of a lay democratic party among the Jews, marked by its obsessively legalistic interpretation of Mosaic law; hence, anyone more careful of the outward forms than of the spirit of religion.

p. 172 **teapoy**: a small three-legged table or stand, erroneously associated, because of its name, with the making of tea.

p. 172 **cellaret**: a case for holding wine bottles.

p. 172 **senna**: dried leaves of the various species of the shrub Cassia, used as a purgative.

p. 172 *esprit de corps*: literally, 'spirit of body' (Fr.); loyalty of a member to the body to which (s)he belongs.

p. 173 **a coal of fire burning on their heads**: cf. Proverbs 25:21: 'If thine enemy be hungry, give him bread to eat; and if he be thirsty, give him water to drink: For thou shalt heap coals of fire upon his head, and the Lord shall reward thee.'

p. 176 **roof-tree**: the ridge-pole (main beam) of a roof; hence, 'home'.

p. 176 **his mortal coil would be shuffled off**: cf. *Hamlet*, III, i, 66–8:

> For in that sleep of death what dreams may come
> When we have shuffled off this mortal coil,
> Must give us pause.

Chapter 21

p. 179 **ease the stings of death**: cf. I Corinthians 15:55: 'O death, where is thy sting? O grave, where is thy victory?'

APPENDIX I: THE CHURCH OF ENGLAND
IN THE NINETEENTH CENTURY

For a great many sociocultural reasons too complex to be discussed here, the Church of England is no longer the dominant social force it unquestionably was during the nineteenth century. Consequently, the easy familiarity that Trollope assumes his readers to have with both the structure and the history of the Church of England can no longer be taken for granted. This short appendix is therefore designed to give a broad overview of some of the issues that form a backdrop to *The Warden*. (For the specific topicalities that gave rise to the novel, the reader is referred to the introduction.)

Perhaps the first thing that needs to be clarified is the hierarchical structure of the diocese. Superintending the diocese as a whole, of course, is Bishop Grantly, who, although formally elected by the dean and chapter of the cathedral, would in fact have been appointed by the Crown, with the perhaps inevitable consequence that appointments to bishoprics tended to be politically influenced. For example, the arch-conservative Duke of Wellington's last act as Prime Minister, in 1830, was to make the equally arch-conservative Henry Phillpotts Bishop of Exeter. (Presumably the traditionalist Bishop Grantly's appointment would have dated from around the same period.) Similarly, in *Barchester Towers* (1857) it is the coincidence of Bishop Grantly's death with the fall of the Tory government that ensures the evangelical Dr Proudie's accession to the see of Barchester, under the auspices of the new Whig administration.

Immediately under the bishop, the hierarchy divides. Superintending and effecting the management of the cathedral are the dean and chapter. The position of dean was another Crown appointment, which is why the perceived threat of the Low Church Rev. Mr Slope's accession to the post (in *Barchester Towers*) causes so much anxiety for Dr Grantly and his troops. The chapter was the body of resident ecclesiastical dignitaries (canons) who assisted the dean in managing the affairs of the cathedral. Prebendaries were those canons whose stipend came from a portion of the cathedral's revenues (a prebend). After 1840, some chapters retained the title for those canons who were now holders of a disendowed prebend.

The rest of the diocese came within the purview of the archdeacon. Unlike that of the dean, the appointment of the archdeacon was in the gift of the bishop, which explains the close familial ties which often existed between the two offices, exemplified in *The Warden* by the father-and-son relationship between Bishop and Archdeacon Grantly. The archdeaconry was then subdivided, the divisions each coming under the jurisdiction of a rural dean, who was directly responsible to the archdeacon.

Finally, the precentor was either (in cathedrals of the Old Foundation) a member of the chapter ranking immediately beneath the dean, whose actual duties as precentor were commonly discharged by the succentor, or (in cathedrals of the New Foundation, and as is the case in Trollope's Barchester) a minor canon or chaplain, who actually performed the duties in person.

The major historical phenomenon that affected the Church of England in the nineteenth century (although it is barely more than alluded to in *The Warden*) was the rise of the Oxford Movement, so called because its centre was at Oxford University. The leaders of the movement were the clergymen John Henry Newman (1801–90), Richard Hurrell Froude (1803–36), John Keble (1792–1866) and Edward Bouverie Pusey (1800–82), the latter giving rise to the pejorative name for advocates of the movement, Puseyites.

The movement's basic objective was to oppose the Protestantism of the Established Church, and to seek a return to Catholic thought and practice within the Church of England. Starting from the High Church position (that would have been shared by traditionalists like Archdeacon Grantly) that the Church had its origins in, and should appeal to, notions of an undivided Christendom (an old Anglican truism that allowed the Church to criticise both Roman Catholics and Dissenters, as not following in the true Christian tradition), the movement went further by asserting that what was needed was a return to the Catholicity of the ancient Christian divines. One can see how such developmental thinking might disturb such a one as Archdeacon Grantly, because the logical conclusion was that the Church's true authority came from its ancients, and hence from the inherent truth of the apostolic succession. Consequently there was no need whatsoever for the Church to be linked to the State, and an early symptom of the movement was its call for the disestablishment of the Church of England.

In effect, the movement argued that while the Roman Catholic Church was an aberrant distortion of the true faith, nevertheless the Church of England had failed to take on board the full implication of the Reformation, which was that the Anglican Church was itself custodian of the true Catholic faith. These ideas were expounded in ninety tracts for *The Times*, published between 1833 and 1841, and the term 'Tractarian' became another name for subscribers to the movement.

The consequent theological and pastoral disputes that permeated the Church were in a large part due to the Tractarians' claims to the inherent Catholicity of the Church of England. And although Trollope's avowed intention was not to portray clergymen from a theological perspective, the reader must bear in mind that the absence of such debate in *The Warden* is itself a means of characterising the isolated world of the Barchester clergy. (Only in the novel's sequel, *Barchester Towers*, does Trollope bring a Tractarian to the cathedral close in the personage of the Rev. Mr Arabin.) [H.O.]

APPENDIX II: 'THE ARCHDEACON'

This descriptive essay by Trollope was first published in the *Pall Mall Gazette*, 11 December 1865, as part of a series of clerical sketches. The complete series of sketches was published by Chapman & Hall, in 1866, as *Clergymen of the Church of England*. Salient features of Trollope's own Archdeacon Grantly are recognisable here, but as the sketch was written after the archdeacon's first three appearances, in *The Warden*, in *Barchester Towers* and in *Framley Parsonage*, this is perhaps not surprising. However, in chapter 5 of *An Autobiography* (written in 1878, and published posthumously in 1883), Trollope does make a claim for the authenticity of his portrait of Dr Grantly:

> My archdeacon, who has been said to be life-like, and for whom I confess that I have all a parent's fond affection, was, I think, the simple result of an effort of my moral consciousness. It was such as that, in my opinion, that an archdeacon should be, – or, at any rate, would be with such advantages as an archdeacon might have; and lo! an archdeacon was produced who has been declared by competent authorities to be a real archdeacon down to the very ground. And yet, as far as I can remember, I had not then even spoken to an archdeacon. I have felt the compliment to be very great.

(Other essays from *Clergymen* will be published in Everyman's forthcoming editions of the remaining Barsetshire novels.)
[H.O.]

A dean has been described as a Church dignitary who, as regards his position in the Church, has little to do and a good deal to get. An archdeacon, on the other hand, is a Church dignitary, who in diocesan dignity is indeed almost equal to a dean, and in diocesan power is much superior to a dean, but who has a great deal to do and very little to get. Indeed, as to that matter of getting, the archdeacon, – as archdeacon, – may be said to get almost nothing. It is quite in keeping with the traditional polity and well-understood peculiarities of our Church that much work should be required from those officers to whom no payment is allotted, or payment that is next to none; whereas from those to whom affluence is given little labour is required. And the system works well enough. There has as yet been no dearth of archdeacons; nor shall we probably experience any such calamity.

Nevertheless, archdeacons are seldom allowed to starve. The bishops have it in their power to look to that, and knowing that in these days starving men seldom can exercise much authority, they take care that their archdeacons shall be beneficed. The archdeacon always holds a living. In former happy days he not unfrequently held more than one, and there are probably archdeacons still living in that halcyon condition. He always holds a living, and almost always a good living. He not unfrequently is a man of private means, and has been selected for his position partly on that account. He is the nominee of the bishop, and is, therefore, not unfrequently intimately connected with episcopal things. He is, perhaps, the son or nephew of a bishop, or has married a wife from the palace, or has, after some fashion, sat in his early days at episcopal feet. He is one whom the bishop thinks that he can love and trust; and therefore, before he has obtained his archdeaconry, he has probably been endowed with that first requisite for a good servant – good wages. A poor archdeacon, an archdeacon who did not keep a curate or two, an archdeacon who could not give a dinner and put a special bottle of wine upon the table, an archdeacon who did not keep a carriage, or at least a one-horse chaise, an archdeacon without a man servant, or a banker's account, would be nowhere, – if I may so speak, – in an English diocese. Such a one could not hold up his head among churchwardens, or inquire as to church repairs with any touch of proper authority. Therefore, though the archdeacon is not paid for his services as archdeacon, he is generally a gentleman who is well to do in the world, and who can take a comfortable place in the county society among which it is his happy lot to live.

But, above all things, an archdeacon should be a man of the world. He should know well, not only how many shillings there are in a pound, but how many shillings also there are in a clerical pound, – for in these matters there is a difference. Five hundred a year is much more in the hands of a country parson than it is in the hands of a country gentleman who is not a parson, – all of which the efficient archdeacon understands and has at his fingers' ends to the last shilling of the calculation. He should understand, too, after what fashion his brother rectors and vicars live around him, – should know something of their habits, something also of their means, and should have an eye open to their welfare, their pursuits, and their amusements. Of all these things the really stirring archdeacon does in fact know very much.

The archdeacon is, in fact, a bishop in little, and as such is often much more of a bishop in fact than is the bishop himself. To define, – or rather to make intelligible by any definition, – an archdeacon's power and duties, would be very difficult; as also it is very difficult, or I may say impossible, to do so with reference to a bishop's functions. The archdeacon holds a court, and makes visitations. These visitations may be made pretty much at his pleasure. He must, I believe, make them once in three years, but may make them every year if he thinks fit. He inquires as to the administration of the services, seeing that the canons are maintained, but has no power to alter aught; and as there seems to be much difficulty in knowing when and by what the canons are maintained, and when and by what they are not maintained, we may imagine that the inquiries of a discreet archdeacon into the practices of a respectable and efficient parson will not be too close or searching in this matter of the canons. It is, however, easier to see whether the windows of a church are in repair, and whether the roof keeps out the rain, than it is to be intelligibly and efficiently explicit on the subject of canons, and, therefore, the outward structure of the parish church gives very safe employment to an archdeacon. The little difficulty as to church rates which sometimes follows upon an order for repairs is not uncongenial to the archdeacon's mind. It hinges upon politics, and upon a vexed political question in which the archdeacon, as a strong local Conservative, has hitherto had his victories. There remain so very few subjects which are still grateful to him in the same way, that church rates, with all their little impediments and embargoes, naturally present themselves to him as pleasant matters. And then the archdeacons receive reports from the churchwardens, if church-wardens have anything to report, – any scandal of which to tell, or evil practices on the parson's side of which complaint has unfortunately become necessary according to the judgement of those churchwardens! By the word 'scandal' let not the uninitiated reader be led to think that undignified tittle-tattle with his neighbour's churchwardens is the duty or the employment of an archdeacon. Open moral misconduct in a clergyman's life is supposed to be matter of justifiable public scandal – the scandal arising with the clerical sinner, and not with those who tell of the sin – and, as such, is, by the constitution of our Church, an especial subject for the care of our archdeacons, and indeed, under them, of our churchwardens. But in such matters archdeacons are liberal, and much prefer to wink an eye than to see too much. We may imagine that a churchwarden, misunderstanding his mission with regard to scandal, and taking upon himself too promptly the duty of watching the moral conduct of his parson, would not receive much comfort from a visiting archdeacon. No one knows better than an archdeacon – no one knows so well as an archdeacon – that it is needless and absurd to look for a St Paul in every parsonage. He would, indeed, be very little at his own ease with a local St Paul, much preferring a comfortable rector, who can take his glass of wine after dinner and talk pleasantly of old college days. St Pauls, however, do not trouble him; nor is he troubled much by the scandals of his clerical neighbours; but he must be troubled sorely, I should think, by the increasing number and increasing influences around him of those 'literate' clergymen who – from want of better, as we must in sorrow confess, – are flocking to us from Islington, Birkenhead, and suchlike fountains of pastoral care. The man who won't drink his glass of wine, and talk of his college, and put off for a few happy hours the sacred stiffnesses of the profession and become simply an English gentleman, – he is the clergyman whom in his heart the archdeacon does not love.

Thus the archdeacon is a bishop in little as regards his own archdeaconry, which may probably comprise half a diocese; and as an energetic financial secretary at the Treasury may, under an uninstructed Chancellor of the Exchequer, have much more to do with the finances of the country than the Chancellor of the Exchequer himself, so may an energetic archdeacon have a much stronger influence on his clerical district than the bishop who is over him. He is the bishop's eye, or should be so, and may not improbably become the bishop's hand.

But the archdeacon, in spite of all his power and authority, though he be so great among his brother parsons, is hardly in the way to better promotion. High promotion in the Church now comes from political influence or from the friendship of Ministers, – from those things, combined of course with high clerical attainments – and an archdeacon is not often in the way to obtain political influence or the friendship of Ministers. As deans live in towns, so do archdeacons live in the country; and like other country gentlemen they are always in opposition. And then they are men who have been made what they are by the bishops, and, therefore, are known well in their dioceses, but are not much known beyond them. They culminate in their own local dignity, and, knowing that they do so, they make the most of it. An archdeacon who is potent with his bishop, and who is popular with his clergymen, who works hard and can do so without undue meddling, who has a pleasant parish of his own and is not troubled by ambitious or indifferent curates, who can live on good terms with the squires around him, understanding how far it is expedient that he should be restricted by his coat, and how far he may go in discarding hyper-clerical constraint, is master of a position in which he need not envy the success of any professional gentleman in the kingdom. But he is not on the direct road to higher things, and will probably die in his rectory, an archdeacon to the last.

If an archdeacon be ambitious of moving in higher clerical matters than his archdeaconry affords him, he generally looks to gratify that desire by sitting in Convocation.[1] This method of doing something more than routine duty is easier and less likely to fail than the other method of publishing a volume of sermons. Sermons are not read now as they were some thirty or forty years since, and Convocation has lately held its head a little up, obtaining recognition in the newspapers, and appearing to do something. An archdeacon is just the man to believe that Convocation can do much; and this faith on his part is evidence of a moral freshness and a real earnestness which adds a charm

[1] The move to give Convocation a more important position in the affairs of the Church of England dominated Church affairs from about 1850 until the close of the century. Convocation itself was a kind of 'parliament of clergy', long instituted but, since 1717, not allowed to meet except formally. However, the many doctrinal crimes that dogged the Church throughout the nineteenth century persuaded many that some form of assembly was needed to debate and legislate upon Church affairs.

to his normal character. Who can bring himself to believe that a bishop believes in Convocation – a bishop, that is, who takes his seat in the House of Lords, talks to other peers, and knows what is going on in the well-instructed blasé London world? Such a one cannot but see, cannot but know, that Convocation is a clerical toy, a mere debating society to which belongs none of the vitality of power. But the archdeacon, fresh from the country, believes in Convocation, and works there with some real conviction that he is one of a clerical Parliament, and that he is animated by true parliamentary life.

But it is in his own rectory that an archdeacon must ever shine with the brightest light. I have said that he is a bishop in little, and I may also say that he is the very chief among parsons; and as the country parson – the country parson with pleasant parsonage, pleasanter wife, and plenty of children – is the true and proper type of an English clergyman, to which bishops, deans, canons, and curates are mere adjuncts and necessary excrescences, so is the archdeacon the highest type of the country parson. He is always married – an exception here or there would but prove the rule – he generally has a large family; of course he has a pleasant rectory. He must be an earnest working parish clergyman, or he would hardly have been selected as an archdeacon. He is necessarily – I may say certainly – a gentleman. Alas! that the day should have gone by when the same might have been said of every clergyman bearing orders in the Church of England. He is a man of the world, as I have above explained, and as such it is not probable that he will be a fanatic, though living examples may probably be adduced that fanaticism can exist under an archdeacon's hat. And he walks just a head taller than other clergymen around him, receiving that pleasant attitude from the modest authority which he carries. Of all attitudes it is the most pleasant. He who stands high on a column can hardly talk pleasantly with those who stand round his pedestal; and that haranguing with loud voice from column top to column top is but a cold ceremonial conversation. Who can imagine two archbishops slapping each other's backs and being jolly together? But an archdeacon is not raised by his dignity above a capability for jovial intimacy, and yet he walks with his head pleasantly raised above the heads of other parsons around him.

APPENDIX III: *THE WARDEN*, E. S. DALLAS, JOHN DELANE AND *THE TIMES*

In chapter 5 of Trollope's *An Autobiography*, the novelist concludes his discussion of *The Warden* with the following paragraph:

> I will here say one word as a long-deferred answer to an item of criticism which appeared in *The Times* newspaper as to *The Warden*. In an article – if I remember rightly, on *The Warden* and *Barchester Towers* combined – which I would call good-natured, but that I take it for granted that the critics of *The Times* are actuated by higher motives than good nature, that little book and its sequel are spoken of in terms which were very pleasant to the author. But there was added to this a gentle word of rebuke at the personalities, – the personalities in question having reference to some editor or manager of *The Times* newspaper. For I had introduced one Tom Towers as being potent among the contributors to the *Jupiter*, under which name I certainly did allude to *The Times*. But at that time, living away in Ireland, I had not even heard the name of any gentleman connected with *The Times* newspaper, and could not have intended to represent any individual by Tom Towers. As I had created an archdeacon, so had I created a journalist, and the one creation was no more personal or indicative of morbid tendencies than the other. If Tom Towers was at all like any gentleman then connected with *The Times*, my moral consciousness must again have been very powerful.

Trollope was responding belatedly to a review of *Barchester Towers*, which appeared in *The Times* on 13 August 1857, and which contained the following criticism:

> [The novel] may be regarded as not unreal, in spite of a tendency to caricature which Mr Trollope continually displays, and especially when he has to deal with subjects out of the clerical sphere. The remarks which in this vein he has made on the influence exerted by the conductors of the newspaper press on public appointments are too insignificant to be seriously criticised; yet, as this is the second clerical novel published within a very short period (the other is the

Perversion of the Rev. W. Conybeare) in which an account of newspaper management is given by persons who know absolutely nothing about it, we beg to suggest that if any one hereafter chooses to write on the subject he will first of all study it and have the charity to admit that among the conductors and the writers of the public press it is possible to find men who are not only men of talent, but also men of honour.

It is likely that the review was written by Eneas Sweetland Dallas (1828–79), who, from the mid-1850s onwards, was one of the most brilliant and prolific journalists on *The Times*'s staff. 'Neither biography, politics, literary criticism, nor any other subject came amiss to his comprehensive intellect', states *The Dictionary of National Biography*, thereby implicitly endorsing Trollope's claim that the journalists of *The Times* were ready to pronounce on almost any topic whatsoever.

The nub of Dallas's criticism in his review is clear: that Trollope is practically slandering the integrity of 'the men of honour' who work for the newspaper. Dallas's sense of injury becomes clear when one realises that he had an almost fanatical devotion to, and regard for, *The Times*'s editor, John Thadeus Delane (1817–79). Delane had become editor of *The Times* at the age of twenty-three, and held the position for thirty-six years, during which time the newspaper achieved the stature and influence that are criticised in *The Warden*. Delane, it is true, sought the same anonymity that Trollope's Tom Towers seems to revel in, but it is fair to say that, although occasionally angering whichever vested interest he sought to oppose (and expose), Delane was a sincere man, committed to defending what he perceived as the public interest.

Nevertheless, it would appear that some of Trollope's other criticisms of *The Times* remain not only fair, but also startlingly accurate; furthermore, the evidence for this comes, ironically, from E. S. Dallas himself, in his correspondence with the Edinburgh publisher John Blackwood.

For if 1855 was the year that a little-known novelist called Anthony Trollope published a story entitled *The Warden*, it was also the year that an equally little-known journalist called Eneas Sweetland Dallas was angling, with some desperation, for a permanent job on *The Times*; and in his correspondence with his great friend Blackwood, the eager Dallas unwittingly confirms the truth of some of Trollope's satirical jibes at the newspaper. For example, the following extract, from a letter dated 5 September 1855, reveals Dallas in a panic over apparently transgressing *The Times* dictum that anonymity (and, as Trollope would have it, lack of accountability) was paramount. Dallas is fretting over a newspaper report revealing that he is going to work for Delane:

> I have been greatly distressed today in receiving from Mr Morris[1] a note enclosing extracts from some of the Edinburgh papers in which I am mentioned as reviewing for *The Times*. This appeared first in the *Edin. News* with which Hogg's *Instructor* is hand in glove. I promised an article to the editor of Hogg for this month, and to obtain some delay was so imprudent as to mention that I was writing a review of Tennyson for *The Times*. Hence the report. I have unfortunately shared my feelings of extreme anxiety to obtain this appointment with several of my friends, but I trust it is not too late to remedy this imprudence. I shall do my best to disguise my style in the articles I have in hand, so that the report may die away ... I cannot tell you how sorry I am that I did not sufficiently see the importance of entire secrecy in writing for so powerful an organ as *The Times*.[2]

There is something faintly absurd in Dallas's paranoia leading him to the conclusion that he must 'disguise' his style in order to 'reclaim' his anonymity; but the fact that he *is* so paranoid, and that Morris thought it necessary to reprove him by sending him the clippings wherein his employment at *The Times* is revealed, as well as Dallas's frank admission at the end of the above extract, would all seem to imply that the newspaper took the withholding of its journalists' identities far beyond the stage where it could be viewed as merely a technical measure designed to facilitate editorial impartiality. Consequently, the 'godlike' appearance of *The Times*'s pronouncements that Trollope so deplores in his critique of the *Jupiter*'s lack of editorial/journalistic accountability, can be seen to have been jealously guarded by those in senior positions on the newspaper's staff.

Another of Trollope's criticisms borne out by the Dallas/ Blackwood correspondence is the charge of charlatanism, inher-

---

[1] Mowbray Morris was the general manager of *The Times*, and Delane's right-hand man.
[2] This and the following two extracts are taken from original manuscripts held in the Blackwood Collection at the National Library of Scotland.

ent in the claim that the self-consciously broad-ranging and authoritative opinions trumpeted by *The Times* were necessarily penned by people who could not possibly be infallible, as the bullish and declamatory tone of *The Times*'s leaders often (if implicitly) proclaimed them to be. *The Dictionary of National Biography* may have gushed over Dallas's 'comprehensive intellect', but the journalist himself, newly employed by the newspaper, confessed the impossibility of being authoritative on everything, in a letter to Blackwood dated 18 November:

> I hope to get on well at *The Times*. They want me to write leaders, and I shall only be too happy. I am just going to write one on the Scottish Universities. I have written a literary article on Modern Science apropos of 'The Plurality of Worlds'; next Delane wants a couple of articles on Prescott's book.[3] And then I hope to take up Finlay[4] ... When you have a little leisure I should feel obliged by you giving me a hint as to politics. I daresay I shall pick my way in time, but I should feel more confident if I had your advice ... [T]he worst is that I feel I have not had a political education: that however will come in time – only I am confused by the multitude of subjects – historical, financial, social, constitutional, and personal.

Not only did *The Times* expect a rigid preservation of its writers' anonymity; but also, on the basis of this letter, Trollope's accusation that the infallibility of the *Jupiter* was really an arrogant presumption of authority over a range of subjects about which it knew nothing (if, indeed, anything) would seem to be justified.

Finally, the last extract from Dallas's correspondence (undated, 1855) demonstrates just how much Dallas venerated Delane, and perhaps goes a long way towards explaining the reviewer's indignation over Trollope's accusations in *The Warden*:

> You will be sorry to hear that Delane has been very ill. Fancy him looking pale![5] He has lost a good deal of blood although he is now in a fair way of recovery. What a loss to *The Times* were he away

---

[3] William Hickling Prescott (1796–1859) published a number of books on the history of Spain. His *Philip II* began to appear in 1855 and was completed in 1858.
[4] Presumably referring to George Finlay (1799–1875), the expert on Ancient Greece. His multi-volumed *History of Greece* began publication in 1844 and was finally completed in 1877.
[5] Delane had a notoriously florid complexion.

... The more I see of him, the more I admire him, and the less I wonder that *The Times* is the first journal in the world.

Given the esteem in which Delane was obviously held by his staff, it is hardly surprising that the apparent accuracy of some of Trollope's criticisms of *The Times*, linked inextricably as they are to an implicit attack on Delane (through the personage of Tom Towers), should have provoked the review of 1857 to such heights of indignation. [H.O.]

TROLLOPE AND HIS CRITICS

Trollope's reputation, both during his lifetime and after, has suffered mixed fortunes. When *Framley Parsonage* came out in 1863, the *National Review* could declare:

> So great is [Trollope's] popularity, so familiar are his chief characteristics to his countrymen, so widespread is the interest felt about his tales, that they ... form part of the common stock in trade with which the social commerce of the day is carried on.

(National Review, XVI, 1863, pp. 28–9)

But following his death in 1882 came a waning of his reputation. For forty years his books were obscured by other favourites. Then, after the First World War, there was a modest revival, as the Victorians began to be assessed more dispassionately, and in the Second World War Trollope became favourite reading. The revival flourished through the 1950s and 1960s, and by the 1970s and 1980s critical commentary reached flood proportions. *The Warden*, as much a long short story as a conventional Victorian novel, caught the eye of early reviewers as something new in fiction, though it has often been seen as the precursor of greater things.

Notice in the *Leader* (unsigned), 17 February 1855

Early reviews of *The Warden* were mostly friendly (much more so than for Trollope's earlier novels); but it received more pointed attention after the appearance of the sequel, *Barchester Towers*, in 1857.

> In these days when people sit down to compose fictions, having nothing in the world to write about, a novel with a subject claims honour as a work of unusual merit. *The Warden* has the first great recommendation of being a story based on a good and solid foundation. Mr Trollope has a subject which it is worth while to describe, if we can do so briefly without damaging the legitimate

interests of his plot. He starts with the very recognisable fact of a public charity, in a cathedral town, which has been fairly and admirably founded in bygone times, and which is very dishonestly managed at the (modern) period of the story . . . Here, assuredly, is a new and an excellent subject for a novel – a subject which Mr Trollope has, in some respects, treated very cleverly. The character of the Warden is delightfully drawn, with a delicacy and truth to nature which deserves the highest praise. Equally good in their way are the feeble old Bishop, his truculent and intensely clerical son, who has married the Warden's eldest daughter, and the old men who live on the mismanaged funds of the charity. The defective part of the book is the conclusion, which seems to us careless and unsatisfactory – as if the author had got tired of his subject before he had done with it . . .

This certainly promises well for the author's future, if he gives us more books. Assuming and hoping that he has not written his last novel yet, we will venture to point out to his notice two defects on his manner as a writer which he may easily remedy . . . The first of the defects is, that Mr Trollope speaks far too much in his own person in the course of his narrative. It is always the reader's business, never the author's, to apostrophise characters . . . The second defect of manner which we have noticed in Mr Trollope is a want of thorough earnestness in the treatment of the more serious passages of his story. The mocking tone is well enough where the clerical aristocracy, and the abuses on which they live, form the subject for the treatment. But where the main interest touches on the domain of real feeling . . . it is vitally important to the true effect of the scene on the reader, that the author should at least appear to feel sincerely with his characters. This Mr Trollope . . . seems to avoid.

Henry James, 'Anthony Trollope', from *Partial Portraits*, London, Macmillan, 1888

Though Henry James was originally no great admirer of Trollope, he wrote a generous assessment after Trollope's death, in *Partial Portraits* (1888). The essay includes such famous phrases as Trollope's genius lying in 'a complete appreciation of the usual', and *The Warden* being 'simply the history of an old man's conscience'.

The Warden is a delightful tale, and a signal instance of Trollope's habit of offering us the spectacle of a character. A motive more delicate, more slender, as well as more charming, could scarcely be conceived. It is simply the history of an old man's conscience.

The good and gentle Mr Harding, precentor of Barchester Cathedral, also holds the post of warden of Hiram's Hospital, an ancient charity where twelve old paupers are maintained in comfort. The office is in the gift of the bishop, and its emoluments are as handsome as the duties of the place are small. Mr Harding has for years drawn his salary in quiet gratitude; but his moral repose is broken by hearing it at last begun to be said that the wardenship is a sinecure, that the salary is a scandal, and that a large part, at least, of his easy income ought to go to the pensioners of the hospital. He is sadly troubled and perplexed, and when the great London newspapers take up the affair he is overwhelmed with confusion and shame. He thinks the newspapers are right – he perceives that the warden is an over-paid and rather useless functionary. The only thing he can do is resign the place . . . and he does resign in spite of the sharp opposition of his friends. He does what he thinks right, and goes to live in lodgings over a shop in Barchester High Street. That is all the story, and it has exceeding beauty. The question of Mr Harding's resignation becomes a drama, and we anxiously wait for the catastrophe. Trollope never did anything happier than the picture of this sweet and serious old gentleman, who on most of the occasions of life has shown a lamblike compliance, but in this particular matter opposes a silent, impenetrable obstinacy to the arguments of the friends who insist on his keeping his sinecure – fixing his mild detached gaze on the distance, and making imaginary passes with his fiddle-bow while they demonstrate his pusillanimity. The subject of *The Warden*, exactly viewed, is the opposition of the two natures of Archdeacon Grantly and Mr Harding, and there is nothing finer in all Trollope than the vividness with which this opposition is presented. The archdeacon is as happy a portrait as the precentor – an image of the full-fed, worldly churchman, taking his stand squarely upon his rich temporalities, and regarding the church frankly as a fat social pasturage. It required the greatest tact and temperance to make the picture of Archdeacon Grantly stop just where it does. The type, impartially considered, is detestable, but the individual may be full of amenity. Trollope allows his archdeacon all the virtues he was likely to possess, but he makes his spiritual grossness wonderfully natural. No charge of exaggeration is possible, for we are made to feel that he is conscientious as well as arrogant, and expansive as well as hard. He is one of those figures that springs into being all at once, solidifying in the author's grasp. These two capital portraits are what we carry away from *The Warden*, which some persons profess to regard as our writer's masterpiece. We remember . . . to have heard a judicious critic say that it had much of the charm of *The Vicar of Wakefield*. Anthony Trollope would not have accepted the compliment ... He would have said, very justly, that it gives too small a measure of his knowledge of life.

Bradford A. Booth, *Anthony Trollope: Aspects of His Life and Art*, London, Macmillan, 1958

This early full-length study was largely responsible for academic recognition of Trollope (another is by A. O. J. Cockshut, 1955). Although the critical principles now seem old-fashioned, the book is a milestone in Trollope studies.

In discussing the polemical aspects of *The Warden*, a critic is in danger of losing perspective on Trollope's achievement. What side he himself favoured in the matter of church vs. almsmen is of little importance. The point of interest is that an ethical problem in the life of an old man is made to bear the weight of a mid-Victorian popular novel. Such a moral dilemma as is pictured here became more familiar in literature after the success of the problem drama of Ibsen, but Trollope anticipates by several decades the shift of interest away from conventional romance ... Only once again, in *The Last Chronicle of Barset*, did he concern himself deeply with an issue so significant, one which would enable him to take soundings of the troubled human spirit ...

The significance of *The Warden* in Trollope's development as an artist is that at its conclusion he recognised that his strength lay almost entirely in the intense realisation of character. 'There is no gift', he observed, 'which an author can have more useful to him than this'. When in the future he forgot that this is so, it was at the peril of his novel, for he had little else to offer.

What Trollope offers in *The Warden* is almost enough for a fine novel. As he saw, the sustaining element is the clerical portraits, especially that of Harding ... In the serenity of his temper, the humbleness of his spirit, and the inviolability of his conscience he is a supremely good man. Yet he is not one of the waxwork paragons of Charlotte Yonge or Elizabeth Sewell or Mrs Henry Wood. Perhaps this is because, having no doctrinal axe to grind and, more importantly, no didactic purpose, Trollope could afford to make the cathedral and the vicarage simply the setting for some very human beings. He was also shrewd enough to balance the unworldly idealism of the warden with the busy temporalities of the archdeacon. Grantly provides the contrast which sets off Harding's selflessness, but his function is independent as well as complementary. He gives body and strength to a very slight novel because he is a man as steady in his faith as he is volatile in his emotions.

R. H. Polhemus, *The Changing World of Anthony Trollope*, Berkeley, University of California Press, 1968

The critic here examines *The Warden* in its contemporary context.

The changing times of the fifties provided wonderful opportunities for social comedy. There is something inherently funny in the clash of newfangledness with old fashions, in a meeting, for example, between a free-thinking bohemian and a staid bishop. In Barset the new and the old continually jangle against each other, but somehow, the jarring of the past and future improves the quality of life.

Especially in his books written from 1853 to 1858, Trollope developed and became master of the comedy of change. He liked to juxtapose radically different kinds of behaviour in the face of changing conditions and to show the folly, the variety, and the joy of mid-Victorian life. His novels of the period have their black – sometimes very black – moments. We find in them, as in so much Victorian literature, an elegiac note for a way of life that was passing. He made no attempt to gloss over the problems or the maladjustments of the times. But for the middle classes, at least, the decade was promising, and happy endings seemed realistically possible. The Barsetshire of these early books makes the phrase 'Victorian compromise' come clear; it is a place where the claims of the world and the individual conscience can be reconciled.

With all its light and sometimes awkward playfulness, *The Warden* is a very serious novel. Trollope barely does allow the comic possibilities in the story to win over its tragic potential. We have here, in its simplest form, the typical Trollopian situation of a man whose mode of life is suddenly challenged by changing conditions in his world . . . The problem which Trollope poses for Mr Harding lies at the heart of all his best fiction: 'Now that I must rearrange my life, what should I do in these new circumstances?' How his characters go about resolving this question forms the most valuable part of his writing. *The Warden* is a prologue to all of Trollope's work in tone, subject matter, and particular concerns. The . . . fear of dehumanising utilitarianism, the celebration of modest private life that we find here, remain constant in his writing . . .

Of all the Victorian novelists, Trollope best understands the relationship between a man and his work. The sanctification of work by the Victorian middle classes, and their professional pride, caused new problems. Neither Grantly nor Tom Towers, for example, can separate his opinion as a private citizen from what he considers to be good for his professional status. In *The Warden*, Trollope begins developing his theme that work comes more and more to determine identity, that what a man does tells him who he is. Clergymen in all the Barset novels are tempted to regard the ministry as a job rather than a calling and to see themselves as a worldly professional class. The drive for professional prestige muffles individual conscience ...

... London power has changed Barset at the end of the book. It is not as cozy for Harding as it was at the beginning. *The Warden* has a touch of the pastorale about it ... But pastorale is a genre which blooms, after all, in times of urbanisation, and it almost always shows man's will to fashion for himself 'the good old days'. Trollope's whole image of Barset shows that he both longs for the communal comforts of country provincialism and recognises the slow, inevitable suburbanisation of modern life ...

And yet despite the low-key tragedy of the hospital, the comic possibilities of the novel are realised. The marriage of John Bold and Harding's daughter Eleanor shows human affection triumphing party spirit. But the real comic affirmation in the novel is Harding himself. Mr Harding, a single man, matters more to Trollope than the hospital community, and *The Warden* becomes one of the best expressions of Victorian faith in individualism.

Ruth apRoberts, *Trollope: Artist and Moralist*, London, Chatto and Windus, 1971

Ruth apRobert's theory of 'the shaping principle' ('It is Trollope's art to advocate for each one of his characters: he makes the best case possible for one, then juxtaposes this with the demands of the other, defended with a similar passionate sympathy') is here applied to *The Warden*.

How then can we talk about Trollope as an artist? – a man quite insouciant as to point of view, intruding himself without shame or compunction, quite as ready to tell as to show, naïvely faithful to chronological order ... What can be the controlling element ... ?

To begin at the beginning is to begin with *The Warden*, which is, as generally agreed, the start of his *œuvre* ... The significance of its shape has been missed ... This novel especially has suffered from our tendency to categorise: [it] has been hard for us to think of it in terms other than ... the novel of social purpose.

The trouble with this is that the purpose is not very clear. As propaganda, *The Warden* seems to fail. We are, in fact, puzzled to find what side Trollope is on. Is he in favour of reform or not? Apparently he does not quite know his own mind, and he suffers from a terrible indecision. [One] critic ... finds the novel a symptom of Trollope's illness: which is the Divided Mind. This is called his *plight* . . .

So . . . We know that sinecures are by definition immoral and must be reformed. We – or Trollope's contemporaries – know, too, that the Ecclesiastical Commission is in session, and that reform is in process . . . Trollope is not trying to expose an abuse, nor is he trying to demonstrate the beauties of the status quo.

His art lies in his carefulness to do neither, to avoid the *partis pris*. For it is his delight to regard the juxtaposition of the two *partis*. He has a Divided Mind, and it is no plight but rather a distinct artistic advantage. *The Warden* involves both sides in a beautifully ironic demonstration of incongruities . . .

The potency of the work is simply not in its story. It is, rather, within this situation that Trollope has taken, and in the way he exploits it. What he does, is to insist on the incongruities, by sharp juxtaposition of different perspectives. What is called his 'realism' functions to this end, and it functions like this: Not only are we told that Mr Harding is a good man, and not only do we see him and know him as virtuous . . . but further, we love Mr Harding. We are involved . . . But then we are involved with John Bold, too . . . and we must love him for his principles. Readers sometimes observe that Bold is not a very sympathetic character, as though to imply that Trollope somehow fails there. But surely the limits of his charm are part of Trollope's scheme. Bold is in the right, and so the balance must be shifted away from him; Harding is in the wrong, and so must be made as attractive as all the novelist's virtuoso powers can make him . . . It is only by casting off the demands of conventional 'plot' that Trollope is free to exploit his situation so thoroughly. He wrings his *donnée* with the sort of relentless exuberance that characterises great art.

J. R. Kincaid, *The Novels of Anthony Trollope*, Oxford, Clarendon Press, 1977

Kincaid, unlike the Victorian reviewer, warmly endorses Trollope's use of 'the dramatised narrator', and stresses the conscious art of Trollope's composition.

In my view, it is a mistake, and a common one, to ignore the primary rhetorical purpose of these two novels [*The Warden* and *Barchester Towers*] and to read them in terms of some 'reconciliation-of-opposites' theme. I do not believe that *The Warden* balances the views of Bold and the archdeacon . . . Instead of the movement towards balance common to many other Trollope novels, *The Warden* ... describes patterns of disruption and consequent expulsion. Bold does not really have a 'case' ...

The Warden appears to have been begun with some spirit of reforming zeal ... As far as the issues are involved, the novel does tend to do battle with both Bold and Grantly, but issues become trivial as the novel advances. It is almost as though Trollope discovered a new moral system on the way to writing a light topical satire. As this new intention takes over, the balance is upset completely, and the archdeacon is shifted as close to the centre as he well can be. The original intention makes the switch awkward, though, and the narrator is forced at the end to apologise for the picture of the archdeacon, saying that he is a much better man than he has been shown to be.

He is that, of course, according to the terms in which the novel ends. In fact, the only thing holding him from the centre is a certain coarseness that blinds him to the futility and danger of fighting for mere issues. But in its inception the novel imagined itself also to be interested in issues, and thus there are touches of materialism and hypocrisy added to the character: the copy of Rabelais, the narrative commentary which insists that he is 'hard-hearted', and a marital arrangement that anticipates the one later used with the Proudies. All this is a mistake, as the narrator is forced to admit ...

In terms of values, however, it is Bold's position, not the archdeacon's, that is dangerous ... John Bold's decent position is decent only in the abstract, and when decency is thus abstracted it becomes nearly indecent. Failing to recognise for a long time the complex ties between men and morality, he becomes almost totally a public man, a terribly self-conscious reformer ... The narrator comments sarcastically, 'I fear that he is too much imbued with the idea that he has a special mission for reforming. It would be well if one so young had a little more diffidence himself, and more trust in the honest purposes of others – if he could be brought to believe that old customs need not necessarily be evil, and that changes may possibly be dangerous.'

John Bold is not a bad man. He has, in fact, had the proper instincts all along. But he has been taught to 'quiet them within his breast' by the great organ of the new insanity, the *Jupiter* ... In a world like this, the only positive moral act is the act of withdrawal. Mr Harding, 'not so anxious to prove himself right as to be so', turns his back entirely on the doctrine of success ... His act is a moral one and asserts a connection between will and act, between the public and private life ... It is gloomy in the sense that it gives up external and obvious power altogether. It temporarily sacrifices appearances ... in order to define and defend the integrity of the complete moral being.

SUGGESTIONS FOR FURTHER READING

A. O. J. Cockshut, *Anthony Trollope*, London: Collins, 1955

D. Smalley (ed.), *The Critical Heritage*, London: Routledge & Kegan Paul, 1969

Coral Lansbury, *The Reasonable Man: Trollope's Legal Fiction*, Princeton: Princeton University Press, 1981

N. John Hall (ed.), *The Trollope Critics*, London: Macmillan, 1981

T. Bareham (ed.), *The Barsetshire Novels*, London: Macmillan, 1984

Stephen Wall, *Trollope and Character*, London: Faber and Faber, 1988

Victoria Glendinning, *Anthony Trollope*, London: Hutchinson, 1992

Sherman Hawkins, 'Mr Harding's Church Music', *English Literary History*, 29, 202–23, 1962

Ramon Saldiver, 'Trollope's *The Warden* and the Fiction of Realism', *Journal of Narrative Technique*, 11, 166–83, 1981

Jerome Meckier, 'Trollope Rewrites Dickens in *The Warden*', *Studies in the Novel*, 15, 202–23, 1983

Thomas A. Langford, 'Trollope's Satire in *The Warden*', *Studies in the Novel*, 19:4, 435–47, 1987

TEXT SUMMARY

Chapter 1   Hiram's Hospital
Describes the provisions in John Hiram's will for the setting-up of the
bedesmen's hospice in the cathedral town of Barchester, and the present
warden of the hospital, Mr Harding.

Chapter 2   The Barchester Reformer
Description of Archdeacon Grantly. As the administration of charities
by the Church of England becomes a matter of national controversy,
the provisions of Hiram's will are challenged by the young reformer
John Bold.

Chapter 3   The Bishop of Barchester
Bold awakens Mr Harding's doubts about the latter's moral claim to
his income from the hospital. The bishop tells Harding that such doubts
are groundless.

Chapter 4   Hiram's Bedesmen
At the instigation of the lawyer Finney, the bedesmen assert their right
to a yearly income of £100, and petition the bishop.

Chapter 5   Dr Grantly Visits the Hospital
. . . and tries to hector the bedesmen into submission. Harding's doubts
grow.

Chapter 6   The Warden's Tea Party
Bold ignores his sister's entreaties to him to drop the case against
Harding: 'Because I esteem Mr Harding, is that a reason that I should
neglect a duty which I owe to these old men?'

Chapter 7   The Jupiter
Harding is aghast to read a leader criticising him in the powerful
national newspaper the *Jupiter*.

Chapter 8   Plumstead Episcopi
Description of the archdeacon's lavish rectory, as well as satirical
portraits of three contemporary bishops of the Church of England.

Chapter 9   The Conference
The archdeacon tries to persuade Harding that both his income and his
position are unassailable.

Chapter 10   Tribulation
Unhappiness prevails at the Harding residence. He and his daughter comfort each other: 'And in what sorrow will not such mutual confidence give consolation?'

Chapter 11   Iphigenia
Eleanor tries unsuccessfully to 'sacrifice' herself for the sake of her father.

Chapter 12   Mr Bold's Visit to Plumstead
... to inform Dr Grantly that he intends to drop his suit against Harding ends in violent disagreement, as the archdeacon declares that the Church itself may not be willing to abandon the case.

Chapter 13   The Warden's Decision
Harding resolves to journey to London: 'I will have this matter settled some way: there are some things . . . which I cannot bear'.

Chapter 14   Mount Olympus
Description of Tom Towers, of the *Jupiter*.

Chapter 15   Tom Towers, Dr Anticant and Mr Sentiment
Towers tells Bold he is not prepared to relinquish the case. Parody of Carlyle, and satire of Dickens.

Chapter 16   A Long Day in London
Harding whiles away the day uncomfortably, as he waits for his appointment with the attorney-general.

Chapter 17   Sir Abraham Haphazard
Description of the attorney-general. Harding makes known his intention to resign the wardenship.

Chapter 18   The Warden Is Very Obstinate
... and refuses to be bullied into submission by Dr Grantly.

Chapter 19   The Warden Resigns
... while the archdeacon visits the diocesan lawyers, who suggest that Mr Harding might exchange his living with Quiverful of Puddingdale.

Chapter 20   Farewell
Harding refuses to accept 'the Puddingdale scheme'. He bids farewell to the bedesmen.

Chapter 21   Conclusion
'Our tale is now done, and it only remains to us to collect the scattered threads of our little story, and to tie them into a seemly knot.'

ACKNOWLEDGEMENTS

The editor and publishers wish to thank the following for permission to use copyright material.

Oxford University Press for material from J. R. Kincaid, *The Novels of Anthony Trollope, Clarendon Press*, 1977;

University of California Press for material from R. H. Polhemus, *The Changing World of Anthony Trollope*, 1968;

Random House for material from Ruth apRoberts, *Trollope: Artist and Moralist*, Chatto & Windus, 1971;

Every effort has been made to trace all the copyright holders, but if any have been inadvertently overlooked the publishers will be pleased to make the necessary arrangement at the first opportunity.